Steven Baker

Love across the Decades

The Book Guild Ltd

First published in Great Britain in 2016 by
The Book Guild Ltd
9 Priory Business Park
Wistow Road, Kibworth
Leicestershire, LE8 0RX
Freephone: 0800 999 2982
www.bookguild.co.uk
Email: info@bookguild.co.uk
Twitter: @bookguild

Typeset in Aldine401 BT

Printed and bound in Great Britain by CPI Group (UK) Ltd, Croydon, CR0 4YY

ISBN 978 1910878 903

British Library Cataloguing in Publication Data.
A catalogue record for this book is available from the British Library.

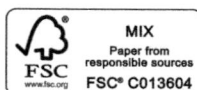

*For the staff at the Worthing Hospital and the Royal County Hospital,
Brighton, who helped me through heart surgery in 2014*

1.

Luke and Maggie

The Depression Kids

The Great Depression crept over the British Isles in the 1930s with all the effects of poison ivy spreading across a once well-kept garden. But now the garden was stained with the unemployment and misery of millions who eagerly looked for the light at the end of the tunnel. Few people had ever imagined that the Depression would last so long. After all, Britain was the centre of the industrialised world. Amongst its resources it could yield iron ore, coal, tin and wood. Lancashire was famous for its textile industry. Shipbuilding took place on the Clyde. Tin was mined in Cornwall. Britain was surrounded by splendid fishing waters. Dairy farming, agriculture and manufacturing industries provided a sound economical base. The Depression could not possibly last.

But it did, and it was not until the advent of the Second World War that the armed forces showed many people the exit door from a life of struggle. This story is about two of those people: Luke Price and Maggie Maguire, who came from opposite ends of the country. Both were locked into a mundane existence and one which was far from promising. Luke and Maggie both sought a different world, and found each other.

Luke Price was born to be a fighter; not only as a young man who did not hesitate to employ his fists if he was challenged to do so, but as one of life's fighters. At the age of 21 he was a proud Newcastle boy with firm straight views on life. He did not worry himself about being liked or respected by others. To Luke this was trivial in the scheme of things. The most important values he had been brought up with were honesty and integrity. In Luke's mind if these were in doubt then a man's character had little worth at all. Luke was a 'speak as you find' man who had no fear of a scrap. Besides, he had been an aspiring young boxer. He never intentionally sought a fight. His individuality and strength often acted as a red rag to a bull for those eager to take him on and make a name for themselves. He defended himself well.

For all the years of his life people consistently underestimated Luke Price. It took time to get to know him properly. At times Luke came across as aggressive, a fault caused by his inability to temper his strong opinions. Luke's strong points were his typical Geordie industriousness, a personal respect of others even if he did not particularly care for them, and an ability to run the gauntlet of life's experiences, emerging unscathed and unbloodied despite taking some pretty heavy blows.

In his home town of Newcastle upon Tyne Luke had worked by day as a manual labourer on building sites. But as the full effects of the Depression hit home he considered other ways of boosting his purse. He turned to prizefighting and in a short time had gained a good reputation as a scrapper. Unfortunately his rise inflamed the jealousy of some of the local lads who viewed him as a contest for a street fight.

The Spatler brothers, four burly hoods saw him as an easy victory. They in their ignorance completely misjudged the pluck of the young man. One dark, damp night Luke made his way home unaware that the Spatler brothers were waiting for him. Luke pulled his flat cap firmly on his head and stopped to light a cigarette, covering the flame with his jacket. He was just about to cross the road when on this dark, lonely and isolated street the four Spatler brothers came into sight. In their early twenties, they were already known as local ruffians to steer well clear of.

'If it isn't the little tough guy, Luke Price,' sneered Bill Spatler, the elder brother at 24 and possessed of far more fat than muscle.

Alan, slightly younger, eyed Luke with contempt. 'Hey, Luke, seeing as you're riding high on your prizefight win how about sparing a bob or two for us without any work?'

Luke at once stiffened his backbone, preparing for a fight. 'I've not go' no money on me lads,' he said coolly. He began to clench his fists.

'Yeah!' snapped Ian Spatler with a disbelieving look on his face.

Tom Spatler moved forward. 'Let's see inside your jacket then.'

Luke angrily retorted, 'It's now't to do with you Spatler brothers. You've been making trouble for folk too long. I'll not stand your nonsense.'

'Give us a couple of bob and we'll move on,' Tom said persistently and he pushed his hands forward to help himself from Luke's jacket. Luke immediately deflected Tom's hands.

'I give ye fair warning,' he said in a voice that sounded lethal.

At this point the Spatler brothers surrounded him.

Luke moved stealthily, raising his fists in a sparring manner. 'So it's a fight you'll be wanting is it boys? Four against one, eh? What odds? I'll take you on. One at a time or all at once. Makes no difference to me.'

Bill raised his fists, 'You're all wind and no sails, Pricey boy.'

He was to regret that remark almost immediately. Bill was knocked flying by Luke who pulverised him with a sledgehammer punch. Luke immediately turned his attention to the other three and struck blows that took each of the brothers by surprise.

However their brawn served them well and they fired back with painful knuckle blows. The result was one almighty scuffle in which Luke and the Spatler brothers found themselves fighting among knocked-over dustbins and piles of rubbish. Luke was the toughest of Geordies. His fists packed fast and powerful punches. He asserted his ascendancy over his opponents.

From out of nowhere it seemed, a couple of policemen came dashing down the street, blowing their whistles. Luke landed two final punches on Alan and Ian Spatler. They fell back alongside Bill and Tom who were already knocked out and lay spread-eagled on the floor.

Not only was Luke a boxer but he was a sprinter too. He wasn't going to hang around helping the police with their inquiries. He had better things to do, like getting home for his supper and a good night's sleep. Luke was off and running. He raced away down an alley. He leapt over fences and backyard walls, and ran across a road to the safety of his home.

At his parent's home Luke straightened his attire, brushed himself down and walked into the downbeat terrace house as if nothing had happened. When Luke walked into the front room his mother and father were listening to a big band show on the wireless.

'Hullo Ma. Hullo Dad,' Luke said boldly, removing his cap.

His mother smiled at him. 'Hullo son. Tea's made. Help yourself.'

Luke helped himself to a cup and sat down next to his parents.

His father studied a bruise on his face. 'Have you been sparring for another fight?'

'You could say I've been sparring,' Luke replied, smiling to himself.

If only his Dad knew he had just taken on four brothers and left them rueing the day they had ever crossed him.

There was something Luke wanted to announce, something that had been on his mind for a while. 'To tell you the truth Dad,' he said between gulps of tea, 'I'm going t' give the fight game away. I've no chance of becoming the next Jack Doyle or Len Harvey any more than I have of playing f' Newcastle United. I'm thinking of going to London to find work, a proper job. And if I'm no successful I'll keep walking and walking and walking till I get summat that pays a fair day's pay for a fair day's hard graft.'

Luke's mother gave him a knowing look, not realising he was in a serious mood. 'You've been souring your brain with ale that rots your muscle sinews. You'll no get work this time. If you're going walking in search of work it's only good shoe leather you'll be wearing out. And you'll be passing by plenty other lads all looking for work that does not exist.'

'Are you serious then, Luke?' asked his father.

Luke was firm and sincere in his reply, 'I am that, Dad. I'm sorry Ma. I've got to be giving it all my efforts. There'll be life on the road that I've not seen before. If I no succeed then I will be returning with o' bag of tales that'll entertain you here on a rainy night.'

Suddenly Luke's parents realised with surprise their boy was most definitely serious.

★★★

Within a few days Luke was saying farewell to Newcastle upon Tyne, his parents, and — although he didn't know it — the relatively carefree days he had known till then. He sat back in the comfort of the train, happy to be travelling and attempting to improve his lot in life.

It was Luke's first visit to London. After Newcastle and Whitley Bay he found London to be vast, exciting and colourful. For the first few days he took in the sights of Nelson's Column, London Bridge, Buckingham Palace and Piccadilly Circus. Then Luke began the fruitless search for work. He had not realised the depths of the Depression even in a prosperous city like London.

Being a manual labourer not afraid of hard work, however humble or arduous, Luke thought it would only be a matter of time before he found something. The days of searching turned into weeks. At factories and building sites the 'No Vacancy' signs were out. If a job was advertised there would be hundreds queuing up to be interviewed. Dismay turned to frustration and that in turn became a deep seething anger at the futility of it all. He just wanted to work.

So too did several million others. One day Luke saw a man with sandwich boards walking towards him. He was startled when he saw the handwritten notice. It read: 'I HAVE WALKED THE LENGTH AND BREADTH OF BRITAIN SEEKING WORK. FOR GOD'S SAKE WILL SOMEONE PLEASE EMPLOY ME! I WILL DO ANYTHING!' Luke looked on in amazement. What chance was there for him?

It was not in Luke's nature just to give up and go back to Newcastle. He had not come all the way to London merely to be forced on the dole. But as he carried on with his search, the grim news on newspaper placards everywhere made him realise that he would soon have to swallow his pride and join the queue.

When the money ran out the pangs of hunger drove him to a soup kitchen at a Salvation Army hostel. He joined the sad-looking men and women who waited their turn to be served. Luke looked forlornly around him at the misery of the people waiting to receive a bowl of soup. His normally hard eyes brimmed with emotion.

At nights he slept on the London Embankment, or a park bench if he was lucky enough to beat some other poor soul to it. On freezing damp nights the cold would seep into his body. Frantically he would rub himself up and down to keep warm. He was unshaven and looked dirty and unkempt. It was becoming increasingly hard to muster the energy for anything now.

Sometimes he would look across to the Houses of Parliament. Luke had no time for politicians. Except for people like Bevan and Shinwell he thought of all the others as 'shiny arses' who had never known hunger or unemployment. The Prime Minister Stanley Baldwin, as well as trying to cope with the Depression, had an abdication crisis looming. All this was light years away from the cold harsh reality of Luke's world. Today he would have to sign on.

The dole queue stretched right along the street. Luke shuffled along, unsure about joining the men and women in the line. For such a hard-bitten young man he found it humiliating to be standing there. He couldn't believe all these people were standing there for the same thing.

'Are all these fellas standing in line for the dole?' Luke asked a man in the queue.

'Nothing else mate.'

Luke looked up and down the line in disbelief. His amazement turned to a deep, burning anger. 'What a way to treat decent folk who only want to do a day's work!' Luke blew his top. 'It r'art makes my blood boil! We have to stand in line for a handout that's a miserable pittance, and if that's not enough we're made to feel like flamin' beggars!'

The man he had spoken to was quick to respond. 'What else can you do son? I've walked my jack off and there's nuffin! Never mind about nothing. I mean there's nuffin!'

'Well I'll not stand here with my hand out and be trod on like a cowpat in a field! I'll fight this filthy Depression on my own terms! I don't take humiliation kindly!'

Luke walked off fuming. Several people looked on in admiration at this stubborn, plucky and pig-headed young man.

'Good luck, son!' one man called out to him.

Luke called back to him, 'And you, fellow! Don't give in to anyone!'

He had to walk his anger off. It was terrible to Luke that someone such as he could not find even the most menial of work to get by. He walked on and on that day until he encountered a group of demonstrators outside the Savoy Hotel. The dishevelled men carried placards and shouted in unison, 'Give us work! We want work!'

Luke stood watching in fascination. One of the group, a man in his forties noticed Luke's ragged appearance and approached him. 'You look in a bad way, lad. Are you unemployed?'

Luke gave him a wry smile. 'Shows, does it? What's going on here then?'

The man came back swiftly and sharply in a reply that sounded as if it had been rehearsed. 'We're demonstrating for more work for us without jobs, and against the inequality of this land where there's a huge divide between rich and poor. We're about to hold a sit-down campaign in the hall of the Savoy. Why don't you demonstrate with us? What are your politics?'

'I don't hold with no one,' replied Luke. 'I'd vote for a monkey if I knew he'd give me a job, put food in my belly and look after me in my old age.'

The campaigner slapped him on his back cheerfully, 'Come on! With views like that you should tell people. Don't sit on the fence. Come and join us. We're going in.'

'You're going in there?' Luke was surprised to see the demonstrators start to enter the Savoy Hotel. 'Why not? I might nick a biscuit and when I go home to Newcastle I'll tell my ma I ate at the Savoy.'

Luke joined the demonstrators. Much to the annoyance of the guests and waiters, the party of unemployed men and women marched in carrying their placards. They immediately sat down in the lobby. Luke took his place reluctantly but was soon joining in enthusiastically with the chants of the group.

'Give us work! Give us work!' they yelled. 'Break down the barriers between rich and poor! Break down the barriers between rich and poor!'

The words were repeated continuously. Luke looked towards the end of the hall. The head waiter was talking to some of the staff and he pointed to the demonstrators. He issued his staff instructions. They responded and entered another room.

For a while the demonstrators continued to shout at the top of their voices. From the end of the hall the head waiter walked up to them. He smiled at the group in a most disarming and engaging way that quite mystified them. What was he up to? Were the police about to break through the doors and arrest them?

'Ladies and Gentlemen, could I have your attention just one moment?' he shouted, throwing his arms up in the air in an outstretched movement indicating he wanted silence.

'Let the man speak!' cried Luke, who believed in fair play. The crowd hushed straight away, following the request from one of their own.

'Thank you,' the head waiter said with another charming smile.

'The management of the Savoy wish me to convey to you that the point of your protest has been demonstrated clearly and concisely; it has been completely understood and we would like you to know that you have our sympathy in this matter. We also know that many of you have not had a square meal in days. The manager of the Savoy has expressed to me that if you would care to take afternoon tea in the room behind me, beef and chicken sandwiches together with rolls and salad, cakes, tea and coffee are available for your refreshment on the house, courtesy of the Savoy Hotel. Would you care to follow me?'

Almost at once the group of demonstrators rose and followed the head waiter. Luke turned to the man who had beckoned him to join them. He was grinning from ear to ear. 'Thanks for inviting me, mate! I made the right decision to join your mob!'

Luke and the others could not believe their eyes at the array of glorious food that lay before them on the tables in the Savoy dining room. The head waiter and his staff looked on approvingly and it must be said sympathetically, for it could so easily have been themselves looking in.

'Alright, eh?' remarked Luke to his new friend. 'My ma will think I'm giving her a leg pull when I go home and tell her I came to London to find work and had afternoon tea and sandwiches at the Savoy. She'll say I'm a teller of tales.'

The man acknowledged him with a smile. 'I don't want to discourage you, my young friend, but London might be a fine city if you've a place of work, a place of lodging and plenty of pennies in your pocket. It's no place for a sturdy lad like you without work. Why don't you get on your bike and head for the country?'

'The country? And what would I be doing there?'

'Dunno, son. Try some of the farms. Maybe you'll get a job on the land.'

An hour later the once-hungry demonstrators left the hotel. Luke and the campaigner left together.

'So where do you think I should go?' asked Luke.

'Wiltshire,' replied the man. 'They reckon it's good dairy farming there.'

'How do I get there? I haven't got a penny to scratch my backside with!'

'Walk. Run. Hitch a ride.' He looked at Luke intently. 'You can always jump on and off a train. Discreetly of course.'

Before Luke could reply a double-decker bus roared past. It was a moment of fate, for if Luke had peered on board the bus he would have caught sight of an attractive girl who sat there with her mother. Her name was Maggie Maguire.

★★★

Maggie Maguire was not a normal run-of-the-mill South London girl. She was demure and pretty, dark-haired and with a very kind face. But this masked the determination of a girl eager to break away from the background of villains her family had long associated with. Like Luke, the man she would one day marry, Maggie was not a shrinking violet when it came to expressing her equally strong opinions. Her one weak link – or strength as it may have been perceived by some – was her unswerving loyalty to her widowed mother May.

Now May Maguire was by no means a straightforward character either. She was capable of being tyrannical, matronly, rude, overbearing and demanding in loyalty from her family. For all of her faults that were obvious to see May, was a tough old South London bird who gave no quarter and never made concessions. Her life had been hard in all respects. May's late husband Alf Maguire had been a well-known local criminal who had been in and out of prison for all of his short life. He had died while serving a stretch, leaving a bitter May to bring up five children on her own. She wanted only the best for her four sons and daughter. However May made the age old mistake of thinking that she always knew what was best for her children.

On the bus that day, Maggie sat with May. She looked towards the Savoy Hotel.

'I heard there was a demonstration there today,' said Maggie. 'A lot of unemployed people went down and sat in the lobby.'

'Funny place to walk with placards and then sit down!' snorted May, 'I wonder what they were trying to prove.'

May was a pushy sort. After taking her daughter shopping she made a point of going home by way of a local gymnasium. The man who ran it was an affluent young spiv called Louie Malone. May was permanently trying to match Louie and Maggie together. It was strictly a no-goer. Maggie just wasn't interested. Louie had other ideas, though.

Louie Malone had grown up in the area they often referred to as 'The Alley' and he had known Maggie for most of her life. Louie was a spiv, a gang leader and con-merchant. Not yet 30, he had already amassed an interesting empire consisting of a boxing gymnasium, a billiard hall, a dance hall behind which lay a secretive gambling den, and it was rumoured that several shops in the locality were merely fronts for illegal activities organised by Louie. On the surface he was a charming man with an uncanny resemblance to Errol Flynn. In reality Louie was a dangerous man to cross. If anyone tried to move in on Louie's territory he would solve the dispute himself. If the problem was too big Louie always knew people who could remove it. He was cocky, arrogant, vain, good fun to be with and had a sense of humour, sometimes directed at himself which was quite disarming. His smarmy self-confidence was overwhelming.

At the boxing gymnasium, one of his little empires, Louie watched a trainer put two good fighting prospects through their paces. He cut quite a dash in his trilby hat and double-breasted suit. Every so often he fingered his thin moustache.

The trainer stood to one side, yelling instructions at one man. 'Lead with your left. That's it. Now cover as he strikes. Cover... cover... with both your hands. Move forward! Right! Left! Right! Now cover! I said cover! Don't leave yourself unguarded around your abdomen. Straight left! Hard right! Cover! Strike again. OK. Keep on that way for a few minutes.'

The trainer stepped out of the ring and walked across to Louie.

'How are they doing? Reckon we've got a potential couple of champs there we can make money out of?' Louie always had an eye for the main chance.

'Not just yet, Louie,' replied the trainer. 'They lack continuity. That's their main problem. First couple of rounds, no sweat. Half a dozen or so and they tire quickly. Not able to go the distance. They've got to learn to build up their strength and maintain it.'

'Put the boys through the works. Make endurance their middle name. I pay you to make them winners.'

'I'll do my best, boss.' Various boxers around the gym who were skipping or slugging punchbags stopped to look as they caught sight of May and Maggie entering at one side of the gym.

'Would you credit it, Lou? A couple of pieces of crumpet have just walked in.'

Louie tilted his hat back and smiled. 'That's not crumpet. I know those girls. They're May and Maggie Maguire from my alley. I'll take care of them.' Louie walked across to greet them.

Maggie felt uncomfortable and could not hold back her annoyance. 'Why have you brought me here Mum? As if I didn't know!'

'Because I think you should see a bit more of Louie,' May snapped back quickly.

'You're always pushing me towards Louie,' Maggie protested.

May did not have a chance to reply as Louie came to meet them.

Louie removed his hat and bowed gently. 'Hullo ladies. You shouldn't really be here. A nice piece of skirt is not too good for the boxers. It distracts them and breaks their concentration. However I am, as always, entirely yours. What brings you here to my little kingdom?'

'I thought Maggie would like to see you at your place of work,' May replied, as always taking the lead in any given situation.

'What do you think of my kingdom then, Maggie?' Louie asked, sincerely interested in her opinion.

'Baffles me how you've got all this and you're not yet thirty,' Maggie replied.

Louie looked as if he had a sudden surge of pride. 'Oh you've got to know the right people, learn to develop a bit of clout and know-how. I've got a few friends with muscle.'

Maggie looked around at the well-built boxers in the gym. She smiled at Louie. 'Yes, Lou. You've certainly got friends with muscles.'

★★★

They walked along silently. By the time May and Maggie were nearly home it was apparent that Maggie was quite annoyed.

'Don't you like Louie?' May asked, knowing what the answer would be.

'He's not for me, Mum.' Maggie replied crossly.

May was adamant. 'You could do a lot worse. He's worth a bob or two.'

Maggie came back quickly and sharply. Her view of the future didn't include the one of the slum suburb they walked through. 'I could do a lot better! And just because a bloke has a bit of money that doesn't mean to say I'm going to marry him. We all know about Louie's past, don't we? I will get married when, and if, I feel like it! Preferably to a man I love.'

At this remark May's lips twisted into a sardonic smile. 'Love! Huh!' She was almost spitting blood. 'Love! That's the stuff of girl's magazines. Love may be fine but it doesn't pay the bills, my girl. You stick with Louie and you'll never know a life of drudgery.'

'I know all about Louie, the people he's bought and sold, his brushes with the law and the roughhouse tactics he's used to get what he wants. Just because he's grown up on the manor with us it doesn't necessarily mean he and I were destined for wedding bells.' Then Maggie revealed something that had been on her mind for a long time. 'I'd like to get away from here. To the country.'

'You'd leave here?' exclaimed May. The idea of it amounted to treachery in her mind. 'After the way I brought you and your four brothers up after your dad died in prison? You'll never leave here! What do you want to leave London for? This is your home. The country would be too quiet for you.' After a beat of silence the sometimes nasty side of May came to the surface. 'Besides, my girl, you haven't got the courage.'

Maggie stopped walking for a moment. A look of certainty spread over her face. She looked at her mother intently and spoke in a voice that was cold and chilling. 'Don't you ever, ever put me down like that, Mum. One day I might surprise you.'

May was left standing half-surprised, half-shocked. Maggie stomped off home, seething with anger.

Home for the Maguire family was a few tawdry rooms above a betting shop. Maggie's brothers Frank, Clive, Mac and Bill were all in their twenties. During the course of the evening they sat playing cards and drinking. The room was full of smoke. Ashtrays were filled to overflowing. May sat knitting while Maggie contented herself reading a magazine.

Aware that there had been an argument earlier on and the two women weren't on speaking terms tonight, Frank tried to ease the situation.

'Why don't you join us for a game of cards, sis?' he asked amiably.

'You know I don't like cards, Frank,' Maggie replied gently.

Mac immediately made a comment. 'Girls aren't interested in cards or the good things in life like football, billiards and snooker.'

The remark brought a smile to Maggie's face. 'No wonder you haven't got a girl, Mac, if that's all you think about. You're the same, Frank. I've got four brothers all of a marriageable age and I've not been to one wedding yet.'

'You'll probably be wed first,' Frank said with certainty in his voice.

Clive waded in. 'Yeah. What is it they say? A woman should get married as soon as possible, and a bloke should hold out for as long as he can.'

'That's a prize piece of nonsense, Clive,' May said, never failing to put her sons' opinions down when it suited her to do so.

Bill Maguire, although an inveterate gambler and drinker, had a little more sense and strength than his brothers. He wasn't quite under the thumb of his matriarchal mother, but he always spoke his piece in a firm and quiet manner.

'I think I agree with him, Mum. Not much point in planning anything in the long term.'

'Why's that?' asked Clive.

Bill explained. 'This Depression. If you've got a job you have to hang on to it. Old Charlie down the pub reckons we might be putting uniform on in a few years to fight another world war.'

'None of his warmongering nonsense in here please, Bill,' May said with a hint of repudiation.

Just then there were several knocks on the door. 'Now who can this be?' May put her knitting down. She stepped forward and opened the door. It was Louie. He removed his trilby and bowed like a cavalier at the court of King Charles. 'Hullo, Lou. To what do we owe this pleasure?'

Louie came straight in without being invited. He beamed a smile at Maggie who quickly averted her eyes. The Maguire brothers nodded their heads and smiled at him. Louie knew who he had come to see.

'There she is. Maggie, prettiest girl in the alley.' Maggie raised her eyebrows. Louie grinned at her obvious discomfort and looked across to the card game, 'How are you boys? You should play cards with some of the big fellows I know. Win against them and you'll be sitting pretty for a while.'

'Their stakes are a bit high for us, Louie. We're only working men,' Mac pointed out.

'Ah, you don't have to be poor all your life,' Louie said in response. 'Actually the reason I called round is to ask young Maggie there if she'd care for a walk this evening.' Maggie looked up and smiled, more at the arrogance of the man than anything. 'What about it then, doll?'

'Yes why not?' Maggie replied. May looked up in surprise. 'Yes, I'll go for a walk with you Lou if only to tell you I'm not romantically interested in you. And for you to act like a gentleman and treat me like a lady, if you know how.'

Louie grinned at her and stroked his moustache. 'I've always liked your up-front style, doll.'

It wasn't so much a walk down the street as Louie demonstrating how big his empire had grown. There were lights twinkling from various buildings. A tram car rolled past. Louie stopped and leaned against a lamp post. Always an extrovert, he could never resist being flamboyant wherever he was. He took out a Cuban cigar, lit it and stood back surveying the brightly painted buildings he owned that added colour to a drab slum suburb.

'What have we stopped for?' Maggie asked suspiciously.

'I wanted to show you something, doll,' he answered.

'And that's another thing,' she snapped, 'will you stop calling me "doll"! You make me sound like a piece of plastic without a brain.'

Maggie's retort brought a smile to Louie's face. 'I just love it when you get irate. I've called you doll for as long as I've known you. I don't mind breaking the habit of a lifetime to win your favour.'

'To win my favour?'

'That's right. We could go places together.' Maggie started to listen to Louie very seriously for a change. 'Yes, around here Louie Malone is top dog now. I've put quite a lot together in these parts. Look over there Maggie, my sweet. There's a boxing gymnasium with real fighters in it, lightweights, heavyweights. Blokes with class in every punch and victory in their eyes. There's a billiard hall. An all-night café with an after-hours grog room for fellows wanting a spin on the dice, a gamble with top poker players and quality liqueur available for the asking. Down the road there's a dance hall, a laundry, a tailors, a pawnbrokers and a garage with trucks for hire. All of it spins money.

'And do you know who's behind it? Me! Good old Louie Malone who's been building it up for fifteen years since I was a fourteen-year-old alley cat kid. I came from the alley to the manor by way of the back street and now I'm a big name on the thoroughfare. People come up in the street and say "How are you, Lou?" When I was a kid with trousers so shiny and the sun shone on my behind I got kicked. Now they think the sun shines out of my behind and I've got respect. Real respect. I'm not doing bad considering there's a Depression on.

'Want to be part of it Maggie? You and I were meant to be together. We'd have some good times. I'd guarantee it. We'd make a good team.' There was exuberance in his voice. 'We'd knock 'em dead, girlie.'

'Never, Lou,' replied Maggie without hesitation. She looked at him almost sympathetically. 'Oh, I know my Dad and yours were blood brothers.' She let that sink in, because of the rumours that Alf Maguire and Danny Malone had spilt other people's blood in their time. 'I even know, although I'm not supposed to, that there was a time long ago when my mum nearly married your dad. I get the feeling that's why she keeps pushing you and me together. My own father was in and out of prison until he died there. Mum held us together after that. I owe her that much. But I don't owe her the rest of my life. All my brothers have got reputations as street scrappers. I don't want a life round here. Always walking the tightrope of the law. Living one step ahead of the constable. I'm tired of this place, the alley, the manor.'

'You're bored?' Louie couldn't understand it. 'Where are you going to go then, doll? Further east or up west? There's only one direction I'm going and that's to the top of the pile. I'm not a cocky street kid any more. In time I'll own businesses left, right and centre, you wait. Come with me, doll. Be my lawfully wedded.'

Maggie shook her head. The lady wasn't for turning, 'I'm sorry, Lou. I've heard stories about your rise. I want to marry a hard-working, good-hearted man and live a life where I'm not expecting the police to come rat-tat-tatting on the door in the middle of the night. I grew up with all that when they used to come for Dad after he'd done a job. Besides, I don't love you. I know life would never be dull with you. But you're not what I want.'

'You'll eat your words in time, doll.'

Maggie smiled at him. Even though he was an unscrupulous rogue and capable of being a thug, Maggie felt something for him, although even she was at a loss to work out what those feelings were. But love was not one of them. 'Walk me home, Lou,' she said pleasantly, taking his arm.

★★★

The man that Maggie would marry one day was sitting on a crowded train bound for Wiltshire. Luke was fast asleep when a ticket collector gave him a jolt.

'Can I see your ticket please, son?'

Luke opened his eyes and stifled a yawn. He suddenly realised he was being asked to show a ticket that he had not bought.

'Are we in Wiltshire yet?' he asked trying to delay the problem that would soon follow. He knew he should not have tried to board a train like a hobo in the Wild West.

'Next stop, son,' replied the ticket collector. 'Can I see your ticket?'

Luke looked apprehensive for a moment. He had never been a dishonest man. It wasn't in his nature to do something of a deceptive nature. For the first time in his life in a moment of desperation to get away he had done wrong, now he was going to get caught. It was the humiliation of being branded dishonest that really worried Luke. He made a false display of fumbling around in his pockets for it. How did he handle a situation like this?

'It's in my bag in the luggage rack outside,' he lied.

The ticket collector knew he was lying but gave him a benefit of the doubt. 'Would you mind fetching it?' he asked politely.

'Sure,' replied Luke. He immediately rose from his seat and walked through the carriage. Taking his bag from the luggage rack, Luke considered what he must do. The train was moving at a dangerous pace.

The ticket collector looked towards the end of the carriage to see what was holding Luke up. His suspicions were aroused. He walked through the carriage and looked outside. The carriage door was wide open. Luke had leapt from the speeding train.

In the pitch dark of night, Luke found himself bouncing down the grass embankment of the railway. He landed sprawled in a field. Raising himself slowly he heard the sound of the train speeding into the distance.

Luke allowed himself a smile. 'So this is Wiltshire,' he murmured.

★★★

Maggie stared around at her bedroom. Soon she would be leaving this place that was her home, the alley, the manor, and Louie Malone and her own domineering, matriarchal mother May. After packing her suitcase she tidied her bed and placed a letter on it together with a small bunch of flowers for May. For a few minutes she took a lingering look at the room. Then, taking a deep breath, she plucked up her courage and walked quickly out down the stairs without disturbing the others, who were sleeping soundly.

The morning fog obscured almost everything in view as she left the rooms above the betting shop. Maggie was just about to walk off in the dark when a shadowy figure materialised.

'Sis! What are you doing?' It was her elder brother Bill. He had the appearance of a man who was the worse for wear after a night out on the town.

Maggie put one finger over her mouth, 'Shhh. I'm leaving. I'm going to Wiltshire to find work. Uncle Joe used to speak warmly of the place. I've got to go, Bill.' She scented the alcohol fumes in the air. 'Anyway, what are you doing coming in at a quarter to six in the morning? You've been out drinking all night, haven't you?'

'That's right. I have been on the booze, at Louie's den. I've been playing the cards. And I've lost my week's wages the day after I got it.' He should have looked ashamed, but Bill had owned up almost proudly.

'Bill, you're so unreliable!' Maggie said with dismay. 'You know Mum relies on you for that money. You of all people! The one brother I really thought had some sense. Look, I'm going to catch a train to Wiltshire this morning. Come with me and we'll talk at the station. I'll explain.'

Bill and Maggie sat in an early morning railway café for a long time, talking. When Bill was sober and sensible he was a marvellous listener. Of all the Maguire family Bill had broken the mould. He was kind and compassionate, although his rough exterior hid these qualities.

'I've left Mum a note,' Maggie explained, 'and some flowers for her on my bed. When I get a job I'll send money home to help her out. I had to make the break quickly, and cleanly, without anyone trying to talk me out of it.'

Bill was of the old school. He could sense when someone was not telling him the full story. Especially if that person was his little sister. 'Why are you really going, sis?' he asked gently.

The answer came flying at him with unexpected fury. 'Because I'm fed up with the villainy around us! I'm fed up with Mum trying to push me towards Louie, and I'm sick of Louie thinking he's meant for me. If I stay in the alley I'll end up in a dreadful way of life that will bring me misery for the rest of the days I live. I want the peace of the countryside, where no one knows me. Tell Mum and the boys I love 'em all. I'll come home again for a visit sometime.'

There was a short silence as Bill absorbed the impact of the words. Never in his life had he heard his sister speak so candidly. In his own direct manner he assessed the situation. 'You've given up your job in the raincoat factory. You're leaving home. We'll miss you. I will. I know that. My little sister, the little girl who used to cry when her dolly broke, and who'd bring home stray cats for us to look after until we found them a good home.'

He was sadly reflective. Then a spark appeared in his bleary eyes. 'Maybe you were too nice to hang round some of the folk we know. Don't worry about Mum. I know she can be a bit hard at times. It's all a front. I'll see she's alright.'

Another silence followed. This time Bill broke it with a revelation of his own. 'I was out thinking about my future too, last night. After I played cards I got myself well and truly boozed. I might have got drunk but I was seeing far straighter than I have for a long time.'

Maggie looked at him curiously. 'What do you mean, Bill?'

'I'm twenty-one now, Maggie. Fit. Smart. Like you I want something more. I'm going to join the Royal Navy, and like you I'll make sure Mum gets a good bit of my Navy pay.'

'Oh Bill. I'm so proud of you!' Maggie embraced him with delight.

Her congratulations were short-lived. From the window of the café a train could be seen arriving at the platform.

'The Wiltshire train has arrived. Time to go, Maggie.' Bill put his arm around his sister and escorted her across the platform.

★★★

Luke made his way through the country lanes of Wiltshire. He was a somewhat lonely figure. He was also very hungry. For ages he had walked without seeing anyone or anything and after a while he began to enjoy the isolation. Luke delighted at the sounds of a country silence and the sight of golden cornfields. Yes, thought Luke, this was a place he could grow to like.

Some shiny apples hung tantalisingly from a tree in an orchard. He could not resist the temptation and took a couple, putting them in his pocket. Before moving off he took several more and put them in his bag. They would sustain him for the rest of the day.

When the shadows of the night began to fall Luke found himself searching for a place to rest comfortably. He found it in the shape of an apparently empty barn. He walked around it until he found the door. He had no trouble forcing it open. Inside the barn there were bales of hay and piles of straw.

With a smile of relief he hurled his bag to one side and lay down on the straw. He put his hands behind his head and looked up at the barn roof. A little bit of light filtered through a hole in one of the beams. It was good to lay back and rest.

'This will do nicely,' he whispered to himself. 'Better than silk sheets at the Ritz any day.'

Hours of exhaustion and tiredness immediately caught up with him. Within seconds of closing his eyes he had fallen into a deep sleep.

Seven hours later the morning light filtered through into the barn. Luke was still fast asleep. The door of the barn opened slowly. An elderly countryman entered. He brandished a shotgun. His eyes caught sight of the silent unkempt, unshaven sleeping figure of Luke. He raised the shotgun, momentarily aiming at Luke but then he directed the barrel towards the hole in the barn roof. A shot rang out. Luke nearly jumped out of his skin. The man held the gun pointed towards him.

'Stay your distance, young man,' he growled in a countryman's burr. 'Aaron Heath's the name. I own the farm this barn's part of. You're trespassing, young fellow-me-lad. Do you know that?'

Luke was understandably nervous. 'I… wasn't doing anything. I was just grabbing a night's sleep in your barn.'

Aaron looked at him up and down. His eyes were those of a man who missed nothing, although they had softened slightly. 'Tell me straight. From here you look like you need a good scrub with carbolic and coal tar soap. Are you on the run from the police? Now be honest with me, son.'

'No I flamin' well am not on the run!' Luke protested sharply.

Aaron raised the rifle sharply. 'I don't doubt ye. You've got an honest face. Trifle sharp in your voice, though. While I've got this here shotgun in my hand I'll take ye down to the farmhouse and you can have a cup of tea. I'll have to check with local Constable, though.'

A short while later Constable Davidson duly arrived at the farmhouse belonging to Aaron and Grace Heath. They all sat around the breakfast table, enjoying more of a pleasant get-together than the apprehension of a possible criminal on the run. Grace and Aaron, both in their fifties, spoke in a slow and almost warming manner.

The Constable sipped his tea and winked at Luke pleasantly. 'He seems to be alright Aaron. He's like nobody pinned up on our noticeboards. So you're a Newcastle lad come south to find work, then? What do you want to do?'

For some reason he couldn't fathom, Luke felt comfortable with these rural folk. 'I'll do anything. Where I come from we have no shirkers. I'll give a hard day's graft at anything.'

Grace waved a pot of tea in front of them. 'Another cup of tea, son? Constable Davidson?'

'Yes please, Grace,' replied the Constable.

'Right nice of you,' beamed Luke.

The Constable looked at him in a kindly manner. 'Well, I'll be the first to wish you luck.'

'I think I'm going to need it. It's right tough going out there at the moment. All over London I've not seen a vacancy I could work at.'

Aaron's eyes, which had seemed fierce at first, now showed a degree of warmth towards Luke. Perhaps it was the young man's directness and straightforward manner that reminded him of his own qualities. After a beat of silence he waded into the conversation.

'I take it ye've not eaten properly for a while, lad?' Aaron asked. Luke nodded his head. 'I'll not give ye charity. That would be insulting your pride. But how would you like to do a few hours' work for me baling hay? In return I'll have Grace wash and press your clothes while you toil in overalls. And I'll put a plate of bacon and eggs with mushrooms, toast and tomatoes, and a piping hot cup of tea in front of you. You can take a scrub in a tin bath full of hot water and soap suds. What say you?'

'I'll start this minute!' exclaimed Luke. He was on his feet, ready and willing to work.

Luke worked hard that morning, baling hay for the farmer. Aaron showed him what needed to be done, and Luke took to the task with enthusiasm. The thought of a plate of good food and a scrub in a hot bath was an enticement to work productively. He laboured for several hours, piling up bale after bale.

Towards midday Grace walked up to him with a mug of tea. She seemed to be very impressed by Luke's efforts. 'Here you are, young fellow,' Grace said pleasantly, handing him the mug which he took gratefully.

Luke mopped his forehead. 'Much obliged to you Mrs Heath,' he said with a smile. Grace watched him as he took a sip of tea. 'I think you deserve that. You've worked hard, Luke. I've heard that Geordies are an industrious lot.'

'I'll not tarnish that reputation then. I've really enjoyed this past few hours. All my muscles have been nicely exercised and the air I've been inhaling has been the freshest and the purest I've ever scented.'

Grace could not resist a smile. 'That's Wiltshire air, young man. Now if you want to finish that bale, come on down to the house. Soak yourself clean in the tub. Put on your freshly washed and ironed clothes and there'll be a hot nourishing meal for you, farm fresh cooking.'

'I'm most thankful to you for your kindness and hospitality.'

'Don't mention it, son.' Grace's kindly eyes twinkled.

Back at the farmhouse a freshly scrubbed and cleanly clothed Luke tucked into the meal. Grace and Aaron looked on in approval.

Luke was an experienced street fighter who could sense when people had something on their mind. It was clear to him that Grace and Aaron had a look of intent about them. Not malicious, but that of people who were about to ask a favour or a helping hand.

Luke scraped his plate and decided it was an opportunity to dispense a compliment to these two fine people. 'It's been a while since I enjoyed a meal so much. That was right delicious. After my morning's work and that beautiful meal I could do another ten hours hard yakka. I'm right grateful to you both. I'd like to thank you both. Before I go on my way, if there's anything you'd like me to do for you I would consider it a real privilege to do it and ask for nothing in return.'

Aaron and Grace looked at each other quickly. It was Aaron who spoke first. 'We had a young lass ring us from the station 'bout half an hour ago. She was the niece of Joe, a fellow who was with us for a fair few years. Well, as a favour to old Joe we're going to give her a job milking the cows and helping Grace here. Farm's pretty big for us two. Looking after the hay bales and ploughing the fields takes fair amount of my time… and strength I must add.'

'What Aaron is saying,' Grace cut in, 'is that we saw how hard you worked this morning. You're a good strong lad not afraid of hard work. I'm going to have this young lass helping me. Aaron needs someone to help out. If you said no, fair and well. But if you said yes, even if you work with us for just a few months as a general farmhand, your food and lodging would be all in. We've a snug little room adjacent to the stables.'

Luke looked astonished. He could hardly believe his luck.

'I'm serious now. Would you be interested?' Aaron asked.

'I've got to be honest with you,' admitted Luke, 'your offer is kind and unexpected. It's taken me fair by surprise.' He rubbed his chin and thought deeply for a moment. 'You'd take me on, on the strength of a morning's work and my freshly scrubbed appearance?'

'We would,' replied Grace hopefully.

'Then in that case,' Luke replied knowing this was a chance in a lifetime offer, 'I'll work damn hard for you and earn every penny you pay me twice over!'

Luke and Aaron shook hands warmly. For Luke this was the start of a new life.

★★★

Aaron drove to the station to collect Maggie. He was pleased that his wife would have some assistance and a soulmate. In the same way he had warmed to Luke, there was something about Maggie that he found endearing.

All the way back to the farm, Maggie peered out of the window at the scenery. Aaron could tell by the expression on her face she was excited.

'You'll love it here Maggie,' he said encouragingly. 'Your Uncle Joe took to it like a duck to water. Grace and me, we were most surprised to get your call. But we hope you'll be happy working with us. Matter of fact, we took on a new lad from Newcastle just this morning. Name of Luke. Between the four of us I think we'll work rather well.'

Maggie turned to him. Her eyes were glowing. 'I'm very much looking forward to it Mr Heath.'

'Call me Aaron. I've never been one to stand on ceremony.'

Luke met Maggie for the first time that afternoon. With a full stomach and feeling fresh after his scrub, he was working hard turning over hay. Unexpectedly, Grace walked towards him with Maggie by her side. Luke turned round and was quite taken by surprise when he caught sight of her. Maggie in turn politely smiled at him. Although a rough diamond, Luke remembered his manners and removed his cap in the presence of this young lady.

Grace introduced the two. 'Luke, I would like you to meet Maggie Maguire. She is a lass from London who'll be working with me.'

Luke stretched out his hand to shake Maggie's gently. Even in the touch of her soft hand there was something appealing about her. 'A pleasure to meet you Miss,' he said softly.

Maggie looked quickly at the haystack where Luke was working. 'Hard work?' she asked matter-of-factly.

'Nowt's trouble t' me. I'm enjoying this.'

Grace turned to Maggie. 'C'mon, I'll show you the milking sheds now.'

The two ladies turned and walked off. For a moment Luke leaned on his pitchfork and smiled in admiration at Maggie. He had always had an eye for the ladies, but this one really sparked something off inside of him. He did not know it then, but this was love at first sight.

At the dinner table that night, Grace and Maggie sat opposite Aaron and Luke. Maggie was reticent about talking about herself but she had shown great interest in the running of the farm. Luke tried to avert his eyes whenever they made contact with Maggie's.

'Tomorrow, Luke,' said Aaron suddenly, I'll train you with a horse and plough on the fields.'

'And tomorrow, Maggie,' added Grace, 'I'll show you the art of milking a cow.'

Maggie grinned between mouthfuls of food. In her heart she felt happy to be here on this farm.

So too was Luke. That night in his bed he pondered over his dramatic change of fortune. He wrote a letter home, telling his parents about his adventures since leaving Newcastle.

★★★

The attraction between the two took time to develop. Luke always behaved courteously and in a gentlemanly fashion. Maggie seemed to be more interested in her work. One day Luke walked past the milking sheds. He stepped to look inside. Maggie was manipulating a cow's udder very carefully.

'How goes it Maggie? Mrs Heath has given me some lunch for you.'

Maggie looked up in surprise. 'It's going well. I'm just about ready for those sandwiches.'

Luke handed her the lunch. He was in two minds to ask if he could join her for a lunch and conversation. 'I'm about to have my sandwiches in the field. Would you like to join me?'

It was in Maggie's nature to be suspicious of men. But to her Luke just seemed like a man of simple nature. 'Yes. I'll just finish here and I'll join you.'

They sat quietly on a wooden gate, enjoying their sandwiches. It was peaceful and quiet. Maggie felt quite safe with Luke, although she was at a loss to find a subject to talk about. But it was Luke who spoke first, making one of his daily declarations about luck and good fortune that had come his way in these dark Depression years.

'My aren't we lucky?' he stated, in a voice that sounded as if he was addressing an unseen audience in the vast field before him. 'You'll not hear me moan about my lot in life. I've got a job in the fresh air I enjoy which keeps me fit and agile. I get a right tasty plateful of bacon and farm fresh eggs for breakfast, and a clean bed to sleep in. I couldn't ask for more.'

'I'm very lucky too,' Maggie felt inclined to remark. 'I've got a lovely room at the other end of the farmhouse. Every morning I just love flinging open the window and taking a few breaths of fresh air. What I like most about this place is how at ease I feel here.'

Luke was quick to detect a hidden meaning. 'What do you mean, lass?'

'Although the days are long, they're pleasant. I don't feel tense or under pressure. It's a good feeling.' Maggie hesitated, then for some reason even she couldn't fathom, a remark about her background slipped out. 'The part of London I come from... well, it's not particularly nice. Some of the people I grew up with had run-ins quite a lot with the law. Even my late father.'

Luke went straight to the point as usual. 'They were villains, you mean?'

Maggie nodded, almost in shame.

'It's alright, Maggie,' Luke said, trying to put her at ease. 'I've been involved in a few things I've been fair ashamed of. I have fought fairly and squarely in the ring trying to make a living. I fought cleanly with the best of them. I was now't too successful, though. I got beaten on points mostly. Fighting for me didn't stop there. I'd fight in the streets too if someone cut up a bit rough with me. This is my kind of life, though. I miss my Ma and my Dad of course.

'You wouldn't believe as we sit here in the peace and quiet, and sunshine that out there in the big cities there's a Depression on, and lads from Jarrow have marched across this land to make their point. It could be on the other side of the world.' He paused for a moment. They both sat in the absolute silence of a lovely sunny day where the air felt fresh and clean. 'Grace was saying,' he continued, 'that there's a barn dance on in Trowbury village this Saturday night.'

'We call them knees-ups in my part of London,' Maggie remarked. And then she added, 'Are you going?'

'I think I might. Why don't you come along with me? You don't have to spend the evening with me if you see a lad that's willing to dance with you. I won't show up a classy looker like yourself. But I scrub up pretty well, and can behave like a gentleman.'

Maggie was flattered. 'Luke, it would be a pleasure to go with you.'

Luke was equally delighted. 'Right,' he said with a beaming smile. 'Well, we're on for Saturday night then, aren't we?'

★★★

Country dances in those days were really quite wonderful. In such a small village community folk came from all around to join in the fun. For Luke and Maggie this was the first country dance they had ever attended. In the Trowbury village hall the happy scene was one of a band at the centre of a makeshift stage that was more used to having amateur dramatics performed against a painted backcloth. Couples happily adjusted their dancing steps to the different tunes the band played, which varied between traditional country music and the 'Lambeth Walk'.

All around the hall smiling men downed pints of beer. Women of all ages chatted together. Luke looked typically one of the lads in braces and open-necked shirt with his hair greased back and shining. Maggie was pretty in a plain-coloured dress, but it was her glowing complexion and shining sparkling eyes that set her apart from the rest.

The band began to play a slow tune that was the signal for swooning couples to fall into each other's arms and glide around the floor. Maggie looked sideways at Luke, desperately hoping he would ask her to dance. Occasionally she hinted with her eyes, but to no avail.

'Doesn't look as if anyone's going to ask me to dance,' Maggie sighed with make-believe innocence.

Luke gave her a grin in return, he was canny enough to recognise the hint. 'Well, how about I ask you then?'

'Thank you, I'd love to.'

Luke and Maggie took to the dance floor. The tunes changed frequently that night. They danced to the 'Lambeth Walk', they did the 'Hokey-Cokey' and finally to a tune that generated one almighty barn dance in which all and sundry pounded hard down on the floorboards.

It was the beginning of the romance for Luke Price, the fighting Newcastle boy with principles and integrity stamped all over his character, and Maggie, the battling London girl who sought hard to put all of her past well and truly behind her.

They sat outside the hall for a while. Inside, the music continued.

'Gosh, that just about wore me out. I'm a bit exhausted. Good fun though! I must tell you something Luke. It's…' Maggie hesitated. 'It's my birthday today!'

'Your birthday!' Luke was surprised. 'Why did you na' tell me? I would have splashed out on something fine for you.'

'I'm twenty today. Twenty! Can you believe it?'

'Oh you poor old thing Maggie Maguire! Twenty! Past your prime already! I'm twenty-one, twenty-two any day now. But let me wish you happy birthday, lass.'

Luke kissed her quickly on the cheek. He drew away, but he was aware that Maggie was looking deeply into his eyes, giving away her true feelings for him. Luke felt slightly embarrassed by this.

He made an observation of his own. 'For a girl who tells me she's been brought up in a rough style of life you've got a fair and soft complexion. Your eyes seem to me to show a mixture of kindness, and maybe a little hurt as if you've suffered some pain. If you have, I'll not press you to talk about it. I'll take you as I find you. And I like what I see before me.'

Maggie was lost for words. Luke had impressed her. In him she saw a young man of youthful vitality, but wisely spoken beyond his years. He was strong, sincere and a man who fought, but only in defence.

Finally she found some words. 'Are you all straight and direct like that in Geordieland?'

'I know I am,' replied Luke self-assuredly, 'I couldn't be true to myself if I wasn't direct to the point of blatancy.'

'I like you, Luke,' Maggie said suddenly. The statement surprised him. 'I feel I can trust you.'

'Nice of you to say that, Maggie,' admitted Luke. 'I'm only being friendly, like, but would you like to go… courting?' He felt embarrassed asking the question. 'That's a strange word isn't it, "courting"? Whoever invented such a word?'

Maggie smiled at him and touched his hand warmly.

They walked back very slowly to the farmhouse, just taking their time and talking. Before going to their separate rooms they were silent for a while. There was something calming about the mood.

'Well it's been a grand night and it's a leisurely Sunday tomorrow, so there's no need to be rushing around. I'll be going for a stroll along the canal banks after lunch if you feel like joining me.'

'Luke,' Maggie said abruptly. Luke looked at her curiously. Maggie stepped forward, taking the initiative. She kissed him lovingly and slowly. Luke responded by holding her tightly and adding his own pressure to the kiss. Maggie released herself gently and then walked away, leaving Luke to look on in deep affection. He ran his tongue over his top lip, savouring the kiss.

★★★

In London, Maggie's brothers Clive, Mac and Frank walked along with their brother Bill who was distinctive by the fact that he now wore the uniform of the Royal Navy. Approaching them from the other end of the street came Louie Malone, flanked by two of his minders.

Clive eyed him. 'Would you believe it? Our old mate Cardsharp Louie.'

'Yeah, with a right couple of rough boys,' said Mac.

'You don't owe him any money do you, Bill?' Frank asked with a sudden urgency.

'Not blooming likely!' retorted Bill. 'My days of lining his over-full pockets are well over.'

Louie approached with his friendly pleased-to-meet you smile, although what he really thought of the Maguire brothers was anybody's guess.

'Well, well, well! Bill, I thought I hadn't seen you splurging your cash on the gaming table and soaking yourself in grog down at the den.'

'I've got better things to do these days,' said Bill.

'So I see,' Louie said with a smirk at the sight of Bill in uniform. 'I take it you're with the boys at Pompey ready to fight for our non-existent Empire if the call comes.'

Frank, a true patriot, took Louie on verbally, 'You've always done alright out of this country, Lou. Even in tough times like this. If the call does come, blokes like you will have to join up the same as everybody else.'

'Might do you a bit of good to take orders from somebody else for a change,' said Mac.

Louie was unperturbed and wore a broad grin. 'Believe me, boys, I'd still find ways of making a few quid out of the Army if I was called up.'

'Now that I can believe Louie!' Bill said with a laugh.

'How's that lovely sister of yours?' Louie asked, 'Where's she been hiding herself these days?'

Mac could hardly conceal his delight. 'She's gone.'

'Gone!' Louie was genuinely astonished.

'Yes,' replied Frank who was also pleased to put one over on Louie for a change. 'Yes, Louie old mate, she got treated like an easy tart by the likes of you. She was sold short by a lot of people round here. My sister had more courage than we ever gave her credit for.'

Bill had the last word. 'We all underestimated her. She's got herself a new life on a farm in Wiltshire. See you around.'

The brothers moved off. Louie pushed his hat back. 'Well, what about that then?' he gasped. His minders looked at him blank-faced. 'What are you two ugly orang-utans staring at? Come on, boys, I'll buy you a round.'

★★★

Market day was always an enjoyable experience. Aaron drove Luke and Maggie with him. He was aware that the two were mutually fond of each other and he watched them both with amusement. 'You two are getting on alright then?' There was a mischievous twinkle in his eyes.

Maggie quickly glanced at Luke to gauge his reaction. Luke was as ever quick off the mark. 'We're getting on fine,' said Luke. And he went on to say, 'I think we all work well as a team. Are you still happy with the work we're doing? If you're not we'll double our productivity.'

Aaron let out a hearty laugh. 'No need to do that, son! You've done mighty well in all the tasks I've given you. If young Maggie doubles up on her work she'll have to squeeze poor old cows' udders twice as fast!'

Luke had a wry smile on his face. 'That's true. You might get more milk from the udders but it would bring tears to the cows' eyes!'

Aaron went off on his own at the markets. Maggie had a few things to buy for Grace while Luke was free to wander around on his own. At one stall he saw some beautiful flowers for sale. A thought flashed through his mind. It was a chance to further his romance with Maggie. He bought two bunches of flowers.

A short time later Maggie walked towards Luke carrying two wicker baskets of household goods. Luke smiled at her and produced a bunch of flowers.

'These are for you,' he said boldly.

Maggie gave him a look of surprise which turned to a delightful smile. 'Oh Luke, you old romantic!'

Maggie leaned over and gave him a quick kiss. Aaron turned round from where he was examining the cattle. He caught sight of Luke and Maggie laughing together, and smiled knowingly at the sight of the blossoming romance.

This did not go unnoticed by Grace either. Back home, Grace and

Aaron looked out of the kitchen window in the early evening to see Luke and Maggie sitting beneath a tree in the distance.

'Nice of Luke to give me the flowers on your behalf,' said Grace putting them in a vase. 'I see Maggie got a bunch too.'

'Yes. They're a nice couple of kids,' admitted Aaron. 'Got to admit I took a big chance employing young Luke. The first time I saw him in the barn he looked like a lad on the run from the police. I've always been a good judge of character. But I was wrong. Luke is a fine hard worker and a straight-talking boy. He's been a real help to me.'

'Maggie is very happy here,' Grace pointed out. 'I know Luke came down here to find work, but I think young Maggie is running away from something. Maybe she was unhappy at home. I don't know.'

'Shouldn't ask, Grace.' Aaron looked out of the window at Luke and Maggie. 'I wouldn't be surprised if yonder romance over there graduated from cosy chats and affectionate kisses to something more permanent.'

Grace tried to sum it up. 'Can't tell. You never can. They are just a couple of Depression kids thrown together by fate.'

That seemed to sum up Luke and Maggie perfectly. They were Depression kids, victims of circumstances who fought to change their lives and had found each other.

Unaware they were being talked about in the Heath farm kitchen, the two of them sat beneath a tree in the orchard talking about things in their past. Maggie had told Luke about Louie Malone.

'This bloke...' Luke began uneasily, 'this Cardsharp Louie, he seems to have some sort of hold over you. Sounds like a right scallywag to me.'

'He was,' agreed Maggie, 'but he was also a charmer too. A lot of stories used to circulate about him in the manor.' She smiled and added, 'Of course, some improved with age and different people could embellish them. I just thought, as we've become really close this past year, that I should be totally honest with you.'

'I admire you for that, lass,' said Luke quietly, and his face was a true picture of sincerity. 'You and me, we're both ramrod straight when it comes to the truth. I may never be a gentleman with shiny clothes and a public school educated accent, but I'll always be honest and hardworking. When it comes down to it I don't care if somebody doesn't like me, I don't even mind if they don't respect me. Being liked or respected is not essential in my life. But I do care if someone doubts my honesty and integrity. Me old dad up there in Newcastle always used to say t' me, if your honesty and integrity is in doubt then you've nothing left at all.'

'You've got a lot in common with your old dad,' Maggie complimented him. 'I think you'd get on well with my brother Bill.' She suddenly became wistful. Bill was the gentle giant. 'I got a letter from him the other day. He's in the Royal Navy at Portsmouth. One of the good old lads at Pompey. He's expecting to be sent overseas. There's talk of him going somewhere like Singapore or Hong Kong. I'm very happy for him.'

'Have you got any ambitions, Maggie?' Luke asked suddenly.

'My only ambition until recently was to leave home and live in a peaceful place. I think I've achieved that.' There was a look of calm and serenity on her face.

Luke decided this was the perfect opportunity to ask her a question he had previously delayed. 'How do you really feel about me?'

Maggie looked at him warmly, but her voice was laced with a certain amount of shyness. 'Do I have to tell you?'

'I'd like to hear it from you,' Luke insisted gently.

Maggie reached out and touched his hand. 'Not today. Not just yet.'

Luke felt resigned to this answer. 'Fair enough, lass, I'll not press you.' For the moment, Luke would have to be content with this.

★★★

It was a few days later that a dramatic turn of events took place. Maggie was helping Grace pick crops in the field when the sound of a car drawing up at the farmhouse could be heard. Grace looked up in surprise, for visitors to her farm were few and far between.

'Don't get any motor cars drawing up here. Must be lost. You carry on a minute, I'll just go and see.'

Grace left Maggie, who carried on collecting and soorting the vegetable crop. Maggie was surprised at the length of time Grace was away. When she returned her face was stern.

'Something wrong?' Grace touched Maggie on the shoulder.

'I hope not, Maggie,' she replied. 'I don't want to worry you but there are a couple of young men here to see you. One is in uniform and the other is a civilian.' Maggie knew instantaneously. 'They said they're your brothers.'

Maggie's face was a picture of shock. 'My brothers?' she gasped, and her eyes flashed across to the farmhouse. Her brothers Bill and Mac were standing by the car. Her voice was apprehensive. 'That's my brother Bill in uniform. And the other one is Mac.'

Grace, knowing they were the bearers of bad news, looked at Maggie in a soft and sensitive manner. 'Go across and see them.'

Maggie nodded to Grace and walked across the fields. At the farmhouse she embraced Bill and Mac. For a moment she was lost for words. Maggie looked up and down at Bill in the uniform of the Royal Navy.

'Bill, you look so well suited. Almost as if you were born to be a sailor.'

'I think I was, sis,' he murmured gently.

Maggie turned quickly to her other brother. 'It's good to see you, Mac. I'm sorry I left the way I did.'

'Don't be. I'm happy for you,' Mac replied. His face changed quickly to the expression of one who is a bearer of bad news. 'It's trouble, I'm afraid. We wouldn't have driven here if it hadn't been.'

'Mum had a stroke,' Bill said softly. Maggie looked horrified. 'Oh, she's recovering. She's a tough old bird. But she wants to see you. I'll run you back… that's if you want to come. I'm sailing out to Singapore in a few days.' He looked at Maggie, who was clearly showing signs of distress. 'Will you come?'

'Alright, Bill,' Maggie replied after a few moments. 'I'll come.'

Luke was working his way through a potato patch. A horse and cart were nearby. Luke placed mounds of freshly picked potatoes on the cart. Aaron appeared on the field, and Luke could see there was a sense of urgency about him.

'Maggie's gone.' Aaron had said it so quickly and quietly that the effect on Luke was of disbelief.

'Gone? Where?'

'Her mother took sick in London. Two brothers came down to pick her up.'

'Is she coming back?'

Aaron patted him on the back warmly. 'I sincerely 'ope so. Young Maggie is a great help to Grace.'

That night Luke decided to drown his sorrows at the village pub. It was always a place of warmth where anyone alone would soon find themselves embroiled in a happy conversation with the landlord. Luke stood at the bar and sure enough the friendly publican, recognising one of his regulars, came across with a smile.

'Hullo young man. On your own? What'll it be?'

'A pint of real ale please.'

'Real ale is what we serve here. Real ale is what you'll get.' The publican proceeded to pour Luke a pint of what he considered was the finest beer in the English-speaking world. 'Where's that nice young lady you're normally with?'

'Oh, she had to go to London. To see her sick mother,' Luke replied with a hint of sadness in his voice.

'Nothing too bad, I hope.'

'I hope not.' The publican topped the pint mug and handed it across to Luke, who gave him the exact change. 'There you go.'

Luke took a sip of his delicious ale and winked delightedly. The publican watched him take the drink. 'You're enjoying that, Luke! Been at the Heath Farm for a while now, haven't you? What will it be… let me see… 'bout a year now? Still enjoying it?'

'Loving every minute of it, mate!' Luke exclaimed. 'I never thought life could be as good as this. I'm only a farm labourer but there are few jobs that would give me as much satisfaction as this. I really feel I earn my bread in the sweat of my brow.'

'You know something, Luke?' the publican asked, and then proceeded to tell him anyway. 'People down here in the farming community have always taken a huge amount of pride in their work. The comradeship amongst folk round here is something pretty strong too.'

'Maggie was telling me how she feels at ease down here. No pressures like she would feel in the city. I know what she means. Considering there's a Depression on in the world, we eat wonderfully well at the farm. There's bacon and ham hanging up in the cottage kitchen. We grow our own garden peas, runner beans, the most delicious potatoes I've ever tasted, tomatoes all rosy red and sweet, onions, turnips, parsnips, there's our own poultry, farm eggs and butter. My old ma in Newcastle would envy me this.'

'You sound like a happy man. I came from the Midlands, an industrial area, as a matter of fact. When I came here it really was a breath of fresh air seeing lush fields bounded by hedges and streams and rivers, rabbits running free, pheasants, partridges, hares, even deer and on occasion badgers and foxes. I could go on and on really… cattle chewing the cud, fields full of sheep and cows. This pub has always been a happy place. I like seeing the couples coming in. Perhaps we'll see you in here with your young lady again.'

Luke peered deep into his beer glass. 'I hope so. I've never met a lass that I warmed to so quickly and felt so happy to be with.' He added sadly, 'I truly love that lass.'

★★★

All the way back to London, Maggie had felt a sense of dread. After the easy-going ways of the countryside, the slowness of pace she had become accustomed to in Wiltshire seemed to quicken the nearer to London she came. The rush of people going to their destinations was noticeable. By the time the car drew up in the old neighbourhood Maggie could see the old familiar cocky swagger of the local lads. Reluctantly, she was back in the alley.

Mac leaned across and opened the door for her. 'I won't ask if you're happy to be back.'

'It's alright, Mac,' Maggie said with a resigned smile. 'We better go.'

The three of them left the car and went up to the drab rooms above the betting shop. Bill opened the door slowly. Inside, May was seated in a Queen Victoria pose with Frank and Clive sitting on each side.

'Hullo, Mum,' said Maggie. May did not say a word. She stood up and walked across to her in an unprecedented show of affection. May put her arms around her. This was the signal for Bill to clear the room.

'Right lads,' he said, raising his thumb backwards to indicate to his brothers, 'Out. Pub. My round!'

May and Maggie talked for a long time together. The stroke that May had suffered hadn't lessened her feisty spirit too much. Yet surprisingly at first she appeared to make concessions. This surprised Maggie, as she knew her mother much better than that.

'I'm sorry I've been so blooming hard on you all these years. Always pushing you, criticising you, even telling you that you hadn't the courage to leave here.'

'Don't go on, Mum. Please. I'd rather you didn't. The point is, how are you now? A stroke is a serious business.'

The real May emerged from the brief period in which she had played the role of another person. 'I've got a constitution made of molten metal, love. You don't live in an area like this without being brought up a fighter. I'll have to take a bit more care of myself. No more gin and cigarettes. In fact none of the hard stuff at all for me. I might be an old cow my girl but it'll take a lot to damage my udders!'

'You haven't lost your sense of humour, Mum.'

'Things really are changing, aren't they? You are very happy in your new way of life. Billy boy is going off to Singapore. Singapore, I ask you! I told him he better watch out for those long-fingered Asian girls. If they see a big lad like my Billy they'll be all over him like creeping ivy. What about you, Maggie? Are you really happy? You wouldn't like to stay if I asked you?'

Maggie realised her mother was trying to use the present predicament to her advantage. The old streetwise ways returned, taking over from the easy-going country girl. Maggie tried her hardest to be strong and firm without being hard-hearted.

'Mum, if you need me to stay while you recover, I will. But as soon as I know you're well, I want to go back to Wiltshire. Don't think harshly of me, Mum.'

'Would you leave your old mum when she's ill?' May asked in a quiet voice. It was a miserable performance that wouldn't have passed a drama school audition.

Maggie smiled at May's feeble attempt at persuasion. 'My old mum, stroke or no stroke, can spit fire, fury and brimstone with the best of them when it suits her. And if I know my old mum she's tougher than most men, who'll give back a damn sight more than she's had to take.'

'You really have come a long way, my girl. Not only have you got independence, you have got a bit of fight there after all.'

'And I know where I get it from too!'

'Good for you, Maggie. Like mother, like daughter.'

So on the surface a new relationship between May and Maggie seemed to have been established. May appeared to be respecting Maggie's right to her own individuality.

In her own room, Maggie raised the window slightly and then unpacked her case. Although this was her home Maggie felt a great deal of unease at being back here. This unease was further borne out by a familiar voice that drifted up from the street below.

'Hullo, Dave. How's it all going?' It was Louie Malone on the street below, meeting an old burly bruiser.

'Not so bad, Lou,' Dave replied affably. 'I just saw May's boys down at the Pirate and Beggar pub. Old May's going fine.'

'That's the shot. May is a fighter just like her old man was. She'll be up and about in no time.' Lou looked up at the light in Maggie's bedroom. He didn't miss a trick. 'Hang on one moment, Dave. You say you just saw the boys down the pub?'

'That's right. Something wrong, Lou?'

'Then who is up there?' He pointed to the lighted room.

Dave grinned at him. It was no secret around the alley and the manor about Louie's intentions toward Maggie. 'Didn't you know? The boys brought Maggie back to see the old girl.'

'Is that right?' Louie gasped in a mixture of amazement and delight.

Before anyone could say something else the window above them was fully opened. Maggie could scarcely conceal her amusement.

'That is right, Lou,' she called down to him. Louie looked upwards and gave her a familiar smirk that passed as a smile. 'But don't worry,' she added quickly, 'I'm not staying. Just as soon as I know Mum is fine I'll be heading back.' She closed the window.

Down on the street below Louie's eyes sparkled. 'Not this time, girlie. You're mine,' he muttered under his breath.

★★★

Already Luke was missing Maggie. Four weeks passed and Luke was doubling up with the work at the farm. He was now milking the cows as well, watched over by the farmhouse cats, who were quick to lap up any freshly spilt droplets.

Grace came up to him one day to see how he was going. 'You don't mind helping out in the sheds do you, Luke?' she asked almost sheepishly. In truth, Grace felt embarrassed that Luke was working twice as hard without complaint.

'I'm right pleased to help.' And he was sincere in his words.

'Trouble is, we don't know when Maggie will be coming back. She's been gone four weeks now. I'm not sure we'll be able to keep her job open.'

Luke stopped working. His face was a picture of shock. He appeared to think of a possible solution. Without hesitation he suggested an idea to

Grace. 'Would you think it wrong of me if maybe I had a few days off and went up to London to see her?'

'You've worked here well over a year now without having any time off to go home and see your folks in Newcastle.' She paused. 'Why not, Luke? I could discreetly give you the address.'

Within a few short hours Luke was on his way.

★★★

Louie did not give up his pursuit of Maggie. He would appear unexpectedly. One morning as Maggie walked down the street, a car pulled up with a sudden squeal of brakes. It was Louie. He had obviously been choosing his moment.

'Hullo, doll. Where ya going?'

'To the city. To find work.'

'Does this mean you're staying?' Maggie did not reply. She looked at him more in sadness than anything. 'Let me give you a lift, doll.'

Reluctantly, Maggie entered the car. Louie started the engine up and moved off. There was a silence as Maggie fumbled for words.

'I hear Bill sailed out,' said Louie after a while. His ear was always hard to the ground these days.

'Yes,' Maggie said quietly and then she felt included to add, 'he's going on a grand tour. He's got to make stops at Gibraltar, Malta, Naples, Sicily, Alexandria, Suez, Colombo, Rangoon, Singapore, and I believe his convoy may go up to Hong Kong and across the Pacific.'

'Seems like Billy boy is going to be a bit of a traveller. Naturally he's visiting all the great ports of the Empire. Churchill and Eden seem to reckon there'll be a war soon. So maybe he'll get a front seat at the stalls. Still, it's all bull dust to me, doll. The only life I'm concerned about is the one I've got today. How about going out tonight?'

It had gone too far already. Maggie was going to tell him straight. 'Listen to me Lou…'

Louie came back, persistent to the end. 'Go on, doll. Just a friendly night. There's dancing on at the den tonight if you just want to twirl.'

Maggie gave up. Perhaps this was fate dragging her back to the life she had so much strived to get away from. 'Alright, a friendly night it is. And that's all it is!'

'Good stuff!' Louie said delightedly. He knew it was only a matter of time before he and Maggie became a permanent fixture.

That was what he thought. But for once in his life Louie was going to meet his match in the form of real competition from Luke Price. Luke arrived in London that night and immediately set out to find Maggie's London address. When he found the area and the squalid street Luke realised why Maggie had so desperately wanted to get away from it.

He found the betting shop and walked up to the rooms above it. The air stank of rotting vegetables and coal dust from the nearby railway sidings. The whole area looked badly in need of cleaning and a fresh coat of paint on every house. Larrikin lads swaggered through the streets like punch-drunk prizefighters eagerly looking for their next bout. A few drunks reeled out of a corner pub and one promptly threw up in the gutter. Some street corner kids shouted raucously at passers-by, eager to prove they were as cocky and confident as their elders. A few women, heavily made-up, headed out on the town in a predatory manner for the new loves in their life.

What a dump! What a godforsaken wretched area! Luke could bear the sight no longer from his vantage point above the betting shops. He checked the address again and rapped on the front door.

It was Clive who answered. 'Yes, mate?'

Luke removed his cap as a sign of courtesy although even he was at a loss to know why. 'How d' you do? Luke Price is the name.'

'Is that supposed to mean something to me?' Clive answered sharply.

'No. but it might mean something to your sister.'

'Maggie?'

'Yes. I've been working awhile with Maggie at Aaron Heath's farm in Trowbury, Wiltshire.'

Clive's expression immediately changed from suspicion to one of a friendly disposition. 'Shuffle yourself inside, Luke. Welcome.'

They shook hands and Luke stepped inside to the Maguire household. Inside the scene was one of a damp apartment with mould on the wallpaper. May, Frank and Mac looked up from the table where they were seated. Luke wasn't sure, but it appeared as if May was lifting her nose in the air as if he had brought some of the smells of the farmyard with him.

'This is Luke Price everyone. He worked with Maggie on the farm.' Clive announced.

Already May was studying him with a discerning eye. Who was this clodhopping clog-booted yokel with the North of England accent? This was what she was thinking. Surely this fresh-faced farm boy didn't have serious designs on her daughter?

'What can we do for you young man?' Her lip was twisted as she spoke.

Luke was clear, courteous and firm. 'I hear you've not been too well and I'm glad t' see you're fighting fit and looking in fine form. I'll not waste too much of your time, but the purpose of my journey has two missions in mind. One is to ask Maggie when she intends to return to the farm. The second… is of a more serious nature.'

'Oh, and what might that matter be?' May seemed to be verbally squaring up for a fight.

'I love her, and I'm going to ask her if she'll consider marriage to me.'

'To you!' May was aghast. 'A clodhopping yokel like you! Not to you she won't!'

Frank showed real anger at his mother's display of rudeness, 'Now that's enough, Mum!' he yelled, for the first time in his life. 'He's done us no harm. And he's come all the way from Wiltshire to see Maggie! I love you Mum but you've not given the lad a fair hearing.'

May suddenly became very stern. Looking very hard at Luke she muttered, 'Alright then. Lad… and that's just what you are, a lad. What have you got to offer my daughter?'

Luke rose to the occasion and as always he made himself perfectly understood. 'I didna' come here to be insulted by a woman short on tolerance. I came to see Maggie because she means the world to me. I love her. I'm a hard-working bloke. I'm dependable and reliable and I've got a strong set of values that'll be hard to beat anywhere. I'm a no-nonsense, no-shirking, straight as a die, find as you speak man, and if the only cross I have to bear in life is having you as a mother-in-law then that's a small price to pay.'

'I like a fighter,' May said, impressed by the young man's presence.

'Well you're looking at one. I don't go looking for battles to fight. That's for the weak who've got nothing better to do than pick fights. But if someone takes me on I repay with interest and triplefold at that.'

May looked at her sons and grinned. For some reason she took to Luke. Perhaps it was because in him she recognised similar traits for character to her own. 'You better go and see how she feels. You'll find her at Louie's den down the road, talking over old times with Cardsharp Louie himself. It's two blocks down the road.'

'I'll find my own way there, and I'll bid you good day.' Luke turned to the door but before he left he could not resist a passing comment. 'For a lady who's had a stroke I'd say you've got plenty of life in you yet!'

★★★

Louie's den was a dark and smoky place at the best of times but on Saturday night when the gambling punters came to play in the back room and the dance band was in full swing then the place exploded into a blaze of electric light. Louie and Maggie sat alone in a corner. It was obvious from the outset that Louie was up to his old tricks again. He kept trying to push Maggie into a relationship with him. But still she kept him at an arm's length.

'We've been over this a dozen times, Lou. You're an old charmer, an old rogue, a villain of sorts some would say. Tying the knot? No. Never. You sail too close to the wind.'

'A lot of people sail close to the wind round here,' remarked Louie.

'I didn't get work today,' said Maggie with a decisive air. 'In fact I made up my mind that now Mum is in good nick I'm going back to Wiltshire.' Maggie's expression changed suddenly. Across the room she saw Luke enter. 'I can't believe it!'

'What is it?' Louie noticed the expression on Maggie's face.

'It's Luke. I work with him in Wiltshire…' her voice tapered off as she tried to adjust to the shock.

Louie looked across the room at him. There was distaste evident in his face. In that same moment Luke spotted Maggie and came across to her.

'Luke! What on earth are you doing here?'

'I've come to ask you two things, Maggie. Firstly, are you coming back to the farm?'

'What was the second thing?'

'And secondly… I love you Maggie. Will you marry me?'

Maggie was completely taken by surprise.

Louie was enraged. He stood up and erupted like a volcano. 'Get lost, knucklehead! She's mine!' Louie swung a heavy punch at Luke who took the blow hard on his chin. He was sent keeling over onto his back.

Silence fell across the den. The band stopped playing. The people looked on in amazement. Louie moved forward like a leopard examining its kill. To his shock, Luke leapt up and faced him square on.

'Cardsharp Louie, eh?' Luke said with a sparkling grin.

'Are you alright, Luke?' Maggie asked quickly. She was stunned, not knowing what to do or say.

'Never better!' Luke said, removing his jacket. 'While you're thinking over the marriage proposal, Cardsharp Louie and I are going to get to know each other better.'

Louie suddenly recognised he was facing a far more formidable adversary than he ever had before. 'How you do you mean, pal?' Louie asked with a trace of menace in his voice.

Luke started to spar with his fists. 'I fight Marquis of Queensbury Rules. What about you?'

'I'll fight Murphy's Rules if it suits me,' Louie replied raising his fists.

For once in his life he had made a grave misjudgement of one of his opponents. Working on the premise that he who throws the first punch is the victor in the final round, Louie stupidly took an uneven swing at Luke.

Now Luke's boxing training in the ring came to the foreground. He sidestepped Louie's ridiculously wide punch and led with his left, striking a sharp uppercut. Louie was down. The look of horror mixed in with amazement that he had been floored was something to behold. Louie was angry. He had been humiliated on his own patch.

All of the dancers and gamblers in the den stood to one side to see what their local gangland leader would do. He rose slowly. His eyes gleamed with hate and anger. Louie came back fast and furiously, sending two swift blows with hyper-charged force into Luke. One struck him in the stomach and one on the chin. But they were not sledgehammer punches – fast punches, forceful punches, yes – but effective in their power, never. Luke returned the same two punches to Louie with considerably more effect. Louie staggered and weaved. He had been hit and hurt, but he was an old street fighting boy with a few tricks up his sleeve.

In the manner of bareknuckle fighters of old, Luke and Louie traded punches. Louie might not have been a boxer, but he had resilience. He could take the blows with the best. The fight began to move across the room. Several times Luke made Louie look ridiculous by dodging and ducking. From the centre of the dance floor Luke and Louie punched their way into the billiard room, much to the amazement of the watching players.

Luke sent a straight right at Louie which propelled him over on his back, landing him in the middle of the billiard table. Louie clutched some billiard balls and threw them at Luke's feet. Luke found himself slipping on them. Louie leapt forward and threw punch after punch at Luke. Luke went down on his back, threw one fist straight at Louie and then leapt up. He grabbed Louie by the shoulders and hurled him through the door onto the dance floor. Luke raced in. Louie jumped up again and called out to the band on stage.

'Keep playing boys! That's what I pay you for! How about "When the Saints Go Marching In".'

Luke disagreed with the choice. 'I'd have preferred "Happy Days Are Here Again"!'

Louie was not devoid of humour either. 'Well you don't own this establishment, do you?' The band began to play Louie's request.

'OK, tea break's over!' Luke struck Louie a heavy blow. Then all hell broke loose. The fight became dirty as Louie used every street fighting trick in the book. They both fought hard, in the process knocking over tables and chairs. Louie picked furniture up and threw it, missing Luke with every shot. Luke could not resist grinning.

'Look at you,' Luke said with a broad smile, 'you can't even fight cleanly.'

But Louie started back into the fight with a vengeance. He struck the pose of a bareknuckle fighter and delivered blow after blow to Luke. The fight moved onto the stage and the two men slugged it out, moving in between the musicians who stepped forwards and backwards as punches were thrown.

Luke grabbed a pint mug from a nearby table and swilled back the contents. Before finishing off the pint Luke tossed the remainder of the beer over Louie. Louie was undeterred and shook his head. He moved forward, jabbing and punching. Poor Maggie stood to one side not knowing whether to laugh or cry. The fight moved all around the dance floor and into the street. The people at the den followed the fight outside. They had not seen a bout like this before, not even the famous Doyle versus Phillips fight at White City in 1939 would reach such epic proportions.

Out in the street Luke sent Louie a sharp heavy right. Louie went keeling back and collided with a cyclist who came riding around the corner. Louie, his anger aroused that he couldn't beat off his opponent, came back sharply and thudded Luke with the hardest punch he had ever delivered in his life. Luke was thrown back, and with great surprise he found himself rolling amongst overturned dustbins. Louie saw this as the opportunity to finish the fight once and for all. He moved in to take one final knockout punch. He swung sharply. Luke grabbed a dustbin lid and shielded himself as Louie struck. The pain of his fist connecting with the dustbin lid soared right up from his fingertips through his funny bone to his shoulders. Louie roared with pain.

But still Louie did not give up. Still Luke seemed incapable of being floored. Two persistent, pig-headed fighters of contrasting fisticuff methods and integrity continued. Louie still had his sharp left. Luke thought he would have had enough of it all by now. He had to admire Louie, if only for his persistence. Louie struck hard left after hard left. In the bout he had learned from Luke the value of heavy powerful punches, and to Luke's distress he was beginning to feel the pain.

The fight progressed along the street to the outside of a café. Bemused customers in the café suddenly stopped drinking their tea and eating their meals as the fight took place in front of the window. They had ringside seats to the longest and most entertaining bout folk had ever seen found these parts. Cars, buses and double decker trams stopped as passengers stepped out and watched in absolute amazement.

Louie seemed to regain strength in both arms now. He was determined to win this fight, after all, this was his patch! He was cock of the walk, nobody beat Louie, the undisputed king of this manor. He could not lose. If he did his credibility would be gone and pretty soon some other young thug could challenge him. In sheer desperation Louie picked Luke up by the shoulders and thrust him through the café window, breaking the glass. Luke's response was to grab a plate of food and slap the contents into Louie's face. Louie staggered around with gravy and potatoes and pie on his face, hardly believing the fight had disintegrated into slapstick.

Luke walked across, breathing heavily, thinking that the fight was now over. He could not have been more wrong. Louie wiped his face clean. It was Luke's turn to make a misjudgement now. Louie simply did not give up. He came rushing at Luke and rained five or six blows in succession on him. Luke staggered back until he was standing with his back against the doors of the Pirate and Beggar pub. This was it. This was the end of the fight. Louie Malone reigned invincible. Or did he? Louie moved in to finish the fight off. Luke appeared to slide down the door. Luke closed his eyes momentarily. He opened them to see Louie raise his fist. Luke quickly opened the door and ducked.

To the astonishment of the drinkers in the pub, Louie came tumbling into the bar. Luke came in quickly as if he had suddenly acquired a new burst of energy. The crowd from the street poured into the pub, doubling the night's takings as Luke and Louie continued their marathon fight. Louie decided to return the earlier compliment by tossing a mug of beer over Luke, who shook his head like a wet dog.

'Call that stuff beer!' Luke said in a jocular mood. 'In Newcastle we give that to stray cats!'

Louie raised his fists. 'Then I suggest you get back to the alleys you know so well!'

This remark brought a smile to Luke's face. But he wasted no time. The fight was gradually becoming an endurance test. Both men were determined not to give way. They fought all around the pub, through the saloon bar, the ladies' lounge and in the snug; then the pugilists slugged it out in the toilets and headed out into a back alley.

Down the alley the fight continued. Dustbins were overturned and rubbish was everywhere. The fight had well and truly gone the distance. Louie was beginning to tire. His shirt was torn. His handsome face was bloodied and bruised. Luke still had his fighter's energy intact but he would have preferred a clean-fought bout in the boxing ring. The crowd followed the two down the alley into a yard full of wastepaper.

This had to be the finalé. Both men knew it. Louie mustered his strength and decided to fight it out in a no-holds-barred brawl. The two of them rolled around, striking and jabbing until a pile of wastepaper showered them like confetti. Wastepaper fell down all over the place as they bounced from one corner to the other. Louie threw a pile of old newspapers at Luke who showered his adversary with paper shreddings. Punches and paper flew. It became not so much a fight now but a scene resembling two children throwing paper arrows at each other.

Louie began to laugh. Luke tried to remain serious but found himself shadow boxing in a maze of paper. He landed one hefty punch on Louie's jaw. Louie staggered back and landed in a mass of soft wastepaper. Luke fell to his knees; surely the fight was over now.

He began to laugh softly. Louie shook his jaw and tried to sit up. He looked at Luke and suddenly he too began to laugh. In a few minutes the two of them were laughing in a Herculean fashion at the fight they had just had.

'I enjoyed that,' Louie said in a fit of laughter.

'Do we go on, or what?' Luke asked.

Louie was more interested in his opponent. 'Where did you learn to fight like that?'

Luke swept his hair back and dusted himself down. 'I'm a former boxer. I did m' training with a fellow called Joe McQuillan who runs a gym in Newcastle. What about you?'

'On every street in South London.'

Luke nodded. He knew Louie could never have been a pro fighter. The crowd of spectators who had followed the fight all the way from the den looked on in puzzlement. Louie smiled at them. 'The show's over now folks. If you go back to the den I'll see you all get drinks on the house.'

The crowd eagerly departed giving Louie the thumbs-up and smiles of approval. It had been such a great fight for the spectators and people found it hard to establish who the clear winner had been.

'I reckon it was a draw, don't you?' Louie asked smugly.

Luke's answer came as no surprise. 'I won clearly and decisively. If you'd fought like that in the ring the ref would have ruled you out.'

'I don't doubt that for one moment.' He looked at Luke, suddenly realising he had a potential fighter in front of his very eyes, 'I've got a gym down the road…'

'Amongst other things, I hear.'

'Never mind about that. Some of the fighters I've got down at the gym couldn't go the distance with Cicely Courtnedge or Jessie Matthews, never mind trying to emulate Jack Doyle. You've got real power in your punches. You can go not only the distance but a surplus of furlongs, pal. Fancy making some easy dough if I managed you?'

'Not a chance. I love the game but that was another life ago.'

'Shame. We could have made some big cash. Well, Luke, there is a good-looking girl called Maggie down the street. You better go and ask her to marry you — if she still wants you. What she sees in a piece of rough like you I'll never know. You've got no class, pal. You've no style. And what's more, you'll never have a shilling to spit on.'

Luke replied with words to match. 'I might not have a shilling to spit on but I'll always earn an honest quid.'

'What a life of boredom you're going to lead,' Louie said half-mockingly. In truth, he had acquired respect and admiration for Luke.

Luke stood up. 'It's you I feel sorry for. You've got your little kingdom. You wear a cut of clothes and style of cloth I'll never wear. But in your way of life you'll always be looking over your shoulder. You fight rough and dirty, and you've not got integrity the way you choose to win a bout. I'll take a life as near to peace and quiet as I can find.'

★★★

For Luke the peace and quiet he craved included Maggie Maguire. He chose his spot carefully to propose marriage. A few days after the fight, Luke and Maggie walked down by the Thames. They found a bench and sat in silence for a while.

Finally Luke decided the time had come to steer the conversation to a level where he could build up the courage to propose.

'Maggie, are you coming back to the farm?'

Without hesitation she replied, 'Yes. And I can't wait.'

'It's a better life there than you'll have here. Grace and Aaron would be right happy to have you back. Don't delay. Come back with me, in the next few days.'

'Alright Luke, I will.'

'I think your friend Louie finally got the message. He certainly took a lot of convincing.'

Maggie smiled at the thought of the fight. 'I've got a feeling the people around the alley and the manor will be talking about that fight for years to come.'

The big moment had come. 'I'm not too good with my words, Maggie, when it comes to expressing some of my most emotional feelings.'

Maggie's eyes showed sensitivity as she anticipated Luke's coming words.

'But the moment I saw you… well, when Grace introduced me to you, it was love at first sight for me. We could have a good life together you and me. I'd take good care of you, Maggie.' He felt inclined emphasise. 'Damn good care of you. You'd not want for anything. I'd see to that.'

Maggie stared deeply into Luke's eyes. For the first time she made a concentrated study of this man who she loved so much. He was fearless, principled, strong, and someone who bore all the finest traits of human nature: loyalty, trust, courage, and a dedication to family values and work. Maggie would be hard pressed to find a better man. Beneath Luke's toughness he was capable of great love and gentleness.

'What say you, Maggie?' Luke asked. His eyes were clouded with emotion. 'Say yes to a wild young Geordie boy like myself. Marry me and we'll live in the country and build a good life for ourselves.'

Maggie gripped his hand almost defensively.

'Does that mean… yes?'

Maggie smiled. She kissed him lovingly. 'Of course, Luke. Of course it means yes.'

Luke and Maggie were married a couple of weeks later in London. Luke's parents came down from Newcastle and May Maguire was as proud as punch on the day of the wedding. All of the crowd from the alley and the manor packed out the church. In just a short time Luke had made an extraordinary impression on the local folk. They liked fighters in these parts. They liked people who were the salt of the earth. Luke shone like a blazing beacon in a pitch black night and he'd married one of the nicest local girls.

★★★

When they arrived back in Wiltshire the two of them felt as near to exuberation as they had ever felt. They stepped out of the railway station and took deep breaths of the air.

'Take a sniff of that air, Luke,' Maggie said. He face showed real delight at being back. 'It's fresh and it's clear. What a wonderful place to start married life. I'm so happy, Luke.'

He gripped her tight. 'So am I, lass. I feel that I'm dreaming, and it's all sweet dreams. I've a job I love and a lass I love so much I've only to look at her and she makes me feel good.' They kissed lovingly for a few minutes. He gazed at her in deep admiration. 'I'll ring Aaron and ask if he can pick us up.'

'No, don't do that.' She touched his hand quickly. 'Let's walk. It's a lovely day and I want to feel it all again.'

'Suits me fine,' smiled Luke. 'Let's go.'

The two of them began to walk down the lane to the farmhouse. Luke looked up at the wonderfully clear blue sky and the dense green and golden fields of the countryside. Maggie was studying it all with delight. The alley and the manor were in her past now. This was where she belonged. For Luke, the marathon fight had been worth it just to be here with the woman he loved.

By the time they came within view of the farmhouse they were smiling delightedly. From within the house Aaron and Grace stepped out. Grace looked up and caught sight of the couple walking towards them. Her face blossomed with happiness.

'Oh Aaron, look,' Grace said nudging her husband.

'By gosh. It's young Luke and Maggie.'

Aaron and Grace waved. Luke and Maggie waved and then began to run, so happy to be back. Luke shook hands with Aaron and embraced Grace. Maggie could not resist kissing both Aaron and Grace, and hugging them both.

There were tears in Aaron's eyes. 'It's so good to have you both back,' said Aaron, a warm smile busting through his tears.

'We've missed you so much,' Grace said happily.

'Do you still want us to work for you?' Luke asked the question out of courtesy, although he knew the answer would be yes.

'Of course we do,' Grace replied.

'You don't have to ask,' Aaron said in a tone of voice that betrayed surprise.

'We have an announcement,' Maggie said suddenly.

Luke put his arm around her. 'Meet my wife,' Luke announced, 'Mrs Maggie Price.'

Aaron and Grace looked absolutely overjoyed. They hugged both of them. Then they moved inside the farmhouse for a celebratory dinner. It was a very happy start to a new life for all of them.

★★★

So what happened to all the principal players in this story? Luke and Maggie were married for a total of 45 years, during which time they had five children. Maggie died in 1982 and Luke several years after.

During the war Luke served with distinction in the Army on duty in

North Africa and Western Europe. When he returned from active service he and Maggie, together with their children, lived in Jersey for some years before going to live in Canada.

Luke gave up farming to work as a long-distance lorry driver from Vancouver to Nova Scotia. They returned to Britain several times for holidays to meet up with relatives.

May Maguire was 100 when she died. In South London they gave the grand old matriarch a send-off in the style of a New Orleans funeral procession. The old girl, who had suffered several strokes, died the way she had lived: persistently stubborn, pig-headed and consistently confounding the doctors at every turn. All of the folks from the alley and the manor came to say goodbye. In the streets the people danced and sang to the jazz band that played that day. Even the traffic came to a standstill for May.

For Luke and Maggie, who had come over from Canada, they had a wonderful reunion with the rest of the Maguire brothers. Luke met up with his old sparring partner Louie Malone. Now married for the third time and with a string of petty convictions and dodgy deals behind him, Louie was still as vain and cocky as ever. But Louie's reign in South London was over. He was just a spiv from another age and the new boys on the block considered him a has-been.

When Luke and Maggie returned home to Canada after May's funeral they felt so pleased to be going back to the freshness of Vancouver. They had many happy years of marriage together and they never forgot where it had all begun: on a small dairy farm in Wiltshire, back in the Depression years.

2.

Jack and Peggy

The Wartime Couple

Jack Moran tried hard to maintain his composure. This was a very hard day that he had to get through. He was determined that he would not show a flood of tears and lay bare his grief for all to see. He knew his late wife Peggy would want him to be strong at her funeral and not mourn, but celebrate the life she had led. Jack was supported by his son Derek, who was in his forties, and always there when needed.

The church minister addressed the congregation and many had come to pay their respects. Peggy had been much loved, much admired. Jack, now a distinguished white-haired man, remembered this woman with whom he had been through so much since those dark days of the Second World War. Derek thought of his mother, the kind and sometimes sad person that Peggy had been, but also of the bright smiles and maternal qualities that had constantly shone through.

'Peggy Moran was a fine, good-hearted woman,' the minister said to the hushed congregation. 'Her affection and love for her family was well known by all those who knew her. She was the beloved wife of Jack for fifty years and mother of Derek, and loving grandmother of Derek's children Natasha and Pearl. Her love and loyalty towards her family will endure for years to come. We remember today her great strengths and positive character.'

Love and loyalty, though Jack. That was what he would miss. He could not bear the fact that from now on the house would be empty without Peggy. But he must not think about that now. There was a wake to get through with invited guests; all of them had to raise a glass and smile in the thankful knowledge that they had known Peggy Moran.

At Jack's house, he had carefully arranged around the living room photographs of Peggy in nicely mounted frames. The picture showed Peggy at various stages in her life: as a young child in Sutton, with her own parents in the doorway of a rose-covered porch; there was a wonderful picture of her as a well-dressed office girl of the 1930s, and in another she appeared as a striking young lady in the uniform of a WRAF. Further around the room on a mantelpiece there was a picture of Peggy as a war bride, with Jack who was in his RAF uniform. Two other pictures showed Peggy as a young mother with baby, and in a family photograph with Derek who was about 16.

The guests were all seated. All of the glasses were filled. The time had come to toast Peggy Moran — the late Peggy Moran. Jack and Derek stood at the front of the room. They raised their glasses and everyone followed.

Jack began a short, emotional speech. 'My friends and loved ones, I want to thank you all for coming. Your support and kindness, your sensitivity and friendship to my son and I at this time of grief for us has been much appreciated. I cannot begin to think of the words with which to say our thanks. If I just say, thanks, you'll know that behind these simple words there are volumes more I'd like to say. Life, as we all so sadly know, is too short, far too short when it comes to thinking of all the things we'd like to do, and then it's too late for what we would have liked to have done, and the things we would have liked to have said. But this shouldn't be a morbid occasion. And we must not mourn. Peggy would not have wanted that. Life is an ongoing process. She once told me that whichever one of us went first, the other was not to mourn but to thank God we had so much time together. Peggy told me that we are not mourning the passing of a loved one but we are celebrating the good fortune of a life well spent.'

Jack took a deep breath and raised his glass to Derek's. 'Ladies and gentlemen would you please join with my son Derek and I in a toast to my Peggy.'

Derek added a few words of his own. 'Ladies and gentlemen. My mother, Peggy Moran.'

The guests clinked their glasses. Jack and Derek raised their glasses towards the pictures of Peggy on the mantelpiece.

The rest of the day went fairly smoothly. Jack and Derek kept their own emotions intact, although they were racked with deep grief. By the time all of the guests had left they felt emotionally drained. They gratefully retreated to their own rooms ready for a sleep which would not come, even though they felt exhausted.

Derek lay in bed, closing and then opening his eyes. In reality he knew that sleep would not come for him tonight. He had recently separated from his own wife and children. Coming so close to the break-up of his marriage, the death of his mother had shattered him. This sort of terrible emotional pain hurt him more than a sledgehammer fist. He was 43 years of age, too old to cry. At least, that was what he thought. Damn it all if he didn't have enough reason to cry! He felt the tears run down his cheeks and in the loneliness of the room he let his grief out.

In the early hours Jack rose from his bed and went downstairs to the living room. He tied his dressing gown belt around him. In his own private grief he studied the pictures of his late wife. With sadness in his eyes he sat down at the table and remembered. Derek appeared in the doorway, wearing pyjamas. For a moment he stood there looking at his dad, knowing what he was thinking and feeling for him.

'Dad?' Derek prompted him gently. Jack looked up. His eyes were clouded with moisture. 'Are you alright? I heard you come down.'

'I'm just…' Jack hesitated. 'I'm just remembering, son.'

Derek gripped him affectionately on the shoulder. 'It's not been an easy day, Dad.' Even though he was trying to be a rock for his father to lean on there was a trace of heartache apparent in his voice.

Derek walked into the kitchen and filled the kettle up, switched it on and took out two mugs. 'Well, I know I want a cup of tea. What about you?'

Jack tried to show some humour. 'You know me. I could never refuse a cup of tea.'

'Right. Kettle's on.' Derek sat down opposite his father. Jack averted his eyes to look at the table surface. It was almost as if Derek could recognise the signs that his father wanted to say something; an early hours confession, perhaps?

At last Jack spoke. 'Was I a good husband to your mum?'

Derek seemed perplexed at the question. It had not been asked in a tone of sentimentality, but in a serious manner. It was surprising, for Jack had always been reserved and was not a man given to candid admissions, self-doubt or displays of temperamental extremes.

'Of course you were a good husband,' Derek assured him. 'No man could have done more than you.'

That didn't seem to be enough for Jack. 'But was I?'

Derek felt he'd better let his father say what he wanted.

Jack continued, 'Could I have given your mum a better life? Since Peg went I've wondered. It wasn't an easy life. We got married in wartime. It was an up and downhill ride after that. Looking back we seemed to have covered so much ground together. At the start of the war I joined the RAF in ground staff. For some reason best known to the RAF I was sent on a troop ship to Cape Town, South Africa. Then I was brought home in 1940, applied for flying duties and promptly sent to Canada to do my aircrew training. After that I was posted to RAF stations like Middle Wallop, Northolt, Ongar ,and then one day in 1941 to Yelverton in Devon where I met your mum.'

Derek got up from the table to make the tea. 'Yelverton, did you say, Dad?'

'That's right. We went back there a few years ago to relive old times.'

Derek handed Jack a mug. He took a sip and appeared to drift off in his own private thoughts.

★★★

The car drew up at the overgrown airstrip. Ponies wondered across aimlessly. A gentle wind blew across the scene and with it a thousand memories of what had once been here. Jack and Peggy stepped out of the car. A smile crossed Jack's face quickly. He could feel the atmosphere of a bygone age. Pulling his coat around him and straightening his hat he walked a few yards away to leave Peggy to indulge in her own memories.

Peggy tightened the scarf on her head. She looked at Jack who was fingering through the grass trying to trace the tracks where aircraft had once taken off. Her own eyes were moist as she remembered a time gone by. In her mind she recalled the sounds of aircraft taking off late at night or arriving home before dawn, some of them just barely clinging together, like a child's broken kite. Up in the sky now were a flock of birds flying south for the winter.

Once there had been the roar of engines, the cacophony of voices and big trucks rolling backwards and forward. Today there was a silence broken only slightly by the sound of the wind whistling through the grass.

Jack came across and rejoined his wife. Together they stood in a silent tribute to friends and fellow aircrew who had not returned. It had been so long ago yet it still seemed fresh in their memories. They visualised the barren empty ground as it had once been; the busy Air Force station with its flurry of activity. For Jack, who had been moved at being here once again, the words of Laurence Binyon's great poem 'For the Fallen' flooded his memory. He felt inclined to utter them quietly, with only his wife as the audience:

> They shall not grow old,
> as we that are left grow old;
> Age shall not weary them,
> nor the years condemn;
> At the going down of the sun and
> in the morning
> We shall remember them.

Somewhere in the heavens above some celestial figure saw to it that a beam of sunshine fell across the ground where Jack and Peggy stood.

Peggy not only remembered the fine people they had once known and the comradeship that servicemen enjoyed. For her this place had always been the start of romance leading into marriage with Jack.

'Hard to believe this is where it all began for us,' she said wistfully.

Jack was equally pensive. 'I can still hear the sounds of aircraft taking off in '41.'

'I used to sit in the lorry over there.' Peggy pointed across the field. 'I was just one of many WRAF drivers, who would be waiting in the vehicle at three and four o'clock in the morning to pick up the dawn to dusk boys.' Jack put his arm around her. 'Bless 'em all.' Peggy drifted into the past. 'Remember the boys in the NAAFI singing that one, Jack?'

Her husband needed no further prompting. He began to sing softly, 'Bless 'em all. Bless 'em all. The Long, the short and the tall. Bless all these Sergeants and WOIs. Bless all those Corporals and their blinkin' sons.' From somewhere up above as Jack shakily sang and stumbled through lyrics he had half-forgotten, a squadron of RAF men seemed to accompany him in his memory.

★★★

Jack sipped from his tea. He looked across at Derek with eyes that were moist with emotion. He was only just holding on.

'Alright, Dad?' Derek murmured faintly.

Jack just continued his rambling nostalgia. 'Yelverton… Yes, it was strange going back there, remembering the way it had been in the war years. I remember the first time I saw your Mum.'

★★★

The countryside of Devon looked peaceful and serene. It was a little bit of heaven, in fact, to the leading aircraftman who drove along the pleasant lanes. Here in this most attractive of counties it was hard to believe there was a world war raging, with places being blown to smithereens. Jack Moran, fresh-faced, almost 23 years of age and a positive young man, took his foot off the accelerator in the old Austin car he was driving as a cyclist appeared up ahead.

For Jack it was his first glimpse of Peggy Mills. Coming towards him was a WRAF. She was about 21 years old with dark glossy hair protruding from beneath her uniform cap. Even at a distance Jack was aware of a friendly face approaching him. He slowed right down. The young lady recognising the uniform waved out of courtesy to him. Jack smiled in deep admiration at her as she passed him.

'Mmm. Now she is nice,' he murmured to himself. He drove on, making a mental note that he must try and meet her sometime.

It would be several more days before he would get the chance, and when it did come it was totally unexpected. One morning when he and several other aircrews were about to depart for a mission over Europe, Peggy in her role as a WRAF driver sat waiting in a lorry outside a debriefing room. In a few minutes she would drive the men across to the waiting aircraft on the runway.

The first to emerge from the hut was an aircrew Sergeant. He was affectionately called 'Bluey'. An Australian in his late twenties, Bluey – or Pat Flanagan – was a suntanned man with mahogany brown skin and jet black hair. He had angered his Irish-born father by joining up with the pommies at the outbreak of the Second World War. Originally from Broken Hill in New South Wales he had led a rather chequered life before joining the RAF.

He and Jack Moran were the best of mates. They couldn't help but be, with their easy-going amiability. The two of them were followed by several others. All of them seemed happy and laughing.

'I take it this is our chauffeur for the big one then, Bluey?' Jack asked pointing towards the lorry.

'This is it, Jack,' Bluey replied with a laugh in his voice. He called out to the others, 'This is the holiday bus. Jump up blokes! Imagine this is the bus for Blackpool.'

'Blackpool!' one airman retorted. 'I went on holiday there before the war. It rained every day. It was the best holiday I ever had, too. Crumpet, fish and chips and beer!'

The men clambered into the back of the lorry. When they were all inside Bluey banged on the wall, signifying to the driver whom they couldn't see, to start up the vehicle.

'Everyone's aboard. Take her away!' The vehicle moved off across the aerodrome to where several aircraft were standing poised for take-off. 'How do you feel, Jack?'

'I'm not sure I feel anything, to be honest,' Jack replied.

'Nor me,' admitted Bluey. 'No, mate, I reckon it's a case of just getting through the day… and the night.'

The apprehensive men sat inside, their stomachs in a knot. Their nerves were on edge. Eventually they arrived at their aircraft. The men stepped out.

'Thanks driver,' Jack said and as he cast a glance in the driver's seat he was delighted to see the young WRAF again.

Her face was so pleasant. Her eyes shone and twinkled. Jack was spellbound as she beamed a dazzling smile, showing a set of pearly white teeth.

'Good luck, boys,' Peggy called out. 'See you in the NAAFI.'

'You can bet on that, darling!' Bluey replied.

Jack gave her a broad and generous smile. 'I'll second that.'

Both of them entered the aircraft. In the lorry, Peggy was quick to appreciate that his smile was more than just a mere acknowledgement.

'Gosh, what a nice man.' Her murmured admission to herself came as quite a surprise. Peggy started the motor up and put the vehicle into gear. For a moment Peggy watched as the doors of the aircraft closed. A look of recognition flashed into her eyes. She had seen him before. She knew that somewhere before the war they had encountered each other.

There was a huge sing-a-long in the canteen a few nights later. Airmen who had been on missions sang to celebrate their returns. Those who were about to fly out sang to boost their spirits. Jack entered. His high spirits were effervescent that night. Every time he returned he could not help but thank God he was alive. It was marvellous and tonight he was going to sing with the best of them.

He made his way to the bar, bought a beer and walked through the staff to join the singers. They were all singing "Don't Sit under the Apple Tree". Jack joined in merrily. He looked down at one of the tables. The lovely face of Peggy looked up at him, and her smile was warm towards him. Jack's heart melted, and he felt a surge of electricity through him as if he was a magnet attracted to her. Even at this short distance in a crowded room he felt love and warmth towards her.

Jack's moment came when he and Peggy met for a date in a quiet country pub. He had casually asked her to meet up with him. He wasn't sure whether she would come, as he didn't realise that Peggy was just as keen to be there. They sat quietly in the snug by an open hearth, getting to know each other. For a few minutes they talked about the weather and the surroundings, until Jack decided the time had come to get straight to the point.

'It was good of you to come. I've seen you around the station quite a bit. I'm Jack Moran from Streatham, London. And you?'

She took his hand in a light shake. 'I'm Peggy Mills.' She appeared to add as an after-thought, 'I come from Sutton in Surry.'

'I know it,' said Jack. 'Nice area if I remember rightly. Funny, until I joined up I'd hardly ever been out of London. I've been all over the shop since then. It's surprised me. In the past couple of years I've been down to Cape Town, across to Canada, and on stations all over England. I've enjoyed it, even if there is a war on. I've flown on missions across France and Holland. I've packed an awful lot in.'

Peggy warmed to him almost immediately. It was his calm, almost bashful manner of speaking that endeared her to him. 'What did you do before the war, Jack?' Her use of his first name suggested to him that she wanted to know him that much better.

For Jack's part he felt comfortable with her. 'I was a carpenter. It's a good trade. I did plenty of work on buildings. After the London Blitz I think there will be a lot of work on again. What about you? What were you doing?'

'I was a seamstress,' answered Peggy. 'So it was a bit of a change for me to come from a tailoring factory to driving large lorries. All the girls I'm billeted with keep wondering how long this fiasco is going to last. When it broke out I recall people saying, almost matter-of-factly, that it would be all be over by Christmas.'

'And now it's '41. I think it will go on for a long time yet, I regret to say. Still, we shouldn't live with that sort of expectation. I think we should just get on with living, don't you?'

'I most certainly do. We've got a lot to live for.'

Jack looked at her with absolute certainty. This was the one. He almost felt he was getting a message from her that she felt strongly about him.

'One good thing about this war though,' remarked Jack, 'you're from Surrey and I'm from London. I doubt if we would ever have met in civvy street.'

Peggy smiled at this remark, for she had in fact seen him before joining the forces. She had finally established where she had seen Jack prior to the station. 'You're wrong there.'

Jack gave her a curious look. 'Why?'

'I once saw you before the war, at the Hammersmith Palais,' Peggy revealed. 'You were on your own. I was with a girlfriend. We were waiting to be asked to dance. My friend spotted you but then two other men asked us and that was that.'

Jack was amazed. 'Do you mean to say I made that much impression on you? I haven't been to the old Ham Palais since... since '38.'

'That's right.'

'My, what a small world. I would never have believed it.'

The two talked for a long time that night. They talked deeply and opening in the manner that people do in times of crisis. Perhaps it was the urgency of the times that prompted people to grab happiness while they had the chance. But neither Jack nor Peggy had any doubts.

Barely three months after meeting, they were married in a beautiful old stone church in Devon with Bluey Flanagan as best man.

★★★

With his marriage to Peggy, life took on a new direction for Jack. He felt thrilled and happy that his lovely young woman had fallen in love with him. The romance had all happened so quickly that Jack found there were things about Peggy he was still getting to know. They came as a pleasant surprise to him.

Peggy had come from a normal suburban family in Sutton, Surrey. Her parents had been rigid disciplinarians who believed strongly in the work ethic. Peggy's mother had worked 16 hours a day cleaning offices, even though she suffered from painful arthritis. Her hard-bitten nature made her a person who carried on life and work without grumbling, despite the hardships of her ailment. But she loved her daughter Peggy dearly; she wanted not just the best for her, but to bring out the best in her. In this she succeeded. The two of them were so unlike, yet of the same ilk.

The cool, beautiful woman who Peggy had become was by no means solely attributed to her strong mother. True, she had learned manners, courtesy and politeness. She had learned respect, duty and how only work and loyalty brought the true benefits in life. Peggy's father was a volatile, short-tempered man who also worked hard in his trade as a toolmaker. He had no time for the grey areas of life. People worked hard or they didn't. People were good or they weren't. The fear of God he put into his daughter worked the other way. Peggy had grown up cool, considerate, and with a first-rate sense of right and wrong.

Perhaps it was many similar qualities that she recognised in Jack Moran. He was probably her male equivalent. Actually, Jack was a working man through and through. His parents were humble people who had known little luxury, if any, in their lives. They were delighted by their only son's choice in his bride.

When Peggy become pregnant with their first child she left the WRAF to live in the nearby village. Jack was delighted when in 1942 Peggy gave birth to a girl. The baby was called Vivien Scarlett Moran. They named her after Peggy's favourite actress Vivien Leigh. Scarlett naturally enough came from the character of Scarlett O'Hara whom Vivien Leigh had portrayed in the film *Gone with The Wind*.

Every time Jack returned from a mission with the aircrew boys, the first thing he wanted to do was get to the village, cuddle Peggy and gaze in wonderment at his beautiful baby daughter.

Bluey Flanagan and Jack become close friends as time went on. One thing that stood out about Bluey more than anything else was a deep love of the land of his birth. He could not resist spinning a few yarns about that place 'out there'. One day they were seated outside on some steps by their barracks. Bluey casually rolled a cigarette.

'How's Peg doing with the little girl?' he asked in a slow, monotone voice.

'Fine,' Jack replied. Even in one word he sounded enthusiastic and his face lit up at the thought of his new family. 'I still can't believe just how lucky I am. Look at what I've got: a lovely wife, a beautiful little daughter. It's a bit difficult getting across to see them between our time in the air. Makes it all worthwhile, though. A family, that's the best incentive to get through anything.'

'My word,' agreed Bluey.

In Jack's new-found happiness he was beginning to think that everyone should be married. 'You never say, Bluey, but is there someone back in Australia waiting for you?'

'I wish there was,' Bluey replied with what appeared to be a glimmer of sadness in his eyes. 'I've been away a while now. Never really forged any long-term relationships. I did a lot of drifting around in my youth. I get that from my old man. he was Irish, he came from the Falls Road in Belfast and went out to work in Broken Hill in New South Wales just before the first war.'

'And your mother?' Jack was curious.

'Oh, she was an Irish girl too, originally from Dublin. The two of them met when they travelled steerage to Australia.' He felt inclined to elaborate more on his own life. 'Yes, I was born to be a drifter. I was a wharf labourer on Pyrmont Dock in Sydney. Then I was a fisherman on a prawn trawler in the Gulf of Carpentaria. In '37 I worked my way on a freighter to Europe. I ended up in Spain fighting in the Civil War there. Heaven knows, when I saw some of the casualties in Barcelona I was sickened by it all. After that I worked on a trawler between Hull and the Shetland Isles. I'm looking forward to going home when all this lot is over.'

Jack was fascinated by Bluey's manner of speaking. He was genuinely interested in the land his friend came from. 'What's your country like, Bluey?'

Now the Australian was in his element. He loved to talk about it. 'It's a very easy-going happy place, especially for families with children who love the beach and the bush land.'

'Did the Depression affect Australia very much?'

'Oh my word,' Bluey said and the memories of these years came flooding back to him. 'Yeah, it was hard to believe a young country like Australia could have been so affected. Something like half a million people were unemployed. There were people sleeping rough on the streets. I'll never forget seeing some of the homeless sleeping in rotten old rusty water tanks on a smelly stinker of a place called Dudley Flats at Port Melbourne. Of course when the war came a lot of folk were glad to join up. It put food in their stomachs, gave them a bed and a place to take fresh showers in. But Australia will be alright. With all its resources, when the war is over it'll be a beaut place to live in for anyone wishing to give it a go.' Bluey suddenly noticed that Jack appeared to be glowing with interest. 'Why, would you like to go?'

Jack looked at him squarely. The seeds of ambition had been sown.

'It could be a good place for a new family,' Bluey grinned at him. 'When the war is over, whenever that may be.'

It was a joy for Jack to visit the cottage in Devon where Peggy and the baby were living. He and Peggy would lean over the cot, almost soaking the young child with looks of constant love. There was within him the overriding urge to smother them both with love and affection. He had never felt this way before in his life. True, he had loved his parents, but that was something different. That had been a love and respect for two very humble people who had taught him kindness, caring and loyalty. In Peggy and Vivien, Jack felt they were his responsibility; his influence and efforts would shape their lives and for him it was important to make them the number one priority in his life. It was for them he lived.

Jack considered that after the war, it would be in all their interests to try a new life overseas. Bluey, with his marvellous way of speaking, had put the idea of Australia into his mind. He knew that as soon as it became clear that the war was coming to an end, even before he had taken his discharge, he would apply to migrate.

When the war came to an end in 1945 it came with a surge of relief across the world. For the servicemen, it was time to go home and get on with their lives. Not everyone would be going home. For Bluey Flanagan the end had come somewhere over France when his aircraft was shot down. Jack had been assigned to another mission with new aircrew. When he had learned of the loss of Bluey he had been inconsolable for days. Pat 'Bluey' Flanagan had been a real mate and comrade. But his influence would be strong on Jack for several years yet. In 1945, after taking his discharge from the RAF, Jack and his new family sailed out for a new life in Melbourne, Australia.

★★★

The voyage to Australia was six weeks in length. On board the liner, Jack and Peggy found that the bulk of the passengers were servicemen fleeing war-torn Europe. Most of them knew little about Australia except that it offered some promise, and something other than grey skies and rationing. Above all, it offered a new life for their children.

At the time the immigration scheme was considered so important that the Australian Prime Minister of the time, Ben Chifley, came to the dock in Port Philip Bay, Melbourne to welcome the vessel. When the ship made its way into the dock Jack could not resist looking for the water tanks at Dudley Flats where Bluey had told him the homeless had slept out in during the Depression.

The voyage through the Mediterranean, the Suez Canal and the Indian Ocean had been an interesting start to the migrants' new lives. For Peggy the voyage was an eye-opener. She had never been out of England before and the ports of call en route to Australia awakened her to a whole new world. When the liner sailed through the Suez Canal, Vivien was fascinated by the sights, sounds and smells of this new experience. Only three years old, she was fast growing into a lovely child. Jack and Peggy beamed in adoration of their daughter.

When they had first set sight on the Australian coastline they had felt excited. The sun shone more powerfully than they had ever known and the sky was a more vivid and deeper blue than they had ever seen in the British Isles. By the time the vessel had arrived in Melbourne the blue sky had become dour grey and rain was falling by the bucket load.

It was the very early days of post-war migration, and Australians still had an innate suspicion of the migrants from Europe. Thirty years, on when much inter-marriage had taken place, the Australian mix would be different and migrants would be greeted with a tolerance and welcoming kindness that did not exist in 1945.

The migrant hostel was squalid, unwelcoming and resembling something like a row of Nissen huts and factory warehouses. Peggy's heart dropped at the sight of it. Jack did not feel too happy about it either. To make matters a great deal worse, there was an accommodation shortage in Melbourne. Houses and flats available to rent were in short supply. It seemed that these dreaded wooden huts – 'A replica of Belsen', one 'reffo' from Eastern Europe declared – would have to be home for some considerable time.

Jack soon found work as a carpenter and was busy working long hours making a living. Immersed in his new life, he struck up a good camaraderie with his workmates. It was Peggy he worried about. Stuck in the hostel all day long with their young child, the happy life Jack had hoped of for her seemed a long way away. The climate, rather than being kind to her face and appearance, seemed to take its toll. It soon became obvious to Jack that since their marriage this was undoubtedly the first major hurdle they were facing.

Every weekend Jack made a point of taking Peggy and Vivien to a different spot around Melbourne. They visited the Dandenong Ranges, the Twelve Apostles, the Mornington Peninsula, Dromana, Glenrowan, Apollo Bay, Ballarat, Bendigo; but no matter how different or interesting, it soon became clear that Peggy was not adapting to the change. Neither, too, in some way was Jack.

Although he liked Australians, Jack could not always fit into the way of life. He liked to work hard and sought security for his family. He earned better money in Melbourne than he could in London but he was not sure of his long-term prospects here. The dreadful thought of years wasted in the hostel unable to find reasonable accommodation elsewhere appalled him. Even a council house in England seemed a better prospect than a Nissen hut.

The social life did not agree with him. He detested the six o'clock swill when the workers rushed from offices and factories to drink as much beer as they could before the pubs closed. Jack much preferred the quiet pint drunk slowly in an atmospheric English oak-beamed pub, rather than the lavatorial bathroom tiles of bars in Fitzroy and Footscray. When the Aussies talked about football it wasn't about English soccer teams such as Chelsea, Arsenal, Brentford or Burnley; it was about the Victorian Rules teams of Essendon and St Kilda. Instead of players like Stanley Matthews and Tom Finney, the blokes in the bar talked of Cazaly and Bunton.

By 1948 Jack and Peggy felt concerned that they hadn't adapted to their new life. With feelings of considerable regret and, it would have to be said, a sense of failure, they decided to return home.

In the years that followed they would often ask themselves what might have been if they had stayed. But all thoughts of regret at leaving were dissipated when they felt the joy at returning home. In Jack's heart he felt a failure. Perhaps they hadn't given it everything they could have. But they did know that rationing or no rationing, rain or no rain, bomb sites and blitzed-out buildings, de-mob suits everywhere, it did feel good to be home.

There was one piece of delightful news for them that they learned on the boat coming home: Peggy was pregnant with their second child. It was a huge boost to their happiness. From the start, Jack felt certain that the child would be a boy. He was right. Early in 1949 Peggy gave birth to a son whom they called Derek.

★★★

The family settled in rented rooms in East Acton. They picked up the threads of their life again in London. Jack, who was a truly hard-working man, put in long, exhausting hours on building sites. He was gradually getting the money together for a deposit on a house. On his free Sundays he walked proudly with Peggy, Vivien and his baby son Derek, who he felt so thrilled to push along in the pram. It all seemed so wonderful, being a young man with a lovely, loving wife and sweet children. But then one terrible day in 1949 his happiness – indeed the happiness of the whole family – was shattered by tragedy.

Jack was at work in a factory putting wood together in a mortice and tenon joint. A team of other workers were all performing similar tasks. The enthusiasm amongst the men was infectious. Jack was whistling happily as he carried out his duties. He liked to work hard and be productive in his job, and he always tried to be happy. One happy, hard-working man seemed to generate the same feelings across the floor.

Amidst the noise of the workshop, a telephone rung. The foreman took the call. Out of the corner of his eye Jack could see the expression on the man's face. Although he could not hear a word because of the factory noise, Jack felt a deep unease as the man looked directly towards him. He suspected that the foreman was going to be the bearer of bad news.

The foreman put the phone down slowly, and walked towards Jack. He stopped and looked at Jack. There was a great deal of sympathy evident in his eyes.

'Jack, you've got a call.' His voice sounded grave.

'Who's it from?'

The foreman looked concerned. 'I think you'd better answer it straight away.'

Jack sensed the urgency of the matter. He walked towards the phone expecting to hear some sort of bad news: a burglary at their flat, perhaps, or maybe Peggy had heard something of a neighbour's misfortune. What he was about to hear was something he could not possibly have dreamed of. Nothing could have prepared him for this.

It was a neighbour on the phone. The news delivered a severe jolting thud. While out in the garden their beautiful daughter Vivien had suddenly developed breathing problems. Almost without warning, she had turned blue, and on her way to the hospital she had died. Peggy had stayed at the hospital and was now under sedation.

The realisation of what had happened hit Jack with a vengeance. In shock he dropped the telephone to the floor. He clutched his face with grief. Oh God! How could this happen? Why? Why? Why?

Somehow that dreadful day dragged into the night, and then weeks of grief followed. The shattering tragedy of Vivien's death brought both Jack and Peggy to the edge of a breakdown. It was hard for Jack to hang on to his own sanity while trying to console Peggy. The worse part of it all was that there seemed to have been absolutely no warning of Vivien's early death. It had just come unexpectedly; it was like the trauma of cot death: sudden, unexpected, and triggering a fierce, heart-breaking grief that would take a marathon effort to overcome.

While trying hard to come to terms with Vivien's death, Jack could see the pain inscribed on Peggy's beautiful face. She had been born to be a mother. The happiness she had shown when she played with her daughter was endearing to watch. Now Peggy had lost her, and with her young baby son Derek, there were dangerous signs that she was not giving him enough attention. It was not her fault, nor was it intentional. The pain had hit Peggy so hard that she found it hard to grasp the reality of it all. Her eyes that had once sparkled with joy were now dimmed with sadness, and her normally flushed cheeks were stained with the oceans of tears she wept.

Jack had to carry on with his work and try his best to keep the family together. He stopped working overtime and on Saturdays, spending every spare moment with Peggy and Derek. It was not a happy home that he returned to each night. It was going to take months, possibly even a few years, before they could put the tragedy behind them and rebuild their lives.

One afternoon Jack came home early from work to find Peggy sitting on the garden swing. He could see that she was still dispirited, and near to breaking point. Her lovely warm face was tear-stained and saddened. It cut Jack up inside to see her like this. He almost felt responsible for the way she was. He dropped his bag of tools and walked across to her. He ran his hands up and down her sides, trying desperately to reassure her. A tear formed in the corner of Jack's eye and ran down his cheek.

'Peg, it's more than I can bear to see you like this,' he said in a soft whisper, his voice cracking in emotion.

Peggy was terribly emotional. 'I just can't come to terms with it.'

'Please, Peg. We must try. We still have Derek.' He desperately struggled to find some consoling words. 'For weeks, leading into months, I've seen you breaking down, grieving, agonising, struggling, thinking and saying if only... what if... We must go on.' The tears were rolling down his cheeks now. 'We must go on. It's a poor consolation but we must always remember Vivien's years...' He broke away to wipe the tears from his eyes. 'Vivien's years, if numbered, were her happiest. And we will always have the memories of that little girl with us, no matter how long we may live.'

Peggy looked down at the floor, then up again. She touched Jack's hand and then began to wipe away his tears. For the first time, Peggy seemed to find strength from the fact that Jack too was enduring his own personal struggle. However, her voice gave a different impression. When Peggy began to speak it was as if Jack was listening to a woman who was completely different to the one he had married.

'I keep thinking of what we had,' said Peggy. What we had. The past tense alarmed Jack straight away. 'The four of us together. It's gone. It's as if our whole life has been taken and shaken and ripped apart.' Then her voice took on a devastatingly sad tone, 'We'll never know what Vivien might have been in life. She could have... should have grown into a lovely young woman with so much to offer. It's not that I don't love you, Jack. I do, so much. But I can't go on here in this house where it happened. I can't go on thinking of what might have been. I don't feel like I can continue now as we are. I feel so responsible.'

Jack was concerned and worried. 'Responsible? What do you mean?'

Peggy spoke in a resigned voice. The words stung and twisted. Jack could only listed in disbelief. 'I think we should... separate. Divorce.'

'Divorce!' Jack's voice was quiet and betrayed his dismay. Divorce? But why? What had he done? It did not seem right that he should be the one to suffer because of what had happened to their daughter. After all, was it not both of them who were suffering? 'Divorce?' Jack repeated. 'I don't understand.'

In fact it was reasonable that he did not understand. Had he been older and wiser he would have realised that Peggy, in the traumatic aftermath of Vivien's death, had undergone a shock that had temporarily thrown her off balance. Peggy just wasn't thinking straight. How could Jack have realised that his wife was trying desperately to detach herself from a situation that had been created by circumstances beyond their control?

It took a while before Jack could even attempt to analyse what had happened. Peggy had been devastated by the death of their child. Overnight she had gone from being a sweet, serene, happy woman to someone who was withdrawn, emotionally shattered, even frightened that life might dish out more pain to her. The calm in her had become fear. The security of her family life had been threatened. She wanted to escape the nightmare.

Instead of seeking more assurance and love from Jack, she withdrew, creating more pain for herself. The love within her had turned to ice. Peggy did not consider any alternatives. The only option she could think of was to secure a divorce and start again, irrespective of any pain it would cause. It just wasn't Peggy's normal character. She was strongly maternal, devotedly loyal and loving, yet in the absence of medical advice or counselling her reason and common sense had deserted her. All she could think of was escape.

For the time being Jack and Peggy carried on as a normal married couple. It was Jack, though, who took more interest in Derek. Very reluctantly, Jack and Peggy made an appointment to see a solicitor in order to start divorce proceedings.

Donald Halliwell was a kindly-looking man in his fifties. Since the end of the war in his work as a solicitor he had handled many similar cases of divorce. He'd seen all types of situations: the soldiers who had come home to their wives only to find that what they had once known had been blown to smithereens in the war years; people who had grown apart or forged new relationships. He knew more about marital ups and downs than any marriage guidance counsellor.

In the office, Jack and Peggy faced him across the table. Mr Halliwell listened sympathetically to their story. He knew instinctively that divorce or legal separation was not the answer to their problems. He looked across at the sad figures of Jack and Peggy. After they had finished speaking he sat in silence, waiting for anything further they might want to say. There wasn't anything they could add, so in his own quiet way he decided to pursue a different line. Not so much in the form of questioning, but in the manner of a gentle cross-examination.

'Let's put this in perspective, then. You both met in the Services and married in 1941. Your daughter, Vivien, was born in 1942. You came through the war together. You also have a son Derek, born after you returned from several years out in Australia. So all things considered, how would you describe your marriage? Mrs Moran, could I ask you first?'

Peggy was hesitant and glanced quickly at Jack. 'It was… it was a very happy marriage.'

Mr. Halliwell turned to Jack. 'Mr Moran? How would you sum things up? What has changed for you?'

Jack looked deeply upset and he struggled with his words. 'Obviously the loss of our little girl has had a shattering effect. But I still love Peggy. I can't understand…' His voice faltered as he tried to regain his composure. 'I can't understand for the life of me why we are sitting here discussing divorce. How we've got to this stage, I don't know.'

Mr Halliwell paused with his assessment of the situation and strived to show some sensitivity. 'It seems, Mr Moran, that the last thing you want is a divorce.'

Jack nodded his head sadly in agreement.

'Do you think I could possibly speak to your wife alone for a few minutes?'

'Certainly,' replied Jack, 'I'll take a seat outside.' He touched Peggy's hand warmly and left the room quietly. Jack walked outside. He had a slight inkling of what the solicitor was going to do now. Perhaps he was going to ask Peggy if there was more to this pending divorce than met the eye. Was he going to ask if Jack was a wife-beater or an alcoholic?

In this he seriously underestimated Donald Halliwell, for the man was an extremely shrewd judge of character, able to sum up people accurately within a few minutes of meeting them.

'You can be quite open with me, Mrs Moran. I'm used to it.' Mr Halliwell was a very kind man who people found it easy to reveal their problems to. 'In my job I've had to deal with divorces relating to all sorts of breakdowns and reasons for it. I've spoken to people whose spouses have been unfaithful; women whose husbands were drunken bullies; men whose wives left them for a wealthier man or a person who offered more excitement than the drudgery of nappies, washing clothes and preparing meals. I've even dealt with couples who developed separate lives within their own marriage to the point that they had nothing in common. I've seen every sort of situation.' He let the words sink in and then asked her very gently, 'Now what category do you fall into?'

'I can't really describe it. I don't feel good about myself in this marriage.'

This answer simply wasn't good enough for Mr Halliwell. He knew he was right to be suspicious. 'Have there been any other problems between yourself and Jack?'

Peggy looked at him curiously. She was slow to grasp the gist of what he was saying.

He elaborated for her. 'I'll be blunt, Mrs Moran. Is Jack a good husband? Has he ever shown acts of cruelty or anger to you? Have the intimacies of your relationship broken down?'

Peggy looked shocked beyond reason. 'No! No!' she gasped in genuine astonishment. 'Jack's a kind and loving man. It's my fault.'

Now they were really getting down to something.

'No, please, it's not Jack at all. It's when our daughter died. That was when I felt our marriage should end.'

Mr. Halliwell took a moment to absorb the words and mentally sum up the situation. He knew that Peggy was on edge, very close to breaking point, and not seeing the way ahead clearly. To begin with, Peggy had just declared that Jack was kind and loving. These were not the words of a woman who had been badly treated. The death of their daughter had changed things. Mr. Halliwell took a gamble and deduced the fact that Peggy simply wanted to extricate herself from the past. Divorce was no answer. He decided to handle the matter in the manner of a father counselling his daughter.

'Could I try and put it into words for you?' he asked sensitively. Peggy listened as he began to analyse the situation as he saw it. 'The way that I am viewing your problem is that with the death of your daughter, the carefully mapped out life you and your husband had was shaken to its foundations. Your whole way of life has obviously changed with sudden and jolting drama. Once you looked forward to the years ahead, the four of you, very happy with good things to come. This tragedy had destroyed your once perhaps blissful marriage. I dare say your faith in life has been shattered. Even your confidence will have taken a terrible tumble, and you're unsure of your love for your husband. Am I right, Peggy?'

Peggy thought carefully before answering. 'I know this may sound strange, Mr Halliwell, but I still love my husband. It's not so much how I feel for Jack. My feelings there have never changed. It's more to do with my enthusiasm for marriage now.' Suddenly her voice gathered pace. 'I need desperately to change the present. I don't feel good about myself, as a wife or mother.'

Mr. Halliwell realised his strategy was working. 'Go on,' he urged her.

Peggy continued, and her true feelings came to the foreground. 'I blame myself for not recognising Vivien's ill-health earlier. I feel like I failed Jack as a wife in this respect.' Her tears began to fall.

Mr Halliwell gave her a handkerchief. He could see the trauma that she was experiencing. Allowing her some time to dry her tears and calm herself, Mr Halliwell sat quietly. Then when she was ready, he stood up. 'Come across to the window, Peggy,' he beckoned. 'You don't mind if I call you Peggy, do you?'

'No. Of course not,' she replied.

Peggy and Mr Halliwell moved to the window. They looked out at the busy street below. Just exactly what was the purpose of this little exercise? Peggy seemed bemused.

Mr. Halliwell looked down at the trams and buses. His voice was gruff and kindly. 'Down there in that street are people of all shapes, sizes, characteristics, opinions and races; many of whom, if you were to ask, would tell you of a tragedy they or someone they know has experienced.' He turned to face her. 'Do you know what distinguishes them from each other? Any idea, Peggy?'

'I'm not sure Mr Halliwell.' Peggy was at a loss to see what he was driving at.

'It's their manner of coping with things,' he replied. 'During the war I was an air raid warden. I went out on duty one night in the Blitz, said goodbye to my wife and three children. Didn't give it a thought.' His face became grave in an instant. 'When I came home the next day, my house was in smithereens. In the space of a whole night I had lost all that was dear to me. My family — gone. My home — just rubble and debris.'

At this Peggy felt sadness for the solicitor instead of herself. 'Oh, I am so sorry. It must have been terrible.'

'It was. But I eventually came to terms with it after feeling grief and solitude and despair I could never have envisaged. Let me stress' — on this point he was firm — 'I have never got over it. Not after nearly ten years. But I have come to terms with it, and that hasn't been easy. The point I am making, Peggy, is that there is life after tragedy. There is life after grief and despair. It's the manner of adjusting to that tragedy and overcoming it that is most important. I can see no clear reason for your marriage breakdown, Peggy. In fact I'm not sure it has broken down at all. You're in a state of deep grief, mourning, still in shock. You're blaming yourself for something that's not your fault, for a failure that doesn't exist.

'On the other side of that door is a kind man who loves you. He's broken-hearted. I urge you to go home with him and start again. Divorce is a long, complicated business that causes as much pain as the reasons for the marriage break-up itself. Go back to that man who loves you and your little boy. Move on to happier times. I'd say your marriage was too good to disregard.'

Peggy felt the tears fall from her eyes. Donald Halliwell had spoken so frankly and assuredly, and she knew every word was true.

Outside the office Jack waited patiently, unaware of the events that had taken place within. The door opened and Peggy emerged. To his surprise, as he stood up to greet her Peggy put both her arms around him. She hugged him as if they had been away from each other for months. Jack was taken completely by surprise.

'Peggy…What's wrong?' The sight of Peggy's tears stunned him. Her sudden display of warmth and affection after weeks of coolness was a great surprise. What had brought about this change in events?

'Jack, I've been such a fool. I've treated you so badly. Forgive me.'

'I don't understand. What's happened?'

'Can we go home? Can we start again? My thinking has been so muddled and confused.'

Jack gripped her tightly. His bemusement turned to happiness. 'Of course, darling.' He could not understand how in the space of a short conversation Peggy had suddenly made a complete turnaround. A short time ago they had been on the brink of starting divorce proceedings. Now they were reconciled, and about to restart their married life together.

From within the office Mr Halliwell appeared. His face was filled with warmth for the couple before him. Jack looked at him, as if to query what had happened. 'I don't think you'll be needing my services, Mr Moran,' he said almost happily, as if he had just accomplished a remarkable achievement. 'I would like to wish you both a long and happy marriage.'

Jack acknowledged Mr. Halliwell with a smile. The two men shook hands warmly. Then a tear-stained Peggy and a beaming Jack walked out of the office, back to their married life.

Mr Halliwell looked at them in admiration and smiled. He turned to his secretary, who had listened quietly without comment. 'Well, if I reconcile any more petitioners for divorce, I might have to look at delivering coal for a living.'

★★★

The 1950s were a very happy decade for the Moran family. They moved to the North of England and began a new life. The tragedy of Vivien's death was something the family never really got over. But the three of them developed a unity that many families would have envied.

They rarely returned to London. The city held little fascination for them any more. After Vivien's death they had wanted to make a clean start. There was one occasion on which they made a special effort to come to London, however. This was the Coronation of Queen Elizabeth II. They were determined not to miss this. Although neither of them were fervent royalists they had respect for the monarchy of the day. The procession and the pageantry of the Coronation were a sight they would remember for years to come.

In London on that most spectacular of days crowds gathered to see their new Queen arrive in all the glitz and colour that characterised such occasions in British history. It was much touted at the time that for the nation this heralded a new Elizabethan Age, and the Queen's spectacular reign would commence with a tremendous show of ceremony. The event was televised live, much to the annoyance of the Cabinet. This was a distinct change from the Coronation of her father, George VI, in 1937 when the government of the day had advised against radio coverage. The reason given was the notion that people listening to it would not show the monarchy dignity and respect in their private homes and public places; a somewhat misguided notion.

But for Jack, Peggy and their four-year-old son, to be there and actually part of this wonderful historical occasion was thrilling and exciting. Jack was wearing a double-breasted coat and trilby hat typical of the time. Peggy looked smart in a coat and hat. Their young son Derek looked on, mystified by the carriages and the guests making their way to Westminster Abbey.

Jack picked Derek up and held him tight to get a better view. 'There you are, son,' Jack said amiably, 'watch this. It's a moment of history you will always remember.'

In later years, the 1950s would take on an afterglow. It was a time of great changes, not just for the Moran family but for British people in general. It was a time of great optimism, of hope, and hard work for the future. It was also a time of ration book austerity, rock 'n' roll, skiffle groups, coffee bars, and bomb sites that were still leftovers from the London Blitz of the previous decade. The last London tram ran in June 1952. Churchill's Conservative government fought hard to retain interest rates at a level of 2.5 per cent. The Labour Party, now in for a long stint in opposition, was set for years of internal ideological strife. British troops were still actively engaged in other parts of the globe after the end of the war. After Palestine, they had served in Korea, then they would be fully occupied in Malaya, and in later years there would be problems in the Suez Canal that would require their attention.

The Moran family, now living in the Lake District, occasionally treated themselves to a night out at the cinema. Amongst the favourite films they saw were *The African Queen*, *High Noon*, *The Lavender Hill Mob* and *Singing in the Rain*. The greatest thing about their family life was the togetherness that existed between them. Peggy was determined to spend a lot of time with Derek now. It had been obvious shortly after Vivien's death that she had neglected her young son. Not deliberately, but during her mourning period she had been unable to cope. Now her strength and determination had returned. The whole family were trying to build a new chapter of happiness.

Jack continued to work as a carpenter in the Lake District. They were living in a small terraced house. It was very sparsely furnished, not that in any sense it was meant to be purely temporary, but it had an aura of comfort and warmth about it. Even in winter the house was warm.

In the 1950s the Morans often sat around the warm coal fire that burned in a beautifully set Victorian fireplace. Those cold nights for some reason were always the warmest of times, the happiest of memories. Peggy would sit reading a woman's magazine which would detail the clothes fashionable ladies wore in Park Lane and Mayfair. Derek would normally be playing with his pet Corgi dog Trigger, occasionally alternating between running his Hornby train set on the floor, or reading a copy of *The Eagle* or a football magazine that described the progress of Leyton Orient and Manchester United. There would be slices of butter and sultana cake next to a freshly made pot of tea on a round coffee table. Jack would eagerly scour the daily papers looking for new opportunities in the classified advertisement columns. From the mantelpiece long-deceased relatives gazed out from old yellowing box camera photographs in metallic frames.

This was a very happy house. Jack loved coming home to it and Peggy felt secure there. This was Derek's childhood home that he would always remember with affection.

'How would you feel about me changing my job, Peggy?' Jack asked as his eyes fell on a newspaper advertisement one night.

Peggy was immediately concerned. 'Change your job? That's a bolt out of the blue, Jack. Have you been thinking about this for a while? I thought you were born a carpenter and joiner. You always seemed happy working with tools.'

'I am,' Jack affirmed, 'but I was just reading in the paper here about a new car factory opening in Birmingham soon. Apparently they desperately need assembly operators.' He thumbed the lines of the Situation Vacant column. 'It's a good salary too, with overtime, shift allowances and penalty payments.'

'Birmingham!' The idea of moving back to the city life held little appeal for Peggy. 'Do you think it would be a good idea?'

Jack tried to explain. 'I'm thirty-six. Still a young man. But I feel I need a challenge, a real change. I've been on the tools as a chippie since I was fourteen. I need a new career pattern. But I wouldn't even consider it without your approval. I always said that marriage was a partnership.'

Peggy smiled at Jack's constant consideration for her. 'We've been married thirteen years. You don't need to seek my approval. If you think it would benefit us all, go for it.'

Jack's eyes shone. He knew how much the house meant to Peggy. It was a very generous gesture on her part. Before he could say anything, his son Derek looked up. 'If we move to Birmingham can we take Trigger?'

The dog automatically looked up at Jack with canine canniness.

'Of course, son,' Jack replied. He looked down into the eyes of the dog and stroked him. 'Trigger is part of this family. Aren't you, boy?' The dog licked his hand gratefully.

Jack was successful in obtaining a job with the Birmingham car factory. In due course they reluctantly sold the house and moved to a similar home just outside the city. At first it was a difficult move. The Lake District had been kind to them. The throb of the city of Birmingham was not too dissimilar to that of the cacophony of London. But Peggy soon got to know her new neighbours and Derek, now six years old, was soon settled at a new school. It was Jack who had to experience the biggest changes of all.

After years as a happy-go-lucky tradesman working with wood, the car parts assembly line was a different set of circumstances. Before, he had worked as an individual. The performance and quality of work was his own responsibility. Now he was part of a team, following a set routine that required his constant attention. To depart from the pattern by error or mistake could create a breakdown in the whole production line. For a while Jack seriously began to wonder if he had made a very grave mistake. However, the hard work and 16-hour days were more than compensated for by the amount of pay he earned. Almost in line with a Prime Ministerial comment that was to be well quoted in later years – he had never had it so good.

The years had passed since Vivien's death. Jack tried never to mention it. He knew Peggy still thought of their little girl often. There were rare moments when Peggy would sit in silence in a room on her own, and examine photographs of Vivien. Somehow she still could not put the tragedy behind her.

★★★

Peggy was out shopping one day in Birmingham when one of her neighbours, a smart dark-haired lady called Judi, shouted out to her. 'Howdy neighbour!' she cried from the other side of the street.

Peggy waved as Judi crossed the road. Judi was a splendid-looking woman in her late thirties, attractive and desirable, but with a remarkable air of serenity about her. She always had the appearance of being permanently happy. Her eyes twinkled. Her lips always looked as if they were about to break out into a smile. Just for being near, her people seemed to become happy.

'Hullo Judi,' Peggy said happily. 'Are you doing the family shopping as well?'

'Just finished as a matter of fact. Fancy joining me for lunch?'

For some reason the idea of woman-to-woman conversation appealed to Peggy. Perhaps because she had been part of family life for so long, the chance to talk of womanly things to another made a change.

'Why not.'

The two of them found a Lyons café and enjoyed the sort of scrumptious lunches that the fabled establishment served. They were two happy middle-class suburban housewives, typical of the time in style and dress. Their personalities could not have been more different, as Peggy found out. Judi was confident and warm. Peggy was in many ways a shy person who felt happiest within her own family circle. Judi was outgoing. She loved people. She loved life.

Quick to assess that her luncheon companion was rather reticent, Judi tried to start the conversation flowing. 'We've never really sat down and talked properly, have we? I've seen you and your family going for walks a lot. My husband said you came down from the Lake District.'

'Yes. My husband Jack came from Streatham in London originally. I'm from Sutton in Surrey. We met when we were in the Air Force during the war. We did go out to Melbourne, Australia to live in 1945 but we came home a few years later to London. Then we went north to the Lake District. Jack is a carpenter and joiner by trade. He wanted a change. That's why we're here in Birmingham.'

'What's he doing now?'

'He's working as an assembly operator for the Holdley car factory.'

'Really?' Judi smiled. 'My husband Paul works there as well. He's in the work study section.'

'Work Study?' This was a new term to Peggy. 'What is that?'

Judi explained. 'Work study is sometimes called time and motion study, I believe.'

'Oh, I know now. Is it all those men with clipboards and stopwatches standing watching to see how long a job will take?'

'That's it. But I know they look at how the job is done and try to work out better ways of doing it, and quicker ways too. It's quite an interesting job. It acts more or less as a service to management. Paul said it could lead eventually to a work's manager job or a section leader. They're running a course at the works. Why don't you tell Jack? It would get him off the assembly line. Could be a step up the ladder for him.'

Peggy considered the prospect. She knew that Jack had not been as happy as he could have been. 'I'll mention it to him, Judi. Thank you for telling me.' Peggy did not know too much about Judi and tried to show an interest in return. 'Do you have any children? I can't recall seeing you all out together.'

'I've got four!' Judi stated proudly, and Peggy could tell that this was her neighbour's favourite subject. 'I've three daughters and a son. We're actually trying for another one.'

'Gosh, you're going for five?'

'I adore children. I'm not shy of admitting my age. I'm thirty-eight and if I had the chance I would have two or three more, but time is not on our side in that respect. Paul and I are both Roman Catholics. My family were Irish. I've six brothers, would you believe! Paul's relatives were Liverpool Irish. Besides him there were five girls and two other brothers. We're a devoutly religious family. Our faith is very important to us.'

'Do you worship regularly?'

'Constantly,' replied Judi and as she went on to explain, Peggy could see why this lady appeared so calm and happy. 'We try and live as normal a family life as most people. We do try and install into our children the most important things like love of people, respect and courtesy, and to lead a life without resorting to aggression or harmful behaviour. Love of all mankind has always been a priority of our faith.'

'I think it's wonderful that you have your faith to fall back on to. I wish I had learned to have some strong religious belief years ago.'

'What do you mean, Peggy?' Judi was suddenly curious.

At this Peggy became pensive and she replied in a slow, thoughtful manner. For the first time in many years she had finally found someone she could open her heart to. 'I've got a little boy, Derek. He's coming up for his ninth birthday soon. But he wasn't our only child.'

Judi looked on, interested and her eyes appeared sympathetic.

'We had a lovely little girl. Her name was Vivien. I gave birth to her in 1942. Derek was born in 1949 after the family had come back from Australia. In 1949 while Jack was at work I collected Vivien from school.

It was so sudden, so unexpected… she seemed cold and clammy.' Peggy's voice dried up as she struggled to overcome the painful memory. 'When I got her home she seemed to have terrible difficulty breathing. She was wheezing, puffing, panting, desperately trying to inhale air. Something was terribly, terribly wrong. Her face went from pale white to red and then blue. It was a horror story. I called for a doctor and an ambulance. By the time she got to hospital it was all over for her. She had died.'

'I… am so sorry.' Judi's face was a picture of deep shock.

'It was a terrible time for both of us,' Peggy continued. 'When it happened I lost complete faith. When I say faith, I mean in myself, as a wife and mother. I came close to having the most terrible withdrawal. I could not communicate. I didn't want to look forward. I couldn't feel interested or enthusiastic about anything. It was as if I had no desire to be part of a family… or even worse, part of anything any more. I just wanted to be completely out of the situation. I felt so awful that I asked Jack for a divorce. It still causes me pain to think of how thoughtless I had been.'

Judi appeared disturbed but continued listening attentively.

'It was when we went to see the solicitor that the man talked to me quietly for a while. I could see that getting out of the marriage would have solved nothing. Looking back, it was such a terrible thing to do. Jack's a wonderful man, warm, kind, gentle. He's a wonderful dad, a wonderful husband too. I think if I had the sort of faith you have, I could possibly have drawn on it at that time to give me some sort of backbone.'

'You have been tested by tragedy Peggy,' Judi said softly. 'I've been very fortunate in that I have all of my children, and my husband and I have been blessed with good health. It's true that we have our faith which sustains us, and it influences our family life. Yet we've not been tested. We've not been tormented in this way. If we were, maybe I would find my faith sorely tried. After talking to you today, Peggy, I am going to go home and give a prayer of thanks that I have all my family together.'

'I hope you didn't mind me talking like this Judi,' Peggy said with some embarrassment, realising how candid she had suddenly been. She attempted to justify her openness. 'You see, for years I've kept this in my mind. I've never really been able to speak about this before. You seem a very compassionate person, if you don't mind me telling you. Thank you for listening to me.'

Judi's eyes brimmed with emotion. 'Believe it or not, Peggy, I am the one that's benefited from our conversation. If you and Jack ever want to come over, Paul and my family will always make you welcome.'

★★★

Jack did decide to follow up the suggestion that he should apply for a work study job within the Holdley car factory. He made an appointment with the works manager and in due course he was called into the office for an interview. A secretary led him into the room.

The works manager rose to greet him. 'Welcome, Mr Moran. I'm Jeff Blue, works manager. Please be seated.'

Jack sat down as Mr Blue looked through the application form he had written.

'I understand you've expressed an interest in joining our work study department?'

The ball was now in Jack's court, and he attempted to make a good first impression. In fact, Jack had read and rehearsed his words days before. 'That's right. I'm keen to make the move from the floor. Being on the assembly line for so long, I've got a few ideas how to improve productivity and efficiency. Not only by making changes on the assembly line but in the general use of resources and by the best use of labour. I can see ways of improving our stores, stock, even on the line itself.'

Jeff Blue was impressed by Jack's apparent grasp of the subject matter. 'Well, you're obviously conversant on the workings of the shop floor. Do you know anything about method study, time study, job breakdown and redesigning duties? Activity sampling? Critical examination?'

Jack was on the ropes immediately. He looked very embarrassed. Mr Blue was quick to recognise this. But Jack was an honest man, he would not try to bluff his way through the interview. With some reticence he told him, 'I'm afraid I have to say I don't.'

'Well, we really need people who are trained in the subject,' Mr Blue said with a decisive air.

There was a long pause. Jack interpreted this as meaning the interview was at an end. In fact, Mr Blue was using an interview technique of allowing a silence for Jack to justify why he should be taken on. Jack did not realise this and he rose to leave.

'Well, thank you very much for taking the trouble to see me,' he said courteously.

'Wait, Mr Moran. Please,' Jeff Blue said quickly. 'Stay seated.' Jack sat down again rather reluctantly. 'I believe you were a carpenter before you joined us?'

'Yes,' Jack replied, although what this had to do with the job in question he wasn't really sure.

'What made you join Holdley, Mr Moran?'

'I needed a new challenge. I wanted to try a new career.' Jack then realised that the interview was still very much in process. 'I'm willing to go on learning and retraining until the day I retire. It's very important to me. I'm a great believer in personal achievement.'

'In what way? I'm interested in what you're saying.' Mr Blue appeared to relax his hands as he concentrated on Jack.

'I believe everyone in life has a particular talent and ability, that for many people sadly remains untapped all their working days. There are many jobs throughout industry where people work in the same routine day in, day out, often in conditions that are unsafe, dampen enthusiasm, destroy incentive and pay little in return. I'm not speaking of conditions here at Holdley, but other factories. I think it is very important to give dignity and respect to working people and to engender enthusiasm and interest in what they are doing. If employees are genuinely enthusiastic in what they are working at, the organisation gets back a quality product and reliable efficient happy workers. I think it's true to say that many people work purely out of economic need, just for the wages packet that pays the mortgage and feeds the children. By involving staff in the decision-making process you can build up their interest and respect. Everyone has something to offer, a potential to be unlocked.'

This satisfied Jeff Blue. 'I'm impressed by your views. I will put you on a course starting next Monday at our training school. Be there at eight-thirty sharp. Thank you for coming, Mr Moran and welcome to the team.'

'Thank you very much, Mr Blue.'

Jack's career was on the rise. By the late 1950s Jack Moran's career was progressing nicely along the social structure. He had started life as a working-class man and now he was becoming one of the middle class;

the people to whom Prime Minister Harold Macmillan was to say, 'You've never had it so good'. And speaking for Jack, he was right.

Everyone's life was on the up and up it seemed at that time. The Moran family were no different. They had endured their years of struggle. Now they were determined to enjoy life as best as it was possible.

★★★

There were still times when Peggy would appear sad and distant. The earlier tragedy haunted her, even though the years had long since passed. Peggy never forgot Vivien's birthday or the anniversary of her death. She would sit in silent memoriam of her late daughter.

On one such day, when Derek was ten years old, Peggy took him and their dog Trigger to the park. Derek was unaware that this day was the anniversary of Vivien's death. Peggy sat silently on the park bench while Derek played ball with his dog. There was a faraway look in Peggy's eyes. She was visualising how her daughter would have grown. With a shattering effect, Peggy realised that Vivien would be rising 17 now! Vivien had been such a beautiful, happy little girl. How could someone so lovely be robbed of life at such an early age? Peggy could never reason why.

Derek came across and sat next to his mother, who remarked, 'You'll wear old Trigger out. He's not a young puppy any more.'

'He still seems fit to me, Mum,' Derek said defensively.

Peggy stroked the dog lovingly. 'For every year of our life a dog has about seven I believe. Therefore old Trigger here is eight in human terms but about fifty-six dog years. You're a loving boy, aren't you Trigger.' The dog appeared to respond with loving eyes. 'Old faithful, that's you.'

Derek noticed a subdued look about his mother. He knew that something was wrong. He was too young and naïve to work it out. Then, a question he had always wanted to ask his mother popped into his mind. 'What was your life like as a child, Mum?'

Peggy smiled at her son. 'Oh, your grandparents and I had a happy life at Sutton, in the old house at Greyhound Road.' She started to remember, and there seemed to be real pleasure in her voice as she spoke of the past. 'It was one of those places and times of my life I feel very grateful for. Your granddad was a bit unpredictable. Very quick and bad-tempered when his moods swung from high to low. Basically a good man who believed in hard work and respect. I learned a lot from him but he put the fear of God into me. I never misbehaved or spoke out of turn because I was frightened he would explode into a fearful temper. It was your grandmother who was the real stabiliser. She could be tough, but she was always fair. My poor old mum worked sixteen hours a day cleaning offices and she suffered from the most painful arthritis. Do you know, I never heard her complain or grumble?'

'Did you have any pets?'

'I had two,' Peggy replied. 'A lovely black and grey tabby cat with huge green eyes and a mischievous nature. It was always rolling on its back and playing or jumping up on top of cupboards. I had a dog too, a lovely golden retriever called Penny. My old volatile dad loved him. Penny was one of those dogs who looked like she had a permanent smile on her face.'

Derek had never heard his mother speak so openly. He pursued the line of questioning with childlike curiosity. 'What sort of games did you use to play when you were a little girl?'

'Gosh you're testing my memory aren't you, Derek? I suppose I should be able to remember things very clearly. I'm not quite forty. Funny thing is, it doesn't seem that long ago. Time is strange. Some things that happened in my childhood could have occurred yesterday. Other things in my adult life seem to have happened a generation ago. I suppose my memory's become selective as the years have passed. I tend to remember only the happier things.' Peggy realised she was beginning to ramble. 'Now then, when I was a young girl I used to play hopscotch, and I had a pogo stick. I used to play netball and tennis.'

'Did you use to play football?'

Peggy burst into laughter. 'Football? Play football? You're joking! Not us girls. Whatever made you ask?'

'I don't know. Just asked.' Derek laughed. When his mother was happy she looked radiant.

'Until I met your Dad I didn't know the difference between a dribble and a foul. Your Dad soon filled me in on football. I could tell you the complete history of Stanley Matthews, Danny Blanchflower, Tom Finney, Jimmy Dickinson, Alf Ramsey, Harry Gregg.'

Derek looked at his mother adoringly. There wasn't an ounce of bad in her whatsoever. There was love and goodness, a dash of sadness perhaps, but a beautiful calm about her. Unlike some children who lived in fear of the iron rule and volatility of their parents, Derek knew gentleness and serenity in his own mother and father. Even when they disciplined him it was with a secure and firm manner. His curiosity compelled him to ask one further question. Even at such a young age he was aware of the inner sadness his mother wore beneath the still waters.

'Are you happy, Mum?'

The question surprised Peggy. She was virtually expressionless. Almost as if to avoid answering the question, she leaned forward and stroked the dog. Then she sat up again, turned to her son, nodded slightly and tousled Derek's hair. He smiled back at her; he was always the adoring son.

★★★

Judi had become something of a soulmate and confidante to Peggy. The two regularly had lunch together. At first glance the two women did not seem to have much in common. Both were strikingly attractive, but Judi was deeply religious and leaned on her faith for support. Peggy's main love was her family. She hadn't any religious leanings but she lived a selfless life. Peggy lived not for herself. It was the Moran family who were her linchpin.

At 41 years of age Judi gave birth to her sixth child. The upcoming christening merited a small party to which Peggy and Jack were invited. The child was happily taking centre stage in a playpen. Paul and Judi led their guests through to look at the little girl.

'Here she is,' Judi said delightedly. Jack and Peggy looked on with moist eyes.

'She's lovely, Judi,' Jack said, and there was a lump in his throat as he spoke. It was like seeing his own first born again. He turned quickly to Paul. 'Got your eyes, that's for sure.'

'Thanks,' Paul said with a grin. He was a sturdy 6 footer with dark wavy hair, a born father who proudly looked on at his latest child. 'The rest of her is her Mum's, no doubt about that.' He looked across to Judi as if there was an important matter they wanted to discuss. Judi recognised the hint and came across. 'Peggy, Jack,' Paul said grabbing their attention immediately, 'There was something we rather wanted to ask you.'

'What is that, Paul?' Peggy asked in anticipation.

Paul's eyes glowed with warmth and when he spoke his voice was filled with the tones of love and sincerity. 'We don't want to delve into the past too much. But since Judi and I have got to know you so well we've grown very much to appreciate your genuineness and openness as people.'

Jack was a little surprised and embarrassed. It was not in the British character to be generous in appraisal of one's personal qualities. 'It's a nice compliment Paul, I…'

Before Jack could find the words, Paul continued quickly, 'We're very fortunate in that we've already been blessed with five children in good health and now we have a sixth, a lovely little girl. We know how much your boy means to you. He's a lovely lad. We know that you once had…' He broke off short of saying 'had a daughter'. The silence that followed spoke more than words. Paul continued, 'We wondered if you would like to be godparents to our little daughter?'

Peggy positively beamed with happiness. She looked at Jack, who was feeling more happiness for her than for himself. 'Oh, how wonderful! Of course. I'd be thrilled. Jack… can we?'

'My words. It would be simply wonderful. I'd consider it an honour.'

Peggy was already kneeling down by the child and playing with it. Her happiness was evident for all to see.

By the time Peggy and Jack arrived home they were bubbling with joy. They sat on the sofa with a hot bedtime drink, revelling in the pleasurable honour that Paul and Judi had bestowed on them.

'Wasn't that nice of them to ask us to be godparents?' It was the third time Peggy had said that. Jack didn't mind. He was thrilled to see the light shine in her eyes again.

'They are a lovely couple, Peg,' Jack said. He was very fond of Paul and Judi. 'I've enormous respect for them. What is it about them, though? There's something so endearing about them. I can't really explain.

'How do you mean, Jack?'

'Well… how can I describe it?' Jack rubbed his chin. 'In life there are certain people you meet and for some reason I can't explain you feel warmth, you like them straight off. It's as if you've known them all your life and you're instantly comfortable with them. You could tell them the most private details of your life and you know they'd be there in your darkest moments, your hour of need. And they would want to help you. I mean, really want to help you. There are others — perhaps I speak for myself only — but when I meet them I feel an automatic hostility to. I know it's wrong, of course. It takes time to get to know most people but as soon as I meet them I can hear warning bells in my mind saying, steer clear of them, they're trouble. With Paul and Judi it's something completely different. They seem to exude love. In fact they glow with love. When I meet them, well it's like I want to throw both arms around each of them and love them.'

Peggy knew how intuitive her husband could be. 'I know what you mean, Jack, and I can explain it for you. They are Roman Catholics. They are strongly religious and live within the confines, or the limitations, or maybe even the rules that their faith demands. But more than anything, what makes Judi and Paul the way they are is that they believe love is the most important thing they can give to humanity, and that love is returned forthwith. I don't purely mean the love that exists in marriage between man and wife, and their family.'

'You've spoken to Judi in some depth, then?' Jack queried in a surprised tone.

'Oh yes,' Peggy confirmed. 'Paul and Judi believe in the Christian act of loving everyone. Hate and mistrust are things that don't exist in their world. It's a wonderful philosophy of life. It doesn't always exist in an ideal world.'

Jack sighed, 'It's almost enviable to have those sort of qualities.'

Peggy touched his hand reassuringly, and then gripped it in the manner that lovers do. 'I love you, Jack,' she said gently. The words surprised him. Neither of them had verbally expressed their love for a long time. 'You've got enough good qualities of your own. Steadfast and sure, that's you. You're my anchor.'

Jack gazed into her eyes with honest amazement. 'You can still say that? After seventeen years of marriage? Is there still some magic there after all this time?'

'Yes, Jack,' Peggy replied with a smile. 'There's still magic there.'

★★★

'I always remember the way she said that.'

Jack appeared misty-eyed as he recounted the memories to his son Derek. Even now, in 1992, all of the years of his marriage flowed back into his mind.

Derek had been listening patiently and courteously to his father. He was aware of the terrible despair that was evident in Jack's eyes as he realised the future was going to be a lonely one. It was Derek's time to say his piece.

'What was it that Mr Halliwell, the solicitor told you back in 1949?'

'He didn't tell me,' Jack pointed out. 'He told Peggy. There is life after tragedy. There is life after grief and despair.'

'Well then, Dad, I'm sure Mum wouldn't want you to be sitting here in sadness. She would be quite firm about it that life must go on.'

'I agree. But this morning I'm remembering a fifty-year marriage. You don't just get up and go on after half a century of married life has finished. Your mum and I weathered a few storms in our time. The war. I never thought I'd survive some of those RAF missions. There was our spell in a stinking set of Nissen huts that passed for a migrant hostel in Melbourne. Then there was the death of your sister, which tore our insides out and brought us to the point of divorce. But somehow we got over all that, and the later years were some of the happiest I've ever known.'

'I know, Dad,' Derek said sensitively. It was his turn to speak of his own private heartache. 'You know, when my own wife and I separated and I only saw Natasha and Pearl on weekends I was quite envious that you and Mum had managed to stay together and ride roughshod over any family problems. Fifty years. That's a long time. Jennifer wanted so much in the way of material things that I just couldn't give her on my salary. I was only ever a working man, a hard-working man too, but she wanted a wine and roses lifestyle on a beer and sandwiches budget. You and Mum... well, you got through despite material things. They didn't mean much at all.'

Jack felt for his son now. He knew that Derek had tried hard to preserve his marriage even though his wife Jennifer had grown apart from him. Derek had been loyal and dedicated, a man like his father who believed in commitment and the sanctity of marriage. Jennifer had become bored with just being a wife and mother. Simply being comfortable was not enough, she wanted more luxurious items that just didn't come within Derek's earnings. There were arguments that led to stony silences. The couple could not relate to each other any more, and the inevitable separation came.

'Your mum and I were of a different kind of people,' Jack explained carefully. 'In our day, marriage was a stronger institution than it is today. Rightly or wrongly it was the days when the man was head of the household and the woman was really all things: mother, cleaner, cook, washerwoman, lover; some of the women's libbers would tell you there were unpaid slaves who had to be on the beck and call of their husbands. I think a lot of women were treated very badly. They weren't treated like equals, given their due respect as individuals who might have had ambitions and hopes of their own. These days women are given far more respect. They are far more treated as partners in marriage than the way they used to be.'

'It broke my heart when my marriage ended. I think a lot of the problems began when Jennifer looked around at other women of her age who had achieved things on their own. Suddenly to be a wife and mother just wasn't satisfactory. She wanted long lunches with the girls, an unlimited chequebook to buy clothes she would probably only wear once a year. And then I realised with heart-breaking pain that she didn't want me any more. She wanted to be the centre of different men's flattery and attention.' He looked at his dad, the pain still so strong in his eyes. 'You and Mum…'

'Yes, son.'

'You were so lucky. You stayed the course. Your marriage held the ground.'

'I was lucky, wasn't I, Derek?' Jack realised the truth in his son's words. He felt inclined to add a few complimentary words for his son's benefit. 'Not only was I lucky to have a fine wife, but I was damn lucky to have a good son in you.'

Derek appeared to be deeply embarrassed.

'Don't be embarrassed. You've grown strong with the years. You've handled your life well. I'm proud of you.'

'Thanks, Dad. You've never said that to me before.'

'I should have told you years ago.'

Derek felt uneasy at his father's open display of admiration. He stood up. 'I'm going back to bed now. I'll leave you to the privacy of your own memories.'

'Thanks for listening, son. I needed to talk.'

'We'll talk tomorrow, if you like,' Derek said gently and he walked upstairs.

Jack glanced quickly at Derek. He was a fine man, 43 years of age, and solidly decent. What a tragedy that he and his wife Jennifer had grown apart over the years. It was not that long ago that they had all been a happy, united family. In many ways Derek was so much like his father. Jack thought to himself that it only seemed like yesterday when they had sat around the television watching the funeral of Winston Churchill. Where had the time gone?

★★★

The world leaders had gathered in London for the funeral of this remarkable man. The familiar faces flashed across the screen as they came to pay tribute to a great man: Johnson, De Gaulle, Menzies, Wilson, Attlee – they were all there. The Moran family watched keenly as the coffin of Sir Winston Churchill was carried by young soldiers, one of whom was seen to express relief as it was lowered down. The weight of it could only be imagined. There was the spectacular fly-past over the River Thames that followed. London had never seen anything like it before.

Peggy's eyes were moist. 'It's a wonder the old man didn't sit up in his coffin and give a victory salute.'

'I half expected him to,' Jack said with a smile. 'I remember seeing him at RAF Northolt during the war.'

'Don't forget VE Day,' Peggy reminded him.

'That's right,' Jack remembered. 'We saw him when we made our way to the Mall.'

That far-off night in 1965, the three members of the family sat around the dining room table discussing the occasion. Peggy was a very observant person with a great sense of history. In another life she could have made a fine teacher or magazine writer.

'Churchill had the biggest send-off any public figure in this country will ever have,' she stated with certainty. 'It's incredible to think of all the things he did in his lifetime.'

'True.' Jack began to list them. 'Apart from being the Harrow-educated son of a one-time government minster in Randolph Churchill and a beautiful American woman, Jennie… that's right, that was her name. He went on to become a soldier in Sudan, South Africa, a journalist and war correspondent. He was both a Liberal and a Conservative at different stages of his career. Prime Minister twice from 1940 to 1945 when Attlee defeated him, and then again from 1951 to 55. What a life he led. As well as all that he found time to be an author, a painter. He was a statesman. He fought in the Boer War and led Britain through its most difficult years.'

This was the signal for 16-year-old Derek to join in the conversation. 'Our history teacher at school has been telling us about Churchill all this week.'

Peggy remembered that Derek had an important appointment that week. 'Has the careers advisor been to your school this week?'

'Yes,' Derek replied quickly without elaborating.

'And?' Peggy was curious to know if her son had been given any useful information.

'Well, he said that as my strong subjects at school were woodwork, art and English, I ought to try something in that line.'

'Did he suggest anything specific?' asked Jack. Derek nodded. 'What do you want to do though, Derek? Never mind what anyone else tells you to do. What would you like?'

Derek realised he was being put on the spot to answer a question that every father asks their son at some stage. 'I try hard at everything,' he answered honestly. 'But physics and maths are too difficult for me. Anything to do with science I find very hard. I like painting and putting wood together.' He added with delight, 'I enjoy it.'

'So…' Jack sensed his son had some idea what he would do for a living.

'I hope you don't mind, Dad,' Derek said almost apologetically, 'but I'm not a chip off the old block. It's not like father, like son. I've been thinking that I wouldn't mind working as a fully fledged carpenter.'

Jack was beaming with pride. He could not resist telling his son the finer points of such a career move. 'It's a damn good trade. It's got a lot of openings. I miss being on the old workshop tools myself.'

'You were never happier than when you chipped wood,' Peggy mentioned.

It was an opportunity for Jack to sum up his own personal achievements, of which he felt very proud. 'It will give you a good start in life, I can tell you this. I've gone from carpenter's apprentice to the Air Force, then as a chippy here and in Australia. Then at Holdley car manufacturers I was an assembly operator. I moved up from there to a position as a work study officer and even though that led to the job I've got now as a management consultant, I don't think that in all of my working life I have ever felt as greater feeling of satisfaction then the days I was an ordinary carpenter. There's a lot to be said for being a skilled woodworker. Everywhere you look you'll see a chippy. Building boats, fitting kitchens, making furniture, in television and film studios building sets, on building sites, in churches, shopping centres, hospitals. And it's a trade that you're always learning.'

This convinced Derek. 'I'll probably give it a go.'

★★★

The year of 1966 was a very special one. England won the World Cup. It was also Jack and Peggy's twenty-fifth wedding anniversary. By a coincidence, both events occurred on the same day and helped to make the occasion a very happy one.

The entire family sat round the television watching the spectacular English soccer team play against West Germany. Managed by Alf Ramsay, the team boasted such luminaries as Bobby Moore, Gordon Banks, Nobby Stiles, Alan Ball, Bobby Charlton, amongst others — but it was the game for which Geoff Hurst would be remembered forever in football history when he went on to clinch England's victory with a hat trick of goals.

That evening the house was full of friends and relatives in very buoyant mood. Jack and Peggy stood in the centre of the room. It was Jack's moment.

'Friends and relatives,' he began warmly, 'I want to thank you all for coming today. On this happy day we are celebrating two marvellous achievements. England won the World Cup, so we better drink to Alf Ramsay and the boys. But more importantly to Peg and me, it is our twenty-fifth wedding anniversary today. Peggy has stood by me for twenty-five years.' He turned and kissed her. 'Thanks, love. I know it's not always been easy but I'm so grateful for your love and support.' Jack raised his glass. 'Everybody, would you join us for a toast? To Peggy and I.'

The partygoers simultaneously raised their glasses and said in unison, 'To Peggy and Jack.' All of their friends and relatives had come. It was a lovely day for all concerned.

Jack was on a good salary as a management consultant. In his late forties now, he had come a long way from being a chippy. Although he would always consider himself a tradesman, Jack had brought a practical down-to-earth and commonsense attitude towards his new role. At the Holdley car factory he had learned new skills as a work study officer; as part of a team reporting directly to the management he had helped improve productivity, efficiency and safety standards. From there he had graduated to a consultancy that dealt with all kinds of employees: professional, technical, administrative, manual, secretarial staff, in all types of industries from commerce to manufacturing. His salary had almost tripled, commensurate with the new responsibilities he was called on to perform.

Peggy and Jack were now at the stage of their lives where they could afford to move to a house of a higher standard than anything they had lived in previously. Jack's work frequently took him to different parts of

Britain, but he and Peggy needed somewhere that was easily accessible. In the past few years Jack had visited a steelworks near Newcastle, a water project in rural Scotland, financial institutions that needed new management structures in the home counties, and shipyards as far apart as the Clyde and Southampton. Surrey was an easily commutable county with mainline stations to and from London. It was there that Jack and Peggy found a country cottage that they both fell in love with.

They studied the thatched cottage from within their car. A 'For Sale' sign stood in the front garden, which was a display in itself of lush green lawns and flower beds. The estate agent had given Jack the key and they stepped out of the car to view the garden. For a while they walked around it in awe.

'It's nice, Jack,' Peggy said, making an obvious understatement. She had never walked around the grounds of such an attractive home before. 'But it looks so expensive.'

'It is,' Jack agreed. 'Don't forget I'm not Jack the Streatham chippy any more. I'm a management consultant on a good salary now. I could take the mortgage on, but if the interest rates suddenly rise sharply we may find ourselves in the position where we cut down right across the board.'

Peggy studied the look on Jack's face. 'Let's forget it. It's not for us.'

Jack knew his wife better than that. 'You want this place as much as I do.'

'You don't have to please me, Jack. Of course I would love it: a thatched cottage, it's a dream. I know I've only been doing part-time office work in recent years. What with Derek starting work full-time I could do a full five days and a Saturday if need be. I don't mind.'

'We'll worry about that when it happens. Let's go inside and have a look round.'

Inside the vacant premises the country cottage proved to be every bit as irresistible as the exterior. It exuded warmth and character in every room. Peggy walked around every nook and cranny, studying the layout of the house. There were beautiful spacious bedrooms that would catch the light of the early morning sunshine in summer. A private den lurked in the corner of the cottage. Here Jack could work on his consultancy reports in peace and privacy. The dining room was cosy and neat. Peggy envisaged having long warm conversations with Jack on winter evenings. This house was the nearest thing to heaven on earth that Peggy and Jack would ever live in.

If Peggy had in mind a vision of a happy, warm home, Jack in his professional manner was admiring the solid workmanship of a cottage built by master tradesmen in an age gone by. He examined the huge fireplace, the hearth and the oak beams. Jack ran his thumbs up and down the beams; he still possessed the old carpenter's eyes of checking the grain of the wood. It was fine and solid. Peggy noticed what he was doing. Jack's eyes shone with delight.

'You love it don't you, Jack?' Peggy asked him. 'I can see you're admiring the structure.'

'Beautiful wood,' remarked Jack. 'Must be four hundred years old. Do you realise this cottage was built years before, centuries before some of the modern methods employed by builders today? And it's still standing. This is something from the age of Christopher Wren. It's standing the test of time.'

'It's a beautiful house, and it's less than an hour by train to your new headquarters in London.'

'I take it you're sold then, Peggy?'

'I can't believe we're even considering buying a house like this. There are some people in the world who would take this as being their divine right to live here; they'd take it for granted.'

'Not us, Peg. We're not made like that.'

'When I think of the places we've lived in over the years. Rented rooms, with a sewerage farm at the back.'

'A migrant hostel in Melbourne,' Jack added.

'Don't remind me,' Peggy said raising her eyebrows. 'And what about the other places? A council house, and then a squalid terrace with an outside toilet in a garden by a railway line. That toilet used to shake every time the fast train came through.'

Jack looked around at the high oak beams. 'I like this house, Peggy. It's been a long journey from Streatham.'

'I adore it, Jack. I think it's the chance of a lifetime to have something like this. It seems unfair to me that you should shoulder the burden as far as the mortgage is concerned. Let me go back to work full-time in the office rather than just the two days or so I've been doing. They have asked me if I wanted to do a full week. I've no reason not to accept. Besides, I'd feel guilty just living in a place like this while you graft away. I was never cut out to be Lady Muck. I'm not going to sit around getting a fat bottom drinking tea with the neighbours. Let me contribute.'

'Alright, Peg,' said Jack putting his arms around her. 'We'll make this a very happy house.'

Peggy was true to her word. Both knew the opportunity of owning a house such as this was a rare one. It was a prosperous time in the late 1960s that would eventually give way to regular economic recessions. Jack took on extra work and Peggy started full-time in her office, working overtime and on Saturdays when the occasion arose.

In her new career, Peggy applied herself industriously to her tasks. Hard work obviously ran in the Moran family. Jack had always been a grafter. Both of their families had been very hard workers. Now Peggy was fully utilising her abilities.

The director of the company, Mr Stallybrass, watched over the staff through a glass partition in his office. He had watched Peggy's progress with a keen eye. The office manager had recently appointed Peggy as supervisor. When Mr Stallybrass's secretary, a young lady with an hour-glass figure called Miss Wyatt, came into the office one day he made it his business to find out how Peggy had been coping.

'You wanted me to do some shorthand, Mr Stallybrass?' she said, knowing full well that was all Mr Stallybrass usually required her for.

'Yes please, Miss Wyatt.' The lady sat down with pen and pad in hand, her tight skirt sliding up revealing a perfect pair of legs. 'Just before we start, how is Peggy handling the supervisor's job?'

'Very well,' Miss Wyatt replied without hesitation. 'The office is ticking over efficiently.'

Mr Stallybrass was curious about Peggy. He was aware of each member of staff, but always made it a point not to mingle with them personally. He was very aloof and authoritative; on occasions he could also be arrogant and pompous. Miss Wyatt waited patiently as her boss appeared to be studying Peggy through the window of his office.

'How long has Mrs Moran been with us?' he asked quickly.

'On a part-time basis, five years. And full-time since 1967, coming up for two and a half years now.' Mr Stallybrass seemed to be waiting for more information. Miss Wyatt thoughtfully added, 'She's a very hard worker.'

'Will you tell her to come in and see me as soon as we've finished?'

'Certainly, sir.'

Shortly afterwards Peggy came into the office. Mr Stallybrass was not known for his tact in dealing with women. Long before equality in the workplace became a legality, men like Mr Stallybrass tended to underestimate the strong points of female employees. He was pleasantly surprised at Peggy's efficiency, her attention to detail, and a concentration span that dealt with the immediate needs of the job in hand. For once he was professionally impressed.

Peggy sat opposite Mr Stallybrass. She was aware that he cast something more than just a cursory admiring glance over her. 'I'm very pleased with the work you've been doing for us,' he stated with an air of pleasure. 'I've noticed a considerable difference in the way the whole office has been performing. Your reorganisation of the filing system, for instance: it's superbly indexed and the information is easily accessible. The accounting system used to be something of a shambles; now it's near perfect. Everything is paid on time soon after the due date. I have to say even the arrangement of the office furniture and equipment is looking better.' He paused and looked at her with an inquiring eye. He was canny enough to know that this former temporary worker had knowledge of management skills. 'Could I ask where you got some of your ideas from Mrs Moran? You obviously have professional abilities that I've not been previously aware of.'

'My husband is a management consultant,' Peggy replied. 'Over the past few years I've read some of his reference books in relation to improving office efficiency. Not only offices, but also factories and industrial plants.'

Mr. Stallybrass's eyes gleamed with delight. He was visibly impressed. 'I see. Perhaps I could meet your husband sometime. Why don't you bring him around for dinner with my wife and I?'

Peggy appeared hesitant at first. Even Jack, with all the responsibilities his position entailed, had never mixed family and business life. In the manner of politicians, Peggy tried to give an answer that did not match the question. 'Well, my son Derek will be staying with us for a while. He has been working in Plymouth. He's twenty-one shortly.'

'Bring him along! If he gets bored in our company he can talk to my daughter. She's nearly twenty-one herself.'

Peggy smiled, but it did not disguise the apprehension she felt.

★★★

Derek looked around the country cottage that his mother and father lived in. He was of another generation who thought differently to his parents. The house was beautiful, a real luxury, but it espoused in every corner the age of materialism. It was a display of just how far in life Jack and Peggy had progressed since the war. In a way the Moran family were typical of their time. They had made the graduation from working class to middle class since the end of the war.

At 20 years of age Derek had grown up in a Britain that had undergone radical changes in the 1950s and 1960s. The rock 'n' roll and coffee bar era of the 1950s had given way to the sounds of the Beatles and the Rolling Stones. The coffee bars had been replaced by the folk clubs from within which the protest songs of Bob Dylan and Joan Baez were heard. Unemployment had not yet risen to the massive 3 million level that was prominent in the early 1980s and early 1990s.

Perhaps it was a time of happiness and relative prosperity compared to the more difficult times before and in later decades, but in 1970 things seemed to be relatively peaceful. Flares and miniskirts hung over from the swinging sixties. A Conservative government led by Edward Heath had been returned to power in the General Election.

Working away from home as a carpenter in Plymouth and on Saturday nights at different sites, Derek quaffed his lager and lime while watching for the availability of seemingly unattached miniskirted girls.

He didn't come home to Surrey very often. When he did, he always felt uncomfortable in the thatched cottage. Not because he didn't like it. Far from it. But because it represented a lifestyle that so many younger people of that time were rebelling against. In truth, however, it was only to be a temporary opt-out. Twenty years on and many of the rebellious youth would be solid citizens, some more conservative and conventional than their own parents had been. Their own children would give them far more concern in the 1980s and 1990s. There would be worse things to worry about in later years: long-term unemployment, street vandalism, joyriding kids, and a breakdown in society not apparent until statistics would show the number of single parents struggling to bring children up on their own. The family unit would become a different kind to that of previous eras.

All that was a long way off as Derek waited in the lounge for his parents. Tonight they were all going to Mr Stallybrass's house for the evening meal. Derek wore a light jacket with wide lapels, a pink shirt boasting a collar with long pointed wings, a pair of dark flares, and some boots with elastic slip-on sides and Cuban heels. His father was slightly more conventional, wearing a three-piece navy suit with collar and tie.

'You are coming to dinner with us tonight?' Jack asked amiably as he walked into the room.

'I'd hardly be going to a rock concert in a jacket like this,' Derek said smoothing back his shoulder-length hair.

'That's true. At the Isle of Wight when Dylan appeared some of them didn't bother wearing anything at all!'

'No. That was Woodstock in the United States,' Derek corrected him. 'Anyway if I was going to a rock concert I'd be wearing purple flares, a floral shirt and…'

'I get the picture,' Jack said with a smile. At that moment the smell of scent and perfume combined with hairspray came into the room, followed by Peggy. Jack looked at her in adoration. A few months away from 50 years of age and she could still turn heads. 'My word, you look good.'

'Thank you, Jack,' Peggy replied with a trace of girlish shyness. 'Well, I didn't really want to go tonight, but I felt I'd almost been talked into it by my boss.'

'Don't worry, Peg,' said Jack. 'Derek and I will do our best to enjoy it. Won't we, son?'

Derek gave his Dad a knowing look. 'Of course. I wouldn't show my own parents up!'

Mr Stallybrass lived in a huge Tudor house in the Surrey stockbroker belt. The house was more than a match for the man's salary, every penny of which he would desperately have need to meet the payments on what Jack determined would have been something of a colossus of a mortgage.

The Morans joined the Stallybrass family at the dinner table, feeling slightly socially uncomfortable at first. To their surprise, Jack and Peggy found their hosts John and Dorothy Stallybrass to be extremely easy going and pleasant. Away from the surrounds of the office the company director shed himself of his arrogance and authority, and the real man beneath the regulation business grey suit revealed his personality. The original 'grey man', John Stallybrass was an entertaining raconteur full of charm and good humour. Peggy was amazed at the differences, so glaringly obvious now, between the man in the office and out of it.

Dorothy was a very likeable woman. Peggy judged her to be nearer the mid-fifty mark. They both seemed to warm to each other instantly. Dorothy was in many ways the exact opposite of Peggy. She had flirtatious eyes, a husky voice and a girlish sense of humour. How Dorothy and John came together was anyone's guess.

Derek found himself placed strategically opposite the Stallybrass's daughter, Jennifer. While the adults talked, it soon became obvious that Derek and Jennifer were eyeing each other up with more than a little interest. They listened politely while the adults talked about their wartime service. A faint smile played around Jennifer's mouth. It was Peggy with her sharp womanly intuition who recognised the first signs of mutual admiration between her son and the boss's daughter.

'I did my Army service during the war in the Long Range Desert Group,' Mr Stallybrass stated very proudly.

Jack searched his memory quickly. 'That was the unit started by David Stirling, if memory serves me correctly.'

'That's right,' Mr Stallybrass confirmed. 'And what a fine bunch of men I served with. We were up and down North Africa like yo-yo's. The great thing about my time in the Army was that we saw sights the ordinary traveller today doesn't get to.' With a cigar in one hand and a glass of Scotch in the other he became broad and expansive. 'I shall never forget the scents and sounds of the desert. Remote oasis, Touareg camps, nomadic Arab wanderers, I can never forget the sight of a lone Arab making his way across the dunes with a camel. It was a magical experience. At night the desert was so quiet, you could hear the quiet.'

Dorothy quickly rescued the conversation before it became an evening of John Stallybrass's reminiscences. 'Were you in the forces, Peggy?' she asked pleasantly.

'I was a WRAF. That was where I met Jack.' She cast a quick glance at Derek and Jennifer who were chatting to each other.

Later in the evening the two youngsters escaped to the conservatory while both sets of parents talked inside. Jennifer Stallybrass was a delectable young lady. Derek had never quite met anyone like her before. Jennifer was 5 feet 4 inches tall with neatly cut brown hair, and blue eyes that echoed her mother's in that they were flirtatious and twinkled with humour. Her figure was slim, yet attractively evoking hints of the woman she would blossom into.

'They're revelling in nostalgia about the war years,' Jennifer said in a voice that sounded as if it had been speech trained at RADA.

'Yes. My Mum and Dad often talk about that time. That's where they met.'

'Probably the highlight of their lives.'

Derek looked at her admiringly as Jennifer lazily stretched her legs. 'I've got a few weeks' holiday now,' he said seizing the opportunity. 'Would you like…?' He hesitated to ask her out but Jennifer was quick to second-guess him.

'To go out? Is that what you were about to ask? Are you asking me out? If you are, the answer is yes.'

Derek grinned at her anticipation. 'You've made that easy for me!' In the background the music of an old Vera Lynn song could be heard. 'That's my parent's signature tune.'

Jennifer just said, 'Oh.'

'They got engaged to that one,' Derek added trying to further the conversation. He thought that if anything positive came of this relationship that same tune — 'Yours', sung by Vera Lynn — could in an ironic sense become their own song too.

Just being near this girl dazzled Derek. In all of his nights out with the boys at discotheques and public houses he had never met anyone like her. Jennifer was of a different breed to the girls he had met. Her background had been one of solid, uncomplicated comfort. Derek's own life had run the gamut of rented rooms, a council house, a terraced house, and a thatched cottage that he occasionally came home to from his digs in Plymouth. There was a world of difference between them, and yet in some ways there was only a coat of paint between their characteristics of personality.

Jennifer turned to him suddenly. 'When they've finished in their nostalgia I'll put on "Baby Come Back" by the Equals.'

Derek felt confident with her now. 'That should bring the situation up to date.' He was certain already about this girl. Almost certainly she would figure prominently in his future.

★★★

Jennifer and Derek started their courtship virtually straight away. They went for long walks along the river at Walton-on-Thames and Richmond, they had picnic lunches in Hyde Park and would sit talking for hours over glasses of shandy at the Star and Garter as if it was a clandestine meeting in some far-off exotic place. For Jennifer the attention and obvious adoration Derek bestowed on her was something she had not experienced with previous boyfriends. Derek was thrilled that Jennifer responded to him. It seemed too good to be true.

This was a real romance for both of them. Neither had ever properly been in love before. True, they had enjoyed romantic attachments, casual flirtations and boy—girl friendships, but this was something different. Every time Derek set eyes on Jennifer he felt genuinely weak at the knees, and was sure his pulse rate tripled at the sight of this lovely girl. In truth, he was intoxicated by her: The way she walked, her warm smile, her eyes that sparkled with a mixture of love and mystery. Even Jennifer's clear white skin and inviting lips were appealing. Derek felt so proud to be out with her.

The two of them together were an attractive couple. Jennifer wore colourful miniskirts and multicoloured tops. Her shoes were shiny high heels that made her legs seem longer than they actually were. Derek in many ways was a younger version of his father, slightly more in tune with the fashion of the times, a working man who was slightly rough around the edges. But these had been smoothed out by his relationship with Jennifer.

Derek had grown up under the thumb of a father who believed that women were hallowed ground and should be treated with respect at all times. His own father had in many ways been the sort of person who would have earned respect from his fellow man and through his gentility and courtesy also appealed to women. In a unique sort of way he was both a man's man and a woman's man. Derek had inherited many of these traits.

In just four weeks their romance had developed very quickly. It was on the Serpentine in Hyde Park that Jennifer began to hint of her deepening interest in Derek. On the lake, Derek rowed a small boat while Jennifer lay back, luxuriating in the sunny weather.

'What's your life like in Plymouth, Derek?'

'Lovely. My digs are a bit rough. I'm glad to get home on the odd occasion. The job's terrific though. I like Plymouth, it's a nice town. The countryside around it is nice too.'

'You've got a good future, then?'

It was the opportunity Derek had been looking for, to be able to expand upon his worth as a future husband. 'Yes. I've definitely got a good future and prospects. I've finished my apprenticeship now and the work is coming in good all the time. I'm looking forward to completing my Clerk of Works Certificate and maybe becoming an estimator in time for a large building company.'

'That's good,' said Jennifer as if she was waiting for him to say something else. Almost as if he could read her mind he stopped rowing the boat and allowed it to drift freely. Derek sat down at the end of the vessel and looked straight at her.

'I know this is rather sudden...' Jennifer looked at him in expectation. 'Will you marry me?'

All she could say was one word, 'Gosh!'

'I'm sorry. Did I shock you?'

Jennifer smiled warmly at him. She felt half flattered, half amazed. But she was also secretly delighted. 'I am a little shocked,' came her reply in a voice that betrayed her surprise. 'You've only known me four weeks.'

Derek said wistfully, 'My dad knew the first time he met my mum that he wanted to marry her.'

'That was different. They were a couple who met in wartime. During the war they lived on a knife-edge, never knowing if there would be life after next week. My parents were the same. They met in wartime.'

'You've not given me a straight answer. I take it... it's a no?'

Jennifer leaned across and squeezed his hand gently. 'I'm really flattered. I always wondered what it would be like when I got a proposal.'

'And?' Derek verbally prodded her.

'It was rather sweet of you. Being here in Hyde Park on the Serpentine in the sunshine.' Jennifer ran her other hand down his arm lovingly. 'Let's have a long engagement first.'

Derek put both arms around her and kissed her. 'That's fine by me, Jennifer.'

'Suits me!' Jennifer exclaimed trying not to allow her bubbling happiness to overflow.

Derek who was thrilled beyond words at her acceptance, tried to remain calm. 'Now that we're both beside ourselves totally consumed with excitement and having got that out of the way, what shall we do next?'

'How about you row us back now?'

Derek took up the oars and began to row back. His face could hold his true feelings no longer. He broke out into a bubbly smile. 'A six-month engagement! What do you think about that?' Jennifer laughed. 'Well, Jen, I think it's wonderful!'

John and Dorothy Stallybrass had quite a shock that night. They were dumbfounded when Jennifer told them the news.

'Get married? Engaged?' Mr Stallybrass spluttered. His distaste was evident for all.

Dorothy echoed the same sentiments, although she kept her true feelings in check. 'Oh no! It's too soon!'

'It won't do at all,' her father said in annoyance.

Jennifer was amused by her parent's expressions. They looked as if they had just got a bill for all the telephones used by the stock exchange. 'Keep your Woolworth's Y-fronts on Dad!' she said in good humour. 'I'm only getting engaged at this stage. I'm not running away to be secretly married with all the other runaway couples at Bethnal Green.'

This remark brought a huge smile to Dorothy's face. Her sense of humour did not desert her for long. 'You mean Gretna Green!'

'Glad you told me, Mum,' Jennifer said with a laugh in her voice. 'I was going to catch the London Underground there.'

John Stallybrass couldn't see anything funny to laugh about. 'But you've only known him four weeks!'

Jack and Peggy were equally surprised at Derek's announcement. 'Four weeks!'

Peggy could also not hold back her surprise. 'Four weeks! That's all you've known her for!'

Derek too could not conceal humour at his parent's reaction. 'Four weeks, eh? Not long is it? That would be about three weeks longer than when you and Dad decided it was right to get married.'

Jack snapped back quickly. 'That was wartime, Derek! And besides, I was older than you.'

Derek realised this was true. 'Of course you were, Dad. I forgot. You were twenty-three. Wasn't it just before your twenty-third birthday?'

A smile managed to form on Peggy's face but she was quick to reprimand him. 'None of your cheek to your dad.'

'Who's being cheeky? Besides, we're only getting engaged.' He threw in a similar line that Jennifer had used to bring humour to the situation. 'I'm not running off to be secretly married at Willesden Green.'

Jack laughed. 'I think you mean Gretna Green!'

'Well, thank God we've got that sorted out,' smiled Derek. 'That's alright then, isn't it? We're all mates and there's no complaint. Good, isn't it?'

'Is it?' Peggy asked him but he had spoken in a good-natured fashion and meant no harm. 'I suppose it is. We better say congratulations, then!'

Jack looked at his son proudly. 'It's not for us to tell you what to do. We all make our mistakes, and good decisions too in life.'

'Don't worry, Dad,' Derek said slapping his father on the shoulder. 'I've got a good head on my shoulders. We're going to have a six-month engagement – perhaps a bit longer, maybe a little shorter. But I'm not silly. I take my responsibilities very seriously.' He added one more remark as if to reassure his Dad. 'I think I take after you in that respect.'

Six months later Jennifer and Derek were married in a Surrey village church. Jennifer looked stunningly beautiful in her bridal gown. It was not only her dress that added to her appearance; her whole being shone with happiness and radiance. Jennifer's eyes shone with love and the happiness of being a bride. The old saying that a woman never looks more lovelier than on her wedding day held true for Jennifer. She looked ravishing.

John and Dorothy Stallybrass were proud and happy for their daughter. It had to be said that they had some misgivings about the marriage. These were private feelings that they kept to themselves. There was no way in the world that they would spoil their only and much adored daughter's happiness. However, John Stallybrass had disapproved of the match from the beginning. His daughter had gone to commercial college and learned accountancy, a profession he hoped Jennifer would become fully conversant in. He had also hoped that she would marry someone like a bank manager or a solicitor who would keep her in a comfortable lifestyle.

It was probably snobbery on the part of John Stallybrass. He didn't mean it to be. He was only naturally concerned about his daughter's welfare. Wisely, he did not express these feelings publicly but it was Dorothy who eased his concern by telling him the good things about Derek's personality. Derek, Dorothy advised him, was a hard-working young man with common sense, firm ambitions to do well in the future and a sense of commitment. Another point in his favour were his parents, Jack and Peggy, whom they both admired. They were calm and kind. If their son was a man in much the same vein then Jennifer would be in good hands and well looked after.

The wedding reception was a very happy one. John and Dorothy together with Jack and Peggy made sure that this was a happy day for all. When the bridal waltz had taken place and the wedding day guests had got down to the more serious aspect of disco dancing, Jack and Peggy sat at their table, taking stock. The band that had been hired for the occasion produced a soulful version of the Procol Harum hit 'Whiter Shade of Pale'. The irony of the occasion had not been lost on Jack who consumed more champagne than he had ever drunk before in his life. The effect was to make him nostalgic about the years that had passed. He looked on at the youthful dancers in a mixture of happiness and surprise.

'I can't believe it, Peg,' he said suddenly.

'What can't you believe, Jack?' Peggy asked slightly amused to see her normally staid husband obviously tipsy.

'I can't believe that we're here now. It hardly seems five minutes since our own wedding down in the West Country, when the world was at war, and I didn't know if I was going to survive those wartime missions.'

'It's nearly thirty years, Jack.' Peggy glanced quickly at the newlyweds, who were deeply in love with each other and didn't care who knew it either. Across the floor, John and Dorothy Stallybrass laughed as they danced together. 'Everyone looks so happy, Jack.'

This remark didn't register with her husband. He merely made his own comment. 'I always thought Derek was like me in so many ways.'

'What do you mean?'

'Shy with women. Didn't understand them.'

Peggy smiled at her husband's admission. 'It's no sin to be shy, Jack. I think you underestimate yourself. You've always been very thoughtful for me. I know it's almost the traditional thing for the downtrodden British women – or at least the alleged downtrodden housewife – to complain about their husbands. I'm not going to. I think you've always understood me perfectly, Jack.'

'Sometimes,' Jack said with a smile.

'I'm not sure who was the more smitten with the other, Jennifer or Derek. How do you think they'll go in their lives?'

'Who knows, Peggy.'

The music turned to something more upbeat. Jack began to grin with delight at the sight of the wedding guests dancing and enjoying themselves. Peggy noticed the change of expression on her husband's face.

'What are you grinning at you, old rogue?'

'I've never been called an old rogue!' Jack replied in surprise. He was feeling enormously happy. His spirits had been propelled along by the champagne he had drunk. 'I'm smiling at all these folk. Here we are in the year of our Lord 1970 and these people are boogying on down to the tunes of the Rolling Stones and the Beatles, and the Amen Corner.'

'So what's wrong with that? It's the music of this time.'

'I know, Peggy, but in our day it was Vera Lynn and Al Bowlly, the big bands of Roy Fox and Ambrose. We used to jitterbug. We used to do the quickstep. Blimey! Look at these young ones! I'm feeling my age. Imagine us in our day getting on down and boogying to Vera Lynn or doing the Funky Chicken to Ambrose or twisting to Al Bowlly. If I'd done that, a couple of little men in white coats would have taken me away on a stretcher!'

'They will do tonight if you have any more champagne!'

'But I feel so young Peggy. I'm fifty-two but I don't feel old enough to be a father-in-law. That's not my son who got married today. I'm sure it was only yesterday I got married. This is all a dream.'

Peggy found Jack entertaining in his tipsy state. 'You'd better have more champagne!'

Jack touched her hand suddenly. 'I know I'm a little tipsy. I'm not used to this blessed champagne. When we first met, Peggy, was I a dashing young man? Was I the most exciting young man you have ever met? Did I drive you wild with desire?'

'Wild with desire?' Peggy exclaimed. 'My, you have had a few glasses too much.'

'I didn't, then. I wasn't the most exciting man you had ever met.'

'No, certainly not!' Peggy was laughing inside. Then she reassured him softly. 'You were the nicest young man I had ever met. Maybe you weren't Errol Flynn or David Niven or Johnny Weissmuller or…'

'I wasn't Johnny Weissmuller, that's for sure!'

Peggy kissed him and gripped his hands. For a few moment they felt as if this had been their wedding day party and they had sat there as the honoured guests. On the floor the band played a rock 'n' roll number from way back in the 1950s. Much to their surprise, John and Dorothy Stallybrass joined the dancers. John and Dorothy twirled with the best of them. They looked at Jack and Peggy, and Dorothy beckoned for them to join in. Peggy was highly amused, and thought it was time to get back onto the dance floor.

'So, Jack Moran,' Peggy said as if she was about to make an announcement, 'You reckon you're fit and still feel young?'

'I feel twenty-one, Miss Peggy,' Jack replied proudly.

Peggy stood up and held her hand out. 'On your feet, Moran!' Her eyes sparkled with fun. Jack stood up as if he had just been given a royal command. 'Come on then, let's get on down and boogey to a little bit of old-fashioned rock 'n' roll!'

'Yeah baby!' Jack retorted in a high-spirited manner. 'They ain't seen nothing yet!'

Jack and Peggy walked onto the dance floor. Jack removed his tie and jacket and threw them to one side. In the middle of the floor they began to dance like old fashioned rock 'n' rollers of another age. Jennifer gaped in amazement. She turned to her new husband who was watching in fascination.

'I thought your Mum and Dad were nice, quiet, shy people,' she said surprised by the expertise her new parents-in-law were demonstrating on the dance floor.

Derek could only smile in wonder. 'I've just got married and I'm still learning things about my parents.'

'I like them, Derek,' Jennifer said in a tone of genuine admiration. 'Your mum and dad are alright.'

★★★

All too soon it seemed, Jack and Peggy became grandparents. In 1972 Natasha was born and the following year Pearl came along. Jennifer and Derek were as blissfully happy as it was possible to be. They lived in Plymouth and for them life seemed happy and settled. Twenty years later they were to separate.

Jack and Peggy carried on with their separate careers, although at home their love and devotion blossomed. Jack's career as a management consultant took him to Europe and North America. On these trips Peggy came along. They were happy times. Since their ill-fated migration to the Antipodes just after the war, neither had travelled overseas. Always they made the most of the opportunities they had both eagerly sought and which life now seemed to hand out to them. By the time Jack retired at the age of 65 in 1983, his career had come full circle. He had worked his way up from the workshop to a management position; his experiences and achievements had made it all worthwhile.

But then tragedy struck his life for the second time in 1992 when Peggy became ill with cancer. Within a few short months Peggy died – as she had always lived: with grace, dignity, uncomplainingly and maintaining a great inner strength.

The night she died Peggy gripped Jack's hand, smiled at him lovingly for the last time and said softly, 'You've been so good to me. I'm going to see our daughter now.' Peggy just seemed to drift away.

Jack stood there in deep grief, realising that the women he had shared so much with had gone. Was is really 50 years ago he had first seen her as a pretty young WRAF riding a bicycle in a country lane in Devon?

★★★

The morning after Peggy's funeral Jack and Derek returned to lay flowers on her grave. There were tears in Jack's eyes. Derek was torn apart inside. Peggy had been no ordinary woman. In her life she had never sought the material things; that had been Jack's duty as a husband, father and provider. Peggy had always seen her role in life as the central figure of the family. To Derek, his mother had been the kind, sometimes distant but demure figure who had always been there for him. He had adored her. The thought that he would not hear that gentle voice again hurt him; the voice that had so often expressed its love, a note of concern for his well-being, even though he had long been a married man; the voice that always responded in with a constant motherly love, interest in his life and a keenness for his welfare. With his own marriage now over, for Derek that voice had represented a consoling tone at his heartbreak, and she had also urged him to boost his spirits, get back up and go on and achieve things.

Moments later, Derek realised his cheeks were wet with tears. He dried his eyes and turned to his father. 'Look at all these flowers,' he said. 'I didn't know you and Mum knew so many people.'

'Surprising how many people you meet in a lifetime, son,' Jack replied. He looked at all the flowers and messages. 'There are wreaths from Paul and Judi, their own children, all of them married with their own families now. Dorothy and John Stallybrass sent flowers, and a beautiful letter. It was so warm and sympathetic. They must have liked Peggy an awful lot. So many people have been kind: Jeff Blue and his family, old friends from Peggy's office, even a few of her old school friends from her childhood in Sutton have sent their condolences.'

'Jennifer and the children too,' Derek reminded his father.

'Everyone remembered. That's the main thing.'

The thought that perhaps Jack wanted to be alone by the grave occurred to Derek. He looked at his father. How would he carry on?

'Do you want to spend a few minutes on your own here Dad?' He asked gently and considerately.

'I wouldn't mind, Derek.'

'I'll wait in the car, Dad.' Derek walked away leaving Jack on his own with his thoughts and memories.

Up above the sun broke through the clouds and the sky became a more vivid blue. Jack stood by the tombstone in sadness. He tried desperately to reach into his soul to find some farewell words for Peggy. Tomorrow he would be on his own in a world which would be that much more lonelier for him. But that was tomorrow. Today he wanted to speak from his heart out to the sky and the sun in the hope that somewhere in a heaven beyond human reasoning Peggy would hear his words. When it was clear that he was totally alone Jack began to speak to the grave. His voice quivered with emotion as the words fell from his lips.

'Although you've left this world, Peggy, I still feel a closeness to you as if you are here beside me. I shall never forget the first time I saw you, that happy young WRAF on a bicycle in a Devon country lane. You won't think it morbid if I talk to you now as if you can hear me from a distant world away. We had fifty full years together in which we tasted every facet of life together, triumph and tragedy, fear and fun, love and laughter, tears and moments of anguish − but we did it, Peg! Oh my, we cleared every hurdle and beat off every hurt that was inflicted upon us, and we stood so well together! I want to thank you from the bottom of my heart for standing by me, giving me the support when I most needed it and for providing dependability for all my married days. If there's one thing in life everyone needs then that is friendship. You gave me that, and loyalty and love, and a fine son who has weathered his own storms with courage.

'Peggy, I don't know how I am going to get through the rest of my days without you but somehow I will. Somehow I'll come to terms with it. Somehow I'll go on. But I do have one consolation and that is you are now with our little daughter Vivien who never lived long enough to become the fine and good woman you were and always will be in my heart.'

Jack paused for a moment and then blew a farewell kiss at the tombstone. 'God bless you, Peggy. Now that the burdens of mortality have been lifted may you enjoy the eternal peace and tranquillity that exists in another place of which we here on this earth know nothing.'

Jack stepped back from the grave. He was feeling emotionally distraught. However, he was still very much in control of his senses. He gazed up at the sky as the sound of an aircraft winging its way towards an exotic destination broke the silence.

★★★

His memory was stirred. He recalled the occasion when, as an RAF rear gunner in 1941, his plane was about to crash-land on the airfield. From below, the drivers on the airfield and the ground staff could see the smoke streaming from the aircraft's tail.

Inside the aircraft Bluey Flanagan, another airman, the pilot and Jack battled hard to keep their wits about them. The aircraft was right on course to land. It was going to be a terrible landing. Each member of the aircrew was petrified at what was going to happen next. They had seen the results of previous crash landings. Yet even in these desperate moments their humour managed to surface.

'Hang in there, cobber,' Bluey called out to his mate Jack, who was literally pressing his hand imprint into the sides of the aircraft.

'I wasn't going anywhere special, anyway,' Jack replied.

In fact, as he returned from that frightening mission over Europe, he did have an important appointment. Aware that his life expectancy during these harrowing war years had been drastically reduced, he had made it his objective to ask the young WRAF called Peggy Mills to marry him.

The pilot called out to the airmen, 'Brace yourselves, lads! Hang on for dear life as we go down, and then every man for himself as we land!'

Down on the aerodrome Peggy sat in her vehicle waiting for the aircraft to land. Suddenly she heard the sound of the spluttering engines of the plane. Peggy wound the window down and looked through. Her facial expression was one of horror. Even from this distance the painted kangaroo on the aircraft that signified Bluey was aboard became easily identifiable. Peggy knew at once Jack would be in the rear gunner's seat.

'Oh my God!' she gasped. 'It's Jack and Bluey.'

Immediately Peggy started the lorry and began to drive. The aerodrome was a flurry of activity. Other vehicles and a fire engine began to move across at great haste. Peggy continued to drive for a few minutes. Then with a jolting suddenness the sound of an aircraft exploding hit the air. Her vehicle came to a halt as Peggy applied the brakes. She began to shake all over. The unspeakable had happened.

In horror Peggy could not look on. Straight away she put her head down on the wheel resting it and closing her eyes. She was in a state of shock. The tears would come later. For now an iciness spread throughout the body. She felt cold and clammy. All she could do was sit in the driver's seat not daring to look. Then after a while Peggy heard someone tapping on the lorry window. At first she did not look up. She did not want to. She plainly ignored it until the tapping got louder. Then slowly, very slowly, Peggy raised her head. Her eyes could not believe what she was seeing. Outside were Bluey, the airman, the pilot and, last but more certainly not least in the order of priorities in her life, the man she loved, Jack Moran.

'Open up, love,' Bluey called out with a broad grin spread out over his face like a beam of sunshine. 'It's so cold I've got ice on my kneecaps and places I wouldn't mention in front of a lady!'

Peggy broke out into contagious happiness. She leapt out of the lorry and hugged each one of them.

'Oh boys! I thought we'd lost you,' she gasped.

'It was touch and go,' said the airman whose name she did not know.

The pilot explained what had happened. 'The moment we touched the ground we leapt out and ran for it!'

'I haven't run so fast as that since my school sports day,' said the airman.

Peggy turned to Jack and gripped his hand warmly. Cautiously she gave him a quick, loving look that spoke volumes in an instant. She knew the boys had just been through a very rough night and she was careful of their feelings. Too much attention to one man might be misconstrued the wrong way, even if that person was her special man. It was an open secret anyway.

'Get in lads,' she said. 'How does a hot cup of tea sound?'

Bluey licked his lips. 'I don't care how it sounds, love. As long as it tastes beaut, who cares?'

'Like tea to a thirsty swaggie on an outback bush track, eh Bluey?' Jack said, slapping his mate on the back.

'Too right,' retorted Bluey. 'And by golly we need it.'

The men jumped up into the back of the lorry. Peggy started the vehicle and cast a sideways glance at the smoke of the burning plane on the aerodrome. Fireman and ground staff worked hard at extinguishing the flames. From the back of the lorry the men looked at the sight.

'Very close call, boys,' the pilot said with a grimace. 'Still, we got away. That's the main thing.' He thumped his fist on the inside of the lorry. 'Take her away, gal! Hold very tightly!'

'Hot tea and bacon and eggs coming up, boys!' Peggy called out from the driver's seat. She started up the engine and began to drive to the NAAFI.

'I can hear those tasty rashers sizzling,' Bluey said almost in ecstasy.

'That's my teeth chattering from the cold!' remarked the pilot.

'Nice girl, that driver,' Bluey whispered to Jack. 'When are you going to ask her to marry you?'

Jack just smiled and sat quietly for a moment. He was thinking very seriously, though. They had just been on a frightening mission which had almost ended in disaster for all of them. Life was so short. Time was a dividend in wartime. Everyday counted for something. He loved Peggy. He felt warm and comfortable in her company. The two of them could make a good life together. It was now or never.

'Peggy, can you hear me in there?' he called out suddenly.

'As clear as a loudspeaker,' Peggy yelled back.

'There was something I wanted to ask you,' Jack said in a voice that clearly echoed the excitement he felt.

The others in the lorry looked up in interest. They were aware that Jack was about to ask something of an important nature.

'Go ahead, Jack,' Peggy shouted.

Jack came back with the most important question he had ever asked anyone. 'Will you marry me, Peggy?'

This was followed by a long, stunned silence. The others smiled in amazement at their friend's audacity. It was breath-taking, waiting for the reply. Jack began to think that he had made a big mistake and he had chosen the wrong time. It was going to be a huge embarrassment to everyone. Just then the lorry pulled up to a sudden halt.

'You've done it now, mate!' Bluey said nudging Jack in the ribs.

'I've blown it,' Jack whispered.

Peggy stepped out of the lorry. Jack heard the door close. Reluctantly he also got out of the vehicle, preparing himself to apologise. He had no sooner stepped on to the ground then he found himself facing a smiling Peggy. Jack suddenly felt his heart miss a beat.

'Ask me again, Jack,' Peggy asked softly.

Jack was amazed to think that this fine young lady might actually answer with the one word he wanted to hear.

'Will you… will you marry me, Peggy?'

Another breaktaking silence followed. The men in the lorry watched eagerly. Bluey was unconsciously miming the answer to Peggy. Words did not answer the proposal. Peggy put her arms around him and kissed him luxuriously. From within the lorry came a burst of applause and good-natured congratulations.

'You little beauties!' cried Bluey. 'Good on ya Jack!'

'Congratulations, you two,' said the pilot.

The airman turned to the other two and beamed a warm smile. 'I don't know. Some people have all the luck.'

★★★

Jack Moran smiled at the memory of that very happy day. He stared down at the grave. There was just one final message he wanted to relay to Peggy, wherever in heaven she may be watching him from.

'Thanks for saying yes. No man on earth was more grateful than me, Peggy.'

Jack turned around and walked to his son's car. Tomorrow, life would go on. His memories would sustain him. He had been such a lucky man to have loved and cherished Peggy.

3.

Margaret and John

The Spinster and the Bachelor

Margaret Gategood lived alone in a pleasant suburban semi-detached house in Wembley. Alone, that is, except for a grey, black and brown cat with shining green eyes. Margaret and Mitzi the cat lived quietly and happily together.

At 39 years of age she was attractive, self-assured, confident and had a certain panache about her. Somewhere in her family background was some Welsh ancestry. Her hair was black, and so too were her eyes that could move mountains; they could change from humour to fury in an instant. Her life was a lonely one, however.

Margaret had a good career as a personnel officer for a large department store. She had her own home, a good salary, an independent lifestyle and many nice clothes in her wardrobe. But there was a yearning within her to be loved and, once again, to be part of a family. Since the death of her parents Margaret had possessed the feeling of being totally alone without a soulmate.

Each night as she drew the curtains in her comfortable bedroom there were other things she desired more than sleep. The space beside her in the double bed was a vacancy for love, warmth and someone else's tenderness. Margaret also had maternal instincts that desperately needed to be satisfied. Often she would see couples with their children and a feeling of envy would sweep over her. With all of her career achievements and material benefits, that sort of happiness had always evaded her.

Hardly had it seemed she had just closed her eyes than the alarm clock by her bedside was ringing furiously at her indicating that it was 6.30 on a cold, grey Monday morning and it was time to go to work. How nice it would be to have someone to live for. Enough of these morbid thoughts.

She reluctantly pushed the duvet off her bed and rose to take a shower.

Casting aside her nightdress she walked naked into the shower. With hot water and rich foaming gel pouring over her sleek figure she would be ready to face another working day. That luxurious feeling of being freshly showered and shampooed made her feel confident. Life for her had to be tackled head on. She approached all things with the skill of the schoolgirl netball player she had once been in a distant life. Goals had to be scored. Purpose had to lead to achievement. Her whole life had to be going somewhere.

These were the thoughts that had been with her when she had left school at 15 to work as a check-out girl with Woolworths in Ealing. Her late father had been a bus driver on the big red double deckers that rolled past her childhood home in Acton Town. Margaret's mother had been a clippie on the route between Acton and Hangar Lane in the smog-filled London of the 1950s. They had duly married and Margaret was their only child. It had been a happy enough childhood, spent in a council house in Acton, but her parents had urged her to study and progress in life. Margaret had followed this advice. She had enrolled at technical college, studied hard for diplomas in personnel management and business administration.

From Woolworths she had moved to Marks & Spencer, and then to a new up-and-coming chain store called Debenworths. Her new qualifications enabled her to make the move from sales to administration and now, at 39, her annual salary of £30,000 a year more than compensated for her years of hard work.

Margaret put on a nice two-piece outfit for work. It smoothed down over her figure just nicely. She brushed her hair meticulously, applied some hairspray and stood up to examine herself in the mirror. As a matter of daily procedure, she checked her appearance once again. Assuring herself that she was in good shape Margaret picked up her briefcase and made her way downstairs.

On cue at exactly 7.30 the cat flap shot open with all the force of a double-barrelled shotgun, and into the house leapt her pet cat Mitzi. She meowed her greeting. Margaret could never really interpret what this sad cry meant. Mitzi was her baby, though, and she loved her as if she were one.

'Hullo little Mitzi,' Margaret said with a smile. 'I wondered where you were. Are you hungry?' The cat responded in the way she always did: she meowed again and rubbed herself against Margaret's legs. 'Come on. I'll give you some breakfast.'

The cat led Margaret intelligently into the kitchen, knowing what her mistress would do next. Margaret took a tin of cat food, mixed it with some cat biscuits, and added a couple of pieces of hard cheese for variation, which for some reason Mitzi always enjoyed. She placed a saucer of milk down by the food. Looking at her pet cat tucking into the food after walking up and down the kitchen floor Margaret determined that there must be an element of the tiger in her.

'There you are, my baby.' She stood back, lovingly looking at it. 'You really are like a little baby needing love aren't you, Mitzi? I'd better put flea powder on you tonight and give you a brush.' The cat continued to ignore her. Margaret added, 'Pity you aren't six foot three, tanned and male with a tender nature. But I love you just the same.' She stroked the cat softly. Then she picked up her case and made her way to work.

Margaret drove, of course. One of the material benefits of her life was a Mitsubishi car, although if pressed on the point Margaret would not honestly have known whether she had the car out of need or just to exhibit her status. There were some people who, with careful analysis, would have considered her one of the children of the Thatcher era. She did not consider it like that. For Margaret, all that she owned had come through years – 24 years, in fact – of continuous employment and hard study, together with the acumen for recognising opportunities when they arose.

In her role as personnel officer with Debenworths she was often called upon to address other members of staff in training sessions. Today she had to speak to some members of the sales area, instructing them as to the possible career routes they could take. In the the training room Margaret fluently, using her own knowledge and experience. Occasionally she would refer to some flip charts mounted on an easel. The charts tended to show the staff departmental structure.

'As you can see from the diagram behind me,' Margaret indicated, speaking without notes but with great authority, 'the running of the store involves a number of different sections. We have personnel, accounts, finance, recruitment, purchasing, stores. And then we have you, the staff serving in the various sales departments. There is plenty of scope for you all to advance within the store to these managerial positions. In a competitive market, department stores have to produce the goods for the customer, and that covers everything from confectionery to clothing, beauty cosmetics to baby needs, car tools to car and house insurance.' She smiled at the astonished expression of one of the staff. 'Oh yes, we even handle insurance through Debenworths. In all of our high street stores we have brokers with their own office ready to advise clients on the sort of premiums they may need. Everyone contributes to a good performance within the organisation. We rely on good manners towards the customer, a need for high retail sales and efficiency throughout. But most important of all, what we need is enthusiasm, a belief among the staff that what they are selling is good quality, that the store they work for is the best in the land. Any questions, anyone?'

A young lady put up her hand. Margaret nodded towards her. 'How does Debenworths compare with other international retail stores?'

Margaret's knowledge of department stores was second to none. 'On the international scale? Well, every country in the world has its own brand name stores if that's what you mean. Woolworths stores are to be found throughout the world. In New York, Macy's is perhaps the most famous. In London of course Harrods has an international reputation. Were you to travel to Australia you would find stores such as Coles-Myer and David Jones across the land. Here in Britain Debenworths is a separate entity. We're a more self-contained store, which means that in a sense we have more variety within a smaller capacity than some of the larger ones. Does that answer your question?'

'Yes,' the young lady replied.

In fact it had more than answered the question. It had served to demonstrate just how knowledgeable Margaret was in her line of work. On the surface she appeared to be a confident, independent authorative woman who needed no one. The truth of the matter was very much the reverse.

★★★

'Well, that's another training course completed,' Margaret said to her supervisor and friend Mary Byrne, who sat across the room from Margaret, working hard at her desk.

'That's good,' Mary replied with a pleasant smile. 'Do you spend all your spare time preparing these courses?'

'Oh yes,' Margaret said in a casual reply. 'All part of a career girl's life. I'm preparing a good one on staff safety and also one on customer service.'

Mary glanced at her watch. It was just after midday. 'Do you feel like taking a breather from the office and having lunch somewhere nice?'

'What a good idea!' Margaret exclaimed. 'I didn't have any breakfast this morning and my tummy is as empty as the Channel Tunnel.'

Mary immediately rose from her chair. She shuffled some papers together and picked up her handbag. 'There's that nice Italian restaurant round the corner. Let's give that a try.'

The two very smart women touched their faces up with make-up and left the office for a long lunch.

Mary Byrne was a dark-haired, cat-eyed, vivacious woman in her late forties or early fifties. She did not disclose her age and the other girls in the office could only hazard a guess as to how old she was. There was a lot more to Mary than the image she presented at first glance. With thick-rimmed spectacles, her hair invariably tied in a bun, and conformist office clothes, one would have assumed her to be a quiet spinster. Certainly she did nothing at work to discourage this notion.

In fact, Irish-born Mary from Dublin, who had been raised in Tiger Bay in the Welsh city of Cardiff, was something of an enigma. She had travelled as a motorbike pillion passenger on the hippy trail to Kathmandu and had ventured even further to Saigon during the 1960s. Twice she had married. Twice she had given birth. Her two sons, one from each marriage, were now 28 and 22 respectively. Both marriages had ended in divorce and Mary was now living with her lover, who was a man some 17 years younger than her. Outside the office Mary took off her spectacles, let her long, well-conditioned hair fall down her back, and her clothes revealed the slim, lithe figure that she kept trim by rigorous exercise. At times she followed a strict vegetarian diet but would occasionally dine out Italian style.

There was much more to Mary. She was on hormone replacement therapy. She lived for love. Not just the act of love, but the giving of it in various forms. If she saw a cat she would stop to stroke it. From the Eastern religions she had learned about as a traveller in India, Mary had a strong belief in karma. If you gave love and did good things, then these would be returned to you in due course. If you did bad things, then punishment or retribution would find its way back. Her idea of a quiet night at home was to indulge in a long relaxing bubble bath with her lover, followed by a session of soothing massages to each other and to top this with a couple of hours of the *Kama Sutra*.

For Mary, who had led such a passionate stimulating private life, the idea of existence without love was an appalling concept. It puzzled her why her younger friend Margaret seemed to lead an almost loveless life. After all, she had the lot. So why was she still alone at almost 40 years of age?

Margaret and Mary dined quietly together in a corner of the restaurant. Mary topped up their glasses with the last of a carafe of wine. An eagle-eyed waiter immediately replaced the empty one with a full one. After talking about matters at the office, Mary steered the subject to the one she was most interested in.

'What do you do in your own time?' Mary asked coyly. Now that the wine had flown easily for the past half-hour, perhaps the candid talk would flow too. 'Have you got any hobbies? In the time I've known you, you always seem to be on your own.'

Margaret seemed glad to be able to speak of her own private loneliness. 'The story of my life, I think,' she admitted. 'I've got my house, a cat called Mitzi, my work. But I haven't got a man. In a week's time I'll be forty. Forty! At times I don't feel any different to when I was sixteen. I still hope maybe I'll meet someone, get married and have a child. Time's running out on that score.' She sipped from her wine glass. 'Where do I go to meet someone?'

Mary wasn't sure, but it sounded as if there was a hint of desperation in her voice.

'I've been looking for a good man for years. I just never seem to have found Mr Right for me.'

'I don't profess to be an expert on the workings of the male mind,' Mary began, seriously underestimating her own experiences, 'but I have to admit I am surprised that a man has never made himself a permanent fixture in your life. After all, you've got the lot: looks, personality, style. So where did you miss out?'

Margaret herself wasn't sure about this. 'Probably I found it too hard to make a permanent commitment.' This was half true. 'I allowed my work to take precedence. I left school at fifteen, began as a check-out girl, worked in different stores, and decided I wanted to get on so I went to night school, studied for my diploma in personnel management. I just can't believe I've got to this age and I've never met the love of my life. Apart from two brief affairs it's just been a list of acquaintances and flirtations.'

'I sympathise, really.' The effect of a girls-only lunch with two carafes of wine was beginning to tell on Mary. 'There is a downside though. I've had two marriages. Both of them were terribly unhappy and they're very bad memories that I try desperately to slot into the back of my mind. The man I live with is lovely, but I'm not sure we will ever marry. He's had one unhappy marriage too. At least you've got where you are and you're not one of the emotionally walking wounded.'

'Do you know anyone you could introduce me to?'

'Not really,' Mary replied. Then she added quickly, 'Why don't you join a dating agency?'

'A dating agency?' Margaret had never even considered the possibility.

'Yes! Why not? There's no shame in joining a dating agency. It's not an admission of failure.'

'I've always thought of dating agencies being for the absolutely desperate.'

'No!' Mary was surprised at her response. For such an intelligent woman Margaret could make surprisingly naïve comments. 'You would probably find many nice people signing up with a dating organisation. When you think about it, how does boy meet girl? In a pub or a cocktail bar? What happens if you don't like to drink? That rules this option out. On a discotheque floor? In your late thirties and forties the clientele is so young, you could be mistaken for one of the bar staff! Where else could you meet someone? At the office perhaps? Certainly not ours! We've got an absence of good-looking, available men of a certain age group. If there were any going spare I might seriously be tempted.'

Margaret pondered over this. 'Well, it's something I've never seriously considered before. I suppose I could give it a try. It might make life more interesting.'

Once the idea had been placed in her head, the more she thought about it, the more it seemed worth making the effort.

★★★

Margaret loved the privacy of her home. It was a place where she could be at peace with herself. Away from the cacophony of the office and the department store she liked to relax by listening to music or the radio. Occasionally she would rent a video and lie in bed watching it.

When she came home that day she threw her case onto the armchair, kicked off her shoes and looked for her cat. Sure enough, Mitzi was fast asleep in a basket. She smiled at the sight of her, curled up like a little baby. 'I expect you'll want feeding soon.'

117

Margaret walked into the kitchen, filled the kettle and prepared herself a pot of tea. After that big lunch at the Italian restaurant it was going to be scones, cream and jam for tea. Coming back into the lounge she knelt down and stroked the cat. 'No wonder so many lonely women have pet cats,' she murmured to herself. 'They're the nearest thing to a baby for us.'

The thought of having a real baby enthralled her. Margaret did not gush over the thought of children, but she did so much want to have one of her own. A loving man and a child would surely crown her life.

It was strange, but she had never planned the route that her life had taken. The entire result had been unpredicted. At school, Margaret was disinterested and left at 15, at the earliest opportunity. Her mother and father had never had any great ambitions in life for themselves. They were content with their lot, content to work on London Transport's buses, to live in a council flat, and to take their holidays locally, never going further than Bournemouth or Bognor Regis. Even their nights out were simple affairs, when they would go to the bingo halls or the greyhound racing at White City.

Margaret had never really felt compelled to hold great ambitions. This had not gone unnoticed by her parents, who desperately wanted their only daughter to achieve things in life other than just leaving school, getting married and having children. This advice she had followed. Margaret's diplomas hung around the room. She wondered hard at times what the sum total of her life had added up to: a successful career in a job and environment she felt happy to be in; a good home and a pleasant, independent life. What else could she want? It always came back to the yearning for a family life.

When she had been a child in Acton her life had been very happy. With parents who were content to make do, never strive for or expect more, there was an absence of stress or tension in the house. Her father said that being a bus driver in busy traffic could be stressful enough, but he never showed signs of anxiety. Both parents died in their fifties, however, and without any aunts, uncles or cousins, Margaret found herself suddenly very alone in the world. From then on she developed a fierce independent streak that had never waned. At least, not until now, as the quicksands of her forties loomed up.

She went to bed early that night but didn't go to sleep too early. From the pleasant contours of her bed she watched an old movie. She was all alone in the darkened room except for the flickering images of William Holden and Jennifer Jones on the screen before her. The film was *Love is a Many Splendored Thing*. The setting was Hong Kong. The story was a moving romance between an American reporter and a Eurasian doctor. But it was not a film with a happy ending, for their love was only to be a brief affair before fate intervened.

Fate. Destiny. These were the masters of our lives. At least that was what Margaret thought. But she really believed in circumventing fate. The film came to an end. The words 'love is a many-splendored thing' kept ringing through her mind. In the final scene as William Holden's voice spoke of 'that many splendored thing', Margaret's eyes clouded with emotion. The theme-tune of the film roared out from the set. Using the remote control she switched the set off, turned off the bedside lamp and plunged into the night-time hours of sleep.

It took a lot of courage for Margaret to enter the Centrepoint Dating Agency, but she took the first step. An hour later she returned to the office. Mary was working hard at her desk. Margaret studiously attended to her own tasks but her mind was elsewhere. What had she done now? What sort of men would she meet? Perhaps she would get lucky. On the other hand, maybe it would confirm for her that she might not be cut out for marriage. Whatever the result, it would be a new experience.

'Guess what, Margaret?' The words from Mary cut into her intense thoughts from the other side of the room.

'Tell me,' Margaret said casually.

Mary adjusted her spectacles, the look in her eyes just briefly suggesting the highly sexual woman she was away from the world of commerce. 'My account figures show retail sales up everywhere in the store except footwear and the pharmacy. Amazing, isn't it? You would think people would always buy shoes. And medicine too. I wonder what the manager will make of my figures.'

Margaret could no longer constrain herself. She simply had to tell Mary what she had done. 'I went to a dating agency today, would you believe.'

Mary smiled with delight. 'Good for you! How did you get on?'

'I had to fill out a form, obviously. But there was a lot to put on it. I had to enter my interests, my status… I felt a bit strange writing "spinster", describing the sort of person I am. You know the sort of thing they ask: are you outgoing, affectionate, shy, reserved? It even asked me how I viewed myself. I didn't want to sound conceited and vain, so I wrote down that I was shy, which I am sometimes with people I don't know. I also wrote down that I was attractive and hard-working.'

'At least you didn't sell yourself short,' Mary remarked.

'Actually, I may have done,' Margaret added. 'While I was filling out the form it suddenly dawned on me that here I am, nudging forty. I'm a bachelor girl with her own house, a good position as a training officer in the personnel department of a top London store. I've got money in the bank.'

Mary at once knew what her friend was driving at. 'In other words, you're a class bird with a great pair of legs, a good figure, and an even better figure in the bank which might attract a few gold-diggers full of smooth talk and empty in their wallets.'

'Exactly. So on the information form, rather than boost myself up I didn't put down on the form that I was a training officer on £30,000 a year.' Mary looked on curiously. 'I said that I worked in a shop and that I love animals and nature, and enjoy watching football.' Mary smiled at this remark. 'If I'm going to meet a caring, considerate man I want him to fall in love with me. Not my material possessions.'

'That's fair enough,' agreed Mary. 'It will be curious to see the kind of man you're matched with. I shall be most interested. Rely on me for expert advice!'

★★★

John Hicks was destined to be the man in Margaret Gategood's life. He was just a little less than 6 feet tall, with brown hair, and by his own description he was not the slightest bit handsome. He was fairly ordinary in appearance. There was nothing about him that suggested he would make a good match with Margaret, except that he was the possessor of a sudden bright smile that could endear him to most people. He was, however, a most genuine and trustworthy man.

In the front window of his butcher's shop in Brentford, John was laying out meat for display. He and his amiable, slightly rotund but very jolly partner Charlie Tomlinson had worked hard to make this a thriving little business. Apart from the racks of lamb, beef and other joints of meat, they sold their speciality: their own brand of sausages, which they put together in all flavours. These included lamb and mint, tomato and sage, Mexican, beef with a mixture of mashed potato and Bovril, and vegetarian sausages made with a recipe of mushrooms, tomato and any other ingredients they thought might add to the flavour. There were other varieties comprising of mixtures using chicken, kidney, liver, mince, steak, stuffing, best end and pork, in all sorts of concoctions using herbs and sauces.

Needless to say their little shop won awards for its sausages and they did good business. John had put up most of the capital for their venture. He kept a tight rein on the accounts and ran the shop with all the control of an entrepreneur. If he had been working for Virgin Airways or ICI he would have managed as well as the top brass. The only difference between him and Richard Branson was that John had chosen the life of a butcher.

Often when things were quiet in the butcher's shop John and Charlie would ham it up, singing at the top of their voices. In and around the area they were nicknamed the Singing Butchers from Brentford. Different customers had different nicknames for them. These included the Crooning Cleavers, the Flash Choppers, the Butchershop Baritones, the Swooning Singing Sausagemakers, and one customer had even dubbed them the Mincemeat Tabernacle Choir.

They loved to sing old standards. 'Love is a Many Splendored Thing', 'Yesterday', 'Blue Moon', 'Blueberry Hill', 'It's Impossible'. Yet in between creating spicy sausages and cutting up joints of beef they could serve up a mean song. If Phil Collins or Frank Sinatra had ever dropped into John and Charlie's butcher shop in Brentford for a couple of spare ribs or chicken breasts, they would have been impressed by the entertainment.

'What are you doing this weekend then, Charlie?' John called out to his friend, who was slicing meat at the counter.

Charlie was hardly ever serious. 'I shall probably chase my missus around the bedroom, and then I'll let her catch me! Seriously, though, I'm taking my boy to see the future FA Cup winners of the twenty-first century, Brentford.'

'Lucky you, eh. Don't laugh, Charlie, but I've just joined a dating agency.'

'A dating agency!' Charlie was mystified. 'Cor blimey. Whatever for?' He in his ignorance could not understand why anyone would want to use one. 'Can't you find a bird down the pub? Get down the disco, son, and let it all hang out!'

John smiled at his friend's no-holds-barred approach to life. 'At forty-one years of age, Chas, going down the disco and chatting up the girls over a pint of bitter is a thing of the past.'

'I would if I was still single,' said Charlie.

'Would you? I wonder.' John came behind the counter to chat to him. 'Sometimes I wish this was England in the 1950s.'

'So do a lot of people, son, but time doesn't stand still.'

'I know that, but in those days most couples seemed to meet on the dance floor at the local Palais or the Trocadero. Not now though. Believe it or not, Charlie, it's very hard to meet anyone.'

'I suppose it is, really,' Charlie conceded. 'I've been out of the single man's world for so long I've forgotten what it was like. Come to think of it, I was very lucky. My wife was a new kid on the block. I saw her at the bus stop one morning and she asked me what time the next bus was due, and I sat next to her. By the time I got off the bus we had arranged to go out, and six months later we were married.'

John beamed a broad smile at him. 'I bet that was the only time you said "Thank God for London Transport!"'

The two of them were the best of friends even though they worked together six days a week. Normally on a Friday or a Saturday they would stop off at one of the pubs in Ealing Broadway for a couple of pints. Tonight was no exception.

Charlie sipped back a mouthful of his favourite Tartan bitter. 'There, that's better. A lovely drop if I may say so.' He winked at his friend good-naturedly, and changed the subject. 'So tell me, John, this dating agency, what's it all about really? Are you getting a bit lonely? Is it the hankering for a family?'

John took a long swill of his beer and paused before answering. 'I think the truth is — speaking man to man of course — is that I probably am a bit. Lonely, that is. Oh, I'm not singing the blues.'

Charlie cut in quickly. 'No, that was Tommy Steele, or was it Guy Mitchell, or was it both of them?'

'Don't speak when I'm interrupting,' John said jokingly. 'Well, put it this way, Charlie. I woke up one morning and suddenly felt the years slipping away. I'm not being morbid, just being realistic. You've got this life and you've got to find someone to love. I've got my work, my house, a cat and a dog. But I've never had a happy family life.'

'I understand, mate.' Charlie was serious for a change. 'It's easy to take it for granted.'

For the moment John had the floor to himself. Charlie could be a good listener when he wasn't acting the role of the court jester.

'When I left school at fifteen I spent seven years at sea. I had a very unhappy home life with a pair of very short-tempered parents, and an elder sister who treated me like dirt as a boy. Anyway I don't want to dwell on that part of my life. I joined the Merchant Navy and sailed all around the world with the Cunard and P&O Lines. By the time I came home my elder sister had got pregnant, married, swanned off overseas. My Dad had died of the big C, and Mum needed a lot of looking after following a couple of heart attacks. I had to look after her for many years until she died five years ago. I suppose I've been in a quandary for a long time, really. Running the shop six days a week hasn't left me with too much time. You may think this sounds silly, but I need someone. I need to give of myself, I need — and when I use the word "need", I really mean, I want someone to love. Someone who'll be there for me. Someone I can look after. I bet you're laughing at me inside aren't you, Charlie? You probably think old Johnno's flipped his lid.'

Charlie looked at him, concerned. John quaffed a mouthful of beer. 'After all the years we've worked together, if you think that then you don't know me at all. Besides, you've only had a pint of Tex! You're as sober as an Old Bailey judge.'

John responded with a smile. 'Alright Charlie, I can take the hint. It's my round, isn't it?'

As John returned to the warmth of his home in Northolt a few nights later, he saw that he had a lot of mail that day. Brown envelopes mainly. It was a fairly ordinary home, just a normal suburban terrace, but it was the home he had inherited on his parents' death. The cat and dog sat close by on a rug. The pets adored their master and he loved them both.

He looked quickly at the telephone bill. Damned thing! The rental cost of his handset cost more than the actual calls he made. He put it to one side. Amazing how the gas and electricity bills always seemed to arrive at exactly the same time. But there was one letter he read with more than passing interest: it was from the Centrepoint Dating Agency. He read it, realising with a slight nervousness that his name had been matched with a possible partner.

It said:

Dear John,

The Centrepoint Dating Agency computer has matched you with a lady of similar interests to yourself. Her name is Margaret; a 39-year-old shop worker. Margaret lists as her interests: animals, nature and loves to watch football. If you would like to meet her, please contact this office.

John smiled to himself. He could hardly believe his luck. He re-read the letter again and again.

'A thirty-nine year old shop worker!' he exclaimed to himself. 'Likes animals too!' He looked across to his pets. 'Hear that, you two? She likes animals. And would you credit it? She loves football! I wonder what team she supports?' It all seemed so incredible to him, almost too much of a perfect match. 'I wonder if she'd like to go and see Brentford play at home?'

★★★

Margaret was doing exactly the same thing at exactly the same moment. Her own cat was sitting on the sofa next to her. Margaret looked through her letters, occasionally stroking the cat as it purred responsively and speaking to it in tones it seemed to understand.

'Well, how was your day, Mitzi?' The cat gave her an adoring look and seemed to blink its emerald green eyes in response. 'That good?'

She looked through the letters and put aside the bills. 'I don't know... bank card, American Express, store account card, Visa card, MasterCard, telephone, gas, electricity, water.' Even on £30,000 a year the bills managed to make an impact. She must get shot of these credit card bills. Then she would have a private bonfire in her back garden, watching her credit cards go up in flames.

For light relief she looked at the cat, who nuzzled her gently. 'You're lucky, aren't you?' she said affectionately. 'All you want is a plate of food and a cuddle. Now what's this?' Margaret stopped to look at a letter from the dating agency. It was similarly phrased to the one that John had received:

Dear Margaret,

The Centrepoint Dating Agency computer has matched you with a gentleman of similar interests to yourself. His name is John. He is a 41-year-old small business owner. John lists as his interests: pets, outdoors and loves watching football. If you would like to meet him, please contact this office.

Margaret looked up for a moment and thought deeply. Then for inspiration, as always, she looked at her cat.

'I've been matched with a forty-one year old small business owner. He likes pets. What about that, puss? A man who likes animals.' But as always, there was a catch. 'And he loves football. Oh dear, I knew I shouldn't have made up that bit about liking football. I wonder what team he supports.'

★★★

Margaret and Mary stood by the office window during their coffee break, sipping from mugs containing the store's own brand. Mary was acutely interested in Margaret's pending meeting.

'And you say this man, John, is a small business owner?' Margaret nodded. 'That covers a lot of ground. A small business owner could be anyone from someone running a used car lot to being the manager of a pet shop. He could also be a tobacconist, a newsagent, a store holder, a plumber. Did he elaborate?'

'No,' Margaret replied. 'I'm not class conscious. I just hope he's warm and considerate. I don't mind what he does for a living, I'll take him as I find him.'

Mary looked at her with mischief in her eyes. 'Even if he's a male stripper who runs a protection racket?'

'Well, you have to draw the line somewhere, Mary,' Margaret said with a smile. 'He seemed quite well-spoken on the phone. In fact his voice had a very friendly tone about it. He came across as a down-to-earth Londoner. I wonder what he's going to expect me to be like? I imagine because I put down on the form that I was a shop worker, I might not be what he expects.'

'Believe me, when he sees you he will probably think all of his birthdays have come at once.'

'I'd better dress down a little, perhaps,' Margaret added cautiously.

'Don't do that,' urged Mary. 'All men when you meet them for the first time are worth making an effort for.'

★★★

John Hicks certainly made an effort that night. When he finished work and returned home he felt a twinge of excitement. Tonight he was going to meet someone new, a person like him who had definite intentions about finding a partner. Now he had made a genuine effort to meet someone, he felt a thrill about the prospects that may lie ahead.

In the 41 years of John's life he had never had a relationship with a woman other than acquaintanceship. During the seven years he had been a merchant seaman he had met some very glamorous girls. But they had mainly been girls on voyages to exotic lands where the sun shone brighter and longer than anywhere in the United Kingdom. Once the voyage was over the girls never wrote or made contact. They had just been brief holiday romances.

Women had always been fabulous unattainable creatures who were normally on another man's arm, not his. John had almost given up the idea of ever getting married. Work and the domestic problems that had bedevilled him for years had restricted his social life. He had never been a man confident in the fact that women may have expressed an interest in him. It would have surprised him that many women may have had more than a passing interest in his decency and pleasant, uncomplicated personality.

Armed with a bouquet of flowers he had dressed up especially for his date. He had arranged to meet Margaret at a restaurant called the Hunter's Lodge. John had no idea what Margaret looked like. He had no idea how he would get on with her. He only knew that tonight was going to be different. It could be the start of something special. He hoped and prayed that it would be.

John entered the Hunter's Lodge and walked upstairs to the bar. He was early and knew he would have a quarter of an hour anticipating the arrival of Margaret. A barman in a tuxedo and bow tie came across to serve him.

'Good evening, sir,' the barman said amiably. He glanced quickly at the flowers. 'Are those for me?'

John smiled at his sense of humour. 'Not unless your name is Margaret.'

'You're meeting a lady, obviously. What would you like to drink while you're waiting?' John hesitated while he examined the cocktail menu on the top of the bar. 'Let me guess, sir. You look like a man who enjoys a good pint of Tex.'

John was surprised at the man's summing up of him. 'That's right. How can you tell?'

'Easy. I've seen you down the pub on the Whitton Avenue.'

John gave him a grin. 'Not much gets past you, eh? MI5 will be seeking your services. Well what do you recommend?'

'May I suggest a Piña Colada, sir?'

A taxi drew up outside the Hunter's Lodge. Margaret stepped out. She stood outside the restaurant and looked at it. Although she was opposite to John in the fact that she was possessed of more confidence than he was, apprehension made her nervy. She was not a novice when it came to affairs, nor did she hold any fear of the opposite sex. But tonight, because this date had been carefully orchestrated and planned with every intention of forming a permanent relationship, Margaret found that even she lacked the courage to make that first step inside.

A full half hour ticked by after the agreed meeting time. John had practically given up. He was sure that his date wasn't going to turn up. He had spent most of the time chatting to the barman in between Piña Coladas. He looked at his watch. 'I don't think the lady is coming, somehow,' John conceded. 'I'll have the same again.'

'Another Piña Colada? Coming up.' The barman turned around to prepare the drink. He cast a backward glance at John. 'Don't worry. It's a woman's privilege to be late.'

'Oh well, I'll just be patient,' John said. But he really had given up on the idea Margaret would be coming.

However, his patience was soon to be rewarded. Margaret had finally found the courage to enter the restaurant. Slowly she walked in, and for a moment she stood at one side looking across to the bar. John was chatting pleasantly to the barman. He sipped on a Piña Colada, and finally accepting that he would not have a date that night, he settled down to making the most of the evening.

John may not have thought so, but Margaret found him handsome. It was his cheery smile, a pleasant openness of manner that entranced her. She decided it was time to make her presence known. Margaret moved forward until she was standing beside him. John immediately turned his head, and when he saw Margaret his expression changed from one of surprise to delight. This lady could not possibly be Margaret. Girls like this surely didn't need to go to dating agencies.

'You're John, are you?' she asked, smiling the best possible smile she could put on display. 'I'm Margaret Gategood, from the Centrepoint Dating Agency.'

John was temporarily lost for words. All he could do was step down from the bar stool and take her hand lightly. 'Margaret?' he repeated almost stuttering. 'Very… very pleased to meet you.'

Neither had expected the other to be quite as nice.

'Very nice to meet you, too,' Margaret said, fully aware that for both of them there was an initial shyness they had to overcome.

John picked up the bouquet of flowers and handed them to her. 'These are for you.'

Margaret looked astounded. 'You didn't have to do this for me! Oh, that's very considerate of you.' She kissed him quickly on the cheek.

He smiled at her. It was a smile that was received well, and returned with affection.

'Let's go into the restaurant, Margaret,' John offered. As he opened the door for her, the barman gave him a thumbs-up sign and winked. John was obviously onto a winner here. At least, that was what he thought.

★★★

Margaret puzzled John from the outset of her arrival. To put it simply, she was just too good to be true. Here she was, a stunning 39-year-old with well-conditioned dark hair, clear eyes, and a well-dressed appearance. Straight away John was questioning why such a delightful woman had never married, and why her appearance suggested she did something more than just work behind the counter in a department store. However he did not bring these questions to the foreground. He was content to indulge in conversation and let the other things rest for now.

'So you live alone, then?' John advanced the conversation from the status of small talk to something that might bring forth more personal information.

'Well, yes. My parents died and I set up house on my own. Apart from my cat Mitzi I've lived on my own for some years. I don't mind it. But it does get a bit lonely.' Then came the first candid remark that gave John an inkling as to the sort of person she was. 'I suppose I've seen most of my girlfriends get married over the years. Some of them are on their second and third go at it, would you believe. Their children are teenagers too. I get worried about not meeting anyone.'

'I know what you mean,' John agreed. He felt that they were on common ground here. 'Virtually since I came out of the Merchant Navy, I was looking after my mother who was ill for many years. It got to be very difficult towards the end.' Here John was revealing himself to her. A look of pain flashed into his eyes as he remembered the severe family problems he had endured. 'When she passed away I look over the house. I've got pets as well, a tortoiseshell cat called Topie and a boxer dog called General Gordon.'

'General Gordon?' Margaret exclaimed. 'That's an unusual name for a dog.'

'Yes it is,' John said with a smile. He could feel himself becoming more at ease with Margaret. 'When I brought him home as a puppy I was wondering what on earth to call him, and I switched on the television and on came a film called *Khartoum* with Charlton Heston playing General Gordon. And I thought, what a great name for a boxer dog. He's a great mate. The dog that is, not Charlton Heston.' Margaret responded to his humour with a faint smile. 'Oh, I think pets are lovely to go home to. It's not quite the same as having a family though.' He paused to think of a way to further the conversation. 'Especially if the family are a calm and serene group who get on well together.'

Margaret was slow to respond, so John prompted her. 'What do you think, Margaret?'

Margaret looked at him in detail. He had a kind face and she had warmed to him considerably. Margaret was quick in her feminine intuition to recognise that John had been trying hard to make an impression on their first date. Perhaps a little too hard. Margaret attempted to relax him.

'What do I think?' Her voice and composure were warm and relaxed. Her manner was soothing and gentle. John could feel the warmth radiating from her. 'I think you seem to be a very nice gentle… gentleman. I feel very comfortable being here with you now, it's almost as if I've known you all my life.'

All my life. It almost sounded clichéd. Margaret was not one given to hearts and flowers, and sentimentality. Yet she was sensitive and skilled enough from her personnel and training experience to identify the good qualities in a person at first sight.

'I suppose we've both been trying hard to make a good first impression. I hope you feel relaxed with me too, ' she went on, as John smiled at her perceptive mind. 'It's always going to be a bit tricky, these sort of dates. You can never be sure just what sort of person you're going to meet.'

'I've not disappointed you then?' John asked shyly.

'Not at all,' she replied.

There was something so right about this meeting. John, who had felt nervous about this occasion, was now completely at ease in Margaret's company. She too felt a certain kind of warmth about John. The two of them were able to be forthright and open about themselves without causing offence to each other. The attraction between them was obvious. They both liked each other. From this first meeting all the ingredients for creating a romantic soufflé seemed to have been set in place.

At the end of the evening, Margaret and John walked along the street to a taxi cab rank.

'Thank you for the evening, John,' Margaret said pleasantly, holding her hand out to be shaken. John took the grip of her tender hand. On the surface, courtesy with cordiality was still being maintained.

'It's been a pleasure and a privilege,' John replied, holding the taxi door open for her.

For a moment it seemed as if each of them were waiting for the other to make the next move. Does she want to see me again? This was John's thought. I wonder if he wants to see me? Margaret was puzzling over this.

Finally John took the bull by the horns, or as he saw it, the bird by subtlety. 'Where do we go from here?' The anxiety in his voice was obvious.

Margaret looked at him affectionately. There was a sparkle in her eyes. Was it warmth? Was it humour? The delay in answering unnerved him. She got into the cab. From within she called out to him, 'Do you want to see me again, John?'

'I would love to.' His voice almost had the hint of a plea there.

'I scribbled my address and telephone number on a piece of paper. It's in your pocket.'

A look of surprise spread across John's face. He put his hand in his pocket and took out the piece of paper. Momentarily he was lost for words.

'Dinner tomorrow night, John?' Margaret pursued.

'Definitely,' John agreed.

'My place,' Margaret said with a happy smile. 'Seven-thirty.'

John stood there in radiant spirits as the taxi moved off. He felt so happy. He was convinced that after years of loneliness it was all going to come good for him. But it was all happening so quickly, and at the back of his mind there were doubts: it all seemed too good to be true.

★★★

Margaret was simply bubbling the next day. She was in her element as a training officer that morning. In high spirits, she expanded on the subject of dealing with the customer, using confidence and courtesy as her theme. Confidence was one thing Margaret had in abundance as she delivered her lecture to some very attentive staff members.

'Dealing with the customer,' she began. 'That is the topic of this morning's lecture. Believe it or not this is an art form. In the course of a day behind the counter the shop assistant will come into contact with just about every conceivable form of customer: the good, the bad and the ugly; the difficult, the disinterested, the rude, the humble, courteous; spend easy, spend what they have, and spend what they haven't got on the plastic card. The shop assistant will deal with all kinds of people, and no matter what sort of person they are, two rules should apply. The first is to be courteous at all times. Courtesy and good service are essential in any store. The customer will not come back a second time if staff are rude. When I was a child there was a slogan used in most British retail stores, and cafes and restaurants I might add. The slogan? "The customer is always right". Remember that. Good service means satisfied customers. Satisfied customers means good business because they may well come back. And if they come back again that means we're doing a good job. The second rule is to have confidence in yourself and what you're selling. Know the section you work in. Learn about the products you deal with so if a customer asks you about it, if you can speak knowledgeably on the subject and appear enthusiastic, then it becomes infectious. Enthusiasm engenders enthusiasm.'

Margaret performed her duties well that morning. It is strange how romance fills the human soul with sparkle. Mary walked up to her at the coffee machine noticing how radiant her friend appeared that day.

'How did you get on?'

'Oh the lecture went very well,' Margaret replied unthinkingly.

'Lecture?' Mary showed more than a twinkle of amusement in her laughing Irish eyes. 'Who cares about the lecture? I want to know how you got on with your date. Go on, don't keep me in suspense. What was he like?'

'I was pleasantly surprised,' Margaret stated honestly. 'I didn't think men like him would go to a dating centre. He was very nice. Good appearance. No show about him. He was very nice. I've said that before, haven't I? He was trying very hard to make a good impression. A little too hard I think.'

'Are you going to see him again?' Mary's question sounded not unlike that of a fifth-form schoolgirl anticipating a date with the head prefect.

Margaret's reply was not unlike the fifth-form schoolgirl who had scored a resounding success. 'Tonight. We're having dinner.'

'You're going to strike while the iron's hot, then?'

'Definitely, Mary.'

Mary pondered her own love life. 'I'll have to do something romantic for my man. A real champagne and flowers night with soft music in the background.'

'Soft music, now that is an idea.' Margaret was on the lookout for anything that could enhance her coming date, or as she saw it, her appointment with destiny.

★★★

At the end of the day, Charlie and John made their way home. Naturally for them too the subject was romance. Charlie was in his element, giving his advice freely without charge except perhaps in the hope that John would buy the first round of Tex or Tartan.

'Handling women, my son,' said Charlie with all the confidence of the acknowledged and respected expert, 'is like handling a piece of someone else's china tea set on the *Antiques Roadshow*. Women are sophisticated priceless creatures for which it is quite impossible to give a valuation. I know. I've got a degree on these things.'

'Degree, Charlie?' John joked with his best friend. 'The only degree you've ever taken is the temperature of your beer! You didn't get your wife on the Portobello Road though, did you? You met her at a bus stop.'

'And I've been paying her fare ever since,' Charlie pointed out with delight. 'Listen to an older man – about one month older, that is, but don't tell anyone – let me give you a piece of worthy advice, my son. Treat women like rose petals. They need to be looked after and pampered. All this stuff about women being equal in the office, Johnny boy, or wherever it is they work, might be good but when they're out with their bloke they won't admit it, mind — they like him to be captain of the ship.'

'Do you think so, Chas?' Now this was an interesting debating point. 'I thought with the equality of the sexes women demanded equal rights in everything.'

'And there's more,' Charlie added. 'They love a gentleman. Always take her flowers. Remember to pull back her chair for her, and never — I repeat, never — tell her a joke you heard a comedian tell his adults-only audience show the previous night!'

John was amused at this. 'Now that really is creating restrictions for me, Charlie!'

★★★

The setting for a perfect romantic evening had been organised. Soft music played gently in the background. Candles flickered. John and Margaret sat at the dining table, both relaxed in each other's company. Surely nothing could bar the progress of their romance.

'I believe you're a small business owner?' Margaret asked out of the blue. This was the first time the subject of work had cropped up in their conversation.

'Yes,' John replied with some hesitation. Although not to put too finer point on it, John felt uncomfortable being known as a small business owner. 'And you work in a shop?'

Margaret blushed with embarrassment at the downgrading of her own position. Why had she simply not told the truth to begin with? 'In a manner of speaking,' she croaked miserably.

It was John who decided to elaborate first. 'Actually, when I say I'm a small business owner what I am really am is a… well, I'm a butcher.' Margaret's chin dropped suddenly as she realised this nice man she was so taken with had also sidestepped declaring his position in life. 'I own the shop, though, and I have one fellow working with me. His name is Charlie Tomlinson.'

'Why did you put your job down as a small business owner?' Margaret's tone had changed rapidly. John wasn't sure, but it was somewhere between anger and annoyance.

'Well, I run the business,' John explained firmly in his defence. 'I am a small business owner. But butchering is my trade. The shop is in my name. I do the accounts and the books. I order the meat. But I work in the shop behind the counter as well.'

'I see.' Margaret's face and voice were grave. John felt embarrassed that he had not been completely honest. He rose to leave. Margaret looked on in shock. 'Where are you going?'

John appeared sad. He replied to her with disappointment evident in his voice. 'I thought I'd better leave, I'm obviously not what you thought I was.'

Margaret stood up and placated him. She touched his arm gently. 'Please don't go, John.' Her voice sounded soft and pleading in tone. 'John… sit down, please.' John sat down as if he had been ordered to do so. 'I know you didn't say anything that was dishonest. It's just that I haven't been quite honest either.'

It was John's turn now to be astounded. 'You haven't been honest?' he gasped. He began to expect the worst. 'What is it? Are you married, or something else?'

Margaret looked at him. He was obviously hurt. He had not been dishonest by any stretch, but he had been made to feel bad.

'No, I'm not married, John, and I'm not involved with anyone,' she assured him. 'I'm a spinster. I said I work in a shop. I do work in a shop. But I'm not behind the counter. I used to be when I first left school, however I worked my way up through several department stores to become a training officer at Debenworths.'

'I have to say I'm a bit perplexed, Margaret,' John stated. 'Forgive me for asking, but why did you give me the impression that you were… well, an ordinary sales assistant behind the counter? Not that there's anything wrong with being a shop assistant... or a butcher, or a cleaner in a sewerage works for that matter. Even John Major has spoken of the classless society. Why did you downgrade what you really do for a living? I don't understand.'

Margaret's embarrassment turned to confusion. 'It's difficult for me to explain.'

'Try,' said John firmly, and he added wistfully, 'I'm a good listener.'

Margaret had hopes for this romance. She knew if it was to lead anywhere the best thing would be to lay all her cards on the table. 'Alright, I'll tell you.' Her voice was calm and composed. Occasionally a flicker of a smile appeared. 'I'm an unmarried woman who is almost forty. I've no man in my life on a permanent basis. I didn't inherit anything from my parents. This is my own house that I worked and saved for, and mortgaged years of my hard-earned working life on. I'm on a damn good salary. Thirty thousand a year.' John blinked in amazement. Margaret noticed his change of expression. 'Not bad, eh? I've got a good car in the garage and money in the bank. With the job I've got, and the prospects...'

'Margaret.' John held his hand up, indicating to her not to explain any more. 'Margaret, I think I understand.'

'Let me finish anyway, John.' Margaret was determined that John should understand her point of view. 'I'm well set up. But I've got to the stage in my life where I am very self-sufficient. The fact that I'm financially well established could be off-putting to some men who are still old-fashioned or, to put it another way, traditional breadwinners. I'm very much a traditionalist. I hope that a man will fall in love with me for who I am. Not what I've got materially or in long-term financial prospects.'

'And that worries you?' John was puzzled. But not surprised in the circumstances. He pursued the matter, making it clear to Margaret that he knew what she was driving at. 'So the fact that you're independent, a training officer with a top department store, the fact that you've got your own house, it all adds up in your estimate that a man might find you more attractive for what you've got in the bank rather than the nice woman you are.'

'Yes.'

'You're worried that a man might marry you because you've got material things.'

Margaret nodded.

'I understand, but I think it's so sad you should even think like that.

When I joined the dating agency I wasn't a gold-digger looking for a solvent wife. I was looking for someone to love. I know it sounds a bit old-fashioned, but I was looking for a person to care for, to give a lot of love and attention to.' There was a mixed tone in John's voice. It was full of sincerity and perhaps a little bit of agony.

Margaret filled both their wine glasses. 'Are you angry with me, John?' she asked suddenly.

'No. Why should I be angry?' John replied. There was hurt in his eyes, however. He took a long sip of wine. 'I think it's a tragedy of the times that women often equate love and material things together.'

'It's not you, John. You're a terribly nice man. It's me. I built myself up to be a career woman, and now that I've achieved some sort of professional and financial success I find that when I'm looking for a husband it's a strong disadvantage.'

John and Margaret rose from the table and sat down in easy chairs facing each other. Relationships could be so complicated at times, thought John. He was really wondering if all this deep talk was worth the bother.

A few glasses of wine had the effect of putting Margaret and John at ease. John had never been a wine drinker. He had always been a pint of beer man. But with a few glasses of wine inside him he could feel a warm glow. Margaret was temporarily lost for words, and John felt it important to take the lead here. He knew that confidence and sensitivity were important to women. He desperately wanted to impress upon her the strong aspects of his own personality, whilst expressing his caring feelings.

'You know, it's a funny thing, Margaret. I'm an ordinary bloke. I'm a working man, just a hard-working six days a week butcher cutting up sides of beef, lamb, pork... cutlets, chops.' There was an element of pride in the way he spoke. The wine was giving a jet-propelled thrust to the flow of words that tumbled from his lips. 'I win awards for the sausages I make, would you believe? Sage and tomato, lamb and mint, turkey and bacon, Mexican, beef and Bovril, kipper sausages – not many butchers make those. Charlie and me, well we even cater for vegetarians, creating them from a mixture of mushrooms and tomato and any suitable ingredients.

'I take pride in my work. It's a humble job. It's the business side that is hard to handle, the accounts and the interest due, the purchasing of my stock. But do you know something? I don't think I'm any less or more of a person than others. I've always felt as good as the next bloke in the crowd. My next door neighbour is a computer programmer, he's got a mind like Albert Einstein. The fellow on the other side, now there's a character for you. You name it, he's done it. He's been a plumber, a sparky, a window cleaner and to top it all, he's a guitarist at night in a Country and Western band. The fact is that when we get together there is not a scrap of difference between each of us. We get together and talk about music and soccer and cricket. Am I boring you?'

'No. Do go on, John.'

He suddenly felt infinitely more confident now; like a music hall entertainer who had found the pulse of his audience. 'If I thought there was something wrong in me being who I am and what I do for a living, I would probably be a recluse. I would possibly have an inferiority complex a mile wide. The thing is, I am happy being who I am. For the most part I am very happy to look back. Not all of my life has been happy, not by a long stretch. But then whose life has not had its ups and downs, the isolated incidents along the way that cause minor upheavals?'

This last sentence sounded as if John had some poetry in his soul. A smile broached Margaret's lips.

'I must try some of your different types of sausages sometime,' she said. 'If they are as good as the way you handle your words then they must be very tasty!' Margaret's voice took on a more settled tone. 'You are a very candid and open man. I admire your honesty. I'm sorry for all that spiel I gave you earlier.'

'Why? I understand perfectly.' John was more sharply intuitive than might have been thought at first glance. He proved now that he realised Margaret's predicament. 'Marriage is a career to many ladies. It's the thing that they invest most of the years of their life in. It was for my mother. And if the mothers of this world ever got together to demand union rates for their job description, their wages claim would outstrip inflation a hundred times over. What I can't understand is why someone like you with all the world at your feet has never married. I know your career has been the mainstay of your life. Surely with your... your...'

John broke off. He knew exactly what he wanted to say but he knew it would be tactful not to.

'My what, John?' Margaret asked gently.

'Well, your beauty, Margaret,' he replied after a short pause. Her eyes twinkled with delight at the compliment. 'With your looks, I would have thought men would fight over you.'

Now it was time for Margaret to make her own candid admissions. 'There have been a couple of affairs,' she confessed. On these she did not elaborate, for they were personal to her and the conclusion to each had been painful. 'I had mostly casual dates; you know, lunches, dinner, that sort of thing.' Then she slightly changed the subject. 'I'm only really a working-class girl. Dad was a bus driver in Acton and my Mum was a clippie.' A laugh crept into her voice. 'Love on the buses! I was brought up in a council flat near the Gunnersbury Road. I went to an ordinary secondary school on a council estate in Northolt. I started work at the age of fifteen and worked my way up from behind the counter to where I am now. As far as marriage is concerned, I know it sounds selfish, but I never felt the need until now.'

'Need.' This word was the common denominator for both of them. 'Need is the same word that came into my mind.'

Margaret decided to interrogate John a little. 'Now, what's your story, John? Why haven't you ever been spliced? Tell me your story.'

'My story?' he replied. 'Same as you. Well, almost. A working-class boy, that's me, I guess. Actually I spent my early years in the prefabs on the old Barrantyne estate.'

'I've heard of that,' remarked Margaret.

'Yes it was in West Middlesex. It was a rough old place too. Apparently the prefabs were thrown together after the war to rehouse families. When it rained the corrugated roofs used to rattle and shake, and as for television and radio reception...' He laughed at the memory of his long-ago childhood. 'My family were lucky, though. When the prefabs were demolished most of the locals went to high-rise council flats in the Hayes and Southall areas. My Dad got a mortgage on the house I live in now. I've never really had the need to move.'

'Your mother and father?'

'Dad died while I was away at sea. He was a greengrocer. Never had a lot out of life, I'm afraid. He had a shocking temper.' John's voice tapered off as he spoke. The look of a man who had been deeply hurt by past traumas flashed across his features. He tried to smile away the memory but there were other hurtful things to remember. 'I had an elder sister who was a bit of a handful. She and Dad used to argue all the time. She ended up running off overseas. Anyway Dad got cancer and died. Mum had several strokes and was an invalid until she died. They were difficult years. Mum took a lot of looking after. It hurt me that I couldn't do more for her.'

John had not spoken about the past with bitterness or anguish. It was obvious to Margaret that he was a sensitive man who had more than amply coped with family problems. It was sad however that he had been hurt by his sister's thoughtlessness and the events that had befallen his family. One thing was strikingly obvious to Margaret: here was a man with reserves of great strength, capable of showing love, loyalty and care for the right person. Margaret touched his hand warmly. John recognised the sign.

'You're a good man, John,' she said in a soft voice. 'It must have been hard for you.'

'It was,' John agreed. 'Mind you, it's not all been trouble and strife. I had seven wonderful years when I worked as a merchant seaman with the Cunard line and then P&O.' A smile returned to his face as he recalled very happy memories. 'I went all round the world, half a dozen times. I met some wonderful people.'

'Where did you go, John?'

'Every continent in the world.' His eyes lit up and he began to wax lyrical. 'I saw some fascinating places in the Med and the Pacific. I've sailed through Suez, through the Panama Canal, and I've been to islands such as Tonga and Yasawa and Nuku'Alofa. It was nice. It was nineteen years ago, though I remember it all so clearly.'

Margaret listened intently. She did not say anything to continue the conversation; her eyes said it all. They were filled with warmth for this man before her. Their conversation together had been candid and warm. Both had spoken deeply of the past, and there were now no secrets between them. Things had progressed well from that first meeting in the Hunter's Lodge restaurant. But it was Margaret who felt that it would be up to her to further progress the situation.

Putting down her wine glass she stood up from her chair and moved beside him. Almost nervously, John stood up as well. They stood face to face. Margaret's face had an expression which he found hard to determine. Was she saying, 'Love me'? Was it a desire for him to take her in his arms and give her the love that both of them had waited so long for? He had mixed feelings: he was nervous and excited, tense and thrilled. John suddenly realised that she was waiting for him to respond. He touched her arm gently. Margaret's eyes were shining. She took the initiative and kissed him. John wrapped his arms around her warm, comforting figure. He had waiting so long for the right woman.

★★★

Charlie was always quick to pick up on John when his friend was worried by something. John had been strangely subdued after his dinner date with Margaret. What was wrong? John should have been on cloud nine, floating on air in fact, but it was as if his dreams had taken a tumble since the previous day.

After Charlie had served a couple of customers, he turned to his friend. John was hanging up racks of meat for display in the window.

'You've been quiet this morning. Anything wrong, John?'

'It's Margaret,' he responded without hesitation.

'I thought it might be.'

John turned to face him. 'I just don't think it's going to work somehow. She's too far above me.'

To Charlie this last statement was an admission of inferiority. He could hardly believe his ears. 'What do you mean, too far above you? She works in a shop like us, doesn't she? What's the problem there, then?'

John stopped what he was doing and wandered around the counter. Charlie put the kettle on. John's downcast look was a sure-fire indication that a mug of tea was needed as an antidote.

'It's not quite the way it seems, Chas,' John admitted. 'She does work in a shop. That bit is true at least. But she's a training officer for Debenworths. Margaret worked her way up from behind the counter to where she is now. I couldn't believe it when I first met her: someone about my age, never been married, looking the way she did. It was all too good to be true.'

Charlie shared John's disappointment. He knew his friend's life had been a lonely one, and quiet. He had hoped John would get lucky on this occasion. 'Why did she tell you she worked as a shop assistant? I don't understand why she wasn't straight with you, John.'

'It's because she's very well set up. Everything she's got has come from hard graft. So she told me that by downgrading what she does for a living, she hoped a man would fall in love with her, not her bank account, not what she's got. Margaret wanted a man she could trust.'

'Well she's got one now,' Charlie assured him.

'I know. But it just doesn't feel right. Oh, I like her enormously. She's a smashing bird. And I'll let you into a secret: I know she likes me. We've both got off to an awkward start, though. Now if we'd both been honest about what we did…'

Charlie was quick to point out one obvious fact to him. 'If you had both been honest about what you did for a living, the computer at the dating agency might never have matched you.'

John acknowledged this by raising his eyebrows, which was his usual mannerism when he couldn't think of anything to say.

'Are you seeing her tonight?'

'No. Not tonight,' John replied pensively.

This was the signal to Charlie for a malt sandwich aperitif after work. 'Fancy a beer tonight on your way home?'

'Any why not indeed, Charlie? Why not?' The suggestion was a good one to John. 'I might even have a couple of pints of Pompey.'

John and Charlie's favourite pub was the Load of Hay. It had been their watering hole since they were teenagers. Once it had been the sort of British pub that expatriates overseas loved to reminisce about, but with brewery takeovers, new management structures and restaurant catering, it was now something of a hotchpotch tavern. It resembled more of a mixture of a fast food outlet, an off licence and a motorway café. The only thing that had been consistent about the pub was the weekly visits by John and Charlie, who were among the elite group of customers who were always invited to the pub's staff Christmas party!

This home from home was the place where John and Charlie had long intimate discussions about their private affairs. There had been nights when the Tartan bitter, the pints of Tex and Pompey had flowed like the River Jordan as each had opened up their soul to each other in the manner that Moses had parted the Red Sea. There was no better place for John and Charlie to discuss things. Charlie always knew that a joke in the right place could help push things along.

'I envy you,' Charlie said in a deadpan voice.

'Why?'

'You think marriage is a wonderful institution, don't you?'

'Yes. I always have.'

Charlie smiled. 'Yes, mate, what you need is a good wife.' His eyes took on a look of wicked amusement. 'You need a good woman you can keep permanently pregnant, barefoot, dressed in rags and chained to the kitchen sink full of crockery and babies' dirty nappies.'

'Sounds wonderful!' Charlie always had a way with words. 'You certainly know the better parts of marriage.'

'Did you hear about the Prime Minister?' Once again Charlie's face was deadpan. It was difficult to tell from his laconic humour whether he was serious or not.

'The Prime Minister?'

'Yes. The bloke who lives rent-free at 10 Downing Street.'

John looked concerned. 'What about him?'

'He was over in Hollywood. He stayed in one of those big hotels in Beverly Hills. He was in the Raquel Welch suite. There were no door knobs. Just two big knockers!'

John tried hard not to smile at the awfulness of Charlie's jokes. 'I thought you were going to tell me something funny, Chas.'

'You don't really want to be here, do you?' his friend fired back quickly. John knew that Charlie was right.

'Go round and see Margaret. Don't let it die before it's been born, mate. Forget all the stuff about her being too far above you. Just because you're a tradesman and she's a good-looking independent girl it doesn't mean to say you can't enjoy each other's company.'

Charlie added, perhaps a little wisely. 'Something stronger than friendship can grow.'

★★★

Just as Charlie and John had the Load of Hay as their regular venue, so Margaret and Mary had the Brown Derby. Their watering hole was something a little more upmarket. Every so often the two ladies escaped to the wine bar, which was just around the corner from the store. It was a pleasant little bar filled with high stools and where soft romantic background music was played. Office workers thronged the place at the end of the day.

Mary had taken to updating her image at work, much to the surprise of the other girls who had long considered her to be a prim, diffident spinster. The new Mary who wafted into the office each morning was an eye-opener to her colleagues. They had never suspected that this conscientious worker had such unabashed sexual magnetism. Gone was the tied bun hairstyle. In its place her long hair fell free. Gone too were the spectacles. Her green cat-like eyes sparkled and glimmered with humour and excitement. It was impossible not to be bewitched, bedazzled or bewildered by them. Her plain office suits had been substituted by brightly coloured dresses and tops. If all these changes were not enough of a shock, Mary had enhanced her complexion by the use of self-tanning cream, all over. Her legs and face were intoxicating to the men in the wine bar, who were almost falling over themselves.

Margaret could not help but notice and to a certain extent admire the effect her friend had on members of the opposite sex. Perhaps it was a combination of Mary's Irish−Welsh upbringing, her own interesting life that had encompassed travel to exotic places and colourful love affairs and marriages. Even more surprising was the fact that Mary had discreetly told Margaret her real age was 53 and that the man she lived with was a mere 36 years of age.

There was almost a sense of envy from Margaret at Mary's constant positive attitude to life and taking it all in her stride. Mary was a good soulmate to Margaret in much the same way as Charlie was to John. Curiously enough, one could have imagined Charlie and Mary, opposites at first sight, to have made a good couple in different circumstances.

Mary and Margaret sat at the bar pondering life over a carafe of wine. 'Are you worried that you may have made a mess of this one?' Mary asked Margaret.

'Yes,' Margaret admitted. 'He really is a very nice man. I know it sounds silly, but the moment I saw him I thought, this fellow's the one. There was something nice about him. I can't really put my finger on it. Do you know something else, Mary?'

'No. But you're going to tell me and I'll be pleased to listen.' In this she meant exactly what she said, for she took an almost sisterly interest in Margaret.

'Over the years I've been so wrapped up in my life I've never really had – no, that's not right – made the time for a permanent relationship. Even in the line of friendship I've few, if any, soulmates. I've got my own house, my own way of life, my career, and after much thinking and much critical analysis, I've finally worked it out. I need love and a family. But there's part of me that feels threatened at the thought of a man in my life on a long-term basis. Do you know what I mean? About permanent relationships and marriage?'

'Too true I do,' Mary said firmly. 'I've two marriages behind me and several lovers too. I can't believe both of my marriages failed. I went into both of them with the best of intentions, and both men I was madly in love with. The first one wanted to be a married bachelor, and the second one wanted me to be his obedient servant at the beck and call to his every whim. He wanted not so much a wife but a woman who was a washer-upper, waitress and lover when it suited him. The only good things to come out of those marriages were my sons, one by each husband. They're terrific boys. One's twenty-eight, the other's twenty-two. They come to visit occasionally. Anyway, I wanted a man with whom I could find friendship, happiness; someone in whom I would find trust and loyalty and decency; someone who would treat me equally and with respect.' She added, with a twinkle in her eyes. 'I also wanted him to be a very passionate lover.'

'Does such a man exist?' Margaret asked apprehensively.

'I live with him,' Mary stated with a broad smile on her face.

'You're lucky.'

'I am. I know that. I'm a fifty-three year old broad…'

'A good-looking sexy one at that who looks at least ten years younger,' interjected Margaret.

'And I've been blessed in another respect,' added Mary. 'Finding Rob was wonderful. I know he's seventeen years younger than me but it hardly makes any difference.'

Margaret put a serious point to her friend, whose opinion she always valued. 'Do we women expect too much from life? Life is not a fairytale. Neither is it all grim and grey. But is there something in our make-up as women that puts dreams in our heads? Do we all believe that we're each something special, and that one day a man with the suntanned build of a Chippendale, the wallet and bank account of a Rockefeller, and the sensitivity of a monastery priest is going to waft into our lives? Yet we also need to be our own person, and at the same time we have the family-making instinct.'

Mary was no slouch when it came to giving her opinions. 'I think it's probably the desire to be loved and the fact that we're the ones who give birth to the children. Until Margaret Thatcher – and I'm not being political here – came on the scene, to some extent women weren't taken seriously in society. There is still the thought in many households that a woman exists as a child-bearer and skivvy. Not any more. A woman can have a career, a lover and children. A woman need not be shy about asking a man out, or going Dutch on dinner dates.'

'I think John feels a bit put out by our differences in career. I didn't think it would make that much difference. I told you I wasn't class conscious. But the fact that John is a butcher, and I am what I am, does seem to make a huge amount of difference. It shouldn't. John's done things in his life that I've never done. Before he went into the meat trade he was a sailor and he's been to New York, the Caribbean, Bali, Indonesia, Tonga — everywhere in fact. He's a wonderful man, humble, honest as the day is long, straight... there's no bull about him.'

Mary noticed the glowing terms with which Margaret praised John. 'Gosh, you really are struck on him aren't you?'

'I am. So much so... Do you know what I'm going to do? For the moment I'm going to let it ride. Then I'm going to go after him and make him the man in my life.'

Margaret had spoken with such firmness that it was hard to believe she wouldn't be successful in her task.

★★★

Perhaps the one person John relied on apart from Charlie was his highly dependable boxer dog, General Gordon. John loved his dog dearly. He was always there for him, wagging his tail and panting a greeting when he came home at night after a hard day's work.

Charlie lived only a few streets away, and occasionally when John took his dog for a walk late at night he would drop by. The light in Charlie's house was still on. Come round any time, that had been Charlie's advice to John. He didn't take up the offer too often but he always enjoyed the occasional drop-in visit. Charlie's delightful wife Jean would always give him a warm welcome and make them all a sandwich and a couple of cups of tea.

John knocked on the door. It was Jean who answered. She was about 5 feet 6 inches tall with light blue eyes and mousey hair. Unlike Charlie, who was an inch taller with dark hair and almost plump, Jean was maternal and well-rounded.

'Hullo, Johnnie boy!' Jean exclaimed in her usual jolly manner.

'Hullo, Jean. I was just passing.' It didn't sound very convincing but it didn't make any difference.

'Nice to see you. Come on in. Bring General Gordon in. He can run around the back yard.'

John entered the house. It was warm and cosy, more of a home of the 1950s than one of the 1990s. Charlie was hard at work performing one of his most favourite roles; that of the couch potato watching *News at Ten*. General Gordon, who was well acquainted with Charlie, ran into the lounge panting and slobbering his long tongue over him like a long-lost relative.

'Hullo, General Gordon!' Charlie said almost as if he had expected him to drop by. 'Your master can't be too far behind you, I bet.'

John came into the lounge. 'Didn't mean to bother you, Chas.'

Without taking his eyes off the dog, Charlie replied, 'She wasn't in, was she. Margaret, I mean.'

Charlie assumed that John's romance had just about run its course. He also assumed that John had come round for a friendly natter to cheer himself up.

'I caught her as she was just coming home.' John sat down. 'Anyway, the upshot of it all is that we've decided to let it go for a while. Perhaps we'll try and pick up together in a few weeks' time.'

Margaret had not revealed the ace card she held closest to her heart. This pause in their affair was only temporary. In a short time Margaret would become the hunter and John would be the unsuspecting prey caught in a trap.

Charlie just took it for granted that his mate John had decided he wasn't cut out for relationships. 'Oh well.' He shrugged his shoulders. There wasn't much he could say really. Besides, the dog had its paws pinned on his shoulders and he was in serious danger of being licked to death.

Jean entered the room. 'Would you like a bite to eat with us, John?'

'If that's alright with you, Charlie.' John was polite as usual. He knew Charlie would never refuse.

'It's not alright with me,' Charlie said abruptly. For a moment John thought the unexpected had happened. Then Charlie's face broke into a huge smile. 'Since when do you need to ask me, old mate? We'll brew up a pot of tea and have a bacon sarnie.'

Tea and bacon sarnie with friends. What more could a man want? John wanted much more. But he wasn't complaining. Jean and Charlie

Tomlinson were lovely people. They and their house seemed to belong to another age. Their friendship and genuine cheerfulness was like the back-street terraced house warmth of the 1950s. They sat around an electric fire that had been designed to look like a grate with roaring flames from burning logs. The deception was a good disguise and it gave the room that extra touch of warmth.

'It's not often we see you here, John,' Jean said affably.

'I don't like to impose,' John answered honestly. 'After all, I see Charlie every day. No, I just wanted to drop in and see you both. I didn't want you to think I was keeping Charlie away from home too often, what with Saturdays and late night shopping on Thursday.'

This was the flimsiest excuse Charlie had heard in a long time. It brought a sly smile to his face.

'That's alright John,' Jean said ahead of Charlie. 'The overtime comes in very handy.'

'We've done alright in the meat trade considering the recession of the past couple of years,' Charlie looked coyly at John and smiled, knowing his friend had come around for a good reason. 'Why did you really pop around, mate?'

John allowed himself a smile at his friend's intuition. 'There are no flies on you are there, Charlie?'

'I can always tell with you. What's up, John?'

'You're a mate, Charlie. A good mate at that. And I know you will always tell me straight without any bull.'

Jean, who sensed that this might be a 'men's only' conversation, looked on anxiously. 'Do you want me to go, John? Is this a private conversation?'

'No. This is your house. My goodness!' John felt embarrassed that his presence there had precipitated such a question. 'Besides, I value your opinion. I've got two questions for you. Tell me straight. Question number one. What sort of bloke am I? Question number two. Do you think I'm too old for marriage?' He added one more question as a postscript. 'And at forty-one, am I too set in my ways?'

'Soul-searching are you?' Jean asked warmly.

'Believe it or not, I am,' John admitted.

Charlie strode in with his down to earth humorous answer to the first question. 'What sort of bloke are you? You're alright, mate. Mind you, your hair's a bit thin, you're getting fat round the backside, you've got bags under your eyes, wrinkles in your wrinkles, your teeth need straightening up and one of your ears is higher than the other – but apart from those minor details you'll pass.'

John allowed himself a smile at Charlie's very inaccurate description. Although he was certainly no oil painting, John cut a good dash and he was a very presentable 41-year-old.

'You're okay,' Jean added. 'To answer your other question, of course you're not too old for marriage at forty-one.' Jean had a similar sense of humour to her husband. 'Don't forget, we're only forty-one as well. If Charlie ever gets crushed to death by a crowd of runaway circus elephants I'll marry you!'

'I won't be taking you to the circus any more,' piped up Charlie with a broad smile on his face.

'Do you know, John?' Jean continued. 'My Uncle Wesley, on my mother's side, got married for the first time at seventy-eight.'

'Seventy-eight!' John repeated.

'Oh yes. But there's more,' Jean went on to say in the manner of a storyteller. 'His wife died when he was eighty. But he liked being married so much he got hitched again at eighty-two. Then she died, and he's just got engaged. He's eighty-five!'

'He's a real lad. Sprightly old bloke too.' Charlie spoke with admiration of the old gentleman. 'Now that's what I call armadillos.'

'You mean peccadillos,' Jean pointed out.

'Suit yourself,' Charlie murmured. 'There's a message there for all of us. Until the final whistle's blown there's time to score a few goals. Could be one there for you too. Don't dwell on this girl Margaret. Get out and do a few things. There's a big dance on at the Town Hall next week for thirty- to forty-year olds. Why don't you go along and show them some of the John Hicks charm? Just take one year off your age and give 'em a good show.'

Good old Charlie. He always made it sound so easy. When John walked his dog home that night he thought that perhaps he had placed too many eggs in one basket. Perhaps he should look around at alternative prospects. But in his heart he knew there was no one else he even wanted to show interest in. If he couldn't have a relationship with Margaret then there was no one else for him.

★★★

The best party music in the world is good old-fashioned rock 'n' roll. Whenever the music is played, people of all ages tap their feet, their mood perks up, spirits rise and aspiring dancers take to the floor with zest and energy.

At the local Town Hall, this particular Saturday night had been given over to a rock 'n' roll revival show for single people from 30 to 40 – give or take a year of two between the parameters of the age group. John reluctantly went along. He had to force himself to go. His thoughts were still enmeshed around Margaret but as they had agreed on a relative cooling off between them he decided to check out other possibilities.

Dancers filled the floor. It was obvious from a first glance that many of the twirlers had long burst the 40 mark, possibly even the big five-O. Still, if they enjoyed themselves, what else mattered? John shuffled around nervously sipping from a glass of beer. A couple of girls made a surreptitious study of him from the side-lines. They were damned attractive. But how does one ask either of them to dance without upsetting the other? John offered them an expression that passed as a smile, although he declined to take up the options that were on offer. He moved along and watched the people with interest.

He felt distinctly uncomfortable. There is something about loneliness and isolation in a person which stands out like a blazing beacon for all to see. It is nearly almost identifiable within a few short minutes of first sighting. It was very evident that night. There were the nervous puffers. Those who chain smoked and relit their cigarettes time and time again. There were the hair tuggers and the tie adjusters. How many times did a girl tug at her hair as she waited for an invitation to dance? The fellows who straightened their ties until one could hold a plumb line against it were plentiful.

One attractive-looking woman sidled up beside him, obviously hoping he would ask her to dance. John smiled at her, and stepped back almost into the shadows. Watching the dancers, John felt his age acutely. This was a curious age to be single. Most people here, he considered, were those who had been married, divorced, widowed. They were perhaps remnants of broken relationships; everyone here had probably had a relationship experience of some kind. Everyone, it seemed, but him.

There were plenty of available women for the men to glance over. Many of them looked anxiously for prospective partners. The men did exactly the same. John did not like being part of this situation. He watched people of all ages making the first approach. It wasn't always the men who made the first dance invitation, sometimes it was the lady. For when it came down to it, taking a chance on finding a person to have some sort of relationship with was a very serious business.

Loneliness was not so much an occasional state of emotion or situation. It was very much an epidemic. People need people. So the words of the song went. No man is an island. That quote was frequently brought to mention. Perhaps it should also have been said that no woman is an island either. But here on a Saturday night in a foot-stomping rock 'n' roll revival show, the state of loneliness was very much on display.

John had always felt that events in life should never be pushed. To those who wait, good things will come. How different he felt now at 41. He realised with great regret and misgivings that everything in life has to be earned, sought out, and tried for. That included jobs, competitions, and winning a girl's hand in marriage. Tonight just wasn't the night or the occasion for him. John placed his half-empty beer glass on a table and walked out into the fresh night air. At least he thought it would be fresh. The rain poured down with a vengeance and the night air was distinctly chilly.

John stood in the shelter of a shop front. He pulled his coat firmly around him. A couple dashed hand-in-hand down the street to catch a bus. John looked on enviously. How nice it was in life to have someone to love. Life is so short. If the span is just an average seventy years, how fortunate is the man or woman who has loved for half that lifetime.

★★★

Margaret had felt the need to go out that Saturday night too. She had chosen the cinema in Harrow as the venue. Cinemas had always had a warm, safe appeal about them. Ever since her parents had taken her to Disney movies as a child she had loved being entertained by the figures on the screen.

On nights like this she felt like a girl of 16 sitting in the back row with a choc ice and eyeing up the single boys in the cinema, who were no doubt doing the same thing. Tonight the usual programme of Arnold Schwarzenegger, Freddie Kruger and Sharon Stone strategically placed under fluorescent lighting was abandoned for a serious of classic romantic films.

Margaret sat alone in the cinema, absorbing the atmosphere more than the romantic melodrama set in the austere era of the 1940s. Her gaze slowly shifted from the screen. The truth was, she was not really interested in the film. She found herself studying the audience. All around her there seemed to be couples. The truth was beginning to dawn on her very harshly. There were young romantics in the traditional back row. There were elderly and middle-aged couples hand in hand. Margaret realised with a sudden jolt that she was the only single or unaccompanied person in the audience. A tear rolled from her eye without warning. It was the stigma of being alone. It was the feeling of a future always spent yearning for a partner; someone whom memories and happy times could be shared with. To some people it wouldn't matter; to Margaret it did matter. Her independence and career were fast giving way to her own well-restrained vulnerability and desire to be loved. Margaret rose up from her cinema seat and left.

Margaret stood alone at the bus stop. Rain pelted down heavily. She stamped her high heels in frustration. Opposite was a small Wimpey hamburger house. The aroma of sizzling steaks and French fries gave her an appetite. Just as she had decided to give in and cross the road to assuage her hunger, the bus to take her home meandered slowly up the High Street. Gratefully she climbed on board.

The bus journey through Harrow on the Hill and Sudbury Court Drive seemed to take forever. The rain lashed against the windows on the top deck. Margaret loosened her wet clothes. Apart from a few people the bus was almost empty. There was a young couple in the mid-twenties who sat a couple of seats ahead of her. Margaret did not intentionally listen to the couple, but their voices carried.

The young man looked at his girlfriend slowly. There was a look of that first flush of love about her. 'Judy…' he began, in a voice that sounded as if it was something between a quiver and a tremble. 'I know this is not exactly the most romantic of places, but there is something I want to ask you.'

Judy looked at him apprehensively. The shine in her eyes suggested she knew the question that would be asked of her. Margaret too listened in anticipation.

'Can I ask you something?'

A glint of humour in her eyes appeared. 'As long as it's not too personal.' There was an air of mischief about Judy. 'I'll pinch your bottom if it is!'

'I'm trying to be serious!' The poor young fellow was trying hard to build up to propose. He took a small box from his pocket and opened it, revealing an engagement ring.

Judy looked at it, amazed. Margaret found this occasion more interesting than the movie she had been to see. From her personal viewing spot Margaret smiled at the sight of their happiness.

'Oh Ray!' Judy looked at the ring in genuine astonishment. She kissed him quickly. 'Oh Ray, it's beautiful.'

'I love you Judy,' Ray said softly.

It was hard for him to utter his words softly without tripping up. He had rehearsed his lines over and over again but the final performance was so different to what he had envisaged. Then came the last act and crescendo before the curtain call.

'I do love you. I was never so sure about anything in my life. I care for you. Will you…'

He paused. The silence was deafening. For one moment Margaret expected a delivery from Clark Gable to Vivien Leigh in the manner of 'my dear I don't give a damn'. Instead, Ray proposed in a beautifully modulated voice.

'I'll look after you and care for you the rest of my days and I promise to show you kindness, consideration, love and affection as well as give you a home and support. Will you marry me? Please?'

Judy didn't reply at first. She gazed at him in adoration and then put her arms around him, kissing him long and luxuriously. When finally she had finished, Ray looked deep into her eyes and smiled.

'I take it that's a yes is it?' he asked gently.

'Of course it is,' Judy replied, her face glowing with happiness.

Margaret looked on with just a hint of envy. What price independence, she asked herself. Marriage is still an institution worth entering.

★★★

Charlie Tomlinson had been following the progress of John's romantic life in the manner of backing a horse in the Grand National. If the local bookie had kept odds on John getting together permanently with Margaret, Charlie would have wagered an even bet on it. The turf was tough. The track was well worn. They had come round the bends with ease. Now they were on the flat and heading down the last lap evenly. Charlie could see only one possible ending. John and Margaret would sprint home together in record time.

It was late on Saturday night in the Tomlinson household and Charlie gazed from the comfort of his easy chair at Jean, who was drying dishes in the kitchen. What a lucky bloke I am, thought Charlie. He looked kindly at the woman who was the mother of his son. He had really got lucky when he had married her. It was about time he told her how much she meant to him. Charlie walked into the kitchen and put his arms around her.

'You're a smashing bird,' he said.

Jean turned around and faced him. 'You're not a bad-looking bloke yourself, Charlie T,' she replied, kissing him gently.

Charlie held her tightly. He constantly joked and generally acted the part of the court jester when he was with his friends and customers. But with Jean his sincerity and love were there for all to see.

'I never tell you how much I appreciate you.'

It was a rare moment of revelation from him. Jean lapped up the silence that followed by gazing deep into his normally laughing eyes.

After a while she replied to him. 'You don't have to.'

'Oh, but I do,' Charlie insisted. 'I need to. I can't believe how I got lucky with you through a chance meeting at the bus stop.'

Jean could respond with good humour too. 'I might have married someone else if I'd gone by London Underground!'

'Thank goodness you didn't.'

'But I would never have missed our honeymoon. Even if it was a week in rainy old Sussex walking up and down the Downs at Findon.'

'It was nice,' agreed Charlie. 'It was the best honeymoon I ever had.'

Charlie clasped Jean tightly and thought how good it was to be loved. Forgetting all the bull and sentimental drivel he had always associated with love stories, deep down inside Charlie realised he was a true romantic who appreciated the love of a truly good woman and a son. The riches of Solomon or the value of the glittering Crown Jewels had nothing on the worth of his family to him.

★★★

Robert Bentley was 36 years of age and Mary Byrne's live-in lover. He was a good-looking young man, slim, not muscular but toned, and with a slightly tired face. His eyes showed sensitivity and an occasional hurt look which was probably the effect of coming from a broken home, a difficult upbringing and being the veteran of a divorce, having extricated himself from a violently unhappy marriage to a woman who had constantly cuckolded him.

So far his career had encompassed working as a garage mechanic, a brief episode as a racing car driver, and a production manager at an auto plant. Currently he worked as a freelance technical author, writing up product manuals and equipment specifications for European car firms. A lot of his work involved him working away on the Continent but whenever the contract was finished he would go gratefully home to the arms of Mary Byrne and the bed they shared.

He and Mary had met at a singles party. Despite the difference in their ages they were drawn together out of mutual loneliness and the passion they knew existed virtually from day one of their meeting.

Mary liked the calm and peace of their home in an elegant, well-refurbished terraced house in West Ealing. It was a haven of love as far as Mary was concerned. A soft music cassette tape played in the background. It was curious music, combining the sounds of Japanese wind chimes, the lush strings of an orchestra and the faint addition of an Indian sitar. It all provided a warm enchanting sound for an evening of love.

Mary and Rob had just indulged in one of their long warming bubble baths followed by a session of tingling back massages and breath-taking slow indulgent lovemaking. Clad only in kimonos Mary and Rob lay about casually on the lounge room floor, sipping from glasses filled with sweet sparkling non-alcoholic wine. Mary stroked the back of Rob's head with her long seductive fingers which pulsated with electricity. Rob was definitely not her poodle or a hen-pecked man who was there purely to give love and receive it. They both had a more satisfying partnership than they had ever had in their previous marriages and relationships.

'You know my friend Margaret, the girl at work I was telling you about?'

'Yes, you mentioned her,' Rob replied.

'She was really getting on well with this fellow, a nice man called John, and then she seemed to pull right back from getting too involved. To make a commitment even on a personal level was too hard for her.'

'It sounds like common sense to me,' Rob stated bluntly. 'Take you and me, for instance. I had a lousy marriage. You had two that broke your heart. Three divorces between us! Maybe there are some people in life who are better off being spinsters and bachelors till the end of their days.'

'A celibate existence, you mean?' The idea appalled Mary. 'There's an old saying: better to have loved and lost than never to have loved at all.'

'I suppose you might be right.' Rob reluctantly agreed. He looked at his lady. She was such a loving woman, and he wondered about the history of her passionate feelings. 'Did you go out searching for love or did it happen naturally for you? I was thinking of your friend Margaret. She's waited all this time, whereas you...'

'Me,' Mary smiled at him. 'I haven't any secrets, Rob. None from you. I've always been passionate, I've always had deep, smouldering emotions ever since I was a child running barefoot in Tiger Bay. I've always wanted...' Her voice was wistful as she felt compelled to speak of things in her past. 'I've always wanted love, to travel, exotic places and experiences.' Rob listened, fascinated by this incredible woman who herself was something exotic. 'My parents were fiery and Irish. Dad was away at sea a lot and we moved from Dun Laoghaire near Dublin across the water to Cardiff and Tiger Bay.'

'Hence your Irish—Welsh upbringing.'

'Yes, it's something of a combination.' Mary stretched her long brown legs across Rob's lap. He made no complaint. 'And,' Mary continued, 'I suppose some of my sense of fun and passion is a little bit Irish, a little bit more Welsh. I'm well-travelled and interested in men generally.' Her blatant admission came as no shock to Rob who had always regarded her as something of a firecracker.

'When I was sixteen I made love for the first time to a boy in the street I lived in. At nineteen I decided to work in Paris and then Switzerland, where I met my first husband. He was a Londoner who was travelling by motorbike to Kathmandu. I joined him as a pillion passenger. Gosh, it was so exciting.' Rob listened, enthralled by the honest and candid way she spoke of her life. 'To be in love with someone and to travel through the best parts of Europe and across the North African desert was fantastic.'

'You were a sort of motorbike hippy?' Rob suggested.

'Oh yes. Beads, tassels, thongs, long hair and an Indian headband. That was me in the sixties. By the time we arrived in India I had found the passion I had wanted so much. We travelled up and down India from Goa to Delhi, Jaipur to Madras; and then we married in Nepal – in Kathmandu. There was no wedding ring, just a curious Nepalese tattoo that went with the marriage when that went out the window. After all that adventure in Kathmandu and a further jaunt to Saigon, home life and a son didn't suit my husband. He was out with other girls. I found another man, moved in with him, had another son, and when our divorces came through we married. That marriage was even worse than the first. I divorced him and brought my two boys up on my own.'

'Does this mean you won't marry me?' Rob asked in good humour.

'Do we need to?' Mary asked, putting both arms around him and kissing him. Her kimono opened unintentionally. Rob stroked her long hair and relaxed in the grip of her arms.

'Perhaps not.' Although if she had wanted to Rob would have married her at the drop of a hat. 'I still have bad memories of my own marriage, Mary. My wife wanted married life and boyfriends as well. When I found she's been with other men while I was out working all day I felt so hurt and used.' The pain surfaced in his eyes. 'When I confronted her about her affairs she said that I didn't allow her freedom and she wanted to find herself, whatever that means. When we were divorced I vowed no one would ever hurt me again.'

'Well I won't hurt you, Rob,' Mary assured him. 'All the same, though, when you look at things in general, it's a world made for couples isn't it? Everywhere you look it's couples together. You go into a restaurant, there are men and women in a romantic corner. You go into a cinema, it's man and woman, boy and girl. The single person, be they the loner, the spinster, bachelor, divorcee, widow or the widower... to some extent they're almost discriminated against.'

This was an interesting statement. 'In what way?' Rob queried.

Mary provided him with a list of what she perceived as being good examples of this. 'The single room supplement on holidays and package tours for example. Being shown the poor table in a restaurant. The uphill task of a single person trying to get a mortgage, whereas they might have a better chance being part of a working married couple. The estate agent who would rather sell to a family man than a single person who might not fit into a particular neighbourhood. Even worse, the prejudice that exists in small communities towards the lone person, the unspoken assumption or the malicious gossip about a single man or woman's sexual preference, especially if they are loners by nature.'

Rob pondered over her words. 'You feel that's prejudice?'

'Yes,' Mary replied without hesitation. 'Sometimes if people see someone constantly alone they might start to draw their own conclusions. Often wildly drawn, in fact. Silly people might say or think: oh but he or she is always on their own – there must be something wrong with them. And people do. Especially youngsters who can't understand what real loneliness is all about.'

'Isn't that more ignorance than prejudice?' Rob volunteered.

'Probably a mixture of both,' Mary conceded. 'Anyway, what are we worried about? We've got each other.'

The way she had made that last comment filled him with warm feelings. 'Too true. And that's fine by me.'

★★★

John sat at home, relaxing on the settee. He sat back and sipped from a mug of tea. His dog General Gordon leapt up on one side of the sofa, much to his amusement. The cat Topie was not to be outdone and jumped up on the other cushion. John smiled at the sight of his pets seeking affection. He put down his mug of tea and stroked both animals. 'Nice to come home to you,' he said quietly, with love in his voice. When all was said and done, pets were something reliable and friendly to come home to.

★★★

Margaret emerged from the shower. She tied her bathrobe around her and flopped down into an easy chair. Almost on cue, her cat Mitzi came into the room and rubbed herself against Margaret's legs. 'Good to see you,' she said stroking the cat's silky but slightly moulting coat. Margaret thought of John. How on earth could she keep the romance going? He was definitely the man for her. It was up to her to make the running.

★★★

John and Margaret didn't make contact for a couple of weeks. When they did meet again it was the result of an impromptu decision by

Margaret who took a chance on bumping into John at Brentford football ground.

It was a good decision. John never missed out on a home game. Since he had been a lad he had followed the fortunes of Brentford. Even when he had been at sea he had listened into the English football results on the BBC's World Service broadcasts. On this particular weekend Charlie was taking his eleven-year-old son Sam to the ground, and John would meet up with them there.

'Hullo mate!' Charlie exclaimed as John strode in about ten minutes after the game had started.

'Hullo, Chas.'

Charlie's young son Sam smiled his lovely childish smile at him. John tousled the boy's hair. He was very fond of him. 'How are you, young Sam? Who's winning?'

'Brentford! One-nil!' Sam exclaimed.

'And a mighty goal it was too,' Charlie added. 'It was a beautiful shot. From mid field right to the back of the net.'

'Good for them!' John said with delight. The crowd roared as the match built up to an exciting moment. After a few minutes of good attacking play the referee blew the whistle as an obvious foul had taken place. John, Charlie and Sam sat together like a family enjoying what to each of them was the greatest game of all.

The game progressed to a one-all equaliser and then Brentford came back with a superb goal created by the centre forward passing to another player who immediately took his chance by pocketing the ball in the left-hand side of the net. The look on the opposing team goalie's face was one of absolute despair.

'I told you, Johnny boy,' Charlie beamed with delight, 'Brentford are the future aristocrats of European soccer and FA Cup winners in the next ten years.'

This he sincerely believed. After all, years before, pundits had dismissed the hopes of such teams as Watford, Portsmouth and Brighton, only to find they had underestimated the capabilities of their players.

At half time John wandered out to the tea bar. He casually meandered along in the queue, then much to his astonishment someone tapped him on the shoulder.

'Hullo John,' a voice said.

He turned his head. An amazed smile spread across his face.

'Margaret! I can't believe it. You're not a Brentford supporter, are you?'

'Not really,' Margaret confessed.

The thought crossed John's mind: had she come here purely to see him?

'Are you pleased to see me, John?'

'Of course,' he replied.

'I'm not really a Brentford supporter. But my late Dad was.' There was a tone of nostalgia in her voice. 'He used to support Brentford when Jimmy Hill used to play for them.'

John at once realised Margaret was talking about the 1940s when the distinguished sports commentator had been a young player.

'Blimey!' he murmured in astonishment. 'That was a long time ago! Pterodactyls and dinosaurs roamed the earth then!' A considerable exaggeration, but John had been put slightly off his stride.

'I was hoping I'd bump into you here,' Margaret said, revealing the true purpose of her visit to the ground.

'Will you join me?' John asked. 'Of course you will. Come and meet my mate Charlie and his son Sam. Charlie's a lovely fellow.'

'I'd love to,' Margaret replied.

John led Margaret up to meet Charlie and Sam. Charlie beamed with positive delight at the sight of his friend's girlfriend. He was to say later on in a quiet moment to John that he had never seen such a splendid joint on two legs.

The romance was definitely back on. John and Margaret took up where they had left off. Margaret visited John's home for the first time and found she was enchanted by his constant companions General Gordon the boxer dog and Topie the tortoiseshell cat.

'So these are your faithful allies?' Margaret said, warming to his pets immediately.

'Do you think your cat would get on well with them?' John asked. The question was a gentle hint that something more important was about to be asked. 'I was wondering how you would feel about getting… getting…'

'Spit it out John, I can't stand the suspense!'

It was time for John to show some real confidence and authority. They sat across from each other in armchairs and John leaned forward. The look in his eyes was betraying his real feelings. Margaret could almost sense what he was about to say before he had even uttered a word.

'I've wanted you to love me from the start,' he admitted. 'I nearly lost the initiative last time. Look, let me put it this way. I'm an old bachelor. Well, not too old, I'm forty-one. I've got a business, I'm on a good income, I could look after you. The first time I saw you I just knew.' He looked at her longingly. This really was much harder than he had ever envisaged. 'What do you say? What do you think? Do you reckon we could make a go of it? A marriage? That's what I'm talking about. A good, old-fashioned, long-lasting, secure happy marriage.'

Margaret reached forward and slipped her hand into his. 'John, I'm flattered. I'm thrilled. I knew when I met the right man I wouldn't waste any time. And I'm not going to now. You're a good man, John. You've no airs or graces. Can I add something else?'

'Of course.'

'When I joined the dating agency, John, it wasn't out of sheer desperation for a man. I thought a computer match would be something different. I know it's crazy, but I just knew straight away that there was something good between us in the offing.'

Margaret hesitated and looked at him to see how well he was absorbing this. John looked on patiently. 'I do want marriage. And a baby.' There was more than a strong hint here that if they were to marry, John would be expected to deliver a baby with all the speed of the Pony Express travelling through Indian country.

'I'll do my best,' John reassured her.

'I've reached the age of forty, which for many women is more than just a half-way point in life. I'm a spinster, a bachelor girl, looking for love and companionship and a family life.'

John did not want to disturb the mood of the moment but a sudden thought entered his head. 'What about your career?'

'I could carry on. Or if you prefer I'd give it up completely.'

'I wouldn't want you to give it up,' John replied adamantly, knowing how much her career meant to her.

Margaret moved across and kissed him. John got up from his chair and they both sat down on a comfortable sofa.

'You're thoughtful too, John,' she said.

'You've spent a long time working your way up to where you are now. It would be selfish of me to ask you to give it up when we're... when we're married. Although obviously if we have a family – and I don't want to dwell on the subject too much – that would have to be sooner rather than later. This would mean you having to take time off to have the child and be with it during the early years.' He looked at her inquiringly. 'This is not a decision you may regret later on, is it?'

'I was never more certain. As for my career, family comes first. We'll work something out.'

This sounded like confirmation as far as John was concerned.

'So it's a deal, then? The marriage between a spinster and a bachelor is announced. The marriage between a butcher who owns his own business and a lady who works as a personnel and training officer for a top department store. I never dreamt I would ever find someone like you. I think I'm one of the luckiest fellows I know.'

Margaret threw her arms around him and kissed him. 'I'm the lucky one, John.' She held him so tightly that he thought she would never let go. 'I finally found a good man to take me on.'

John looked deeply into her eyes. His expression was one of pure joy: the pair of them had made the ultimate decision to marry.

Four weeks later John and Margaret were married at Ealing Congregational Church. It was a very small private function with only a few people in attendance.

Charlie, Jean and Sam looked on happily. Jean was in tears, for she knew John had undergone many intensely lonely years and now he had found someone who would surely bring him happiness. Charlie performed his role as best man with all the zest and wit of a North Country comedian appearing in a working man's club. He was so happy for his friend. What a smasher John had married! He hoped that John and Margaret would find happiness for many years to come.

Mary, who had vowed never to marry again after two broken marriages, was visibly moved by the ceremony. Perhaps she was remembering the reasons her two marriages failed. But maybe it was a feeling of joy for Margaret. Sometimes other people's happiness is a joy to behold, and Mary and Charlie, two completely giving selfless people, could only experience the same emotions. Both agreed that two very nice people had found the right partners.

4.

Gillian and Keith

The Second Timers

The effects of the 1991 recession could be seen everywhere in the High Street as Gillian Hodgson shopped for her family. The tabloid headlines seemed to scream: unemployment rises, more lay-offs, further economic downturn. As if the headlines weren't grim enough there were stores that had closed down; some of these were institutions which had fallen foul to the grimmest economic climate since the Great Depression of the 1930s. People in bus queues talked of their worries about holding onto their jobs and paying the mortgage. No one looked very happy, and to make matters worse it was a rainy, windswept day.

For Gillian Hodgson most of the past 20 years seemed to have been one long perpetual struggle. At 39 years of age she was a divorced mother of three children. Her face was kind and attractive but there was a look of tiredness and defeat about her, of one who had known much struggle and disappointment in life. There were hardly any signs of the laughing miniskirted girl she had once been.

Gillian was well wrapped up in a raincoat and a hood over her brown hair which concealed some of the premature grey strands that were beginning to show. Armed with shopping bags there was just one final destination — Sainsbury's, to buy the children their evening meal — and then she would gratefully board the bus to take her home.

Inside the store she practised her usual ritual of making the very little cash in her purse stretch beyond the limits of elasticity. Gillian chose her items carefully, only buying the things she knew that her children really liked. Along the frozen food counter the eyes of an attractive woman seemed to be studying her. Gillian looked back at the woman with an icy stare. Then with absolute amazement she found herself looking at an old classmate she had not seen in 23 years.

'Hullo! Remember me?' the old friend said to Gillian in a delighted, enthusiastic voice. 'I'm Lyn English from St Thomas's Comprehensive, just in case you've forgotten me!'

Gillian's face broke into a happy smile. After all these years, to think recognition was still possible. 'Of course! Class 5G. Back in 1968.'

Lyn walked up to her. The two of them embraced and looked at each other closely. They were a world apart now, though.

'Well! Who would have believed it? Gillian Sprake! After all these years. It doesn't seem that long ago you and I were playing in the netball and hockey teams at school.'

Gillian smiled at the name her friend remembered her by. 'Sprake was my maiden name. It's Gillian Hodgson now, my married name.'

Lyn glanced at her watch. Then she studiously observed the tell-tale lines of her friend's face.

'Look, Gillian. Have you got time for a coffee? I'd love to talk about old times and what you've been doing all these years.'

'Well…' Gillian was deliberately apprehensive. 'I don't think you'll find me all that interesting these days.'

Lyn was intuitive enough to realise that life had not been beer and skittles for her school friend. But there were happier times to recall. 'Come on, Gill,' she said warmly. 'I'll treat you.'

Gilliam and Lyn found a nearby coffee shop. Together they sat down at a table and reacquainted themselves with one another. Almost from the first moment of their meeting, each had sensed that the other had lived a life totally the opposite to their own. It was something of an understatement to say the contrast between the two ladies could not have been more marked. Lyn looked considerably younger than her 39 years. There was hardly a line or a sign that made her look a day over 30. Gillian was looking her age plus five years, and Lyn was observant enough to notice this; she was also courteous enough not to mention it. Lyn had a prosperous air about her, whereas Gillian had the appearance of one who had not known too many of the good things in life.

It took a while for the two to start talking in the manner that old friends do. At first they spoke about the weather, what a tough year 1991 had been, and the things they had piled high in their shopping bags.

Gillian had not really wanted to speak too much of her own life but her curiosity about her friend got the better of her and she began to steer the conservation rather reluctantly to a more personal level.

'So, where are you living these days, Lyn? What are you doing?'

'As you probably know, I married Malcolm English from school,' Lyn replied in a tone of enthusiasm.

'I remember. He was head boy. And you were head girl.'

'That's right! You do have a good memory, Gill.'

'I used to read the *Northford County Times* every week, especially in 1973 when we were all turning twenty-one. I was curious to see in the weekly wedding photo column which of our old school friends were getting married. I remember seeing your wedding day photo in the paper. To tell you the truth, I always thought you and Malcolm would get married.'

'We had a lovely wedding at Northford Village Church. A lot of old school friends were there. We had bagpipes, a great reception, and a honeymoon in a relative's cottage in Findon by the Sussex Downs. It rained all the time but we were like children, sliding down the hill in the mud and feeding the horses.'

Gillian looked slightly downcast. Her own marriage and honeymoon did not have such romantic memories attached. However, she attempted a smile and tried to change the subject matter of the conversation.

'Are you working, Lyn?'

'Yes. I worked as a laboratory assistant until I had time off to have my two boys. Timothy, he's fifteen now. And Robert is twelve. Malcolm is a company director for Laurelson, that's the engineering company in Slough. When I went back to work I took a computer programming course and I've been doing that ever since. We've been living in Pinner for some time.' Gillian was slow to respond in talking about herself. Lyn prompted her. 'And you?'

'Oh, me...' Gillian was most hesitant. She knew the subject could no longer be avoided. 'I got married in 1971. I was only nineteen and it was something of a shotgun wedding. Too young. It didn't work, we got divorced. It's been a battle ever since.'

'Sad,' said Lyn. There was a pause as she absorbed Gillian's words. 'Any children?' she asked.

'Yes. Three.' The smile returned to Gillian's face. Her children were the reason she lived and breathed. 'The oldest is nineteen, the same age as me when I got married. The others are eighteen and seventeen. I brought them up virtually on my own. Until I got on the housing list and got a council house it was nearly all rented rooms and back of the house flats. I've never lived in a house of my own, never had a mortgage. As for work, I had little or no help from my ex-husband. He went abroad to live after our divorce and the maintenance cheques were spasmodic, so a career was out. I had to fend for my family on my own. I did part-time jobs, temporary jobs, factory jobs, cleaning jobs. You name it, I did it. I had no choice, though.'

Lyn was subdued but very sympathetic. 'You may find this hard to believe, but I admire you.' Lyn had spoken with emphasis and it was hard to doubt her sincerity. 'I don't envy you, but I do admire you battling it out the way you have done.'

Gillian was warmed by her honesty and warm words. 'I really had no choice, Lyn.'

'I have to admit that so far in my life I've been lucky,' Lyn said in contemplation, taking a sip of coffee. Her eyes showed warmth and compassion. Although her lot in life had been good, Lyn was not averse to understanding the difficulties others faced. 'When I look at other people around me and see how much unhappiness there is in the world I never complain or grumble. I've no reason to. I think when you're young and naïve there's this feeling that life is a fairytale and there'll always be a happy ending, but the truth of it is that it's a battle for most people. Some are born to drift easily through without ever having any hassles. Others – well, like yourself – they're fighters.'

'There are a lot of them about too. Single parents, divorced mums, divorced dads. People working all hours for their families. Disabled and handicapped people. All trying to make a decent, normal, happy life for themselves. I've never had any savings or money in the bank. My whole life has been a case of getting by, just getting through, making do with what I've got, which is very little. I've still got my pride though, pride in my children, pride in that I look after them and do my best.'

Lyn added a further compliment of her own. 'And you've got strength, an inner strength.'

Gillian smiled and touched Lyn's hand. 'If that's all I've gained since I left school then maybe it's been worthwhile.'

The two ladies had a long chat that afternoon. They covered a lot of old ground and revived a few old memories of times gone by. In the space of an hour or so all the years fell away. At the end of their reunion they walked along to their separate bus stops. A double decker bus pulled up and Gillian joined the queue.

'It's been wonderful to see you again, Lyn,' she said wrapping her arms around her in a warm embrace.

'Now you know where we are, Gill, make sure you come round and see us.'

'I will.'

Gillian picked up her shopping bags and boarded the bus. They each looked at the other in deep fondness. The passage of life had treated them so differently. Lyn stood there wondering why life for some people was so good, and why for others it treated them so unfairly. She did not realise it, but of the two of them, for all her struggles Gillian's life had been far more interesting than her own.

★★★

Gillian returned home to her modest council house. Before entering she stood outside looking at the cracked paintwork and some of the chipped brickwork. I really must do something about that, thought Gillian. The next time she made out her shopping list some paint brushes and a pot of emulsion would have to be included. Her budget was always being stretched, despite careful planning.

While she prepared the evening meal for her children Gillian's thoughts began to drift. It was so nice seeing Lyn again, but it was also extremely sad. Lyn could look back on her years since leaving school with much satisfaction. Gillian felt that so many personal battles after the divorce had robbed her of utilising all the potential she had. It troubled her that she hadn't been able to achieve all that she might have done.

Bringing up a family and running a home was one thing; it was a much underestimated task. But now that the children were in their teens there was the rest of her life to consider. The thought that she might marry again had often passed through her mind. Since divorcing her husband Terry there had been no one. She did not know what it would be like to love again. One thing she felt absolutely certain about was if she ever found a man willing to take her on, love would be returned threefold. There was also the question of work. Did she want to spend the rest of her life like a domestic servant, scrubbing floors and greasy, uncleanable ovens, and wiping round other people's toilet bowls? It was time to find real work. Another thing that bothered her was the council estate she lived on. For most of her life she had lived in grubby conditions, it seemed.

This estate was not like the one she had been brought up on. Her childhood and youth had been spent on one of the first post-war council estates to be built. That one had been erected on the site of a former racecourse. Almost every street and cul-de-sac on that estate had been given the name of a famous racecourse somewhere in the world: there was Happy Valley Close, named after the one in Hong Kong; Randwick Crescent after Sydney's famous track; Flemington Crescent from the track where the famous Melbourne Cup was run; and then there were others: Kentucky Derby Avenue, Les Landes Lane, Curragh Crescent, Epsom Avenue, Kempton Close, Aintree Road and Chelmsford Way. In her youth the children had been precocious, energetic, cheeky, wild and freewheeling, but here now the environment was violent and dangerous.

Gillian yearned to move away from this area of rundown council houses and huge tower blocks where joyriding, mugging – even of the elderly and infirm – and drug dealing were a way of life. She had done her best to protect her children from the unpleasantness that surrounded her. By involving them in sporting clubs, making them study hard and conscientiously vetting their friends she had succeeded. But she could not be their mother protector all the time and sooner or later, if they weren't already, they would have to learn to be streetwise. It was a hard, aggressive and highly competitive world that her children were growing up in, unlike the days of the swinging sixties when it seemed that the fruits of life were available to all who tried and worked hard. Like good mothers everywhere, she wanted the best for them and prayed that they would not make similar mistakes to those she had made as a youngster.

Women like Gillian were of a special breed. They may have been raised in the decades of the 1950s and 1960s, but like women throughout the ages, when luck and good fortune deserted them, they were solid, reliable, plucky battlers who lived for the good of their families. Gillian did not blame anyone for the hardships of her life. Her life was separate from other people's. She did not envy anyone, nor was she jealous. The sole purpose of her existence was to provide for and guide her children.

At the dinner table that night sat her children. There was Samantha, now nineteen, glowing, blossoming and resembling her father more strongly. Then there were her sons, 18-year-old Mark, and John who was 17. Gillian looked at them in adoration. Her boys had grown up to be polite, well-mannered and aware that life could only give back the rewards if the efforts were made, and that despite the promise of roses at the end of the road there would be many disappointments en route.

'Guess what?' Gillian said suddenly. The others looked at each other. It was John who responded.

'What Mum?'

'You'll never guess,' Gillian said almost excitedly. 'I was shopping for tea when I saw this lady looking at me strangely by the frozen food counter, and I stared straight back at her. Would you believe it, she and I used to go to school together!'

'Really?' Mark said in surprise.

'Really. I've not seen her since 1968.'

John was also surprised. 'And she recognised you?'

'Yes,' Gillian spoke softly. 'She had hardly changed.' Her tone sounded slightly regretful. 'Unlike me. She did very well in life. Still married to a boy she met at school. She was a lovely girl at that time, now she's grown into a smashing lady. It was so nice to see her.' She noticed Samantha was looking a little thoughtful and appeared reticent. 'Are you alright Samantha? You're quiet tonight.'

Samantha looked up and made an attempt at a smile. 'I'm alright,' she uttered in a meek tone.

It sounded very unconvincing. Gillian suspected something was wrong but carried on the conversation. 'I must get out the photograph album and the old school magazines tonight. It will be interesting to see how we've both changed.'

Memories when stirred bring back so many things: laughter, tears, nostalgia for those relatives who once laughed around the Christmas dinner table who are no longer with us, the thoughts of old friends and where they might be today, the regrets about hopes and aspirations that never quite materialised. So it was with Gillian as she sat on the lounge settee that night looking through old memorabilia.

The television was turned down low so that Cilla Black appeared to be miming in the manner of Marcel Marceau. There was a time not so long ago when both she and Cilla Black were that much younger. Gillian looked through her photograph album of times gone by. There were black and white photographs of her taken on childhood holidays at Butlins and Warners camps, at seaside resorts from Clacton to Bognor. Various school photographs showed her as a teenage hockey player, playing netball, and with the rest of class 5G in 1968. She looked at one of herself as a youngster in a miniskirt. Who was that girl with the lovely slim figure? Surely it could not have been me, thought Gillian. Then she stopped and paused over her wedding photographs. It was a Register Office wedding. Her eyes were sad at the sight of these memories. She closed the book and put it to one side. Must not dwell on the past, she told herself.

From behind, Samantha entered the room cautiously and quietly, then stood as if she was about to make an announcement. Samantha steeled herself.

'Mum.' Her voice was quiet. Her manner was cold. There was a look of fear in her eyes.

Gillian turned around to face her daughter. She recognised the look of apprehension on Samantha's face. 'What is it, Sam?'

'Mum. I've got something to tell you.' She took a deep breath and gulped. 'I've been to the doctor.'

Gillian stood up straight away and went across to her daughter. She was ashen-faced and when she spoke there was a tremor in her voice. 'Samantha. Are you… alright?'

Samantha lowered her head almost in shame. After a moment she raised her eyes to meet her mother's.

Almost at once Gillian realised just what it was her daughter was about to tell her. 'No. You're not…?'

Samantha nodded her head sadly.

Gillian was devastated. 'Oh no! This is history repeating itself!'

'Oh, Mum. I'm so sorry.'

Gillian was close to tears but with all the will power in the world she didn't let them fall. 'How many weeks are you?'

'About twelve.'

'Twelve!' Gillian looked thunderstruck. 'Sam, why couldn't you have been more careful? I wanted so much for you to complete your time at college and go on to university.' Her voice sounded full of frustration and anguish. 'I didn't want you tied down to motherhood at an early age like I was, stuck in an unhappy marriage like your Dad and I were.' She stopped and looked hard at her daughter. 'Who's the father?'

'Barry.'

'Barry?' Gillian remembered meeting a gangling youth that Samantha had brought home. Surely it wasn't him. 'You mean that boy who came home from college with you one night?'

'Yes.'

He was the one least likely to be, thought Gillian. Barry was no teenage romeo. It was all too much for Gillian. Her anger began to surface.

'All those years I spent taking dreadful, menial jobs to get you and the boys off to a good start in life! Look at me!' Gillian could scarcely conceal her feelings. 'Look at me, Samantha! I was brought up on a council estate, and because of the circumstances of my life — divorce, your Dad not giving me the help I needed — I've had to bring you up on my own with barely enough money to get us through each week.'

Samantha started to cry. Gillian reached over and hugged her tightly. She realised her anger had swamped her now.

'Samantha. Come on. I'm sorry I exploded. Come on, Sam. Get a grip on yourself.' An afterthought suddenly occurred to her. 'Do the boys know? You haven't told your brothers have you?'

'No. Not yet.'

'They'll have to know of course, but not just yet.' Gillian's eyes were red and strained from withholding the tears she would shed later. 'Look, darling. I'm tired, I'm upset, I'm not thinking straight. And I'm very confused. You look tired and worried yourself. We both need a good night's sleep. We'll talk about it tomorrow. Go and get some sleep.'

Samantha turned to walk away.

'Sam?'

'Yes Mum?' she replied, turning around and revealing a hangdog look.

'Samantha, I want you to know I'm still your mother. I love you and I'll stand by you whatever happens.'

Samantha tried to force a smile. It was a miserable attempt though.

★★★

Terry Hodgson woke early in his bungalow in a pleasant suburb of Cape Town. The telephone was ringing and it was still only 5.30 a.m. Who on earth could this be? He looked at his sleeping wife Lissan next to him. That one could sleep through an earthquake or a rock concert. Reluctantly he rose from the bed, put a towel around his waist and walked past the children's bedrooms, gazing in at them to see if they were alright. He smiled at the sight of his son and daughter. They made him feel so proud to be a father.

In the lounge he picked up the telephone receiver. The moment the voice came over the line he realised the call was from England. He listened intently as the caller gave him very sad news. His heart seemed to stop for a moment as he absorbed the details. By the time he had finished taking the call his eyes brimmed with tears. He sat in an easy chair for ages, numbed by what he had heard. All he could do was sit and stare.

Lissan came into the lounge quietly and looked at her husband, who was unaware of her presence. She was a Dutch-born South African girl with model looks, long blonde hair and a golden tan. She was a born-again Christian.

'What's wrong, Terry?' she asked gently putting her tender hands on his shoulder. Terry squeezed her hand lovingly. 'I heard you speaking on the phone.'

'I've got to go back. Back to England for a while.'

'Why, darling?' Lissan asked, sitting casually on his knee. She noticed the tear stains on his face and fingered his cheeks. 'You've been crying. What's wrong?'

Terry explained. 'That was Aunt Bede's next door neighbour. Aunt Bede was out in the garden yesterday when she keeled over and died from a heart attack.'

Lissan hugged him. 'My darling, I am so sorry,' she said, running her fingers through his hair. 'I know how much she meant to you.'

'Yes. She was a wonderful old girl. I owe her a great deal. After my parents were killed in a car crash she brought me up. She didn't have to, but I got an awful lot of love from her.'

'What will you do now?'

'I must go back and pay my final respects to her. There's the estate to sort out as well.' He looked at her lovingly. 'Do you mind if I leave you and the children for a few weeks?'

'Of course not, but I shall miss you terribly.'

'I won't stay any longer than I have to.'

For a moment they sat with their arms around each other. Lissan, who was about five years younger than Terry, was madly in love with him. She was affectionate and loving. He constantly marvelled at his luck in meeting her and making her his second wife.

'There's something else I must do while I am in England,' he said with an edge of concern.

Lissan knew instinctively what this was. 'You are going to see your first wife and children.'

'I'd dearly like to,' Terry replied almost defensively.

'You must see them,' Lissan emphasised. She was wiser and more compassionate than her husband realised. 'I know the pain you went through when your marriage broke up. I know you pine for your children too. Every time Samantha sends you a letter and photograph your eyes light up. It's been years since you've seen them. Make the most of this opportunity, Terry. At least Bede came here to see us and we all had happy times together. It's your children you have to talk to, get to know them again.'

'And Gillian too. I've felt dreadful, almost disgusted with myself that I didn't give her more help, that I wasn't able to.'

'Then see her, Terry. Talk to her, but come back soon to me.'

Terry put his arms around her and gave her a long passionate kiss. 'I love you so much, Lissan. I was so lucky when I married you.' He ruffled her nightdress as he hugged her tightly to his bare chest. The warmth and love he knew from this woman was worth more than gold.

He went into work at his office that morning and explained the position to his supervisors. Understanding the importance attached to his request they immediately granted him several weeks leave and advanced him his salary. That same day Terry went to the South African Airways office in Cape Town to book his flight home.

Later that night Terry said a tearful farewell to Lissan and the children. He boarded the jumbo jet with mixed emotions. He had not been home in 13 years. The engines began to throb. The sign requesting passengers to fasten their seatbelts flashed up above the aisles. Going home, I'm going home, he thought. Back to the land of green rectangular fields and red buses, of lukewarm bitter and regional accents, to the land where Cup Finals were played at Wembley and Hampden Park. He suddenly felt a surge of excitement within him. After all these years, he would be seeing Gillian and the children soon. He asked himself how they would greet him.

★★★

Gillian could not sleep. No matter how she tried, her anxiety and worry got the better of her. Samantha's pregnancy had come as a shock to her. It was also a bitter blow. Gillian had invested such high hopes in Samantha, she had wanted so much for her to have a good career. But now the birth of a child would alter the passage of her life.

After the years Gillian had scraped and scrimped to give her children a good start in life, she felt as if she had been betrayed. An old saying she had once heard came into her head: 'when daughters grow up, they always break your heart'. Samantha had certainly done that. She had made the same mistake as her mum, who had paid for it over and over again. Yet she loved Samantha with all her heart.

In this day and age single parents were not outcasts from society as had been the case in previous generations. They still faced difficulties. The problems of the past were an ongoing thing. Time had not erased the age old uphill battles faced by unwed parents. An even more terrifying thought entered Gillian's head. Would Samantha marry that loud, brash youth with the manners of a thug, called Barry? It angered her that Samantha had become involved with this young man. She knew that it was impossible to control every facet of her children's lives. God knows she had tried. The pain took over and the tears began to fall.

Life had seemed to be so romantic back in 1968 when Gillian was a 16-year-old schoolgirl sitting in a class of 30 other girls and boys. The 1960s were a sparkling, changing, lively decade remembered with much nostalgia by those who were young then; it was also a much-criticised period which sociologists related with the permissive society and the breakdown of family life. There was no doubt that it was an exciting time to be young. It was an era of change and innovation.

The beginning of the 1960s saw the Russian Cosmonaut Yuri Gagarin become the first man in space. On the 21st July 1969 the American Neil Armstrong gained immortality by becoming the first astronaut to walk on the moon's surface. In the years between, the newspaper headlines were filled with the details of the working class heroes who had risen from the back streets to live in millionaire mansions. The airwaves were filled with the music of the Beatles, the Rolling Stones, Donovan, Dylan, Baez, Cream, Procol Harum, to name just a few. In the sport of boxing there were champions such as Cassius Clay, Joe Frazier, Ernie Terrel, Henry Cooper and Brian London. All over the world, girls tried to emulate the immensely popular models, Jean Shrimpton and someone called Lesley Hornby who found fame as Twiggy. Football produced some of its greatest ever players: Jimmy Greaves, Denis Law, Geoff Hurst, Bobby Moore, Jackie and Bobby Charlton, Georgie Best and Alan Ball. Yes, it was an exciting time.

In the classroom Gillian would often sit staring at the expanse of the blackboard. Her mind was never quite on her studies. At the back of the class, while the lecture was taking place often her mind would be on other things. She would normally be glancing through a magazine. The years had passed but the memories stayed strong.

One occasion sprang to mind as Gillian lay in bed thinking back over the years. Gillian recalled a particular afternoon which must have been a few months before the O-level examinations in 1968. The geography teacher was a grey-haired man, probably then in his late forties. He spoke of the diminishing British influence overseas. Gillian was not really interested in the geography lesson. She quietly sat at the back of the classroom reading a magazine called *Romance* while the teacher droned on. His eyes were sharp and he kept watch for those who weren't paying attention.

'Many countries that were once part of the Commonwealth and perhaps what were once pointedly referred to as the Dominions have broken away from British rule. India gained its independence in 1948 after a long struggle. Does anyone know who the last Viceroy of India was?' He looked around the class. No one seemed to know. His gaze fell on Gillian, who suddenly realised his eyes were studying her. Gillian closed the magazine in embarrassment. The teacher walked down to see what she was reading. 'Perhaps Gillian can tell us. Who was the last Viceroy of India, Gillian?'

'I wasn't listening, sir,' she stated honestly but shamefacedly.

'I can see that!' the teacher snapped in annoyance. He took the copy of *Romance* that Gillian had been reading. 'Read these magazines in your own time. Concentrate on your studies or you won't pass your CSE let alone your O-levels.' The teacher walked to the front of the class and continued the lesson. Gillian blushed in embarrassment at being singled out. 'The last Viceroy of India,' continued the teacher, 'was Lord Mountbatten. Lord Mountbatten of Burma.'

It was in sporting activities and athletics that Gillian really excelled. She always entered into the spirit of these events with great enthusiasm. Had she received encouragement and a strong guiding hand by a firm, disciplined trainer there would have been no doubt that within her lay the courage and stamina of someone who could have gone on to represent her country at Olympic standard. Sadly her talent and potential in this area was never quite tested to yield all that it could have done.

In the 1968 school sport's day Gillian came first for her house team of St David in several track events, which included the 100 yards, 220, 440 and the mile. She always ran with fury and pace, pushing her chest forward as she pounded through the tape. In sports shorts and top she was already developing signs of the fine-looking young woman she would become.

At 16 she was an all-round athlete. On the netball court she would weave in and out of her opponents, dodging and manoeuvring the ball, finally leaping up and placing it squarely in the net. In the game of hockey she was a fast and skilful player.

The school examinations that year were hard for all concerned. Most of the pupils had tried hard to revise, but as with every exam it was almost impossible to predict just what the questions would be. Seated at a single desk, as were all the other pupils, Gillian made a valiant effort to complete her O-level papers. She was confused and baffled. Looking around her she could see that quite a few others wore pained expressions. One of them was a tall, brown-haired boy called Peter who had a crush on her. The two of them smiled at each other.

Every year a dance was held for the fifth formers. The year 1968 was no exception. The hall, which was normally used for assemblies, was filled with 16-year-olds dancing to a group on stage formed by their class mates. It was a four-piece group comprising a lead guitarist, a bass guitarist, a keyboard player and a drummer. There was also a turntable, and they played many of the records of the time, such as 'Dock of the Bay', 'Knock on Wood', 'Honey' and 'A Whiter Shade of Pale'.

Gillian stood at the back of the hall talking to a girl called Shirley, when Peter walked in.

'Peter is on his own I see,' Gillian said in almost a whisper.

'Do you like him?' Shirley asked observantly.

'I think he likes me. He seems alright. I wish he'd ask me to dance.'

'Obviously you do,' Shirley smiled at her. 'Do you want me to ask him?' Gillian nodded shyly. 'Right. Just wait here.'

Gillian watched nervously as Shirley went across to Peter. She looked on as the two spoke. Peter pointed to himself in surprise. He meekly complied with the request and came across to her. The band had finished their number on stage. Someone had put a slow record on the turntable, 'The Last Waltz' by Engelbert Humperdinck.

'You want to dance with me, Gillian?' Peter asked her shyly, in a voice betraying obvious surprise she would even consider the possibility of it.

'I'd love to,' replied Gillian with a mischievous smile.

Peter nervously took her in his arms and they began to dance, a little clumsily at first as did most of the couples on the dance floor, but they soon got into the swing of it.

'You're the first girl I have ever asked to dance,' Peter said, struggling to find a way of making conversation.

Gillian smiled warmly at him which made Peter feel even more nervous. Peter was approaching 6 feet in height and towered over Gillian by about 5 inches. He was genuinely nervous, definitely shy; typical perhaps of his adolescence. But he felt thrilled to be holding Gillian. Since they had both started at St Thomas's Comprehensive, Peter had always had a crush on her. He enjoyed the feel of her soft hands and the scent in her luxurious brown hair that was cut in a sort of page-boy style. Gillian's brown eyes were soft and sensitive, but could change expression so that they twinkled with good humour or gazed at a person with compassion and understanding. It was hard not to fall in love with her at first sight. She was capable of appearing vulnerable, yet fun to be with.

'Have you got a job to go to when you leave school?' Gillian asked suddenly.

'No. Not yet,' Peter replied. He felt slightly more relaxed with her now. 'Depends how I get on with my O-levels, if I pass any at all.'

Peter often gave away his lack of self-confidence and occasionally there surfaced signs of a deep inferiority complex. But if these things showed themselves in him as a 16-year-old they were never to be found in him as an adult, for in the years to come he was to travel more widely and adventurously than any of his classmates could ever have predicted. Here, dancing with him now, Gillian saw only a rather shy boy who had long had a crush on her. When they both left school neither of them ever met again, although Peter would remember her for the rest of his life with warmth.

'I've got a job,' Gillian said proudly. 'I'll be starting work as a typist-secretary with a record company.'

'Good luck!' Peter wished her.

'Thanks,' replied Gillian. 'Have you got any idea what you'd like to do?'

The music stopped. There was a pause between dances and the pair sat down together.

'I don't know yet,' Peter said honestly. He looked at this lovely girl beside him. He felt comfortable with her and began to talk freely. 'My Dad says I should get a trade behind me. I don't know what I'd do though. I'm not an academic. I like English, art and woodwork but I'm not too good at anything else.'

'You'll find something,' Gillian said encouragingly.

'I expect I will in time.' Now he had found a willing audience, he told her of his hopes. 'I know I'd like to travel.'

'Travel!' This was interesting. 'Where would you like to go?'

Peter replied without hesitation. 'The Pacific, down under, the Far East. I always watch *Whicker's World* on television.' He obviously had firm intentions. 'I don't just want to grow up and get into a routine. I want to do something with my life.'

Gillian gazed deep into the eyes of this 16-year-old. 'You're a dreamer,' she said, not meaning to be offensive. 'But a nice dreamer.'

'Maybe I am,' said Peter with a smile. And you're beautiful and lovely he thought to himself. You're also very nice, he added in his thoughts. The only problem was, he didn't have the courage to tell her.

★★★

It was in 1970, a couple of years or so after leaving school, that Gillian met the young man who would be prominent in her life. Frequently at the office Gillian was asked to work overtime. The extra money came in useful. Besides, she was a very conscientious and industrious worker with a good eye for detail. Gillian enjoyed the job and she had made some good friends amongst the staff. One of these was a girl called Wendy. The often worked until eight or nine o'clock at night and would travel home together.

Wendy was a tall and happy girl with a very scatty sense of humour.

She was rarely serious and was always good fun to be with. She was about a year older than Gillian. Her clothes were fashionable; whatever was new she would be wearing it: hats, miniskirts, hot pants, two-piece flared floral trouser suits, extravagant flowing dresses, sandals, beads, flowers in her hair, she would wear them all at some stage. Men adored her and gravitated towards her, although she had the strength of personality not to lead any of them, on while always being polite.

'Eight o'clock Gill,' Wendy announced. 'Overtime's over. Time to go home.'

'Whoopee!' exclaimed Gillian.

'And that's it for this week.' Wendy put the cover on her typewriter and started to put her coat on. 'You were nineteen last week, weren't you?'

'Yes. I had a nice little party with Mum and Dad and my brother last Saturday.'

'Would you like to come out tomorrow with me and a couple of girlfriends?' Wendy made a show of whispering. 'We're all looking for boyfriends!'

Gillian's eyes sparkled with delight. 'Sounds good. Where are you going?'

'I've heard glowing reports of King's Road. We thought we'd kick off at the Trafalgar and move on to the Chelsea Potter and then later on to the Chelsea Drugstore. What do you think? Are you with us?'

'Count me in, Wendy!' Gillian said excitedly.

'Seven-thirty at Sloane Square Station. See you there,' Wendy instructed her. King's Road, Chelsea. What a venue for Saturday nights in 1970.

It was a typical girl's night out, with four happy young females seeking some excitement. Gillian and Wendy, looking exceedingly glamorous, toured Chelsea that night with two other lively girls called Penelope and Amanda. By the time they arrived at the Chelsea Drugstore it was late on Saturday night and the dance floor was lively and colourful.

In a discotheque atmosphere a disc jockey was playing records such as 'Jumpin' Jack Flash' by the Rolling Stones, 'Back Come Back' by the Equals, 'With a Little Help from My Friends' by Joe Cocker, and 'Baby Now that I've Found You' by the Foundations. A lot of mini-skirted girls were dancing with young men in the flared trousers and colourful shirts typical of the 1960s and early 1970s era. In other parts of the room girls and males eyed each other up studiously, occasionally taking a sip of their drinks.

Gillian and Wendy together with Penelope and Amanda stood

nervously waiting around for something to happen. The discotheque floor was crowded and there was a mixed aroma of lotions in the air. It was possible to scent hairspray, eau de cologne, perfume and anti-perspirant all at the same time. A lot of people were going to a great deal of trouble to impress the opposite sex that night.

The four girls didn't know it but they were the star attraction that night. They were so immersed in themselves they were hardly aware that young eligible men circled them like wolves ready to pounce. Amanda and Penelope were 19 and 20, respectively. Penelope was a 5 feet 2 inches tall girl who could break out into constant giggles and outbreaks of laughter which only an earthquake could stop. She wore hot pants, a pair of cowboy boots and a cap that covered her blonde hair. Penelope was a friend of Wendy's who lived in Fulham. Amanda was their mutual friend but her background was very different. She was an ex-Rodean pupil and while working at a trendy riverside café at Eel Pie Island she studied at the University of London. Her attire made her appear to be the hippy of the group, as Amanda wore a long flowing dress, sandals, an Indian headband and braiding in her hair.

'What are you all drinking?' she asked her friends suddenly.

'Mine is a Bacardi and Coke,' replied Gillian, who was enjoying every minute of being in a King's Road discotheque.

'I'll surprise you, Amanda,' said Wendy. 'Make mine a lager and lime.'

Amanda turned to Penelope. 'And last but not least, what about our young friend?'

'I'll have a Strawberry Blonde please, Amanda,' Penelope said with a giggle.

'Careful Penelope!' Amanda admonished her with a smile. 'Too many of those and you'll be so wild on the dance floor we'll have to carry you off.'

'That's right, I almost forgot to tell you Gill,' Wendy added, 'you should see Penelope when she gets going. The bosenova, the twist, the funky chicken, the make it up as you go along and hope for the best… she's a right little raver!'

'You're embarrassing me!' Penelope protested blushing and giggling at the same time.

Amanda checked the drinks order again. 'Right. So that's a Bacardi and Coke for Gill, a lager and lime for Wendy, a Strawberry Blonde – and a definite hangover for Penelope! And mine is a champagne and orange. I shall return in due course ladies.'

The supremely self-confident Amanda turned around and walked through the revellers on the dance floor towards the bar. A number of male heads turned at the sight of this very pretty young girl. Almost as if they had been ordered to do so by royal command the young men stood to one side to let her pass. Such was her presence that even without her saying a single word people responded to Amanda.

It was then that Gillian first set eyes on Terry Hodgson. Amanda had parted the dancers, and on the other side of the room stood three young men. Gillian's eyes shone in admiration at the warm smile which came from one of them. He was a little taller than her. He had long hair, typical of the time, but he was tidy and well dressed.

On the other side of the room Terry Hodgson looked at this lovely girl trying to bring himself to ask her to dance.

'Nice looking dollies aren't they?' remarked his friend Ray.

The other friend, whose name was Ken, piped up, 'The question is, how do we get to meet them?'

Terry looked across at Gillian, who stared back admiringly. For Terry there was suddenly no one else in the room. It was as if he and Gillian were the only people there. The moment was one that they would both remember the rest of their days. That first sighting of the person they would one day marry. For richer or poorer, in sickness and in health.

Gillian appeared vulnerable, sweet, warm and attractive. Through some hidden magnetic power Terry felt himself drawn to her. Was it the fact that across the room there was a young woman who combined the appearance of being safe, yet sexually alluring? It was remarkable. This was love at first sight.

Terry would have been dumbfounded had he known that Gillian was thinking the same way. Gillian's eyes sparkled, they shone in fact, at the sight of this slim young man with warmth and geniality in his face. Now this was a man she would feel proud to be seen with.

'Let's not do these things by halves, lad,' Terry said anxiously. He was thrilled at the sight of Gillian. Before the end of the night he was going to get to know this girl. 'You two can fight over the other three. I want to meet that one with the brown hair. She's a gorgeous little thing.'

'Well, that's Terry sorted out,' conceded Ray. 'There's three stunning looking birds left over, Ken. How do we get started? I'm not very good at chat-up lines. We get one and a half girls each!'

Terry watched as Amanda returned to the girls carrying a tray of drinks. There was no more time to be lost.

'Ever heard the motto, "he who dares wins"?' Terry asked. 'Well I have. Let's go, Ken. Come on, Ray. Let's not be bashful, we might be exactly what they're looking for!'

'You'll win a price for self-confidence,' said Ken with a laugh. 'You're the leader Terry. Let's get this show on the road! Come on lads, the girls are panting for us!'

At once Terry, Ken and Ray walked across the room in an attempt to meet the girls. In their brash display of make-believe confidence they strode through the dancers in the manner of three gunslingers heading for a shoot-out at the OK Corral. Wendy was quick to spot them.

'Prepare yourselves, girls!' Wendy warned them. 'We've got company.'

Terry, Ken and Ray moved in. Penelope enjoyed every minute of watching the three young men nervously brace themselves and rehearse their big minute.

'Have you come to chat us up?' Penelope asked with a giggle.

'That's the general idea,' Ken responded with a smile. 'I'm Ken.' He introduced his friends. 'This is Ray and that's Terry.'

'I'm Penelope!' And then she burst out into more fits of giggles.

'Don't mind her,' laughed Wendy. 'Penelope would laugh at anything. I'm Wendy.'

'I'm Amanda,' the next one in line said. 'That's three down. One to go!'

'I'm Gillian.' Her eyes met Terry's. The attraction between the two was apparent for all to behold. Terry cut out the introductions and immediately got down to business.

'Would you like to dance, Gillian?'

Her response was equally swift. 'Don't let me stop you,' she replied, placing her drink on the nearest table. To the fascination of the others, within a few seconds of meeting, Gillian and Terry headed out onto the dance floor.

That night in 1970 would always have a warm feeling attached to it for both of them. Surprising, when considering how events would turn out. But as they danced happily together they were in the initial stages of a romance that would change the course of both their lives. Had Amanda not gone up to the bar to buy a round of drinks and made a pathway through the crowd, Terry might never have set eyes on her. It was a point to remember in later years.

The records that they danced to in the Chelsea Drugstore that night they would always remember. 'Mighty Quinn' by Manfred Mann, 'Those Were the Days' by Mary Hopkin, and rather symbolically, but not prophetically, 'Let the Heartaches Begin' by Long John Baldry. The pair of them were only 19. They were too young to know the difference between love and infatuation.

When the slow dance numbers were played, Gillian seemed to melt into Terry's arms. He was experiencing the same feelings that her first dancing partner had felt two years before, when Gillian was a pupil at St Thomas's Comprehensive School. Terry felt warm and happy holding her. He took advantage of the moment and the mood in a pause between records. While the disc jockey changed the record on the turntable, Terry and Gillian stood together on the dance floor.

'Would you like to come out sometime?' He asked her softly, feeling confident that the answer could only be a positive one.

'Yes. I'd like to, Terry. When?'

The use of his first name encouraged him all the more. 'How about next Saturday? I thought perhaps we could go to the pictures in the afternoon and for a meal afterwards.'

Gillian was enthusiastic but she didn't want to give away too much by appearing to be over-eager... even if she was. She just nodded and smiled.

Terry excitedly suggested a movie that had just been generally released. 'Have you seen Mick Jagger in *Ned Kelly*?'

'No. I'd like to see that.'

'Alright, we'll see that then.'

Another record sounded out from the turntable. It was called 'Everlasting Love' by a group called the Love Affair. Gillian and Terry began to dance.

★★★

Terry Hodgson was a young man of contradicting characteristics of personality. He was very much a jack-the-lad character. Terry was always on the look-out for fun and usually found it. He had lived with his Aunt Bede since he was 13, his parents having been killed in a car crash. At home with his aunt he was quiet, considerate and well-mannered. He had to be. His Aunt Bede was a fiery spinster who made it clear to him that the orderly life she lived was not to be disrupted. So at home he behaved like a saint, and outside he was a roisterer and a good-time boy.

It was difficult for anyone not to like Terry. He would always invite himself to a party and take a few friends along with him. Born and raised in Putney, he was a Chelsea supporter through and through, and it would have taken a national emergency to stop him cheering for his team at Stamford Bridge on a Saturday. From an early age he had had an eye for the girls. If a new pair of female legs appeared on the block, Terry would be there checking out the face of the owner. It had never entered his head to be a Galahad, he always dreamed or perhaps fantasised that he would be a member of the love 'em and leave 'em brigade. At least that was what he thought until he met Gillian.

Gillian was something different to him. She evoked in him all the traits of personality that he was unaware he possessed. He wanted to protect Gillian, he wanted to wrap his arms around her and love her. At times the feelings he had for this girl both surprised and frightened him.

The following Monday after their first meeting Terry sat in the office where he worked as a trainee draughtsman, and kept thinking about Gillian. He smiled when he thought of her. Gillian too was doing exactly the same thing in the office that she worked in. Each of them was besotted by the other, and unaware of how intense their feelings would grow.

Gillian and Terry's first date was at a cinema in Leicester Square where they went to see *Ned Kelly*. The two of them were hardly interested in the film. Gillian glanced at Terry occasionally and he squeezed her hand suddenly without warning. She did not reject it and entwined her fingers through his. It did not matter that up there on the big screen Mick Jagger and Mark McManus and the rest of the actors playing the part of the Kelly gang were involved in the final shoot-out at Glenrowan. Gillian and Terry only had eyes for each other.

Over the next few months they went out at every opportunity. They held hands and talked and joked together. At restaurants they would sit and dreamily stare into each other's eyes. Often they would have days out at Brighton or go for picnics at Burnham Beeches or the Ruislip Lido. Both had never been so happy. But there was a price to be paid for their happiness.

At 19, Gillian's youth and carefree days were about to end. Gillian was distressed and worried at the news she had received that same day. In the hallway she nervously rang Terry. Next door her mum and dad were watching *This Is Your Life* on the television, which had been turned up rather loudly.

'Terry. Terry, I must see you,' she said in a quiet voice that was broken up with emotion. A dramatic pause followed as Terry queried the urgency of the call. 'I'll explain when we meet.' A further pause followed as Gillian avoided telling him her news. All she could do was to add, 'It is important.'

And so it was. They met a short while later in a park. Gillian sat next to Terry and told him the news. Terry was understandably perplexed. He leaned forward in exasperation covering his face with his hands as he attempted to come to terms with it. He looked at her almost in the hope that it was not true.

'A baby? Are you sure?' He asked as if it could change things and conceal the past. 'But... we're both so young.' Terry was agonised. 'We're only nineteen. Nineteen for goodness sake!' He was shaken. His voice was reflecting his fear at being tied down. 'What are we going to do? What on earth do we do now?'

Gillian was near to tears. It sounded as if Terry was more concerned for himself than both of them. 'I thought... I thought you... loved me.' Gillian started to cry.

Terry realised he had been terribly insensitive and he took a handkerchief and dried her tears. 'I'm sorry. I didn't mean to hurt you.' He looked at her, ashamed. 'I do love you Gillian. It's not that. It's getting... well, getting married before you've lived a life.' He leaned forward and held her tightly. 'I'll marry you Gillian, if that's what you want me to do.'

A wave of fear came over Gillian. Was that what she really wanted? She loved Terry. She needed him. Her feelings of love were overpowering. But the sudden prospect of marriage and motherhood so quickly was a shock to the system.

'How do I tell my parents?' she uttered in dismay. This was going to be more difficult than actually going through the wedding ceremony. The last people in the world she wanted to hurt were her parents.

Predictably that night, Gillian felt a mixture of embarrassment and shame as she prepared to tell her parents. In the lounge her father and mother looked up from the sofa as Gillian and Terry entered. There was a look of dismay on Gillian's face that gave her mother the suspicion that something was terribly wrong.

'Mum, Dad. Terry and I...' Her heart was broken. Tears flooded her eyes. 'Oh, I am so sorry. Terry and I, we want to get married.' Her father and mother looked at each other with blank expressions. Gillian added the reason why. 'I'm... I'm pregnant.'

★★★

That had been 20 years before. Now Gillian at 39 was lying awake considering the same situation that had befallen her daughter. Tears were in her eyes tonight. This time she was the parent, and it was her daughter who had caused her to feel deep concern. Surely this was a case of déjà vu.

The next morning Gillian tried to carry on with her normal day-to-day activities in spite of her worries about Samantha. It was Saturday morning, and soon the boys would be off to play soccer. That would give her the chance to talk to Samantha in private.

The boys walked through carrying sports bags as Gillian hoovered the carpets. 'You're off to soccer now are you boys?' she asked good-naturedly not wanting to show any signs of the heartache that troubled her.

'Yes Mum. Back about five. Bye,' Mark said in reply and he and his brother John smiled as they left the room.

'See you boys later,' Gillian said smiling back at them. She was so proud of them. Don't break my heart she thought. But one day they probably would.

Gillian stopped hoovering. The door slammed as the boys left the house. Almost at that same instant her daughter Samantha entered the room. She looked at her mother as if waiting for an instruction.

'Sit down, sweetheart,' Gillian beckoned to her. They both made themselves comfortable in armchairs facing each other. Her voice took on a consoling and reassuring tone. 'I'm not going to get angry or be hard on you in any way. I just want us to sit down and discuss the situation logically.'

Samantha was more at ease this morning. 'I've thought about it too, Mum. It would be against my nature to have it adopted. I'll take the responsibility. I'll look after it.'

'Alright. You've made one decision. Now, what about Barry? I presume you have told him?'

'Not yet, Mum.'

'Sam, you have to tell him. He has the right to know.' An uneasy thought entered Gillian's head. 'How do you think he'll react to the news?'

'I'm going to see him this afternoon.' She appeared grave at the prospect and then tried to reassure her mother. 'I might even go now.'

'Get it done as soon as possible,' Gillian responded. Aware of the future difficulties that Samantha might face as a single parent, she felt inclined to speak her mind. 'Work out where you're both going. I lay awake thinking about it. I lay awake thinking about a lot of things in the past. Your Dad, me, especially you.' Her eyes became cloudy and moist.

'When I was younger I had my head in the clouds. I used to dream of a glittering white wedding in a country village church swept down the aisle by a lovely prince-like man who I'd stay happily married to for all the years of my life.'

Samantha wondered, was there a touch of cynicism there? Disappointment perhaps? She listened respectfully as Gillian poured out her feelings.

'I can't say I'm not disappointed in you, Sam, but I'm the last one to speak. I've never made any secret of the fact that I was expecting you when I married your Dad. Looking back now, it was a terrible mistake me and your father marrying. You might have had a happier upbringing if I had brought you up alone. As it turned out by the time we were both twenty-two I had given birth to three children in three years. Oh, don't get me wrong, I love all three of you very much and nothing will ever change that. But in those days the single parent, the child out of wedlock, it was still frowned upon. Your dad and I married, and almost from the beginning it wasn't working. Your dad, he wasn't earning enough to keep us. We were living in dreadful damp rooms in a noisy part of Willesden Green. Within five years the marriage was floundering. He wasn't happy. I wasn't happy. We tried hard to make a go of it. but it was no good. Every night there was a terrible row over something and we'd have days where we couldn't even bear to look at each other, let alone sit down at a table to eat as a family together. We didn't want to share a bed together.'

Samantha looked dumbstruck at the facts her mother had just presented.

'Oh yes, that's how bad it got.' Gillian had observed her daughter's apparent discomfort. 'By 1978 we were divorced. He was out of work. I hardly ever got any maintenance. You know the rest. He didn't come to visit for a few years.' She paused. When she resumed speaking her voice had a chilly feel about it and there was a slight tremor there. 'The next thing we knew was when we had a letter from him telling us he'd got married again, had two more children and gone off to South Africa to work as a draughtsman for a mining company.'

'I know all that, Mum,' Samantha said sympathetically. 'I know you've had a hard time.'

'I'm glad you do!' Gillian responded firmly. 'Because it's your decision, Samantha. I am not going to pressure you. I would prefer you to be married, but not if it means you'll be devastatingly unhappy, that your baby who deserves all the love you can give it will be brought up in an unhappy household. Whatever you and Barry decide, I'll stand by you. If you want to take up a career or go back and study, I'll look after the child during the day or whenever. It's your choice.'

Samantha stood up. 'Thank you, Mum. I'll go and see Barry now and tell him.'

Gillian also stood up. She put her hands on Samantha's shoulders. 'For goodness sake make the right decision.'

★★★

On Saturdays Gillian normally took her lunch alone. The boys would be out playing soccer and Samantha would be elsewhere. Today Sam would be telling her boyfriend the news of her pregnancy. Gillian didn't feel much like having lunch but she forced herself to make some. She stood in the kitchen preparing a meal. Outside the window cleaner Keith whistled happily to a tune he could hear from the radio in Gillian's kitchen. Unfortunately the tune was 'Everlasting Love' by the Love Affair, a tune that struck a note of poignancy with Gillian as she always associated this with the occasion she met her former husband in King's Road so long ago.

She was already very upset over her daughter; she felt tired and distressed, and the combined effects caused her to break out into tears. Her tears could not have come at a more inconvenient moment. Keith knocked on the kitchen door to collect his payment. He was a happy smiling man of 41 with an affable manner. In his well-worn routine he greeted Gillian in a cheerful 'speak from a script' manner.

'Good morning, Mrs Hodgson! That'll be two pounds please.' Gillian reached for her handkerchief and wiped away her tears. Keith was bemused straight away. 'I didn't think it was that bad!' Gillian tried to cover up her tears. 'If it makes you cry that much I'd better make it a quid!'

Gillian tried to get a grip on her emotions. 'I'm sorry to embarrass you, Keith. Family problems. You know…'

Keith looked at her sympathetically. 'Don't be sorry, darlin',' he said in reassuring tones. 'If you need a shoulder to cry on I'm here. I'm a very good listener.' He was observant too. 'I know you're on your own with three kids 'n' all.'

Gillian somehow managed to smile through her tears. 'I wouldn't want to bore you with my problems. But if you want to have a cup of coffee and a chat you'd be most welcome.'

'Don't mind if I do,' said Keith, stepping inside the kitchen.

Keith and Gillian sat talking and sipping their coffee for a long time. Gillian was glad to have another adult to speak to. Especially a male who could apply a down-to-earth attitude to a situation. Keith was a good listener; he was true to his word. Gillian spoke to him of the long years she had battled for her family. She spoke of her hopes for Samantha and how they had all been dashed by the impending arrival of a child.

'So there it is,' said Gillian concluding her conversation. 'My daughter Samantha, she's made the same mistake that I did and now she's expecting a baby. God bless its little heart.'

'I understand.' Keith appeared thoughtful. 'I can image how you must be feeling. I'm a father myself. I've got a daughter, a lovely girl of seventeen. I dote on her.'

'I didn't know you were married Keith,' Gillian expressed surprise for she had known him a long time.

'Was married,' Keith corrected her. 'I've been divorced twelve years now. I still see a lot of my daughter. She only lives a suburb away with her mother.'

'What's her name?'

'Tracy. She's a good kid. She was born deaf. But she learned to speak by lip reading.'

'Really?' Gillian was learning something different about the man who had cleaned her windows for years. 'You must be proud of her.'

Then Keith said something that further surprised her. 'Would you like to meet her?'

'Me? Meet her?' Gillian wondered for a moment if perhaps Tracy was outside in the car.

Keith explained. 'I'm having a barbecue at my house next weekend. Any time after ten o'clock Sunday morning. Come along if you like. Bring your children. I'd love you to come.'

'It's very nice of you.' Gillian seemed apprehensive. It had been a long time since she had ever gone to any sort of social engagement. 'Can I think about it?'

Keith was relaxed about the reply she gave, knowing that people who make firm commitments often break them. 'Nothing to think about. The invitation's open. Come along if you feel up to it. I won't think anything the less of you if you don't.' He added hopefully, 'But I'd love you to come.'

★★★

Samantha and her boyfriend walked down the street in a sombre mood. If her mother could have viewed the scene she would have seen a virtual recreation of the earlier occasion when Gillian had first told Terry of her pregnancy.

Barry had mixed feelings. He felt angry, frustrated and bemused. He was a college student who could not grasp the fact that his own desires had brought this dilemma upon him.

'This isn't happening,' he said coldly. 'I just don't know what to say.'

'It broke my mum's heart when I told her.' Samantha spoke as if she was saying the words to herself. 'Mum was expecting me when she married. She had her heart set on me going to university and having a career. I hurt her so much. It's probably like a re-run of what happened to her.'

'Don't make me feel any worse than I do already,' Barry moaned, his voice clearly showing signs of anxiety. Then he lost control. 'Damn it! Damn! Damn! Damn!' Samantha touched his arm. Barry stopped and leaned against a lamp post. 'I'm sorry, Samantha. I've never been faced with something like this.'

It was an obvious remark. Samantha felt for him as much as she did for her own plight. She decided to state one option. 'Barry, if you don't want to get married…'

She had scarcely made this comment before Barry's face turned ashen. It was plainly obvious that he had not even considered the possibility of marriage.

'Get married? Married? Tied down?'

He could hardly have been clearer about his true feelings. Samantha

189

looked at him with sudden distaste. She could see that he was not even a fraction of the man she had hoped he would be. Responsibility and duty weren't words he recognised. Samantha turned away, she could not bear to look at him.

'Is that what this means to you, Barry?' she asked on the edge of shedding tears. 'To be tied down to me? Even if we don't get married we could live together.'

Barry looked at her in dismay. Even this option wasn't one that he would consider.

'No?' Samantha's voice took on an air of concern. 'What are we going to do?'

'I don't know,' he responded quietly. Then angrily he added, 'I just don't know!' He thumped the lamp post. He was a young man full of frustration and annoyance.

★★★

Gillian and Samantha faced each other in the lounge room. It was hard for Samantha, who realised with much pain apparent in her voice and face that she had a difficult time ahead of her.

'I think I'm going to be on my own where the baby's concerned. I don't think Barry is going to take too much interest in it.' Her face was sad and her voice was close to faltering. 'I'm on my own.'

Gillian hugged Samantha and held her tightly, like a young mother holding a clinging, frightened child. There was agony in Gillian's eyes but it was not for herself, it was for Samantha. The light seemed to catch Gillian's face, showing the love and warmth she had for her daughter. There was much unspoken dialogue in her expression.

'I'm with you Sam,' she said quietly. A tear formed in the corner of her eye. 'I'll help you through.'

★★★

If Keith Porter had been in the Army he would have been the cheerful squaddie who could bring cheer to any grim situation. In reality he was a hard-working man who spent his days as a telephone engineer, several nights a week as a barman in a public house, and the weekends as a window cleaner.

The reason for this was that after an amicable divorce he had taken out a rather expensive mortgage on a terraced house of his own. His daughter Tracy often came to stay. The divorce had provided Tracy with two homes in adjoining suburbs. There had been no fierce custody battles and Tracy divided her time equally between her parents.

Keith was never more happier than when he held a barbecue at his home. He always invited a mixed cross-section of people to these gatherings. He was in his element, turning over sausages and chops on a charcoal grill. Families with children played together and ate at garden tables where salad bowls were placed in the centre. Keith handed out paper plates full of meat to the adults and children.

'There you go, son. There you are, lovely. Get tucked in.' He was the master of ceremonies on these days. Keith forever cracked jokes and kept the humour flowing.

His daughter Tracy was there. She was a lovely teenage girl who on the surface appeared as normal as any other of her age. However, she was afflicted by deafness and had to face people square on in order to lip read. Her voice reflected the fact that she had never heard a human sound. It was beautifully modulated, as she always pronounced to the best of her ability. But there were clues in her voice that everything she said was carefully plotted, word for word. Tracy walked up to Keith at the barbecue.

'Hullo darling. How are you?' He turned to face her.

'Alright, Dad,' she replied pleasantly. Her eyes were focused on the movement of Keith's lips more than his facial expression.

'There's a lady outside with her sons and daughter.' Keith's eyes lit up. At once he thought of Gillian. 'She said you'd invited her.'

'Did she? Would you bring her in, Trace?'

Tracy nodded and wandered off. Keith put an apron on. He filled up several glasses and prepared several new paper plates for his guests. He felt very enthusiastic about seeing Gillian socially. The truth was that in so many ways they were a very good match.

'Hullo, Keith,' a soft feminine voice said to him. He turned around and found himself facing Gillian, Samantha, Mark and John. Tracy stood close by, watching curiously.

'Gillian!' Keith exclaimed with delight. 'Hullo lads. Hullo young lady. You've met my daughter, Tracy?'

Gillian who had known from the previous conversation with Keith of the need to face Tracy when speaking, immediately responded. 'So, you're Tracy.' She was very impressed by Keith's daughter. 'Your Dad's told me about you.' Gillian shook Tracy's hand gently. Tracy smiled but she looked back at Gillian with curiosity. 'Oh, your Dad does the window cleaning round in my street. These are my boys, Mark and John, and my daughter Samantha.'

The youngsters warmed to each other instantaneously. There was something about Tracy's gentle nature and apparent serenity that made the boys want to protect her. Keith took pleasure in the fact that they had all responded well.

'I'll introduce you to everybody in a moment. What can I get you all? Chops? Sausages? Chicken legs? Shish kebabs?'

Gillian and her children had not indulged in any social activities for a long time and made a point of trying to enjoy the event as best as possible. A bit later on, when Keith was washing dishes and plates, he gazed through the kitchen window and saw Gillian and her family laughing and smiling with the couples at the outdoor tables. Tracy smiled at her Dad as she dried the plates for him. She was quick to notice the expression on her father's face.

'Gillian's a nice lady, isn't she?' Tracy asked him.

'A very nice lady,' Keith replied.

'Is she your new girlfriend?' Tracy was intuitive too.

'No, but...' Keith stopped short of saying hopefully.

'You'd like her to be?' Tracy added.

Keith stopped what he was doing. He looked directly at her so she could fully understand him. It was a move that he had performed so often, it had become a natural response to Tracy.

'Yes. I've known her for a while,' Keith explained. 'Since I started doing the window cleaning round, in fact. She's on her own. Long divorced, like me. I believe she's had a bit of a rough trot for quite a few years. I'd like to get to know her better.'

Tracy looked at Keith as if there was something on her mind. 'Dad, do you mind if I ask you something?'

'Of course not, darling. Go right ahead.' Keith knew her expression.

'Well, you and Mum...' She hesitated. 'You talk to her a lot. She talks to you as a friend. I've never seen you get angry with her, I never saw you argue. You still seem to get on well with her. I never saw you get upset with her in any way. I know Mum's got her – well, her men friends – but she still seems to like you, so what happened? Why did you and Mum split up?'

Keith thought hard for a moment. Tracy tried prompting him. 'Was it because I was deaf and I had to learn to lip read and I caused you problems because I was difficult to take care of?'

This was heart-breaking for Keith to hear. He put his hands on her shoulders and looked at her adoringly. 'I don't want you to ever blame yourself for what happened between your mum and me. Do you understand sweetheart?'

'I try to, Dad.'

'You don't have to try,' Keith advised her in a warm, fatherly manner. 'When you were born and it became clear that you weren't going to be able to hear like other little girls and boys it caused some tension, some distress for your mum and I, true. But the tension we went through was caused not by you, but a mutual worry that when you grew up you wouldn't be able to mix and make friends, and that you would be a lonely little girl always standing on the outside looking in on everybody's fun. But your achievement in learning to lip read… believe me, darling, it is a wonderful achievement which has brought an immense joy to both of us. I'm very proud of you, Tracy, and I know your mum is too.

'Don't ever blame yourself for Mum and me separating. If the truth be known, I think your mum and I probably grew away from each other, like many couples all over the world. Some couples have got the capacity to grow together and pull together and everything is done in their joint interest. Others unfortunately drift apart.'

He paused to grapple for words. His face showed sensitivity as he looked deep into Tracy's eyes. 'Your mum and I tried hard to make it work, but we knew we couldn't go on. It wasn't that we argued or didn't get on. It wasn't as simple as that.' The memory seemed to hurt him and an expression of regret flickered in his normally happy eyes. 'We had got to the stage where we had very little in common. Even day-to-day conversation became strained. One thing that we did have in common when we were divorced was that we were determined that both of us should be available to you, whenever. That's why your Mum, despite living her own life, has always lived near to me.'

'I understand, Dad. I thought for a long time I may have been the reason you and Mum split.'

'Definitely not!' Keith made a point of emphasising this. 'When we divorced I was the first one in my family to have a broken marriage. In my father's day, if a marriage didn't work out the wife told her burly brothers and they paid a visit to the husband to find out why. Different story today. Divorce and separation are regular occurrences. I came from a very closeted background where almost all of my relatives seemed to be conditioned to living life in stages. You know the sort of thing: you go to school, you leave school, get a job, get a motorbike, meet somebody, get engaged, buy a car, get married, live in a flat, then struggle to get a house. It's almost as if that was expected of us. Well, now I know perhaps a little too late – but not with too much regret – that we're all individuals. We don't have to follow like sheep. If we want to, we can dare to be different.'

'How, Dad?'

'Well, Tracy, when I was at school all the boys I knew – including me – we never thought what else we could do with our lives. It amazes me how we could have had blinkers on, thinking there was only one direction to go: to grow up and then get married. Now that I look back I can see I had many options. In those days New Zealand, Canada, Australia, the United States and South Africa were prosperous countries with plenty of employment opportunities. Not so these days, but I could have emigrated then. I could have joined the Army or the Merchant Navy, or maybe learnt a really worthwhile career. But instead I took a succession of jobs, some of them menial, some of them worthwhile. And then I met your mum, fell in love with her, got married. And do you know what else, Tracy?'

'No.'

'If I had my time again I'd probably do it all the same anyway.' Keith spoke with an element of pride at his admission. 'Just to have you again and watch the way you've grown up and achieve with the odds stacked against you – well, it's been the biggest thrill of my life.'

Tracy knew that her dad really meant it. A lovely warm feeling enveloped her, triggered by the obvious love of her father. 'If you and Mum hadn't taken so much time to help me I might not have made it this far.' Keith put his arm around her and kissed her on the cheek. 'Gillian's coming, Dad.' Keith looked out of the window and saw Gillian walking towards the kitchen. Tracy took the initiative to leave the two alone. 'I'll go back outside now, Dad.'

Tracy left the room and went out into the garden, smiling at Gillian as she passed her. Gillian entered the kitchen, and Keith winked at her as she came up to him.

'On your own with the domestic jobs, Keith?' she asked him, feeling slightly guilty that he was inside drying dishes while others enjoyed themselves outside. 'Can I give you a hand?'

'No, I'm fine here, thanks. I've just about finished.' He looked at her closely. Beneath the tired and weary look on Gillian's face there was still a strong hint of a warm and attractive woman. 'Are you and the kids enjoying yourselves?'

'Yes, it's lovely. It's so long since I've been to anything like a get-together I'd almost forgotten what it was like. The last party I went to was one with jelly and custard and trifle, which my children were invited to when they were little.' She laughed at the memory of it. A glance around the room prompted her to make a further remark, as if to keep the conversation going. 'You've not done bad to get this nice little place on a window cleaner's wages.'

Keith smiled at her assumption that cleaning windows was his only occupation. 'Oh, I just do that on a Saturday. I work as a telephone engineer with British Telecom during the week, then one or two nights a week and occasionally on a Sunday I earn a bit helping behind the bar at a pub called the Load of Hay, on Mandeville Road.'

'You work pretty hard then.'

'Yes. But it's partly social too. I'd rather be serving behind the bar than drinking on the other side. I think I meet more people and socialise better than if I was in the public bar trying to work out how I could talk to someone. My job as a telephone engineer during the day gets me out and about. I install subscribers' apparatus in homes and offices all around town. On Saturdays as you know I do the window cleaning round. I like to keep active. This is important to us single people.' Keith looked at her in a kindly way. He was trying to draw her out to speak more. 'Gillian, have you ever thought of trying to make better use of your time? I know you've got some problems at the moment. But maybe you might find it would take your mind off things.'

'You might be right,' Gillian agreed. She liked this man. He cared sufficiently enough to make this suggestion. She pondered over these words. 'Samantha looks as if she'll be having to plan life as a single parent.' Keith wore an expression of understanding. 'I'll be busy trying to help her through the next six months. I would like to do more with my time though. At the moment life seems to consist of several cleaning jobs, getting the kids their meals, settling down to the TV and following the fortunes of *Eastenders* and *Emmerdale Farm*, *News at Ten* with Trevor McDonald, and on Saturday nights playing the *Generation Game* with Bruce Forsyth.' Keith smiled at her wit. 'Really, though, how can I improve my lot?'

'Well, I can think of two things,' Keith replied without hesitation. 'The first is that we go back outside and enjoy the barbecue. The second... well, following on from what you were just saying about Saturday nights, would I be out of line if I asked you to come out for a meal at Tiffany's ballroom next week?'

Gillian was at first slightly uneasy. 'Oh, I'm not sure, Keith.'

'Nothing in it,' he reassured her. 'Just a friendly night on the tiles — or the ballroom dance floor. It will at least get you out of the house for a while.'

After a moment's deliberation Gillian seized the opportunity. 'Why not? Why not indeed? Of course I will, Keith.'

★★★

It had been a long time between dates for Gillian Hodgson. She had just turned 18 when Terry Hodgson had first asked her out. That had been one marriage and one divorce away, with three children all grown up into teenagers now. The past truly was a different country. Nearly 40 now, Gillian gazed at herself in the mirror. Dressed neatly and made-up carefully, she didn't look bad; a little frayed around the edges perhaps but tonight on the dance floor with Keith she would be 21 again and cutting a dash with the best of them.

Oh, if only I knew then what I know now, thought Gillian as she walked to the door to await Keith's arrival. She sat down in a chair in the hallway and crossed her legs. Not bad legs either, she reminded herself. They seemed to blend perfectly with her tiny feet that fitted into a pair of black patent leather stiletto heels. Her skirt and blouse showed off the best aspects of her figure. Three children she had given birth to, but her waist and stomach seldom varied in size. Even her brown hair, dotted with grey, was shiningly enhanced with a good conditioner and highlights.

She felt confident and happy. After all, she was going out with a thoroughly nice and cheerful man. Keith was one of the lads – anyone could see that – but he liked women, he respected women. Gillian felt safe with him.

In due course Keith arrived and he drove Gillian to their venue for the evening. Keith was only a slight man in build, but dressed in an open-necked shirt and velvet blue jacket he looked striking. The two were well matched. Anyone meeting them for the first time would have been forgiven for assuming they had been married for years.

Tiffany's was one of the old-style ballroom dance halls that had once been so prominent in England before the advent of the discotheque. Keith and Gillian sat at a table eating a meal and watching the dancers. It was like taking a step back in time to the 1950s, all that was missing was the long swirling dresses and teddy boy outfits. It was very much a family ballroom, with dancers of all ages; most of them were in the 30 to 40 age group. On stage a set of musicians resembling a cross between the Joe Loss Orchestra and the Glenn Miller Band belted out a mixture of tunes covering popular hits spanning three decades. One tune they played, 'Out of Time' by Chris Farlowe, summed up the setting and style of Tiffany's. It didn't seem to belong to the present decade.

'I forgot there were places like this,' said Gillian.

'Me too,' remarked Keith. 'Reminds me a little bit – and only a little bit – of the old Hammersmith Palais.'

'That's where my parents met!' Gillian exclaimed. 'They were in the services during the war and met on the Palais dance floor. Apparently it was a ladies invitation and Mum spotted Dad and called out to him, "Oi shortie, fancy a knees up wiv me then?"!' Keith and Gillian laughed. She was at ease now and continued the story. 'Then eventually Mum took him home and Dad proposed to her in the garden. For years afterwards Dad used to say Mum led him up the garden path and she led him round by the nose after that.'

'Funny, isn't it, how places and records can conjure up old memories?' The band on stage struck up 'Little Brown Jug' by Glenn Miller. 'Do you dance?' He advanced it further. 'Would you like to dance?'

'Do you know something, Keith? The last time a man asked me to dance I ended up in a seven-year marriage.'

'Well I've got a great idea. Why don't you ask me to dance? And the answer is, yes, I'd love to!'

Gillian stood up and smiled. 'There's not much I can say to that is there? Except, let's go!'

Gillian and Keith moved out onto the dance floor. There were couples who jitterbugged, others who made up their own movements, and some who were expert dancers. It had been so long since Gillian had danced but the rhythm within her that had lain dormant for two decades was soon reactivated. With Keith's guidance she was soon twirling and swaying with the best of them. No one else would have noticed anyway; once on the ballroom floor the dancers were caught up in their own private world and performed only for the benefit of their partners.

When the music had finished the band took a short pause. With their silver instruments catching the roof lights and the musicians clad in white dinner jackets and bow ties, their presence dominated the room. The house lights suddenly dimmed. Almost as if on cue the band stood up and began to play another Glenn Miller tune, 'In the Mood'. Couples took it as the perfect opportunity to hold each other tightly. On the dance floor people clung to each other, in varying degrees of love and romance.

Gillian relaxed in Keith's arms. She felt security and warmth with him. Keith smiled at her and looked deeply into her eyes. It was a look that spoke volumes. The two swayed gently with the music. When the tune came to an end they both returned to their seats.

'I enjoyed that, Keith. Just for a few moments I felt considerably younger than my thirty-nine years.'

Keith found the remark a little strange from a woman who he felt still had much to offer. 'Gosh! You make it sound as if you're expecting a telegram any day now from the Queen.' He genuinely felt that she needed reassurance. 'I think you're a warm and nice-looking girl in her late thirties who probably underestimates just what she's got going for her.'

Gillian blushed red with embarrassment. She was not used to warm words such as this. 'Oh Keith...'

'No, please let me finish,' Keith interjected. 'I mean what I'm saying. When you look at people of our age — say late thirties, early forties – in photographs of the 1950s... well, people looked generally much older than they actually were. Perhaps because of the way they used to dress in those days. Not only that, but they thought older, they were older in spirit if not in body. That's because by the time they'd got to our age they had lived through a depression, a world war, a time of austerity and rationing. When they got to 39 years of age they had already lived 50. The point I'm making, Gillian, is that today's woman is a different breed altogether. You've only to look at some of those television presenters and newsreaders who are in their late forties and early fifties. Some of those girls are smashing, real head-turners in fact. Believe it or not, Gillian, you're probably in the prime of your life.'

'Since we spoke last week I've been thinking of ways to improve my life. Do you know what, Keith? I want to get myself fit and trim. When I was at school I used to play hockey and netball. And I could run the 100 yards, the 220, the 440, I could even pace myself for the mile. I'm not talking about getting fit for the Olympic Games, but instead of feeling slouchy and apathetic and constantly yawning all the time, I'm going to go along to a fitness class three nights a week where they exercise to music.'

'Good for you.' Keith felt thrilled at the positive way she had spoken. He was to be further impressed.

'I've also been along to the Job Centre to find out about a training course. I used to be a typist. I've been out of practice for a long time. Not that I've done any work in that line for a long time. But next week I start a three week course in brushing up on my typing and using an Amstrad WordStar word processor. I'm hoping when the recession is over to try and get a better job.'

'Blimey! You are determined to change things!'

'What you said, prompted me,' Gillian said with a soft smile.

The band on stage started to play another musical number more current than the tunes that had appeared in their repertoire so far, 'Lady in Red'.

'I think for too long, Keith, I've given up. I've just become resigned to things. But now I ask myself, why? I'm not saying I'm becoming a feminist. I'm not saying I'm going to become aggressive. But I am saying that I'm going to try and put more into my life.'

Gillian stood up, took Keith's hand and led him back to the dance floor. They began to dance in show ballroom style.

'I like this tune,' said Keith.

'Yes it's every young girl's song of romance,' Gillian pointed out. 'You remember how as a child when Christmas got near you would feel really excited thinking about how many presents you were going to get?'

'I still do.'

'There's a sort of enthusiasm – an excitement about life – you have as a child that seems to go as you get older. When you're an adult, especially if you've had a lot of failure, some of those feelings seem to turn into cynicism, even envy of other people's happiness. I felt that a while ago when I bumped into a girl I used to go to school with. Everything she's touched has turned to gold.' Gillian looked into Keith's eyes. She knew he was a good listener. 'I want to feel good about life. I want to feel happy, and energetic.' Gillian suddenly appeared to be embarrassed for revealing her true feelings. 'Am I making a fool of myself?'

'Not at all Gillie. Not at all.'

Keith drove Gillian home that night. He did not make a pretence of trying to stretch the evening out. It had been a pleasant interlude. They sat in the car for a while. Gillian had felt her confidence return that night, and Keith was someone who she felt could be relied upon.

'Thanks, Keith. It's been very nice,' she said softly, like a girl who had just been on her first date.

'Perhaps we can do it again sometime,' he said hopefully.

Gillian was careful not to appear too keen, although in reality she was feeling excited about him. She smiled warmly at him, and went into the house.

Keith's face was indicative of happier things to come. His eyes shone with almost juvenile delight at the prospect of seeing her more often. He was delighted that Gillian had responded so readily to his ideas for improving her life.

★★★

Gillian was soon attending a fitness class at Michael Hunt's Health Spa, where she found to her amazement many ladies such as herself, all taking steps to tone up. In shorts and sports top, Gillian exercised in time to recorded music. A lady instructor at the front of the room set the pace by demonstrating and changing the movements every few minutes, which the class responded to.

The next stage of Gillian's attempts at transforming her life came when she attended a course at an employment training centre. With other trainees she made the effort to update her word processing skills. Through the guidance of an enthusiastic lecturer she was soon beginning to grasp the fundamentals of an Amstrad WordStar word processor.

She felt entitled to be happy now. On two counts, she had made significant efforts to take her life in a new direction.

★★★

Terry Hodgson had been in England for a few weeks now, attending to his aunt's estate. It was distressing for him to sift through Bede's belongings. Terry felt that part of his own soul had died with her. His aunt, after all, had been his last relative in England... almost his last. He had not forgotten his ex-wife Gillian and their three children. He knew he must see them again.

When all the legal problems had been attended to he hired a car and drove to the area where Gillian lived. He booked into a local hotel and then went straight to the council house where his ex-wife lived. Terry sat in the car for a while, studying the house.

He suddenly felt deeply ashamed. And not only that, but he also felt a sense of guilt. Why? The council house that Gillian lived in with their children was shoddy, with peeling paint, and on an estate that had also fallen into disrepair. Terry lived in a comfortable bungalow in a tree-lined suburb with his second wife and two children. Gillian's life had been fraught with struggle and penny-pinching to get by. Terry had improved his standard of living with a move to South Africa in the late 1970s. His whole way of life had been completely the opposite of that which Gillian lived.

The more Terry thought about it, the more it seemed that he should start the car up and drive away. What right did he have to come back into their lives after so many years away? He felt the tears well up in his eyes. I can't stay, he thought. I must go.

'Terry? I can't believe it. Terry! What are you doing here?'

The words came at him through the half-opened window of the car. Terry turned to see his ex-wife staring at him. The look on her face was one of sheer amazement. There was even the suggestion of a warm smile, as if she was genuinely pleased to see him. He stepped out of the car and embraced her.

'Hullo, Gillian, it's good to see you again.'

They looked at each other both well aware that when they had been married they had been teenagers. Both were 39 now, and mature, intelligent adults. Their outlooks on life had changed considerably.

'You'd better come in, Terry.' She looked at him sombrely. 'I have something to tell you. About Samantha.'

'Samantha?' Terry didn't like the tone of her voice.

'Come in. I'll tell you all about it. She's alright.'

Inside the house, Gillian brought Terry up to date on the activities of their family. Terry was understandably stunned.

'What a shock!' he gasped. 'The first time I've been home to England in nearly thirteen years, and I've learned I'm to be a grandfather. I can't believe it! It only seems a moment ago I was holding Samantha in my arms when she was a little baby.' He looked at Gillian sympathetically, who was returning him a similar look. 'I'm sorry to bring it up Gillie, this is history repeating itself.'

The irony of it was not lost on Gillian. 'I said exactly the same thing.' A tiny smile played around her mouth. 'What are you doing home anyway, Terry?'

'Gillian, I'm only here for a short time,' Terry began to explain. 'As you know, I was brought up by my Aunt Bede. Well, she died recently, and I had to come home to sort out her funeral and estate.'

'I'm sorry about Bede. She was a very nice lady.'

'Yes. She was a fine old girl. A bit rough around the edges but one of the old school.' Terry smiled at the memory of her. Then he looked at Gillian preparing to make a candid admission that could awake old memories. 'I've got a lot of apologies to make to you for things that happened in the past.'

'Terry… don't.' The last thing Gillian wanted at this time was to revive old unhappy memories.

'Hear me out Gillian, please,' Terry persisted. He really did want to purge his conscience. It had to be now, or he would never say it. 'I'm sorry that after we separated, apart from the odd letter and Christmas card and the occasional maintenance cheque, I wasn't able to look after you the way I should have done. Forgive me, if you can.'

'It has been a struggle, Terry,' she confirmed. 'I can't tell you just how difficult it has been.' Terry appeared stern at the thought of it. 'But life goes on.'

Terry sought to further explain. 'During the late seventies I was made redundant and I'd got married again to a Dutch girl, her parents lived in South Africa. And anyway, I went out there, where my two children were born. I know I haven't been a proper father to our kids and it weighs on my mind heavily. The point is, I wonder if I could spend a bit of time with the children?'

'Of course,' Gillian said with an element of surprise as if he thought she would even consider denying Terry the opportunity to do so. 'You're their Dad.'

'Do you think I could take Samantha out to lunch? I'd like to talk to her a bit. I feel like I've let you all down a lot. If I'd been around maybe Samantha might not be expecting so early. If I'd been able to give you more help...' His guilt and self-condemnation was so strong.

'How can we tell?' She knew her ex-husband was being unnecessarily hard on himself.

'Another thing, Gillian. What with settling my aunt's estate I've got a bit put by now.' Terry put his hand inside his jacket and pulled out a cheque. He handed it to Gillian. 'This is for you. In lieu of past maintenance payments that I missed. Perhaps you could split it up with the children.'

Gillian examined the cheque. She was amazed to see that it was for £3000.

'I can't accept this, Terry!' Just the thought of the size of the cheque frightened her.

'Well, if you don't want it, please take it on behalf of the children. Or perhaps put it aside to help Samantha when she has her baby. Keep it as a secret between us. No one need know it came from me.'

'In that case, Terry, I'll see to that.'

'Now, Gillian, what time do the children come home?'

★★★

At the Load of Hay, Keith Porter was serving behind the bar. Normally he enjoyed this evening job because of the social side of things. But the recession was noticeable even in the bar trade: customers just weren't coming in even for their regular pints of bitter. It had been a fairly quiet night and Keith was just about to read the evening paper when a hotel guest walked to the bar.

It was another of those ironies that the customer was Terry Hodgson. Neither of the two men knew who the other was or that they were linked to the same woman.

'What can I get you, sir?' Keith asked him affably.

Terry had not drunk in an English public house for so long that many of the brand names of beer were new to him.

'I'll have a pint of the stout that sounds like a bloke from County Cork,' he said jokingly.

'Ah, you mean the stout with the name that sounds like a law of its own,' Keith added in jocular mood. He began to fill the glass with draught stout. It shone in the light like black gold. 'A lovely drop too, if I may say. That'll be £1.80, please.'

Terry grimaced at the price. He had been away a long time and his pub memories were of the 50p pint. 'Do you mind if I put it on my bill? I'm staying here in the hotel. I'm in room twenty-one. I'll settle up in full when I leave.'

'No problem,' said Keith. He took a pad and made a note. 'Room twenty-one.' He watched Terry take a sip of the drink. 'Nice, eh?'

'Good stuff,' agreed Terry. 'It's been a long time since I sat in an English pub like this. Brings back memories of a misspent youth.'

'Misspent or well spent?' queried Keith.

'Misspent, well spent – what's the difference? Depends which way you look at it really.'

'Been away for a while, have you?'

'Well over a decade now,' Terry told him. 'I've been living out in Cape Town, South Africa for many years. I'm home to sort out my aunt's estate as well as see the children from my first marriage.'

Keith was genuinely interested. He always found other people's stories educational to listen to, particularly where they had taken up an opportunity that he might have done.

'What's it like being home again?'

'Strange, really.' Terry felt as if he had found a friendly priest in Keith and he was uttering the words of a sinful confession. 'To tell you the truth, I can understand the saying, "the past is a different country". Things have changed too much in the years I've been away, I don't feel part of this country any more. People, attitudes, politics, even the physical make-up of England, it's all changed. I'm enjoying being home but I'll be happy to go back. I lost my aunt recently, who was really my last surviving blood relative. I saw my kids tonight. I've not seen them for years and they've grown up marvellously. My ex-wife did a wonderful job in bringing them up.'

'You wouldn't want to resettle here then?'

'Probably not,' Terry replied considering the possibility. 'My wife is a Dutch-born South African girl and I have two other children now. I've thought about it from time to time. I've too many memories here, with my divorce from my first wife and the long estrangement from the children of that marriage.' He stopped to sip from his drink. 'I'm a draughtsman for an international mining company in Cape Town. They have offices in Switzerland and Holland, so it's a possibility I might move there at some stage.'

'I take it you're not enamoured with England, then?' Keith asked.

'I've been away too long,' Terry answered. 'It's funny, you know. I love England, I cherish being brought up here. I still feel immensely patriotic at times, really moved by ceremony or the occasions like the FA Cup, Remembrance Day, the Changing of the Guard, the tennis at Wimbledon or the Test Matches at Lords… But in my thirty-nine years on this earth I can't remember a time like this.'

'You mean with the recession?'

'Yes.' It had been so noticeable to Terry. He was glad to have an audience who would listen to the views of a returning expatriate. 'Britain in 1991. What a sad and grey year compared to the times of my youth.' He spoke now more in sadness than criticism of the country he still felt deep loyalty to. 'I've never seen the people so tired and dispirited. Every time I pick up a paper it seems to be higher unemployment, homes repossessed, bankruptcies, businesses going into liquidation, whole factories and industries closing.'

'We had a boom in the eighties,' Keith pointed out. 'I suppose the more people built up for themselves in the way of assets and personal debt, the more they had to lose when the crash eventually came. And boy, are they losing it all now! A few years ago I couldn't have stood here and talked to you all night, I'd have been rushed off my feet, serving as many customers as a football crowd. You should have seen it then. There were car makers and chippies and sparkies and brickies' labourers all coming in, buying whole kegs of beer and having roast dinners with their wives and girlfriends. Look at it now, there's you and I, and not even the regular drinkers coming in for their 'arf pints.'

'It amazes me,' said Terry. 'When I was a boy at school the teacher used to talk about all the great British industries that had been established. Let me see…' He thought hard for a moment. 'Ah yes, Mr Maloney at school used to talk about so many: textiles in Yorkshire and Lancashire, tin mining in Cornwall, coal mining throughout the British Isles, shipbuilding on The Clyde, fishing fleets from Hull and Grimsby and Cornwall. I still remember going on holiday as a kid to Penzance and being fascinated by the lobster pots.'

'Happy memories, eh?' Keith asked with a smile.

'I suppose so. Whatever happened to the wonderful days of the sixties when the world came to London? Do you remember it all?'

Keith grinned. It was his turn to reminisce now. 'I do indeed. My Dad bringing home the overtime. Harold Wilson in his mac with his pipe. Family holidays in Spain and Majorca. England winning the World Cup in 1966 and Cassius Clay versus Henry Cooper and…'

'The Beatles, miniskirts, Julie Christie and Jean Shrimpton, and the King's Road, Chelsea. Manchester United versus Benfica. The Stones in the Park. A choice of which job instead of whether a job. Will we ever see such days again?'

'Gone forever, mate. But life is too short to dwell on the past and be melancholy. You can't be young and naïve all your life.'

'Yes, I think you're right. When I saw my children tonight and how they'd grown up, I felt as if a whole lifetime had passed me by.' Terry looked around at the empty restaurant in the hotel. 'Would I be able to bring my daughter into the restaurant here for dinner tomorrow night?'

'No problem. Just bring her right in.'

'Another thing.'

'Yes?'

'You've been listening to me spout on about how I've found things in England. Would you join me for a drink?'

'I'd be delighted,' said Keith. 'I'll help myself to a shandy.'

'Put it on my bill,' Terry said with a flourish. Another thought occurred to him. 'I didn't catch your name.'

'Keith.' Terry shook his hand.

'A pleasure to meet you, Keith. My name's Terry.'

Keith poured himself a drink and raised it in a mock toast. Terry raised his glass which Keith replenished without waiting for another order.

'To the good times,' Terry said.

Keith added to the toast. 'To the good times. May they roll again soon.'

The two men clinked their glasses and knocked back the contents, unaware of how they both had a common link in Gillian.

★★★

Keith was very busy in his daytime job as a telephone engineer, rewiring internal cables and installing new extensions. The day after he had met

Terry Hodgson for the first time he was working in a large office block. He had just unravelled a long piece of coil and wired it to a block terminal when he happened to glance out of the window. To his surprise, he saw Gillian crossing the road. What was she doing in town, he wondered?

In actual fact Gillian was in the process of further trying to improve the quality of her life. She had come into town to check out the job prospects at employment agencies. Rather than face a lifetime of working at soul-destroying jobs purely for economic need, Gillian was going to try and find something of substance. But it was going to be a case of moving mountains. At 39 years of age without any real qualifications or experience behind her, trying to find work in a recession was going to be close to impossible.

At one job agency Gillian studied the vacancies in the window. It was frightening just looking at the desired experience for some positions: must be computer literate, knowledge of accountancy systems required, keyboard skills and shorthand a must, educated to university degree level, a diploma in business studies essential. Gillian nearly gave up before she had started. What was the point of even trying to be considered? For a moment she was about to walk on, then she had a change of heart and remembered an old saying: 'nothing ventured, nothing gained'. At least she would try to find out whether there were any options available to her. With a sense of nervousness about her she entered the office.

A while later, Gillian had filled in a form about her personal and working life. The young lady who interviewed her was well versed in her role as a recruitment agent, but even she was at a loss as to how to help Gillian find work. However, she was professional and courteous, and read through the form trying to find something that could attract an employer's attention.

'Right, so you've recently completed an employment training course.' The young lady continued to read through, line by line. 'You left school in 1968. St Thomas's Comprehensive. Then a short spell at Pitman's Secretarial College followed by a job as typist for a record company. Then you got married, and after you'd given birth to your children you had a series of...'

Gillian quickly interjected to prevent her own embarrassment. 'Factory jobs, cleaning jobs. I was divorced, and I had my family to look after. I had to work at whatever.'

'I understand,' the recruitment agent said sensitively. 'You completed a typing course. You've brushed up on your shorthand. Also you've just learned the basics of world processing with an Amstrad WordStar course. Very good. Let me see, you're thirty-nine years of age.' The words twisted. She read further down the form. 'You've given as you reasons for wanting to return to full-time work: "keen to resume a full time career in a commercial or administrative field. I have spent many years bringing up my children and I am now ready to take up my career again."'

The recruitment agent looked at her and spoke firmly and honestly. 'As you know, 1991 has been a year of recession. Small businesses are going bankrupt. Companies are trimming staff. Job vacancies are at an all-time low. Even many of the big established firms have had to cut back on their staff. It would be wrong of me to give you false hope.'

Gillian prepared herself to leave. It had been wrong of her to even try at this time, she thought.

'So basically,' she began to say in a tired, resigned voice, 'you're saying there's nothing for me. You can't really help me.'

The recruitment agent was equally honest. 'As far as the big firms are concerned, yes. I'm afraid the situation at present is far from being good even for highly qualified people.'

'That's sad,' Gillian said quietly. In reality she was seething with anger for it had taken her a lot of nerve to try this far. 'I'm genuinely keen to return to work. I'm prepared to work hard and tackle anything.' Her anger and positive attitude became apparent. 'In fact, I'd even go so far as to say I'm looking forward to getting my teeth into something constructive. I feel I've got a lot to offer, I think I've got potential that's never been fully utilised. I might even add that I've got a maturity gained through battling my backside off to bring up my kids. I may not have the qualifications, the educational background or a history of good quality jobs, but I've got good common sense, I'm very positive, I'm not afraid to tackle anything, and if I could organise the lives of three children and myself on next to nothing for nearly twenty years, then I can organise an office.'

Gillian suddenly noticed that the young lady in front of her was smiling.

'Marvellous! You've convinced me!' The recruitment agent was delighted by the way Gillian had spoken. 'Let me add that to your CV.' She wrote the details down. 'Keen and enthusiastic lady. Mature personality. Eager to work hard. Has unlimited potential. Desires long-term career.' Gillian looked on in amazement, realising that her outburst had prompted more interest in her. 'Do you know, I might be able to help you after all. Have you ever done any work managing budgets and accounts?'

'No, never.'

'But that's where you're wrong. You have.'

Gillian was startled at what she perceived as the woman's perfunctory tone, but pleasantly surprised.

'Don't underestimate the duties of running a household. Every day you manage a budget. You have to make allowances for gas, telephone, heating, food, clothes for the children.'

'Television licence,' Gillian volunteered.

'Television licence. And I bet you have to perform miracles equal to the feeding of the five thousand with a few loaves and fishes, don't you? Well, believe it or not I might have something you can do. About half an hour ago a man called Ron Nicholls rang me. Ron runs an electrical business in town. Part of it is a shop selling videos, televisions, electrical appliances around the house, that sort of thing. The other half is a contractors: electrical installation, rewiring, odd electrical jobs. He's just lost his personal assistant who's moved abroad with her husband. He rang me asking me if I could find a lady who could fill in for her. It's for three months on a trial basis, then if you both like each other it would become a permanent position. The business is doing well, despite the recession.

'What does the job consist of?' Gillian asked showing interest.

'It's a PA, personal assistant.' The young lady shuffled through some papers. 'I'll give you the drum on the position. "Ron Nicholls, manager of Ron Nicholls Electrics requires mature, sensible lady, eager to work hard with potential for development, some knowledge of word processing required, ability to handle accounts in order of priority. The job has potential for expansion." That sounds like you, Gillian. Would you like me to send a copy of your CV on the facsimile machine to Ron? I might be able to get an interview for you this afternoon.'

'This afternoon?' Gillian was surprised at the pace that was gathering.

'Yes, if I can arrange it.' She was quick to note the look of anxiety on Gillian's face. 'Give it a go, Gillian. You're well dressed, not too showy. You're natural. Some of the best decisions people have made have been the ones that were made spontaneously on impulse. A few seconds each way, and it's surprising how different a person's life could be.'

Gillian absorbed the words, considering the hidden message as well as the irony.

'Alright, I'll try for it. Put my name forward.'

For the second time that day Gillian found the courage to go along for an interview. It may have been a snip for some, but for a person like Gillian who had long been out of the interview circuit this was quite nerve-wracking. Gillian need not have worried. Ron Nicholls was a genial, polite and easy-going man. He was nobody's fool, however, and knew exactly what he wanted in an employee. He had no time for empire-builders or egotists. Ron was running a down-to-earth business. His employees had to pull their weight, give a first-rate performance, a productive day's work, and learn to cut the mustard.

The recruitment agent had spotted some of these qualities in Gillian's character. There was an absolute rightness about Gillian for the position in question. It was up to her now. Gillian had to get across her determination and enthusiasm at the interview. Surely Ron would spot how genuine Gillian was in character, and recognise her potential.

'This is a fairly easy-going place to work,' Ron explained to Gillian, who sat across the desk from him. 'There is a lot to be done though. Thursdays and Fridays can be particularly hectic at times. I need someone to keep stock of sales dockets, to make a daily record of VAT, sort out the accounts with me. Let me see, what else can I tell you? I have a number of electricians working for me. They do jobs in private premises mainly, rewiring plugs, sockets, light fittings, installation. The electricians' timesheets have to be checked against the actual work they've performed, and their pay calculated together with overtime.'

Gillian felt this was the moment to slot in a remark of her own. 'I believe you're in the process of setting up a...'

'A word processing system.' Ron Nicholls second-guessed her. 'That's right. I understand you've just completed a course in that subject.'

'Yes I learnt the basic of the Amstrad WordStar system on the employment training programme.'

'Fine. Well, we'll work on that together,' he said, almost in assumption that he would be offering the job to Gillian and she would be accepting. It was a hopeful sign. 'Now. The hours are nine to five, or eight-thirty to four-thirty, whatever you find suitable to tie in with your family. There will be overtime and Saturday work if required. We're a small business but I've managed to get my employees paying into a private pension scheme run by one of the big companies. In addition I'm trying to encourage members to put a bit by in a savings scheme. I want my employees to be well looked after. The salary for the position is £13,500 per annum. Now, are you interested?'

Gillian did not hesitate. 'Yes. If you want to employ me I'll give it everything I've got.' She thought of the salary: £13,500 per annum, and that did not include overtime or weekend work! It was an absolute fortune to her.

'Good lass! I'll be happy to take you on,' said Ron.

Gillian could have jumped up and hugged him. This man was giving her the chance to change her life from all that had gone before. No more would she clean other people's lavatories or grind away at factory jobs. Suddenly fate and her own determination had combined together to give her a long-awaited chance.

'Thank you very much indeed,' she said, hardly bothering to conceal her delight at this stroke of good luck.

'I was rather hoping you'd accept. What I've been looking for is not so much someone overflowing with certificates, but a no-nonsense sort of person with common sense, the ability to work hard, maturity and a grasp of reality. This business is for practical, down-to-earth people who can pull together as a team, work well as individuals and, more than anything, enjoy their work. I've worked with a few prima donnas in my time, people who thought they were a cut above everyone else, and they invariably put the whole team out. All I ask for is a quality day's work. My motto is: get the job done and get it done well.'

'When would you like me to start, Mr Nicholls?'

'Let me see. Today is Thursday. Would Monday be too soon for you?'

'That would be fine.' Gillian sighed. A definite starting date for the job. It was almost too good to be true.

Ron stood up and shook her hand lightly. 'Welcome to the company, Gillian. Glad to have you aboard. I hope that you will be very happy with us.'

Gillian was in an ebullient mood that afternoon. Having come through her interview son successfully and unexpectedly, she could hardly believe the luck that had come her way. At the fitness club in the evening a tune called 'Keep on Running' by Wayne Fontana and the Mindbenders blasted from the stereo speakers. Gillian and her fellow classmates leapt up and down in the almost sexy moves of aerobics. Things were changing fast in Gillian's life. Luck, fate and her decision to control events had contributed to this.

★★★

Terry would be returning to South Africa in a short while. Before he left, he had much lost ground to make up with his ex-wife and family. To some extent, time had been a healer. The unhappiness of their marriage and the deep scars of the divorce had passed into history. Still, things had to be said. Apologies for the past had to be made.

Terry and Gillian met in a nearby park and walked through until they found a bench overlooking a lake where swans glided past gracefully. For a while they sat together more in the fashion of old friends than ex-lovers and spouses. It was strange, but the divisions they had known as man and wife had been healed.

Terry looked at Gillian with new admiration. The change in her was clear to see. Certainly, the worry and struggle of the years had taken its toll on her. But now with her new pursuits and job, and happier private life, there was once more something of the young girl who Terry had seen so long ago in King's Road. The girl with warm eyes, that was how Terry saw her now. That was how he'd seen her years before.

'Do you harbour much bitterness towards me?' Terry asked quietly and candidly.

The question surprised Gillian. She did not react badly in anger. Nor was she able to answer straight away. It was difficult for her to think whether she did or not. Finally, after a pause and a study of Terry's expression, she found an answer.

'No Terry,' she replied softly. 'I suppose over the years I've blamed you.' She touched his hand quickly. 'But I shouldn't.'

'I suffered in many ways, Gillian,' Terry explained. 'Oh, I know you might take exception to what I say. Please don't. For many years I've wanted to apologise, even beg your forgiveness, and it doesn't come easy for me to say this. I felt that our divorce was a dreadful failure on my behalf, and as a man too. I wanted to provide properly for you and the children. When we separated I found myself unemployed, on the dole. I had a bad enough job trying to provide for myself with food and lodgings. It was awful.'

Gillian looked deep into his eyes. She did not know what to say. It was as if the whole world had turned, and the people she knew suddenly found it important to express their love and apologies.

'I've thought about the past an awful lot too, Terry,' she said in a quiet voice that hinted at one point that she may break into tears. However, Gillian managed to restrain her feelings. 'In fact, the more I think of it, we were two young people caught in marriage far too early. Maybe if we'd had a long engagement and married perhaps a year or two later...' She broke off suddenly. 'There's an old Chinese proverb someone told me once: "To regret the past is to forfeit the future".'

'I've heard that one too,' Terry remarked. His eyes were misty and streaked with red. He became emotional now as he spoke. 'Do you know, Gillian, coming back here and seeing you and the children has awoken so many memories for me, and regrets, and a sense of sadness. I remember the first time I saw you in King's Road, in the Chelsea Drugstore when you were with your friends. I took one look at you and I fell madly in love. I thought it was the stuff of women's magazines. But no, it was real for me. And there was that girl with you who giggled all night long.'

'Penelope,' Gillian remembered with a smile. 'I wonder what became of her.'

'I expect she's still giggling somewhere.' A pause followed as Terry noted the twinkle in Gillian's eyes. 'I love it when you smile. That's how I've always remembered you over the years: the girl with the smiling eyes.'

'After all those rows and unhappy times?'

'Despite all those rows.' He seemed happy to be telling her this. 'I thought about you and the children so often. I was always writing letters to Samantha and the boys. I imagined I would be there in South Africa only a few years, make a bit, and return home. There was even a thought in the back of my mind that...' he hesitated.

'That what, Terry?' Gillian asked.

'I thought that maybe in better economic circumstances when I returned to England with some money and good job experience behind me I might have got a much better job here. Possibly one from which I could have provided or you. I even hoped that in time you and I might have been able to bury the past, forget the divorce, and maybe even... remarry.' Gillian looked amazed by Terry's admission. 'Oh yes, I'd never completely given up on you and the children.'

'I didn't know, Terry.' Gillian's voice was filled with surprise. 'Why are you telling me this now?'

'So much has to be said, Gillian. I surprised myself when I got married for the second time and had two more children. Somehow I knew that life moves on. You and I had gone the distance. It hurt, knowing that there was to be no return. I paid for our divorce by the fact that I never saw the children growing up. It hurt knowing you were bringing them up alone and that I couldn't be there to influence them in some way. To discipline them, help them with their school work and assist them. You did a wonderful job, Gillian. Against all odds too. I was blessed with a second chance when I had my other two children. Every day I keep looking at them, thinking how lucky I am to be watching them grow. Still, you don't want to hear about that do you?'

'I don't mind,' Gillian said with a smile. 'You've changed, Terry. I don't know what it is, I can't put my finger on it.' Now this was interesting. 'I keep thinking of you as… well a bit of a Jack the lad.'

'And now I'm no longer Jack the lad. I'm Terry the man. I've grown up much more, I suppose.'

'It's not that.' Gillian tried hard to describe the change in her former husband. 'You never opened up to me the way you do now. You seem much more honest and revealing about your feelings, you're far more sensitive, but there's not too much bull about you. I know we were still teenagers when we first married. You were far different then, though.'

'I think in my case, Gillian, it's because I became a Christian when I married again. My second wife is a Dutch-born South African girl from a strong churchgoing family. Her influence on me was strong. In difficult situations where I would get angry and frustrated, she would remain calm; I could not imagine her giving in to hatred or resentment. I asked her how she did it and she told me what she attributed her peacefulness to: faith, love, an inner strength from her religious belief. It's calmed me down no end.'

'And it shows,' Gillian remarked.

'With you too,' Terry felt inclined to comment. 'The way you've taken control of your life again.' There was one thing Terry wanted to ask her. He seized this moment to do so. 'Have you ever loved again?'

Gillian seemed shy at the question. 'No.' Her reply was softly spoken. Terry looked at her sympathetically, which prompted a further explanation. 'I've not had the opportunity until recently, when I've been out with my local window cleaner.'

The window cleaner. Terry did not ask any more. He left it at that, happy that at least his ex-wife had a male companion. He nodded his head and smiled.

'I'm glad you have someone,' he said gently. 'Will it be alright if I take Samantha to dinner this evening?'

'No problem.' Gillian and Terry both stood up as if they had read each other's mind. 'Terry… something else.' He looked at her curiously. 'Thank you. Thank you for being so open about things. For your kind words.'

Terry touched her arm reassuringly. 'It's about fifteen years too late.'

★★★

At the Load of Hay where Terry was staying, he took his daughter Samantha to dinner at the restaurant there. It was not going to be an easy meeting. Apart from letters, until this trip he had not seen Samantha since she was very young. Over dinner he faced the impossible task of trying to make up for many lost years. It was too late for him to be a father. At the most, he could be a friend to her.

The restaurant was hardly doing brisk business that night. The service was all the more better for the lack of customers. Terry felt proud to be out with his daughter. He was half inclined to wonder if the waiters thought that this lovely young girl was his romantic date for the evening. Whatever they thought, he didn't care. He was just so happy to be spending time with his first-born child.

He looked across at her with a mixture of emotion and pride. How could he, in the space of an evening, make up for so many years? He could but try.

'I'm glad I got the chance to speak to you alone before I left. There's an awful lot of things to talk about. Thank you for replying to my letters, Samantha, and sending me photographs of you growing up.'

'It was Mum's idea, really,' Samantha stated, not meaning to be insensitive. 'Mum said it was to make sure you remembered us even though you were living abroad. She said that no matter what separated Mum and you, to remember that you were always my father. And that you loved us.'

These words were too much for Terry to hear. Samantha watched her father wipe moisture from one eye. Terry was affected emotionally. For a moment he faltered as more tears appeared. He wiped them away quickly.

Samantha was concerned for him. 'Are you alright… Dad?'

The way Samantha had used the word Dad affected him all the more.

He took out a handkerchief and dried his face. It was hard for Samantha to see her father this way.

'There, there. That's better,' he said in a tearful voice. 'Sorry about that. It's alright. I'm fine.' He made a further tearful admission. 'Your mum is a very sweet girl to say that.'

'Do you still love Mum?'

The question from Samantha came like a thunderbolt. It had been anticipated by Terry, however. On the plane coming over he had rehearsed answers to the questions he had fully expected to be asked by his children.

Carefully he phrased his answer. 'When Gillian and I met again, there was no anger, no malice, no division. We greeted each other like old friends.' He was cautious with the rest of his words. 'I like your Mum. In fact it's not untrue of me to say that I admire and respect her enormously. But our love for each other... Well, Sam, it died very early in the marriage. We were just up against the odds as far as making it work was concerned. Anyway, I am married again, to a wonderful girl. She's a born-again Christian, with a remarkably calm and serene nature. But your Mum, she was my first love.'

The memories flooded back and he spoke as if he was narrating the story of his life. 'I'll never forget the first time I saw her across a disco floor in Chelsea. She had the prettiest, kindest face I had ever seen. I didn't believe in love at first sight, but it was, with your mother. That divorce still hurts. They say time is a healer. I've felt a lot of pain over the years which time has not healed: the pain of being separated from you and the boys, not being there to see you grow up. Believe me, Sam, it hurts – and it hurts – and it hurts. You were my first-born. The day I picked you up and held you in my arms was a wonderful day for me. I was only a lad of nineteen. Yet I felt such a joy at your birth. Such a thrill.'

He became expansive now. 'It's one of life's great pleasures to see your children grow. How they crawl on all fours. The way they try to get their balance and fall over on their botties trying to learn to walk. Their first sounds. The look of recognition and unspoken love that appears in their eyes, and the touch that says in a voice you can't hear: "you're my Daddy". That sense of belonging to someone. It is the most tremendous joy, Samantha.'

'Why are you telling me all this, Dad?' Samantha could see how genuine her father was. It had come as a great surprise to her to discover that he was a caring, well-spoken, gentle man.

'I'm saying this because… because I want you to know, to really realise and understand, just how important you are to me. Some parents never tell their children how much they love them. Not even once in a lifetime. Perhaps because the parents get embarrassed. Maybe they think their kids will find it too schmaltzy and laugh at them. Or perhaps because they just don't know the words. Sometimes people think that to show gentleness and sensitivity is a sign of weakness. It's not. It's a sign of strength. To show gentleness and sensitivity is to show signs of emotion; to let someone know there's blood pulsating through the veins and the heart that beats is full of love.'

His daughter was listening attentively. Samantha liked her father. He was warm and eloquent.

'I'm still finding out things about you, Dad. I was only little when you left. From what Mum said, you were the life and soul of any gathering.'

Terry explained. 'All in all, I suppose I'm very much a product of the sixties generation.' He aped a hippy tone. 'Peace and love man – peace be with you, brother.' He grinned at the memory of an age of long hair, beads and flared trousers. 'I wish that attitude would come back now.'

'It's a harder age now, isn't it, Dad?' Samantha asked, realising how much nicer that era seemed to be in contrast to the present day.

'In a way, Samantha, I think that you and Mark and John are growing up in a less compassionate, more insecure age, when some members of this generation seem to want to take out their anger on the weak, the vulnerable, the elderly – even, it seems, the sick. I wish that in schools they taught the young to love everyone, to respect the rights and privacy of people, and somehow imbued that with Christian ethics, and the old-fashioned discipline that I had instilled in me.'

Terry's quiet anger surprised Samantha. Behind the words of eloquence and the gentle voice there lurked strong views within him. 'If my baby is a boy,' Samantha began to say, 'I hope he grows up with some of your character.' She wanted to compliment him and be open as he had been to her. Samantha found the words she wanted. 'You're so different to what I imagined. I thought you were… well, a tearaway I suppose.

'Barry – that's the boy who's the father of my baby – he doesn't want to know. I'm going to bring it up on my own. I know Mum was pregnant with me and when you got married it didn't work. But I'm determined to bring my child up happily. You don't feel bad about me being a single mother, do you?'

'It's nice of you to seek my approval, Samantha. But you need not. I have to admit that I am still a strong believer in the institution of marriage. Speaking honestly, in spite of the break-up of my first marriage I would have been happier if you'd got wed to a decent fellow first of all. But I'm still the proudest grandfather-to-be I know.'

'Thanks, Dad.'

'There's not the stigma attached to one-parent families the way there used to be. In the days of old, villagers might have driven a single mum out of the area. The family of the nineties is not the same unit that it was back in the fifties. The most important things still apply though: love, care, attention, security, understanding, unity. I wish we had more time to talk.' The hour was late. Terry glanced at his watch.

'Do you like living in South Africa Dad?'

'That's not an easy question to answer really, Sam. It's a beautiful place. It's colourful, exciting. I have a good job, a wife and children who I love as dearly as you all, a nice home, and the country has been good to me in the way of work and the standard of living. Yet I have to be honest with you, I have never been at ease there because of the political situation over the years and I've seen some of the terrible conditions that our black brothers have lived in, Soweto for example. I think change will come, but with it will be huge turmoil for all of us there. Lissan comes from Amsterdam originally, and the company I work for has offices there, where I could transfer to in time.'

'I hope you do.' Samantha sounded hopeful. 'It would be good to see you more.'

Her father smiled warmly at her. What a wonderful girl she had grown into. Surely, she would be an equally wonderful mother to her baby when it was born.

'It's been really lovely, Dad. I'll keep in touch when you go back.'

'You make sure you do,' Terry said firmly. He was determined never to let long years pass like this again. 'Come on, I'll run you home. I've got the hire car outside.'

Terry paid the bill and then he and Samantha walked from the restaurant through to the bar. Keith was serving, and he looked up in surprise at the pair of them. He was stunned to see the daughter of his girlfriend together with the guest he had spoken to in the hotel.

'Hullo, mate. Samantha! What are you doing here?'

Terry was equally surprised. 'You know my daughter, then?'

Keith was almost lost for words. The penny suddenly dropped with an awesome thud. 'Your daughter?' So this nice man, with whom Keith had shared a welcome home drink and convivial conversation, was Gillian's ex-husband. He paused, trying to find something to say. In the end he felt duty bound to explain. 'Yes, I know Samantha. I do a window cleaning round on Saturdays. One of the houses I call at is Samantha's mum's place.'

The penny dropped with a jarring thud for Terry too. So Keith was the window cleaner who Gillian kept company with.

'I won't be long, Keith,' Terry murmured, half in shock. 'I'll catch you for a drink when I come back.'

Terry drove Samantha home. Fate seemed to have tweaked his nose more than once on this trip home.

'So Keith has seen quite a bit of Gillian, then?' he asked.

'Yes, he invited us all to a barbecue at his house. He's divorced. He's got a daughter called Tracy, she's deaf. You'd never know it though, she can lip read.'

'I had a nice chat with him the other night in the bar. He seems like a good bloke.'

'I think he's keen on Mum,' Samantha observed, and then added, 'I don't know if it will go anywhere though.'

Terry was silent for a moment. He had always felt guilty that Gillian had never remarried and found happiness again as he had done.

'Your mum could do a great deal worse,' he said quietly.

At Gillian's house Terry drew the car to a halt. This was a wretched estate to bring his daughter home to. Tower blocks that had been erected in slip-shod fashion loomed up into the sky like ugly dragons scarring the horizon. The houses looked desperately in need of paint and renovation. The old guilt feelings surfaced in Terry's mind. If he and Gillian had never divorced. If, if, if... He had to stop thinking about it.

'I won't come in, Samantha,' Terry whispered. 'I expect the boys and your mum have gone to bed by now. I'll come and say goodbye properly to everyone on Saturday. I feel pretty sure I'll be over again and maybe, who knows, each of you might visit me sometime.' He looked at Samantha adoringly. 'Come here, Sam. Let your old man give you a hug.' Samantha put her arms around him. 'I love you, Sam. I'm sorry I wasn't around for you when you were growing up. But I'm still your Dad.'

'It's alright, Dad,' Samantha said quietly and emotionally. She was thrilled to have discovered after years of his absence just what a kind and sensitive man her father was. 'It was worth the wait to know how nice you are. I love you too, Dad.'

Later, Keith and Terry sat alone at one end of the bar. They discussed the woman both men had in common.

'You've known her a while then?' Terry asked. 'I had no idea. Are you in love with her?'

'Yes.' Keith's reply came as no surprise. It was also something of a relief. Terry could see that Keith was a genuine bloke.

'Do you want to marry her?'

This was a serious question that Terry thought Keith would hesitate to answer. He was wrong. Keith's reply was immediate and direct.

'If she'll have me I'll marry her tomorrow.'

'I'm sure she will. You're a decent, hard-working bloke. I believe in addition to bar work and window cleaning you're a telecom engineer as well. Mark wants to join the Merchant Navy soon. John has applied to the RAF. That only leaves Samantha, and when she's had her baby I'd like them to spend a bit of time with my family in Cape Town.'

'So you're not hoping for any reconciliation?'

'Heavens, no!' The suggestion came as a shock to Terry. He was quick to put down the idea. 'I've a new wife and family. I have often thought of what might have been with Gillian. But no, it's history. I know this is silly, Keith, but I've got a feeling you'd make Gillian very happy.'

At this Keith laughed. 'I never thought I'd be encouraged by somebody's ex-husband!'

★★★

Farewells are often difficult occasions. It was extra difficult for Terry. After years of estrangement from his children a happy reconciliation had taken place which Terry felt grateful for. At the airport, Gillian, Mark, John and Samantha had come along to say goodbye.

All too soon the announcement for his flight home came across the departure lounge: 'Would passengers bound for Cape Town, South Africa on South African Airways Flight SA 323 please board at departure gate eleven'.

'That's it. I have to go. Terry hugged each one of his children. He felt immensely sad about leaving. The hardest moment had arrived. He turned to face his ex-wife, and what he saw for a brief moment was the young Gillian, the girl with warm eyes he had first met in a Kings Road discotheque. 'Gillian… take care.'

The pair of them embraced. For a moment they held each other. The thought flashed through his mind that he had another wife and family in Cape Town to return to.

'Take care of yourself,' Gillian murmured, and then to Terry's surprise he realised she was crying.

'Keith's a good man,' Terry said without warning, reminding his ex-wife of someone who loved her deeply. 'He could be good for you.' He leaned forward and kissed her on the cheek. 'God bless. You're still… still somebody special.'

When they drew back from each other Terry and Gillian gave each other beautiful smiles that were reminiscent of a love that had once existed.

Then Terry turned to his children. 'Bye everyone. Look after your Mum and love one another.'

'Bye Dad,' Samantha said cheerfully, although in reality she was going to miss this lovely man who had shown himself to be such a sensitive soul.

'Come home again soon, Dad,' John said in a hopeful tone.

'All the best,' added Mark.

Terry nodded at each of them, smiled, held back his emotions that threatened to break through as tears, and walked away. Gillian and Samantha stood there watching him; their faces were tear-stained. The boys looked on at their father. If only there had been more time.

It wasn't until Terry had sat down in the aircraft that his own eyes clouded with tears. The runway lights shone in the dark of night. His stomach felt heavy and his heart saddened. Yet this trip had been worthwhile. So many things that had been unfinished in the past had now reached a happy conclusion. He had reacquainted himself with his children. He and Gillian had now become friends. Terry had not really enjoyed this journey back into the past, but going back to the old country had helped him no end.

The future was important now. His eyes lit up at the thought of being with Lissan and the children. One thing was certain, though. He would talk it over with Lissan about transferring to Amsterdam or Geneva. The move back to Europe would be a good one. He felt sure about that.

★★★

Keith and Gillian continued their courtship by returning to their favourite venue, Tiffany's Ballroom. On the ballroom floor the dancers performed the rumba to a tune played by a Latin American style dance band. Keith and Gillian sat this one out and watched the self-styled experts.

It was time for Keith to take the action he had long planned. He built the conversation up to the very important question that would make or break the evening.

'I like Terry. He is a nice man,' said Keith.

Gillian appeared rather sad. Meeting him again had not been easy for her. Keith was momentarily worried that Gillian would dwell on past feelings for her ex-husband rather than look forward to the future and a new relationship. His anxieties were soon quelled. Gillian was not to be underestimated; she too had progressed.

'Strange how a man that I couldn't make a marriage work with has become a good friend.' It was a candid statement that Gillian and Terry would remain on speaking terms only. Keith breathed a sigh of relief. Gillian made a further comment that signified how much further along the road she had moved. 'I feel good, you know. I've got a new job which is really working out well. I keep fit. Life is going well for me.'

Keith took the initiative. 'Gillian. Do you think you would ever get married again?'

Gillian immediately knew Keith was going to propose to her.

★★★

The anniversary card read:

> Congratulations on your second wedding anniversary. I am so happy that two of the nicest people found each other. Best wishes to you, Gillian and Keith. Happiness always, Terry.

Gillian smiled at the message from her former husband. She looked out from the sitting room of Keith's house onto the garden. Samantha was sitting with her young child while Tracy looked on. The two of them waved at Gillian.

This was almost too good to be true. Every day Gillian woke up thinking how lucky she was. Keith had proved to be a good husband. They were living in his pleasant terraced house, comfortable, warm and wonderful to come home to. Her job provided her life with interest and tasks that were worthwhile.

Samantha had come through her crisis. After giving birth to a lovely baby girl she had resumed her studies. Tracy and Samantha had struck up a warm friendship now that they were stepsisters. In fact, Samantha had become so impressed with Tracy's skill in learning to lip read that it had influenced her choice of career. Samantha had decided that she would embark on a teaching course that would in time lead to helping young people with a speech impediment.

Terry had moved his family to Amsterdam from Cape Town. The location was just that much closer now and each of the children had been across to stay with him.

Gillian was thrilled with her new-found happiness. It had taken a long time for her to realise that life is an ongoing proposition, and that sometimes the best is yet to come.

5.

Jane and Alec

The Apprehensive Couple

Jane Walsh was a kind, peaceful 26-year-old shop worker. Basically Jane was a girl-next-door type who had only ever had one ambition in life: to marry a nice man and have a family.

The man she had chosen was Alec McCutcheon. Now Alec was in many respects the perfect partner for Jane. He was a hard-working motor mechanic, fun to be with and confident about himself and the future. Alec was honest too. He knew he wasn't handsome, and would admit it, but he was tidy, neat and pleasant in appearance. He was also reliable.

Virtually the same words of description could have applied to Jane. The two of them were ordinary happy North of England folk who never sought adventure or excitement in their lives. They did not question the apparent inertia of their existence; they accepted that their lot in life was simply to work and wed, without thinking of the alternatives.

Jane was in good spirits as she rode on the bus into Manchester's busy city centre. Today was the Saturday that she and Alec would choose their engagement ring. In just a few short months they would be man and wife. Already Jane's mind was filled with daydreams of the big day. The thought of marriage excited her. It was a ticket to a new world.

It would be a white wedding in an old stone church. The choir would be singing lovely hymns that would echo warm harmonies to the very top of the steeple. Jane would be a beautiful bride radiant with love for her husband. Alec would be stunning in top hat and specially hired suit. In true tradition they would both be very nervous as they took the step to a matrimonial life. There would be wonderful wedding day photographs showing the happy couple leaving the church and being showered with confetti. Then there would be the reception, the wedding breakfast, the cutting of the cake, the amusing and sincere speeches, the telegrams which would be cheeky and filled with double entendres. Finally they would leave the reception early in a hire car with a 'Just Married' notice plastered on the window and tin cans attached to the bumper, which would make enough noise to wake the dead as they sped away to a secret destination. There would be the night of bliss they would both share as they became enmeshed in the warmth of a love that neither had given to another. Oh, what a wonderful day it was going to be!

In truth, Jane and Alec had both fantasised and daydreamed of wedding bells and bouquets, but neither of them had seriously thought of the life they would lead beyond that first glorious day and night of their marriage. They were traditionalists in every sense. They would live life by the book.

The future beyond the wedding day festivities did not even enter Jane's head. All she could think about was meeting Alec and placing the engagement ring firmly on her finger. Then to all intents and purposes she would be someone who belonged to somebody; she could display her ring for all to admire and drool over.

Alec too was thrilled. Unlike many other 26-year-olds he had never tasted the intimate aspects of a relationship with a member of the opposite sex. Not that he hadn't been tempted but he really was one of that rare breed, the man who would always be faithful to one girl, and who would wait until the wedding night to consummate their love.

Jane was in ecstasy that Saturday afternoon as she and Alec chose the ring. The jeweller had seen it all so often before: excited young girls with their fiancés pouring over rings with eager eyes and loving looks. And why not indeed? Wedding days are still traditionally the happiest days of a person's life. So perhaps it would be so for Jane and Alec.

When they boarded the bus Alec put his arm around Jane and with his other hand he gripped her slender fingers.

'I can't believe it,' Alec said, in his absolute delight. 'We're really engaged to be married. I feel so lucky.'

'You'd better be a good husband,' Jane chided him. 'Otherwise my dad will give you a bad time!'

Alec laughed. Jane's father George was something of a character. Often obnoxious, he was in reality a soft-hearted man.

'I like your dad,' admitted Alec, adding lightly, 'even if he is a United supporter.'

Jane was her father's greatest fan and public relations expert. 'He's just a big pussycat. A tabby from the alley, mind. But beneath it all he's soft.'

'It's going to be interesting when my folks and your Dad meet. There's my stepmum who is a volatile Belfast girl; my Dad a tough old Glaswegian and your old bloke a Mancunian. Sparks might fly!'

'And so will the fun. They'll love each other. You wait!' Jane pressed the bell. 'This is my stop. See you tonight.'

Jane took the opportunity to kiss Alec like a newlywed. In the middle of the bus Jane and Alec kissed long and lingeringly, much to the embarrassment of an elderly passenger. Alec was taken by as much surprise as the passenger.

'We just got engaged today,' Alec explained to the gentleman.

'Thank God for that,' smiled the man. 'I thought you'd only just met!'

★★★

George Walsh was a gruff, burly Mancunian, nearly 60 years of age. A widower for some years he was a lonely man, still missing his late wife, but he was a good mixer who could mingle with just about anyone. He was blunt, not afraid to offend or raise debate; but he could also be hugely entertaining, and beneath the brash exterior lay a man with love and sensitivity. George had lived a very full life. He had been a miner in a Lancashire colliery, a trawler fisherman, a Communist Party member who had switched to Labour after a crisis of conscience. He had also been a big band leader, a clarinet player and a vocalist who had been compared at various times to Eddie Fisher and Vaughn Munroe. Through his trade union he had secured a job as works manager and convenor with Denis Miles Engineering where he had worked for some years.

Truly George was a man of many talents who had led a varied and interesting life. Since the death of his wife he had doted on his daughter Jane. Fully aware that Jane was never likely to pursue a career, his dearest wish was that she should marry a fine young man and have a happy marriage with children. A man could not wish more for his daughter.

He was sitting in a comfortable armchair with a glass of Scotch on the coffee table beside him. A video of his favourite television programme was playing: *Bullseye* was on the screen, compered by a very nice man called Jim Bowen. George was warm and comfortable in a nice centrally heated room. He had won £50 that afternoon on the 3.15 races. He was very happy. And any minute now his much-adored daughter would breeze into the house wearing a sparkling new engagement ring.

George was immensely proud of Jane. How a gruff bruiser like himself could have fathered a daughter like Jane was beyond him. After all, he had a reputation for being blunt, opinionated, often sharp and aggressive, although all these facets of his character masked the real man, who was more like his daughter than he realised.

Jane was serene, kind, loving and warm and had been of great emotional support to her father when her mum had died. With George, it took a while to get to know his good qualities. Jane's fine points of character were always on display. She was pleasant and courteous to all who met her. In private, George was a warm and friendly man who had always been there for his family and friends. His employer Denis Miles had great respect for George, who in his function as a union convenor had helped to bridge the gap between shop floor workers and management.

There came the sound of the key in the lock. The familiar sound of Jane's footsteps in the hallway alerted George to the fact that his daughter was home. He prepared himself for his first sight of her engagement ring. George smiled as Jane entered the room.

'Hullo, love. I didn't expect you back so early,' he said, stepping up and switching off the set.

'Hullo, Dad. What are you watching?'

'I was just watching that Jim Bowen. I like him.'

Jane changed the subject to the most important thing in her life. 'Got it, Dad. Take a look — the engagement ring!' Quickly she flashed the ring up against the light in the sitting room. It sparkled brightly like her personality. 'What do you think? Do you like it?'

George took her hand and made a play of examining it closely. Jane could not wait for her father to comment.

'Well, I'm thrilled. I know that much.'

George kissed her on the cheek and squeezed her. 'So you should be, lovely. It's very nice.' It had suddenly dawned on him that the rehearsal was over now. His daughter really was going to get married. 'Tell me, have you and Alec set a date?'

'We thought the first of July would be nice.'

'The first of July.' George mused at the thought of a pleasant summer wedding. 'That gives us a few months to get everything sorted out.' He took another look at the ring. 'I wish your dear mum was still alive.'

The words touched a raw nerve in both of them. Jane missed the chirpy calm of her mother. She could see the tears in her father's eyes. The wedding would have been the one occasion her mum would truly have loved to live to see, and be at George's side.

'You still miss Mum terribly don't you, Dad? I know I do.'

'I do, Janie,' George said in quiet candour. 'You know she always wanted you to marry a nice lad and settle down to a happy life.'

'I always thought Mum had so many good qualities that it would be hard to live up to her memory.'

George rubbed her shoulder gently. 'You're alright, love.' His voice was warm and reassuring. 'You're unique, and you've got a lot of nice traits about you. But often I see a lot of your mother in you.' He paused for recollection. 'Your mum never had huge ambitions. But she reckoned if you could add up the sum total of the years of your life and it equalled happiness, then that made everything alright.'

'I'll be proud to have you give me away Dad. No tears though.' Jane knew that her Dad was capable of shedding a tear on the odd occasion.

'The last time I shed tears,' pointed out George, 'was when a streaker ran out on the pitch at Anfield and scored a goal against Liverpool!'

★★★

Alec McCutcheon felt happy that afternoon. He was now officially engaged, and it was a good feeling. At 26 he was well aware of the fact that he should have left home long ago. Yet every time he had tried to move, his parents, knowing of his future marriage plans, insisted he stay at home to save money. He offered little resistance, but at the back of his mind he always felt as if he was imposing on his father and stepmother. They had not had the house to themselves much during the course of their married life. That would soon change, though.

There was absolutely no bull about Alec's father Jimmy. He was an industrious, hard-working, sometimes hard-hitting, self-employed builder from Glasgow who had come up the hard way. In Jimmy's eyes there was little flexibility for things he had no belief in. Like George Walsh he had a character that could often be misread. The hard-working Scotsman, who loved a bet on the races and followed soccer and rugby league with a passion, in reality had few friends, preferring the company of his family.

After the death of his first wife, when Alec was only 12, Jimmy had not expected ever to marry again. Some years later Jimmy surprised himself by marrying for the second time: his bride was a red-headed Belfast girl called Leonie Yates who now at 40 was some 15 years younger than himself. Leonie was a bundle of fun and energy. Lively and mischievous, she was tremendously supportive of Alec and Jimmy. She was good-hearted with a warm flirtatious manner, but there was no other man for her than Jimmy, whom she loved passionately. Leonie had not been married before and she had been a warm friend to her stepson Alec. She had been unable to have children, and as a result doted on him with warmth.

When Alec returned home that afternoon, Leonie and Jimmy were both watching the Saturday sports results on television. Jimmy sipped from a can of Scottish beer and smiled as the screen showed his favourite teams winning.

'Look at that! Rangers at the top, Dundee won at home, Hamilton doing nicely…'

And then the door opened and Alec entered the room. 'Good afternoon folks. How are we all?' He sounded bright and bubbly.

'Now there's a chipper lad if ever I saw one,' Leonie observed.

'Let me guess,' Jimmy said quietly 'Your horse came in first at the races? You found somebody's pay packet and there was no name on it? What else? United lost and City won?'

Alec enjoyed letting them guess the reason for his buoyant spirits. Finally he decided to make his announcement. 'No, nothing like that at all. Both United and City drew as a matter of fact. I've got a little bit of news for you both.' Alec gestured with his hands, motioning them both to stand up. 'Ladies and gentlemen, would you please be upstanding.'

Leonie stood up in a mischievous mood, realising that Alec was joking. Jimmy joined in the fun and stood up and grinned.

'Congratulate me, then! Jane and I are officially engaged as of today. I bought Jane an engagement ring.'

Jimmy came forward smiling, shook hands with and then embraced his son. 'That's wonderful news. I'm so happy for you, son.' He turned to Leonie, beaming a happy smile. 'I'm thrilled. Imagine that, Leonie! We'll be going out for a free meal!'

It was Leonie's turn now to embrace Alec and kiss him warmly. The delight she felt was on clear display.

'Never mind the free food! I'm very happy for you, Alec. I know I'm not your real mother, and I can never replace the fine woman that she was, but I love you as if you were my own. I hope you'll have a long and happy marriage.'

Alec was moved by the words of his stepmother, who was generous and loving. It was such a tragedy that she had been unable to give birth to children, for in her own way she would have been a lovely Irish mammy.

'God bless you, Leonie,' Alec said gently. 'Dad did alright when you came along after Mum died. You're a flesh and blood relative to me as much as the old fellow there.'

'What d'ya mean, "the old fellow"?' Jimmy was more amused than annoyed. 'I'm not so old that Leonie couldn't find something attractive in me. I well remember the first words she said about me...'

'So do I,' Leonie piped up quickly. 'I said, "Who's that grey-haired fellow with the battered look, the weary eyes and the lived-in-face?" And Jimmy said, "For heaven's sake is that lassie with the flaming red hair and the husky voice talking about me?" Ah yes, it was love at first sight.'

'Well, I'm seeing Jane tonight,' said Alec. 'Perhaps we could organise a get-together with her dad George. Say next Saturday night.'

'That's fine by me.' Jimmy nodded to Leonie. 'OK with you, Leonie?'

'Yes. That's lovely.'

Alec thought for a moment how two such strongly opinionated characters as George and Jimmy would get on. If he had been a little older and wiser he would have realised that they would get on famously.

'I don't know how you'll get on with George,' Alec said cautiously. 'He was a former band leader in the sixties. He used to play all the clubs, like Batley and the Tower Ballroom at Blackpool. Used to sing a bit. Still does if the mood takes him. Always at the centre of things. He's a works manager and union bloke.' Jimmy was listening curiously. Alec carried on with his description of George. 'He was a Commie once but he switched to Labour. You'll have plenty to talk about.'

'Sounds like an interesting guy,' Jimmy said, rubbing his chin.

Alec and Jane met outside the cinema that evening. They kissed and embraced warmly. It was a great feeling to be in love, thought Alec, and to have somebody greet you so warmly in full sight of other people.

'What did your dad say about the ring?' Alec asked.

'He was alright, seemed to be impressed by the ring. I think he was more relieved than anything that the wedding is a few months away, so that he can get things organised.'

'I know this is silly. I've asked you to marry me. I don't mean that's silly. You've accepted, we've got the ring. But we haven't thought about where the wedding is going to be, or the reception.'

They turned to enter the cinema.

'We've got a lot to work out,' said Jane somewhat apprehensively.

★★★

George took the opportunity that night to celebrate. There was a public house that he had frequented in his younger days when he had been a heavy drinker. He rarely touched alcohol or spirits now. A heart attack and a permanent battle with his weight had caused him to take stock of his health. Apart from a small Scotch on Saturday afternoons when he watched sport on television, he led an almost teetotal existence.

But tonight he would make an exception and go to the pub to toast his daughter's future with old pals. The moment he walked into the old establishment familiar faces smiled and people came up to him to shake his hand. It was good to meet old friends again. Little had changed since he was last there, including the band which played on stage. Even the barman recognised him from five years before.

'George!' he exclaimed, shaking his hand warmly. 'A long, long time since we saw you in our snug little alehouse. I thought you had long given up the sin of the demon drink.'

A wicked grin spread across George's face. 'Time for the devil to join the demons!'

'What's the occasion then, George?' asked the barman. 'And it is something of an occasion when you tread the hallowed ground in here. Celebration or commiseration?'

'My daughter Jane got engaged today,' remarked George. 'It's half a celebration, I suppose, and a little bit of commiseration. She's got herself a nice enough lad. The fiancé is a motor mechanic so he should be able to look after her.' The barman listened attentively. 'Daughters, they're so precious. The lads take care of themselves. But when it's your only daughter it's got to be right, hasn't it? Make mine a double Scotch. And whatever you want.'

'That's very nice of you George. I'll have one and drink to your daughter's health.'

The barman fixed the drinks. George looked up at the band playing on the stage. He immediately recognised the saxophonist as being one of his old colleagues from the days he led a big band. There was also a spark of recognition in the musician's eyes as he spotted George.

'Cheers,' said George taking the drinks and proffering a £5 note across the bar.

From the stage the musician wandered down to greet him. 'George Walsh!' he exclaimed, slapping him on the back.

'Ted Burgess!' George responded with equal delight.

'You two know each other?' asked the surprised barman.

'Do we ever?' Ted replied happily. 'When we were miners we used to play for the Dranthord Colliery band, and some years later I joined his big band round the clubs. Look at him, my old band leader, the old showman himself! He's the only ex-Communist I know who can sing like a lark and sting like a bee!'

George looked at his old friend and said with good humour, 'How are you, Ted? Do you still play the saxophone badly?'

'Even worse than when I played in your band, and getting worse by the week.' It was Ted's turn now to take the rise out of his former colleague. 'What about you, George? Are you still as obnoxious as ever?'

George was not to be outdone. 'I'm in a class of my own, Ted. Unmatched anywhere!'

'Good to know you're still holding your own! How about joining the boys for a song? You used to be able to deliver an old-time melody in a manner of Eddie Fisher or Al Jolson or Vaughn Munroe or Issy Bonn or David Whitfield. You were a man of many voices and many songs once.'

'I still am.'

The barman urged him as well. 'Yes, come on, George. Special occasion today.'

'Why's that?' queried Ted.

'My daughter got engaged today,' George answered.

Ted smiled at him and shook hands in congratulations. 'Come on the stage and dedicate a song to her.'

George reluctantly decided to give in. 'Alright boys, you've talked me into it. Don't expect me to do any rap dancing. One song and one song only.'

Ted and George walked up to the stage. It was a long time since George had performed in public. He had performed on many stages in his life. Facing an audience had never been a problem for him. When he had performed with his big band he had played gigs at some of the top venues around the country: Caesar's Palace at Luton, the Tower Ballroom in Blackpool, Batley Variety Club in Yorkshire. He had also performed at miners' clubs, working men's clubs, British Legion clubs, as well as being the supporting act to big-name variety entertainers, often stealing the show.

In his capacity as a trade union official, George had also performed to a different type of audience. At branch meetings he had been vociferous in speaking for the rights of his union members. Curiously enough, he had also appeared at the same venue at Blackpool but this time at the TUC and Labour Party conferences, putting forward a composite motion for consideration.

In the pub George adjusted the microphone and addressed the audience. It was fun to be doing this again. He hadn't lost confidence.

'Good evening ladies and gentlemen, and hecklers!' Just dare heckle me, anyone, he thought. George was a master of the put-down when the occasion arose. But it seemed no one dare challenge him. 'George Walsh is the name. Originally they had a choice of entertainers tonight: me or William Shakespeare. Unfortunately Shakespeare couldn't make it tonight as he has been unavoidably dead for four hundred years and he couldn't sing anyway so I very kindly offered my services. The boys have asked me to join them for a song. My daughter got engaged today and I'd like to dedicate this next song to her. So what better song to sing for a daughter than...' He hesitated and smiled. 'Than "Unchained Melody".' It was an unusual choice but George could belt this song out with the best of them. He looked to the band. 'OK boys, take it away.'

The band began to play. George had a strong resonant voice that carried well across the pub. The audience in the pub were spellbound. He felt good with his delivery of the song. Naturally the audience wanted more. George performed a whole repertoire that night. It had been a long time since he had performed live and he could happily have sung all night if he had been asked to do so.

★★★

'There you are, mate. Get that into you.'

Alec moved out from beneath the car in the garage. He dusted down his oily overalls and looked up into the smiling face of his fellow mechanic, a West Indian lad called Tim. He was a happy-go-lucky fellow in his late twenties, always ready with a smile and a joke. The aroma of coffee awoke a thirst in him.

'Coffee. Lovely. I could just do with that.'

He took the mug from Tim and they both sat down on chairs inside the garage. For a moment they both sat quietly, and then Alec cast a smiling glance at Tim as if he was about to tell him a hilarious joke.

'Okay man, what's the big wind-up?' asked Tim in good humour. He knew his pal and workmate well enough by now.

'Would you like to be best man at my wedding?'

Tim was thunderstruck. He looked at Alec open-mouthed. 'This is a wind up?' he asked again.

'No.' Alec was laughing at Tim's surprised look.

'Are you getting married, Alec boy? Hey man, that's great.' He shook Alec's hand. He was really happy for his friend. 'Congratulations. Jane Walsh of course.'

'Yes, my lovely Jane. Who else?' Tim could see the misty look in Alec's eyes.

'I'd be honoured to accept,' Tim said humbly. 'That's really nice of you to ask me. Why did you choose me?'

'Oh well, you and I have worked together since I left school. We've been good mates for a long time. Soulmates in fact. I reckon we both know each other inside out. So why not?'

Tim was thrilled to be asked. He was, in his own way, a bit of an entertainer. He had no inhibitions whatsoever.

'I'm sure it's going to be a grand do, Alec. I'll have to brush up on my speech-making and get the dinner suit down to the dry cleaners. Me and my lady have been together six years now. Two lovely children, a mortgage, the whole works. Catastrophe and cacophony! And we still haven't got down to the altar yet.'

This revelation surprised Alec. He had long assumed that his best friend had tied the knot years before.

'I didn't know that. I thought you'd been through the whole ceremony. And you've been together six years! Gosh, don't you feel a sense of urgency?'

'Nah.' Tim was instantly dismissive of the whole idea of marriage. 'At least it's no big deal for me. But I suppose we'll get round to it sometime.'

To some extent Alec shared his father's conservative outlook on marriage. He could not understand why two people who were in love would choose to live together and have children without the benefit of marriage. For the first time since he had purchased Jane's engagement ring, he found himself wondering about the situation.

'Don't you feel strange?' Tim looked at him mystified. Alec decided to elaborate. 'I mean, you have a family, but you're not married. I would feel strange; really out of sorts in fact. If I had children and I didn't have that marriage certificate which binds the family together, I'd feel like I was doing wrong by them. Do you know what I mean?'

Tim thought deeply about this for a moment. It was obvious that he was someone who acted instinctively, perhaps even impulsively, and did not always consider the long-term effects of his actions.

'I do get your meaning, mate,' he replied a bit sheepishly but then he came back good and strong, and firmly on the defensive. 'Because I'm not married it doesn't mean to say I love my family any the less. Far from it. My lady and my kids are treasures to me, worth more in their love to me than their weight in gold dust. I give them a lot of love. And boy, do I get plenty of love back from them! I'm a family man through and through, even though I may not be married legally. In fact when you look at it, taking all things into consideration, I'm probably under more pressure from society by not being married. I'm willing to bet you though that my relationship has probably got stronger foundations than the one that's been legalised in a Register Office or at the church altar.'

Tim was really getting down to the reasons now. Alec was curious about his friend's way of thinking. 'Why has your relationship in your opinion got more strength than others?'

Tim was certainly no slouch when it came to defending his own corner. 'I can't speak for all de facto relationships and couples living in so-called sin, but my lady and I have got a degree of trust and honesty about us. I'm true to her, she's true to me. We both made a vow to each other to be loyal and faithful. We love each other, we trust each other. The key word is "trust".'

Trust. The word had a ring to it. 'But isn't that what most marriages are founded on anyway?' Alec asked, almost in protest.

'I'm no expert on marriage. You'd have to see a guidance counsellor for professional advice. My humble opinion – and it is only humble – is that the marriage certificate makes the relationship complacent. People seem to think there's romance in marriage, but they just relax after the ceremony and say this is it, we're married. That's it, no need to work at it any more. Sometimes I think that's why so many marriages in this day and age end in divorce.'

The more Tim spoke, the more convincing he sounded. 'You've got me thinking very deeply now,' Alec admitted. 'Jane and I absolutely adore each other. We want children. The whole box of dice, skittles and chess pieces, to be exact. I must admit I'm looking forward to the day, the marriage ceremony and the starting of a new life. What worries me is how will Jane and I feel about each other a few years down the track? Will she still feel good about me? Will I still feel good about her? Could we grow apart? Maybe I should give it a bit longer.'

'You were pretty confident a few minutes ago,' Tim said with a wave of alarm. 'Don't let me put you off, man. I'm only telling you what I think. Everybody has got their own views on the matter.'

'I'm a traditionalist,' Alec announced. 'I still believe in the white wedding, the blessing of the church, the confetti and the wedding cake.' It sounded more as if Alec was trying to convince himself than Tim.

'There you are, then,' Tim said relieved that Alec had not changed his mind.

But Tim had unwittingly sown the seeds of doubt in Alec's mind about the stability of marriage. For the rest of the day at work the same thoughts kept running through Alec's mind. Was it marriage that he really wanted? Did he really feel ready to enter the permanent institution of matrimony? Could it be that he simply wanted to be with Jane as man and wife, without going through all the legal niceties? Surely, living together was easier than marrying and possibly going through a divorce later on.

All these questions flooded his mind. The thought that really struck him hard was this: perhaps the legal commitment of marriage, the permanency of a union in church, was too daunting at this stage of his life. He suddenly felt like the understudy in a repertory theatre production who had unexpectedly been given the leading role. Was he really ready for it? Was he really ready for marriage?

★★★

'Phew! What a day! Nearly finished,' Carol said to her co-worker Jane at the department store where they both worked in the beauty section. Carol was a tall, leggy blonde of 36. She was the sort of girl who could turn heads at 100 yards.

'It's been a long day,' Jane agreed. Both ladies were on their feet all day long serving customers, with manners bad and good. Jane tolerated, the job fully expecting that soon after her marriage naturally enough she would be expecting the sound of the patter of tiny feet, then she would happily become a full-time wife and mother.

'Are you going off out somewhere tonight?' Carol secretly envied her young friend, imagining that she had a very full social life.

'No. Quiet night. What about you, Carol? Are you off out?'

Carol laughed at the suggestion. 'I should be so lucky. No, I've got to go home and make my husband and children their evening meal. I've got washing and ironing to do. I've got vacuuming to be done, and my husband wants me to help him wallpaper one of my boys' bedrooms.'

Jane looked astonished. 'That is a long day!'

'All part of married life, I suppose,' Carol said matter-of-factly. Both women leaned on the counter and gazed up at the clock. Just five minutes to go. The shop was almost empty.

Jane was eager to learn how Carol felt about marriage after so many years. 'You wouldn't change it, though?'

'Oh my goodness, no!' Carol was prompt in replying and without being asked she volunteered to expand on this. 'My husband and I have our spats now and again like everybody else. But I love him with all his faults, and he loves me with all mine. My children are a bit of a handful though. They've got to the stage where they want everything their friends at school have got. They keep saying things like, "My friend Martin went to Florida on holiday with his parents", and "My friend Peter had a home computer, a bike and a hundred pounds to spend for his birthday". I can't seem to get it through to them that me and their dad work all hours just to meet the daily bills.'

The two of them started to pack up for the night. Jane listened keenly to Carol. She was well spoken and, given her age in comparison to Jane's, had an authority that added weight to her words. When they had finished tidying the two left the shop together and walked to the bus stop. While they waited in the chilly early evening for their separate buses, they talked as women do.

'You know, Carol, thinking about what you were saying earlier, about your children wanting holidays in Florida and home computers, and all those kind of things...' Carol nodded. 'My dad told me once that if you've got food in the larder, clothes on your back, the rent's been paid and the fare to work is in your pocket, then you're doing alright.'

'Believe me,' Carol began sincerely, 'there are times in the early part of your married life when it's a struggle to get just those things. I'm not trying to put you off. If I had my time again I'd still marry and have children. But I do think I'd try and prepare myself more for marriage. On the wedding day everything seems so exciting. But once you've drifted down the aisle wearing the beautiful once-in-a-lifetime dress and you've heard all the relatives' speeches at the reception, the nights of bliss result in a nine-month pregnancy, feeling like a bloated whale in the North Sea, and the inevitable thought that life is not going to be so easy from now on.'

'But don't you feel good that you've got some emotional support from your husband?' Jane then revealed something she had always felt. 'Life for me without marriage and children, I think it could get very lonely.'

'True.' Carol did not disagree with this although she would have been the first to admit that in a changing world the role of women had also been transformed. 'For women, at least until recent times, marriage was virtually a career. Until Maggie Thatcher became Prime Minister, women invested their years of life in the men they married. Not so today. Take the store we work in, for example, women virtually run the show. It's a woman's world today. Not every girl wants marriage today. Or to put it another way, even so much as needs marriage, the way they used to in the old days.'

'Some men I can imagine not wanting to get married,' Jane said, blowing a breath of steam into the frosty air. Not my Alec, she thought. 'There are some who would probably be happy enough to drink beer with their mates down the pub and do nothing but watch football. With us girls, though, it's our natural instinct to be a wife and mother. We're natural homemakers.'

'I think thirty is a good age to get married,' admitted Carol. 'For a man or a woman. By then you know a bit more about yourself. You've got a pretty good idea who you are and what you want out of life. You've probably even had time to establish a real career direction and get experience.'

Jane considered Carol's statement for a moment. Was it a frank admission that she would not lead exactly the same life again? 'It sounds to me as if you would change things if you had your time again.'

Carol pondered over this. 'Maybe. I was twenty-one when I got married, twenty-two when I had my eldest. He's fourteen now. Perhaps I would wait. But I can't dwell on what might have been, I'm pretty happy with what I've got.'

'I'm twenty-six,' Jane stated almost proudly. 'Five years older than when you got married. It makes me wonder if I am really ready. I couldn't bear it if I got married and in a few years time Alec and I ended up divorced. I wonder if maybe I should extend the engagement. I love Alec so much. He's a lovely bloke. I really, really adore him. All the same, perhaps... perhaps we should wait.'

Thankfully Carol's bus arrived and she said goodbye to Jane, whose bus followed immediately behind. Carol took her seat on the bus, wondering if her candid admissions were responsible for Jane having second thoughts about marriage.

★★★

The workers of Denis Miles Engineering works downed tools at precisely five o'clock, unless overtime was available or they had been specially asked to work shifts in order to reach specific deadlines. For some weeks now the staff on the shop floor had begun to suspect that business was not booming as it used to. Now, unless requested, most of the workers were on short time and all the machines were normally closed down by 4.30.

In his capacity as works manager George checked that all the equipment was fully turned off and inactive. He knew that the factory could not carry on functioning as it had been doing for the past couple of months. The order books were virtually depleted of entries. There were no new contracts on the horizon. It was obvious to him that Denis Miles had not arranged for him to come to his own private office without reason.

After he had finished checking the factory plant, George walked upstairs to the manager's office. He gave two sharp raps and entered.

Behind his desk sat Denis Miles, a gruff North of England man. Today he looked particularly grim-faced. On his desk were a pile of bills and a set of files detailing the history of each member of personnel.

'You wanted to see me? I can guess what about.' George stood for a moment, waiting to be asked to take a seat.

'Take a seat,' said Denis, anticipating George's thoughts. George sat down, while Denis sifted through the files and invoices. The expression on Denis's face said it all. The factory would close, as surely as night follows day.

One of Denis Miles's most irritating habits was inviting people to the office and then making them wait while he fussed and organised himself. For God's sake get on with it, thought George. You're not in show business, waiting for applause, a standing ovation and curtain calls, he thought. George glanced at his watch, which was the trigger for Denis to speak.

'Has everyone gone home?'

'Yes. We're the only ones left.' George looked intently into Denis's face, silently urging him to tell it like it is.

Denis sat back, relaxed and sighed. 'You know why you're here, don't you George?' George nodded and pursed his lips. 'The other week we sat down and worked out a redundancy package for all the staff if we hit a rough trot.'

Denis took a deep breath. Here it comes thought George.

'I'm torn apart. I hate to tell you this. The package will have to be implemented. The company that took over Denis Miles Engineering is being wound up.' His eyes became angry and he was quick to recognise a similar look in George. 'Oh yes, we've been sold down the river. In a fortnight's time this factory is going to cease to function. I've tried desperately to keep this place afloat. This was the last of the five engineering factories I've spent a lifetime building up.' His quiet reserve broke and angry words surfaced. 'Now it's all going down in ruins! I knew I shouldn't have sold out to that mob to keep us going. They've gone bust! The factory and the plant have to be sold off and three hundred and thirty-five jobs on the floor are to be lost.'

George knew where his first priorities lay. 'Where does that leave the staff as far as their entitlements are concerned?'

'Those will be honoured to the letter,' Denis advised him. 'It's all separately funded, so pension, superannuation, outstanding leave plus the details we agreed to in the redundancy outline will all be paid. I'm sorry, George, but that's it, I'm afraid.' He gave George a knowing look that suggested an order was coming. 'You in your role as works manager and union convenor will…'

George second-guessed him. 'I, in my role as works manager and union convenor, will inform that staff that they're all out of a job?'

At once Denis knew that this was unsatisfactory. He was telling his works manager to do the dirty work and give the workers on the shop floor the bad news. It was a cheeky thing to do.

'No. No, I'll do it,' Denis said grimly.

I should bloody well think so, thought George. In a way George felt sorry for Denis. It was a tough thing for anyone to have to do: to tell long-serving loyal staff they no longer have a job.

'I seem to be the bearer of bad news these days. At four factories over the last few years I've had to stand up in front of a sea of disillusioned workers and say overtime is out to save your jobs, we must cut costs, overtime is back, there's shift work, there's no shift work, we're on a three-day week, back to full time… And now I have to make the most heart-breaking announcement of all. The factory's finished. Kaput. And worst of all, that is the last of the line of Denis Miles Engineering.'

'You're telling me it's heart-breaking!' George exclaimed, not caring who knew it. He realised with some anxiety that at nearly 60 years of age his working days were almost certainly over. Another ironic thought entered his head. 'I was due to go to the TUC Congress in Blackpool in a fortnight's time. In the old days when my union had a bit of muscle it might have been able to save the jobs on the factory floor.'

'Nobody could save this lot, George,' Denis said bitterly. 'We're history. I know it's of little comfort, but you and me, only a couple of years separate us, and my livelihood is over. No one will give me a job at my age. I've been working since I was fourteen. I've worked fifty years.' His frustration and anger began to appear more visibly now. 'Fifty years I tell you! And I've lost it all.'

He paused to take stock of the situation. He knew that the man opposite him also had his battle ahead of him. 'Surely some of your mates in the TUC might be able to help you out. After all you've had a lot of experience.'

'Varied experience. That's true,' George mumbled.

'You've had quite a life, George,' Denis said in admiration of his employee. 'I've been in the engineering trade all my life. Never did I try to be adventurous in my way of thinking. I always took the tried and tested route that I thought led to security, not to be being obsolete. Look what's happened now. For all of my years building up the business eighteen hours a day, I've come out with nothing. My marriage broke up, the house has been taken, and I've barely enough capital in the bank to meet staff salaries for the next three months. That's it. I've got to close everything down for good in the next two weeks so that we can all get out with some cash in our pockets.'

'I'm sixty next birthday,' George said emphatically. 'My working life is over as well now.'

'But you've had a go at it all,' Denis pointed out to him. 'What have you been? Miner, trawler fisherman, Communist Party member, Labour Party member. You ran a big band in the sixties while by day you worked as a full-time union convenor and works manager for several factories. It's not been a bad life for you, has it?'

This remark rankled with George. 'My life is not over yet!' He was grim-faced. 'I didn't expect my working life to end quite so abruptly. Nor did the three hundred and thirty-five people on the factory floor! What about them and their families? Who'll come to their aid?'

Denis was speechless. There were times when he wished he had been one of the staff on the floor losing their job. Telling them was going to be so much more difficult.

★★★

At home that night George sat quietly in his favourite armchair, remembering his working life. What a time for him to have to adjust to early retirement! His daughter Jane was getting married and would be leaving home soon. He would be left to mooch about in the house all day.

It seemed like only yesterday that he had begun work as a young lad in the Dranthord Colliery. A Lancashire miner's son, he had more or less followed his father by tradition, going down the pits with other lads of his age. For eight long years he had given up the light of day to work hard at the coal face. It had been hard, grinding work which had introduced him to men with strong feelings for the safety of their colleagues and better conditions for the mines. There were so many things George remembered from those days: the terrible accidents that occurred suddenly without warning, resulting in loss of life or disability; some of the older men looked sallow and drawn, and the accumulation of coal dust in the lungs was responsible for the premature death of so many. George had personally known mates – good mates – who had suffered in both instances.

But there were other things George recalled from his days as a miner. He remembered the freshness of the communal shower at the end of the day as the men scrubbed the coal dust from their aching, perspiration-soaked bodies, and the blackness of the mine drifted with the soot and the grime down the plughole. The men would often sing in the shower; the Welsh amongst them would reach vocal heights in their resonant harmonies. There was great comradeship at the Dranthord Colliery. Many of the men were hardened drinkers when the mood took them, yet so many took time for private and public worship of the God they believed watched over the progress of their daily lives in the pits. The families of the miners were great friends and confidantes. In the event of grief, tragedy or widowhood, the other families never forgot the lot of the bereaved. Help was always on hand. There were Saturday night dances at the Dranthord Miners Club, the working men's club, or the local branch of the British Legion.

When George was young he and his friend Ted Burgess became members of the Dranthord Colliery band. It was from there that both men progressed from brass instruments to saxophones and clarinets, and eventually a big band. It was also at Dranthord that George first got involved in politics. He had heard the local Communist Party members speak in a public rally in terms of state ownership and more benefits for the workers. He was politically naïve at the time, and impressed by the sincerity of the speakers, not realising that in theory many of the dreams of these men were unworkable in practice.

George was called up for National Service and found himself posted with the Army to Korea. It never even occurred to him that once his service was over he would do anything other than return to the mines at Dranthord. On the long sea voyage to Korea his whole world was considerably altered. Passing through the Suez Canal and the Red Sea, the sighting of a lone Arab on a camel would occur from time to time. When his time in the service had ended, George returned to the life he had known, his beliefs unchanged until the invasion of Hungary in 1956. He switched his political affiliations to Labour, and he had remained a party member ever since.

There was one other good reason George remembered Dranthord

Colliery with much affection. One of the miners had introduced him to his younger sister, a pretty girl called Mary. George had courted her for a few months, and then on one happy spring day they married. Ah, but they didn't make women like Mary these days. The two of them had many happy years together, until a fatal viral infection robbed her of life. It had been a tragic loss, but his daughter Jane was there to remind him of that happy marriage.

After the Dranthord Colliery mine disaster, in which many men were killed when the pit caved in, George emerged as one of the few survivors. He was trapped for several days, and it was only the skill of the very able rescue teams that had saved him. Immediately afterwards the pit was closed down and many of the men left Dranthord, seeking work in other fields.

George and Mary moved to Hull where he found work as a trawler fisherman. This was hard work of a different kind. After the confines and the claustrophobic restrictions of the coal pit, to be out on a trawler in the icy North Sea for 20 gruelling hours a day was a new experience. He and the crew members cast their nets adrift for huge shoals of fish which they would haul back in all kinds of weather; storms, fierce cyclonic winds and turbulent seas. Braving the elements was equally as strenuous as facing the depths of the coal face.

In a working men's club in Hull, George happened to chance upon an old friend from the collieries, Ted Burgess, who had played in the mine band at Dranthord. Ted was playing solo spots with his saxophone. The two of them decided to form a big band which would play clubs, provincial theatres and variety shows. After advertising for other musicians, George formed a band much in the mould of those which had dominated the airwaves of the 1940s, although now it was the 1960s, the era of the pop group. Apart from reviving the old standards, the George Walsh big band played the tunes of the day in a repertoire that included anything by Lennon and McCartney, to songs composed by the Jagger and Richards team, and Simon and Garfunkel. Almost any top ten hit was played which could easily be transferred to wind and string instruments.

The band made their base in Manchester after touring Britain and Ireland. Some of the musicians were well into their forties and in need of security, so they took steady daytime jobs. George joined Denis Miles Engineering on the factory floor, and gradually worked his way up. The band broke up, and he devoted his efforts to the firm and the union.

Now, George really did not know what the future would hold. His dear wife had gone. His daughter would soon be married. The factory he worked at was to close. Life could really throw up dramatic changes when they were least expected. He poured himself a very large scotch. Bugger doctor's orders.

★★★

At first glance Jimmy McCutcheon and George Walsh were two men of contrasting characters. One would have been forgiven for thinking that put together in a room their sparky personalities would clash. In fact, they were men with similar attributes.

The common denominator in their characteristics was that they were both working-class lads who had followed their fathers into the same job by tradition. Yet each had moved on from his original occupation to a career of his own choosing. No one would have doubted Jimmy and George's macho tendencies, but like so many men of hard, firmly held views on life, the sensitive side of their character was known only by the women they loved and their immediate families.

While George to all extent and purposes had been a socialist for most of his life, Jimmy was something of a political agnostic. He had no faith in politicians of any creed or colour, believing that profession to be full of people who were dubious and insincere. Jimmy was all for the man who got things done. Political news just held up the football results.

This aspect was probably the only one where their personalities parted company. Each man believed in the value of hard work and in setting aside a healthy proportion of their time for good old-fashioned enjoyment.

Jimmy McCutcheon thrived on hard work. He was born to it. His childhood was spent in Port Glasgow, where he often watched the huge ships heave their way down the Clyde from the yards where they were built. On weekends he would go to the Kyles of Bute with his father Joe, and watch some of the wealthier people sail their yachts. Ever since, he had always loved boats and being near the water.

Joe worked in the shipyards of the Clyde and Jimmy had never questioned where he would work when he left school. Like father like son. Jimmy followed him into the yards. It was there he worked until the time came for his National Service. In his spare time Jimmy had indulged in football and boxing. He had half considered a career in these areas. It would have been a dream for him to have played for Glasgow Rangers in a Scottish Cup Final at Hampden Park. But like most youthful dreams it was one that failed to materialise as the realities of life took hold.

Jimmy served with the Army on the beautiful Mediterranean island of Cyprus. Some of the happiest times he knew were spent with friends in Akrotiri, Nicosia and Limassol. With his Army service over, Jimmy returned to Glasgow. He did not return to the shipyards; instead he chose to work on a building site as a bricklayer. His interest in the building trade bourgeoned and he worked enthusiastically, learning every facet of this occupation. He would have been the first to admit that he was not academically inclined. Yet he was a canny enough Scot to seize opportunities, apply good old-fashioned common sense, adaptability and long hours of toil to make something of his life.

In the 1950s the music of skiffle and rock 'n' roll filled the Glasgow dance halls. Jimmy was there every Saturday night, talent-spotting for the girl who might one day walk down the aisle with him. He didn't have long to wait. One night he saw her, a lovely dark-haired girl from Kilbarchan called Kathy McFadden. Jimmy fought his way through the crowd to dance to 'Rock Around the Clock' with her. Within months he and Kathy were married. The early years of their marriage were the same as for most couples: austere and lean, but full of promise of good things to come.

They were wonderful years for Jimmy and Kathy. His own childhood had not been as happy as it might have been, due to a large family and quarrelling parents. With Kathy he had found a happy, laughing, loving girl who he felt thrilled to be near. In the 1950s and 1960s they moved house in Scotland and England several times, until Jimmy decided to start his own building business in Manchester.

It was there, ten years after their wedding in Glasgow, that their son Alec was born. Sadly, Kathy died when Alec was only 12. Her death from liver failure shattered Jimmy. He knew he had been married to the best. Twenty-two years of a wonderful marriage had ended, and he was inconsolable. Alec, who was suffering considerable heartache himself, rose to the occasion and helped his father through the dark days that followed. Early in his life he learned the harmony of good relationships.

A few years later Jimmy was introduced to Leonie Yates. He had not expected to ever fall in love again. In fact he had never planned to. After all, he had been married to a fine woman, and he was convinced that he could never experience such happiness again. Leonie was similar in many respects to Kathy: she was fun, flirtatious and bubbly, and with a cheerful Irish charm that brought humour to any given situation. It was hard not to like her. Jimmy began going out with her on a friendship-only basis, but as time drew on he began to explore the possibility that with Leonie he might marry for the second time.

Leonie was 15 years younger than him. Jimmy was wary of remarriage on this point only. He adored her, though, and knew it would be only a matter of time before he had to make a decision. In her teens, Leonie had undergone a lifesaving operation which had left her unable to have children. With this trauma behind her, Leonie had decided to lead a bachelor girl existence and enjoy life as much as possible without bitterness or rancour for what had happened. Her strong faith had sustained her. Kindness and warmth flowed from her eyes, particularly for Jimmy, who she recognised immediately to be something of a rough diamond with a heart of gold.

Eventually, after some years, Leonie and Jimmy married. Leonie became a warm and loving friend to Alec, who in turn returned great warmth to her. He knew that she was good for his dad, and he was unselfish in realising that it would be time for him to move on to allow them privacy in their marriage. Since Jimmy had married again after a long widowhood, he was mature enough to know that they needed their time together. But he was never made to feel this by them.

Alec's turn had come, with his pending marriage. He and his dad were more like friends than father and son. Whoever was first home made the tea for the other and presented them with a full mug as they entered the house. On this occasion Alec crept in quietly, only to find Jimmy turn around in the kitchen and hand him a large mug.

'Nothing much gets past a canny Scot like you, eh Dad?' he joked. 'I crept in and you still heard me. Thanks, Dad.'

Jimmy grinned at him. 'Must have been my old National Service experience in learning to detect the enemy when they're creeping up on you. So how was your day, then?'

'Pretty good,' replied Alec. 'I've asked Tim at work if he'll be my best man.'

Jimmy poured himself some tea and took a sip. 'He's that West Indian guy from Barbados, isn't he?'

'Jamaica,' Alec corrected him.

'Ah, Jamaica. And he's accepted?'

'Yes he has.' Alec paused and looked deep into his father's eyes. There was something he wanted to ask him. He knew his Dad would always give him an honest answer.

'Dad?' Alec prepared himself to ask a serious question. 'I know you might think this is a silly question. But if you had your time again, would you do anything differently?'

'I don't think that's a silly question at all, son,' Jimmy replied. He contemplated his answer. 'I have to admit that I'm not one who believes in regrets. Life has to go on. The world moves on, and so do sensible people.'

'So no regrets at all then, Dad?'

'If I'm to be frank with you, I have a couple. But they were beyond my control. No, on the whole I'd do much the same again. Most adults ask themselves the same question at some stage of their life. Maybe they've got to the stage where they begin to wonder, is this it? I've been pretty happy workwise. It was hard graft when I was a wee lad working in the shipyards of the Clyde. I enjoyed my National Service in Cyprus, that was one of the happiest times of my life. Even though it's been an up-and-down ride as a self-employed builder, I've made a good living.'

Now came the opportunity for Alec to ask the question he really wanted an answer for. 'What about marriage? Would you do that again? Not everyone would.'

Jimmy looked startled by the question. He seemed to be thinking: what a question to ask!

'Of course!' Jimmy answered snappily. He was not so much as angry as puzzled. 'I could'na imagine why you asked! Some men are damn lucky to find the right person once in a lifetime. Me, I married two of the finest lassies I ever set eyes upon. Not one, two. And damn fine lassies, I repeat. I'm a lucky fellow to have married Kathy McFadden, and then after years of widowhood find and marry someone like Leonie Yates. Your mum going so early shook me rigid to the point of despair, and I went through a terrible amount of deep grieving. She did'na deserve to die at such an early age. I love Leonie, she's kind and warm. She'll admit to a temper, mind, but she's given me, and you, tremendous support.'

'No, don't get me wrong. I loved Mum and I love Leonie. It's marriage itself. The actual institution. I was talking to Tim today and he's been with his lady a long time. They've got two children. They've got a house and mortgage. Seem quite happy by all accounts.'

'Living together?' Jimmy spoke with an air of distaste.

'Yes. That's right,' Alec answered his dad. He sought to elaborate. 'Without being married in a church or a Register Office. I was wondering, with all this divorce around, if there might be some merit in… just living together.' He hesitated, then said what was on his mind. 'I'm wondering if perhaps Jane and I should.' His father looked dumbstruck. Alec pushed on regardless. 'Lots of people do these days. It's not a bad idea, don't you think? I mean, don't you feel it's better for a couple to know all about their faults before they get married?'

Jimmy's face showed utter distaste at the idea. He was not one for keeping his feelings to himself. Alec at once realised he had said the wrong thing. He could from his father's expression how angry he was.

'Well, you're talking to the wrong fellow if ye expect me to say go ahead, son, live in sin. I mean, it's your choice but I'm a very conservative man when it comes to the subject of relationships. I'm not the most conventional person in life, but I don't hold with this idea of living together and having children. Perhaps it's a religious streak I've got that hangs in my conscience, telling me there's a right way and a wrong way of doing things.

'Breakdowns or not, marriage is still the backbone to a man and women getting together. There's no other way, in my book. A good marriage is like a warm glove. Once worn there's nothing else that'll fit quite the same. I'll admit I like my can of liquid amber, and when God created Saturday afternoons and Bank Holidays he did it for men like me to go to the rugby and the soccer, and place a day's pay on a nag that's a probable loser at the races, but come to the subject of marriage, I'll observe its sanctity. I'm no romantic-looking fellow that's been the stuff of women's dreams. I would'na kid myself! But where the two women in my life were concerned I was Mr Stability, Mr Dependable and Mr Faithful.'

'You were always able to make yourself perfectly understood, Dad,' Alec said, half smiling at the tirade that had tumbled from his father's lips. For tonight at least, he decided not to pursue the matter any further.

★★★

Before Leonie came home from work, Jimmy sat quietly remembering earlier times of his life. He had been looking forward to his son's wedding and was feeling disappointed by the doubts Alec was now expressing.

Years before, in Port Glasgow, Jimmy as a young child had heard his parents constantly quarrel about the lack of enough money to live on. There had been six children in that family. It was a tough time during the depression years of the 1930s. Even then as a child, Jimmy had decided that if he married what he wanted more than anything was a peaceful, happy home. The parental rows from his childhood haunted him for many years.

When he first set eyes on Katherine McFadden in the far-away 1950s it was her lovely warm smile that had captivated him instantly. Across the Empire Ballroom in Glasgow, Jimmy could see serenity in this girl. Her face was bright with happiness, her brown eyes sparked with humour and warmth. Katherine blushed crimson when she realised Jimmy was studying her. But there was no way any of the other swaggering teddy boys were going to dance with her that night. Jimmy broke all records to sprint across and ask the girl of his dreams to dance to 'Rock Around the Clock'. If anyone else had dared try to take her from him that night he would have gone 12 rounds in a boxing ring and a back alley brawl to stop them. So smitten was Jimmy with this dark-haired girl from Kilbarchan.

Jimmy thought back to that occasion and smiled at the memory of it. Then it was fast forward to the moment he first saw the girl who was to become his second wife. Leonie Yates was red-haired, with a slim, attractive figure. She simply oozed attractiveness: her face was warm and cheerful, her two-piece suit flowed down over her waist and thighs — without being intentionally so, she was slightly provocative. Men circled her like wolves but she seemed to be unaware of this. Unlike Kathy, she had a fiery temper which she saved for special occasions. Her temper could be likened to a forest fire: while it blazed it was furious, but when it had burned itself out there was peace and calm substituted in its place.

He loved her very much. Leonie had given Jimmy reason to live. In turn, she was not possessive, realising how much Jimmy liked to go to boxing matches, soccer games and have the occasional afternoon at the races. Jimmy was an old romantic at heart. He respected and loved women, and realised they loved the odd gift. Jimmy would occasionally leave a bouquet of flowers, a box of chocolates, some perfume, or simply a card in the kitchen telling her he loved her. The girl from Shankhill Road, Belfast had found in the man from Port Glasgow everything a husband was supposed to be: tough, hard-working, a lover of sport, a man's man and a ladies man all wrapped up into one; a rugged, sentimental, working gent.

At home Jimmy didn't have any irritating habits. He was a peaceful and placid man. He could cook and do housework as well as maintenance and decorating. His home was tidy. He took two showers a day, rubbing himself down afterwards with a mixture of olive oil and cologne. Damn it, he even changed his underclothes and socks every day, and washed and ironed his own clothes to boot! Leonie could hardly find fault in him at all.

From time to time he could be resolutely stubborn and forceful in his opinions, but on this score they matched many of Leonie's. They were a very well-paired couple. Jimmy loved rock 'n' roll, Leonie loved Irish traditional music, but each learned from the other. The only thing that annoyed Leonie was that Jimmy would insist on singing along to the words of 'Flower of Scotland' whenever it was sung on the radio, or by the crowd at Hampden Park or Wembley when an international game was played.

Jimmy was autocratic at work. He had to be, running his own business. On site, wearing his safety helmet, he walked around checking everything thoroughly: concrete foundations, bricklaying jobs, plumbing and electrical fittings. There was not one item of a building he was responsible for that his eyes did not scrutinise critically. He was a tough taskmaster. In all, Jimmy's attitude to life could be summed up in one word: discipline. He applied it to all areas of his life: work, home, and the principles he lived by.

Discipline had come firmly to Jimmy from the earliest periods of his life. If his parents had been argumentative and hot-tempered, one thing that they were united in was that their six children should behave with courtesy, decency and brutal honesty at all times. Anything other than that, and Joe McCutcheon would remind them with a leather buckled belt across the backside.

Outside of the home, when Jimmy had undertaken an apprenticeship scheme with the shipyards he had learned to respect the older men, who were skilled craftsmen and had little tolerance of those that didn't pull their weight. This was further compounded when he received his call-up papers for National Service. No one could answer back to the Sergeant Major or other NCOs, otherwise they would find themselves doing double time on their own with a heavy pack on their back, around and around the parade ground.

All of these experiences helped to mould the character of Jimmy McCutcheon, and it was easy to understand why, when his son talked about going another way in relationships from the tried and tested route, he could not be flexible.

★★★

Leonie arrived home and sat next to Jimmy on the sofa. She listened as he told her what Alec had been saying. Their son had gone out, and they were on their own. Not only was she loving, but Leonie was also intelligent enough to understand both sides of the story.

'It is the nineteen-nineties, Jimmy,' she said, as if that was a suitable excuse.

'That doesn't make it right in my book, Leonie,' he responded quickly. 'I'm old-fashioned in that view and I don't care who knows it.'

'But whether you hold with that view or not, living together without the benefit of the marriage ceremony is a fact of modern-day life. Besides, Alec is twenty-six now, Jim. He's probably looking at things with a different set of eyes to you.'

'I've not made this admission before, Leonie, but I'll tell you this now.' Jimmy squeezed her hand lovingly. 'With you, as Kathy before, I took one look and I thought, this red-haired lassie's got a fine face, kind eyes, and she's drawing me close like a magnet. After being a widower for so long I'd not contemplated a second marriage. But the moment I set eyes on you the word "marriage" was on the tip of my tongue. I was apprehensive at first, and it took a few years. We got there though, and it's been grand. The point I am making is that when we were going out together I did'na say "Let's get it together behind the cowshed!"'

'No, that was the fellow you were having a drink with the first time we met,' Leonie reminded him dryly. Jimmy gave her a smile at this remark.

'I mean, I'm no prude,' Jimmy continued. 'And I am certainly not the dour intolerant man some might think. I might have been a rough and ready lad in my day, but women have always been hallowed ground to me. My dad, fiery tempered fellow that he was, and even though he had many a verbal clash with my lovely mum… well, he brought me up to respect women and to treat them as gently as the soft petals of a rose. Women are to be loved and cared for, I can still hear him telling us kids that. To me, marriage was a wonderful comforting blanket, providing emotional and loving foundations in life. It's also to me a time-honoured tradition.' He rubbed Leonie's arm with deep affection. 'I'll tell you this, lass… Gruff, inflexible, gravel-faced old north of the border bugger that I am, I would not have missed it for all the tea in Sri Lanka and all the Scotch in Glenfiddich.'

Leonie looked at him with a mist in her eyes suggesting that she was on the point of tears. 'Maybe… maybe Alec is just being very cautious. And if it grates a lot that he's considering living with his girlfriend, surely there is some merit in this. Don't get me wrong, I believe in the strength of marriage too, but surely it would be better to learn about each other in this way rather than go straight into wedding bells and end up in the divorce courts later on.'

'I can understand that,' said Jimmy. It was almost a concession, but not quite. 'It doesn't mean I agree with it, though.'

★★★

George had made a spur-of-the-moment decision. The weekend after the redundancies had been announced at the factory, he decided to make a nostalgic visit to Dranthord. It was a long time since he had visited his old home town. Life was so uncertain in the Britain of the 1990s. The fear of another – perhaps fatal – heart attack hung over him. While his mind was filled with worries about the future, he decided to take a look at what had once been his way of life.

The train drew close to Dranthord on a fresh, clear Saturday morning. George wound the carriage window down and looked out at the town for landmarks that he would instantly recognise. The smell of coal dust from a bygone age seemed to enter his nostrils. A gentle breeze blew up across a beautiful meadow, and in the distance the old colliery buildings were clearly identifiable. He was home. The fields he had once played in as a boy came into view. Then there were the first signs of the cobblestoned roads, the ageing terraces where the miners had once lived, and the remnants of the old town.

A childlike excitement filled George's spirits. He felt overjoyed to be back for the first time in nearly 40 years. When the train pulled in at Dranthord station it was almost as if nothing had changed in all that time. The sidings where the coal had been despatched from stood alongside a handsome station platform adorned with pots of flowers and shrubs.

George remembered that Dranthord station had won prizes in the old days for being one of the best-kept in the country.

The steam trains had once run from there, with the great gusts of smoke spiralling from the funnels, streaming back across the lush green countryside. It was the same green countryside where the miners had taken their children for long walks and picnics. Everything was filled with nostalgia for George. Once through the ticket barrier he began to walk along some of the lanes that were full of memories for him.

There were some staggering changes, however. The colliery buildings had now become a museum, displaying coal mining in a bygone age; it also served as a monument to the many men of Dranthord who had perished in one of the worst pit disasters ever recorded in that region. Housing estates, both council and privately built by independent builders, flourished where slums and crumbling stone cottages had once stood against a backdrop of huge slag heaps. The Dranthord Miners Club where George had met his wife Mary was no more. In its place was a shop selling wet fish. It was also part of a shopping complex, boasting a supermarket, multi-storey car park, public library and a row of stores including a newsagents, a lingerie shop, a bicycle shop and a menswear shop.

Things had certainly moved on from the days when the cloth-capped miners had walked through the town in the early hours of the morning on their way to the pits. Socialist speeches had filled the Town Hall in those days. Now capitalist money had brought in new design, intermingled with the past that had once evoked struggle and hardship. The comparison between the ages was daunting.

There was one institution that had not changed. It still stood as it had done 40 years before. A public house with the curious name of the Dranthord Miner's Son stood out, a remnant from the past, against the gleaming clean newly constructed buildings that surrounded it on all sides.

George remembered it from years before as the doyen of Dranthord pubs. When the publican called out 'Time, gentlemen, please', on a Saturday night, it also served as a gentle reminder to many of those folk rapidly approaching their limit they would have to be up early the next day to go to chapel. Back in the days when the lads from the mines used to drink there, at the back of the pub was a private function room. Beautiful meals used to be served there. George licked his lips at the memory of the food. One speciality was the tastiest roast beef served with fresh succulent vegetables, Yorkshire pudding and delicious jacketed potatoes. The dessert was normally plum tart and custard; its reputation carried, and customers came from far and wide to try it. The beer wasn't bad either, George remembered. Locally brewed, it packed flavour and a punch Jack Dempsey would have envied.

For old times sake he decided to pay the establishment a visit, just to soak up the old atmosphere, perhaps, and revel in the nostalgia. Inside the Dranthord Miner's Son public house, George was greeted with a pleasant surprise. The bar had hardly changed. Oak beams laden with decorations in brass and copper criss-crossed the roof and the walls, and in prime position for all to see located directly above a huge grandfather clock was a miner's lamp and helmet. It was a subtle reminder of the coal that had helped Dranthord to flourish.

On the walls were old sepia photographs set in frames, which were a guide to the history of Dranthord. George examined them with a very discerning eye. His eyes registered surprise at the sight of Dranthord Football Club in a photograph taken in 1911. I know that man, George thought. I should do. And so he should, for it was George's late father who had once had a promising career as a left back with the club. Dranthord had been way down in the division, whatever it was back in that era, but several players managed to move on to more prominent teams such as Preston, Blackburn Rovers and Burnley.

There were other photographs which showed the town as it had been: scallywag depression-era kids playing on the cobblestones; old miners of generations before in long-obsolete outfits with grimy faces and eyes that showed a mixture of fear and apprehension; the Dranthord Colliery Band through the agesm since its formation in the early part of the century. There were pictures too of prominent people who had visited. American film stars who had entertained the GIs during the Second World War at an American airbase that had once been close by. The King who was never crowned Edward VIII featured in one picture talking to the local Labour MP of the time, a man who was a fierce left-wing firebrand and scourge of the Baldwin government, but much admired for his defence of the rights of the good citizens of Dranthord.

That was enough nostalgia for George. It was time to taste a drop of the good hearty Dranthord ale. He walked to the bar, which was busy with office staff taking their lunchtime break. George cast his eyes across the varieties of beer that were on sale. It was a bit of a pot pourri: there were traditional British brands together with American, Danish and Antipodean imports. Where was the old Dranthord brew? He decided to ask the barman for it anyway.

'Good morning to you,' George said affably. 'I'd like a pint of Dranthord's finest, if you still serve it.'

The barman's eyes lit up like a beacon ablaze. 'A pint of our famous brew? It's not often folk ask for that in these days of cosmopolitan beers. You must be an old Dranthord man from way back?'

George smiled at the man's perception. 'About forty years back, to be precise. I've just come back to visit for the weekend.'

'Well, I'll be,' the barman began. 'I've got to go into the other bar to get your pint. I'll be back in a minute and we'll have a natter.' Just as the barman turned to walk away he called back, 'I think I know you.'

The man duly returned with a pint of foaming beer, brimming over the top of the pint glass. George handed over a fiver and eyed the barman.

'Two pounds fifty please, George,' the barman said, taking the £5 note. He put the money in the till and gave him his change.

George looked at him in awe. 'You know my name?' The surprise in his voice was very obvious.

'No. 5 Colliery, 1952,' came back the reply. 'Yes, that's right, Number 5 Colliery. You and I were working on that seam when the whole bloody lot caved in and we were trapped for two days.'

George was astounded. He was so stunned that for a moment he was incapable of finding anything to say. He took a sip of the beer and eyed the man.

'Good stuff,' George said licking his lips like a cat that had just supped the cream. 'I've got to be honest, I don't remember you. But Number 5 is right.' He took another sip and sighed. 'Forty years since I was last here and I walk into this pub and someone recognises me. You wouldn't read about it on page three of *The Sun* newspaper, would you?'

The two men shook hands. George drank his pint of Dranthord. It was a strong mixture of yeast and hops that had some secret ingredient known only to the local brewers, who guarded the recipe with great care.

'Alan Tuck's the name.'

Alan Tuck. The name rang a bell in George's memory. 'Alan Tuck! Of course! Now I remember. The lad's used to call you...'

'Friar Tuck,' Alan reminded him. Both men smiled. 'Ah yes, that was so long ago, but my we had some good times then. Dances and parties at the old clubs. Fetes and country shows. Plenty of work then. Blimmin' hard work but it gave us a steady wage, a hearty appetite and a mighty thirst for brew you're sipping, tastiest best beer in the United Kingdom. Good days they were. Course after the big pit disaster all the lads had to move elsewhere. Including you I s'pose.'

'My word. I was all over the show. You?'

'Me. I went into the services, the Navy, in '53 and stayed until 1970. Came out, worked in business for years. Then a few years ago I thought I'd come back to dear old Dranthord.' He suddenly had a brainwave. 'Look, I own this place now, believe it or not. If you're free this afternoon I could drive you around a bit. Show you the place.'

George felt a sense of relief. He didn't feel much like walking around on his own.

★★★

Jane and Alec walked along a busy street, hand in hand. A few days before they had both been declaring their undying love for each other. Now both had feelings of deep apprehension about making a permanent commitment to each other. But if they both had doubts, neither was letting on to the other.

'So your dad's gone away this weekend, then?' asked Alec.

'Yes. He's made his first visit to Dranthord since the early fifties when he left there. I think he was glad to get away. He's not very happy, in fact he's downright miserable. His factory is on the point of closing. All the staff are out of a job.'

'That's dreadful,' said Alec. One thought did enter his head. If George was unemployed and not earning, the burden of paying for his daughter's wedding might cause him stress. That would be one good reason for delaying the wedding.

'I think Dad's got every right to feel angry,' said Jane. 'He was heading off to the TUC conference at Blackpool in a couple of weeks' time. One of the topics he was going to bring up was the need for the country to aim for full employment. Now he's out of work himself, he's an unemployed union convenor.'

'I'm sorry to hear that.' Alec hesitated before bringing up the subject he wanted to discus. 'Jane I know this is an awful thing to ask. I've just got to ask though.' Jane took on a worried expression. 'I've proposed. You've accepted. I do genuinely love you. I need to know. Are you sure about this marriage? Are you sure about you and me as a couple?'

'No. No I'm not.'

Jane's answer flabbergasted him. 'No?' He exclaimed in response. 'You've had second thoughts about us as well?'

It was Jane's turn now to be visibly astounded. 'What do you mean, "You've had second thoughts about us as well"?'

Alec explained. 'I've been talking to Tim at work. You know, he's the fellow I've asked to be my best man. He was telling me that for six years he and his girlfriend have lived together. They've even got a couple of children. How would you feel about living together for a while before actually tying the knot? I do love you, I really do. It does worry me that in time, if we were to marry now, that eventually we might go the way of other couples and end up being divorced.'

'Do you know, until last Saturday when we got the engagement ring I had never even contemplated the possibility of divorce? We're not even married. We're already talking about what things would be like if we divorced.'

Alec looked glum. 'Where do we go from here?'

★★★

Dranthord was a different town to the one George had grown up in. But amidst the new there was the occasional landmark which stood out like a national monument and tribute to the past. Alan Tuck was driving him.

'What do you think then, George? Hasn't changed much has it?' He had asked the question tongue-in-cheek.

'Dramatically,' the other replied.

'I was only joking,' Alan said with a laugh in his voice. 'I suppose when you get older, if your past memories of your earlier years are good there's that huge temptation to get back to your roots. I'd been away a long time too. I haven't regretted buying the pub. But in my heart I'm not sure I did the right thing coming back.'

George felt much the same. He was trying to reason just why he had come back. Perhaps it was all to do with his daughter's pending wedding.

Maybe it was because there had been a time in George's life when he felt that he had it all to look forward to. That time had been here in Dranthord when he had first met Mary.

'See that spot over there?' said George, pointing to a huge meadow. 'Can we pull up by it?'

'No problem,' said Alan. He drove the car to a suitable spot by it and the two men stepped out.

There was a faint sign of moisture in George's eyes as he gazed at the place. This big burly man who did not suffer fools gladly and could be obnoxious when aroused was visibly moved by the sight of a field.

'What is it, George?' Alan could see tears forming in George's eyes.

Over 40 years before, it had been a place where George had walked with Mary. They had been such a happy young couple. In those days George had been a slim, strong young man. Mary was in contrast a fragile-looking girl, the sort who seemed in need of protection. Hand in hand they walked across the fields and along country lanes. The meadow held a special place in George's heart. It was there that he had fallen to his knees and proposed marriage to Mary.

Sometimes country fetes were held in that meadow. The Dranthord Colliery band would play on these occasions, and George would turn out to play the trumpet. Mary would wave to him and beam a glorious smile which would thrill him.

In the distance at the edge of Dranthord was a wonderful stone church. It evoked history in every crumbling facet of its ageing structure. For it was here that just about every person who had been married took their matrimonial vows. Every birth, every christening, every marriage including that of George and Mary had been registered in its records. When men of the Dranthord Colliery had died in the pit disaster of 1952 all of the townsfolk had paid tribute in a moving memorial service that George had attended. After all, he had survived.

The memory of being trapped beneath the rubble in the darkness haunted him to this day. The pitch blackness had been broken by shafts of light streaming through from above. Food and water had been lowered to the trapped men. The air was mercilessly thin and the feeling of claustrophobia all around him had gripped George with a stark terror he could never before have imagined. Above them the sound of voices and people scraping away at the rubble could be heard. Rescue was coming.

It was too late for many men. The corpses of friends and workmates lay all around amidst the broken beams and fallen structures. Some men had died agonisingly. Their cries of pain had permeated through the long night and in the frightening darkness. Then their haunting voices could no longer be heard as the mine laid claim to more victims.

Suddenly the rescue teams broke through with unexpected ferocity. The first face they were to see was that of George Walsh. Light rained down on a coal-blackened face as two eyes filled with fear stared up at the salvation he had never expected to come.

'I never heard the sound of the beams cracking,' George uttered to himself. 'I woke up to find myself trapped in a sea of night darkness. And all I could think of was Mary, my wife Mary.' George broke off as he realised he had been talking to himself.

Alan stood behind him and gripped his shoulder. 'Memories, George?' he asked sympathetically.

'Too many,' replied George. 'Can we go?'

George decided to stay over at Dranthord that night. Alan let him have a room free at the public house. It was only a short stay, but enough memories had been revived. Perhaps one should never go back to one's roots, particularly if all friends and relatives from that time have gone.

When George left Dranthord the next morning he took one last look from the train window at the old colliery buildings and the meadows. I shall never return, he thought. The past is the past. Let's leave it there.

★★★

Back at work on Monday morning, all the workers of Denis Miles Engineering would learn of the pending redundancies. George had known of this since the previous Friday and he knew it would be a terrible blow to his fellow workers.

On the factory floor, when all the staff had gathered together, there was an air of anticipation as if everyone knew what the announcement would be. Denis Miles walked down the stairs from his office and onto the floor. He looked particularly grim as he began to address his staff.

'I've asked you all here today because I have some particularly bad news for you. It's not good at all.' Denis was almost choking as he spoke; for him too it was the end of all that he had worked for all of his life. 'As you know, I've been fighting a battle to keep Denis Miles Engineering open. Originally there were five factories. I've lost four. This one I've been fighting hard for, it was the last of a long line that I built up. In order to keep it going I had to sell it to a company who promised to provide capital for new equipment and provide solid financial back-up in order to keep all the staff fully employed.' He made the next part of the announcement through gritted teeth. 'That company, I regret to say, is in the process of being wound up.' The employees looked at each other in dismay. 'It effectively means redundancy. For all of us. When I say all, that includes me.' Denis could see the look of anguish on all the employees' faces. 'I'm genuinely sorry, ladies and gentlemen. This was my factory, my life's work.'

George could see how difficult it was for Denis. He stepped in quickly in order to alleviate his pain at making such an announcement.

'We still have two weeks of work left before this factory closes. Let's do our best while we've got work to do. If you would all like to come along and see me individually, I'll tell you what the redundancy entitlements for each of you are.'

★★★

George met up with Leonie and Jimmy for the first time that night, all of them feeling slightly apprehensive at their first meeting. But despite the very different and unique personalities of each of them, they got on famously, and Jimmy stuck up a rapport with George. They sat down for a meal together.

'So, George,' Jimmy said in a relaxed mood, 'all the lads and ladies at your place of work are out on their own now?'

'Afraid so,' George replied reluctant to speak on the subject. 'Although they've got a nice bit of redundancy money behind them. That will help them along a while.'

He changed the subject quickly. It was not one he would have chosen at the present time. 'Still, your lad's alright isn't he? He's got a pretty reliable job as a motor mechanic. At least he'll be able to support my daughter.'

Leonie could see that Jimmy and George were gradually taking over the conversation, but she was not one to be excluded from any fun. 'George, we've all been getting on extremely well today,' Leonie piped up. 'You and Jim have been talking like a couple of brothers who've just got together after serving prison sentences in different parts of the world! You've talked about

261

National Service, yours in Korea, Jim's in Cyprus, and Manchester United and Glasgow Rangers, Bill Haley and 'Rock Around The Clock', Matt Busby and Sophia Loren, Norman Tebbit, Norman Wisdom, Samantha Fox… Now I'd like to ask a serious question. And when I'm serious, I'm deadly!'

'With red hair like yours, darling, you couldn't be anything else!' George retorted in good heart.

'George, let me put this question to you,' Leonie continued. 'What do you think about living together?'

He looked at her in amused astonishment. 'But we've only just met!'

'No!' Leonie replied with a broad smile at George's humorous reply. 'I mean, some of the young couples today who choose to live in a state of marriage but never take the marriage vows. What's your honest opinion?'

'My honest opinion?' George could see that this question was leading somewhere. 'Well, I'm an old-fashioned man myself.' He was in good company. So too was Jimmy. 'I come from a family of good mining stock who believed in a right and wrong way of doing everything. I don't suppose they'd hold with the new. As far as they were concerned there was no such thing as a maternity wedding dress and I don't think they would have much of an opinion of a bride that breastfed her baby during the marriage ceremony. I've been radical on some things in my life, but I think if a couple choose to live together that's their business. I wouldn't recommend it to my own daughter, nor would I like it. Come to think of it, I wouldn't be very tactful and neither would I hold back my distaste.'

It seemed Jimmy and George were almost blood brothers. 'I think you share a similar viewpoint to my own George, I respect that.' Jimmy looked at Leonie quickly. 'If I can be a wee bit candid with you, George… I don't want to sound like a puritanical, holier-than-thou, interfering old busybody, but I think my lad and your sweet lassie are getting a bit worried about taking the final steps. It's not that they don't feel all the right emotions for each other. I know my boy and he'll care for your daughter till the end of his days. What actually worries him is the legal ceremony and the aftermath.'

'By the aftermath,' Leonie elaborated for him, 'Jim means the possibility of divorce, that they might separate. I mean, we know that in life finding the right partner is a bit like striking it lucky in the Irish Sweepstakes. Yet when it comes down to it, if you don't buy a ticket, well you've got no chance of winning.'

George was a good conversationalist when the subject was good. 'Looking at it logically, love, most males before their wedding day – and I expect that includes you, Jim – might feel a bit apprehensive about getting married. I know I was. I used to think when I got married that it meant no more nights at the dog track, no nights out on the town with the boys. Then when I gave it a bit of thought I came out with something astonishing. I don't go to the dog track! I don't have any nights out on the town with the boys! Who needs it anyway? In the back of your mind there's always the story from time immemorial that by getting married you're losing something. Your freedom, they'd have you believe.'

'And yet in truth, by getting married, you gain,' Jimmy stated emphatically.

'I agree,' Leonie said in response. 'Marriage to me is a blanket of security. I support Jim, he supports me. But if he wants to go to the sport I'm not going to complain. He's here for me if I need him and he knows that I will always back him up one hundred per cent of the way. Just because marriage is a partnership it doesn't mean to say you have to live in each other's pockets all the time.'

George brought some humour to the situation. 'How many times have you heard the old marriage joke where the Dad says to his son, who is fifty-one years of age and still living at home, "You've got to get married soon, son, you can't be happy all your life!"'

The others smiled at his woeful attempt at a joke.

'I think I've heard that before,' Leonie said with an infectious smile.

George continued his line of explanation. 'I'll bet you anything you like, Jim, Leonie, it's just a case of pre-wedding nerves. Alec has put the ring on my Jane's finger and the realisation of what they are doing has suddenly struck them.'

★★★

Jane was enjoying herself that night in the company of her workmate Carol and her family. They sat on wicker chairs in the conservatory of their very comfortable home. Carol's husband Robert was a nice-looking man, very straightforward and pleasant. He was well aware that his wife Carol was a very attractive woman, unassumingly and delightfully sexy without realising it. Her long blonde hair, slim legs, slightly curvy figure and the occasional 'little girl lost' look mixed allure and vulnerability together. It was a tantalising mixture.

Looking at Robert and Carol together, Jane wondered for a moment what it is about the male and female species that sometimes people apparently with little in common can be drawn together in successful marriages.

'This has been nice,' Jane said, sipping on a cup of tea at the end of a very nourishing meal. From the conservatory she could see Carol and Robert's sons playing football in the garden.

'Glad to have you here,' Carol replied affably.

'I enjoyed the meal and the company tonight,' Jane stated and then decided to ask them a few questions about their marriage. 'Do you mind if I ask you something, Robert?' He smiled at her, fully expecting a controversial question. 'You and Carol, and your nice boys there, are beautifully set up. Nice home, this conservatory, lovely laid-out garden. Did it take a long time to get all this?'

'We only live here,' Robert answered calmly. 'Carol will tell you that. We don't own this house.'

This was a surprise to Jane. 'I thought you did.'

Robert laughed. 'On paper we do. No, we've got a mortgage that would send a chill down your spine if you knew what the repayments were. Another percentage point interest rise and our very carefully orchestrated budget will be playing a very sour out of tune note. The bank owns this house and the bank owns us. We've had to go without a lot of things that others buy which we don't think necessarily contribute to a happy lifestyle.'

Jane was astonished. 'You seem to have everything you need to me.' Carol and Robert's house had a safe, comfortable feel about it.

'The key word is "need",' Carol pointed out. 'We don't indulge in any luxuries. We're not a family that crave the same as others. We don't have a beautifully fitted kitchen, a bathroom elegantly tiled complete with jacuzzi and built-in shower. We don't drink bottles of wine with our dinner.'

Robert added to the list. 'Nor do we have a video player, a home computer, exercise bike, several televisions in the house. We don't subscribe to satellite television. We have one car between us. We don't have a microwave, or a dishwasher or a spin dryer. We don't have a second home. We don't have a nanny.'

The list of things they didn't have increased, as Carol mentioned other extravagances. 'And we don't take holidays in Florida, Benidorm, Cyprus,

Mombasa, the Seychelles or the south of France. There are some people who want it all and will borrow deep to do it. Not us. This house is just a fight to maintain, as well as the upkeep of the boys. Others think it's their right to those things.'

'I know this is strange,' Jane began, and now she was saying what she really wanted to. 'I'm on the verge of getting married, but there is something that's suddenly taken away the gloss for me. It's not that I don't love Alec. Heaven knows I love him so much it's not true. I never thought I would find a fellow like Alec in a million years. Marriage to me... well, I'm beginning to wonder... why.'

Robert knew what she was thinking. It was the sudden daunting commitment which had changed from the idea of bliss to one of an awesome responsibility. He immediately sought to reassure her.

'I think marriage is lovely.' He really meant what he was saying. Many men had looked on enviously as Robert had walked out with Carol. 'But I never thought it was glossy. I'd still recommend it.'

Carol glanced at Robert and enlightened him as to her previous conversation with Jane. 'I was telling Jane before that if I was starting out again, I would prepare myself more for marriage.'

'Well, I guess that preparation has some substance to it,' Robert conceded. 'You just never know in life, do you? If you meet someone and you're compatible and you are madly in love, you go for it. You don't try and analyse it. I think I'm a very lucky man to have married Carol.' He looked at her and smiled mischievously. 'Whether she thinks she's as lucky as I am is another matter altogether!'

'Oh, I've little to complain about,' Carol said, smiling back at Robert. 'I'm sure we'll get round to overseas travel in time and buy all these things later on that we regard as luxuries.'

Carol in her feminine way detected a sign of wariness about Jane. 'You haven't changed your mind have you, Jane?'

'Mmmm. I'm... I'm...'

Carol anticipated what she was going to say. 'Worried that it might not be as good as you hoped?'

'In a nutshell, yes. Alec has even suggested — and he's quite serious about it — that maybe we should try living together first.'

'Do you think that is really what is worrying you?' asked Robert.

'How do you mean?'

'Carol and I have been very honest and up-front with each other.' He gazed at his wife lovingly. 'We've often considered that even though we're happy, we should have waited a year or two before getting married, to achieve other things. Perhaps a bit of adventure for a year or two. I don't mean of the sexual sort, but real travel. Both our parents were in the Forces before they got married and had travelled round a bit, so come the nuptials they were more than ready.'

'Sometimes,' said Carol, holding Robert's hand like a teenage sweetheart, 'I think that every young person should define their objectives in life. I know what I'd do, I would compile a list of objectives — one hundred would be a good number — and then I would work to achieve them all.'

Jane had an answer for this. 'I only ever had one objective in life. That was to marry a good man and have a family.'

★★★

Tim and his de facto wife Marion were standing in the kitchen arguing, while Alec sat in the lounge blissfully unaware of what was going on.

'I don't understand you, Marion. We've been together six years. You've never pressed me to get married before.'

'Well I think it's high time we did,' Marion said sharply.

'Why? Because my best pal is getting spliced? All the talk about Alec's wedding and now you want the whole lot, white wedding, wedding breakfast in a swanky reception centre, family photographs, traditional night apart. Imagine if I go to the boozer before the wedding and some old grannie sees me all togged out like a Savoy butler, she'll be saying things like, you'll be shaking tonight! Bit late in our case, the horse has not only bolted from the stable door but it's made its way through to the finishing line in record time!'

Marion was adamant. 'I still want to make it official.'

'Official?' Tim was mystified. 'We've been together six years, we've got two lovely kids. How can we make it more official than that? Besides, it's cold on the downstairs sofa. You were alright until I told you Alec was getting married.'

'What are you going to do?' Marion asked him with a hint of challenge in her voice. 'Divorce me?'

'After all this time together, you decide this now! Of all times to make it legal.'

'It's been on my mind a long time,' Marion confirmed.

'So what difference is a piece of paper really going to make?'

Marion picked up a tray of food and drink. Before she left the kitchen she gave him a stern look. 'Don't you know?' Marion asked him softly. There was hurt in her eyes, suggesting she was upset that Tim was not more sensitive.

'Go on, tell me!' Tim snapped back, challenging her.

Marion replied quietly, giving him a steely gaze that froze him in his tracks. 'I'll tell you, Tim. It's a reaffirmation of your love for me. It's a matter of consolidating our relationship forever. It provides a legally binding tie for our children. It's a time-honoured commitment. It gives me respect as a married woman. Is that clear enough for you now?'

Tim scratched his head in sheepish bemusement and reluctantly followed her into the front room where Alec was sitting. They both sat down opposite Alec and handed him some food. Tim was slightly ill at ease after the little tiff with his lady and he tried to regain his confidence by appearing to be in a jocular mood.

'So, how are you doing, old mate?' he asked Alec.

'Fine. Lovely. I've got my mug of beer and a sandwich.'

'All geared up for the big day then?'

'No.'

'No?' Tim looked at Marion in amazement. 'No? Blimey! Did I hear you right, mate? I thought after our chat, our many little chats…'

'Don't get me wrong,' Alec said. 'I think Jane and I will get married.'

'You confuse me, mate,' Tim responded.

'So do you,' Marion said directly to Tim.

Alec explained further. 'But I think we'll live together until we're really, really sure.'

'Like us, you mean?' Tim asked innocently.

This brought a smile to Marion's face. 'And after the first six years and two children, a mortgage, even then you may find it difficult to make it legal. I know Tim does!'

Alec could see he had a suitable debating point and decided to push it for all it was worth. 'Okay, so I've struck a raw nerve here. Why did you two never tie the knot? I'm not trying to be intrusive here, but it's obvious you two have had something good going for a long time. You're married in my eyes, I don't think you're any different to any other married couple. What really stopped you from going the full distance?'

Marion and Tim suddenly became quiet. They were used to arguing between themselves, but to be quizzed by a friend was something different.

It was Marion who after a moment's thinking came up with the answer. 'I've often wondered. I think it was the thrill of living with someone. Well, it seemed daring, spicy, different, and it seemed less problematic to simply move in with Tim rather than get married. But as time has gone on things have changed. I love Tim.'

Marion put her arm around Tim, despite the tiff they had just had. They were an interesting pair. Marion was gentle and an English rose, whilst Tim was a happy-go-lucky Jamaican.

'Yes, I do love him,' she continued. 'But now, after being together for so long, I want something permanent. Especially for the children. I'm not a religious person; if truth be told I'm something of an agnostic. Yet I would like our love declared publicly and blessed in the eyes of the Church.'

Tim who had just been dreading Marion telling him to sleep on the sofa until they were married, saw this as an opportunity to be seized. 'Does that mean I don't have to sleep on the sofa tonight?'

Marion's reply came back quick as a flash. 'No!'

★★★

George was on his feet, playing the comedian for Leonie and Jimmy. The three of them had got on marvellously together. While Alec was debating the institution of marriage with Tim and Marion, and Jane was doing the same with Robert and Carol, George was entertaining in the manner of a variety performer.

'I'll tell you this, folks, every time I've been to a wedding, at every reception without fail, either the best man or the father of the bride or everybody's favourite uncle or the bloke that's been assigned to the role of Master of Ceremonies will always come out with the same old joke. You know, the one about the couple who've been together for forty-five years and never got married?'

'Well, I haven't heard it!' Jimmy exclaimed.

'Go on, George,' Leonie urged him. 'Deliver it to us in your own inimitable style!'

George clasped his hands together. 'Right then! There's this couple, Fred and Hilda. Every night for forty-five years, Fred has been going round to Hilda's for his evening meal. They sit and have dinner. They talk. They watch television. Then Fred gets up and goes home to his place. For forty-five years they do the same thing. Day in, day out. One day Hilda says to Fred, "'Ere Fred why don't we get married?" Fred turns to Hilda and replies, "Who'd have us at our age?"'

Jimmy and Leonie smiled at his weak attempt at a joke. 'I've been to a few wedding receptions in my time,' said Jimmy, 'but I've never heard that one. Remind me not to use it next time I got to a wedding.'

George sat down after his impromptu performance. 'Jokes aside – especially mine – do you know what I find about weddings? Just how reluctant people seem to be to get up and dance. It's normally the MC who'll say in a very hushed voice, "Ladies and gentlemen would you please take your partners for the bridal waltz". And a few people will shuffle onto the floor. But they won't last the distance on the dance floor. Now, when I was a band leader there were two types of music that got the feet tapping and the dancers twirling. It was good old big band swing music, and the greatest sound of all, old-fashioned earthy rock 'n' roll music.'

A look of delight appeared on Jimmy's face. 'I'm with you there, George! When I was a lad in Glasgow in the fifties the next best thing to seeing Rangers play was a night at the dance hall when the rock 'n' roll lads played. Not only rock 'n' roll, but skiffle. Remember Lonnie Donegan singing 'Cumberland Gap' or 'Rock Island Line', Tommy Steele and 'Rock with the Caveman', Nancy Whisky singing 'Freight Train', Fats Domino with 'Blueberry Hill', Chuck Berry, Little Richard…'

'Nothing like it Jim. Pure magic! When I was band leader and my boys played that stuff everybody was happy. The musicians, the girls, the lads, the old and the young. Do you know, I've been to functions where businessmen like insurance consultants, computer programmers and even members of the clergy were present, and all of them stood around looking uncomfortable, fidgety and scratching their bottoms. Until someone puts on a rock 'n' roll record and, would you believe it, they're all tapping their feet, the mood of the occasion has been transformed and the spirit of all of them has been uplifted. They're all chatting away merrily and enjoying themselves.'

'Good music is the food of the soul,' said Leonie and she turned to her husband. 'Hard to believe you were an old rocker, Jim. I thought you were brought up in a household where the only music that was played was by Peter Dawson, Jenny Lind and Sir Harry Lauder.'

'I could swivel my hips with the best of them,' Jimmy remarked.

'So could I,' said George. 'I had less of them to swivel in those days, too.'

'Were they good days for you, George?' Leonie asked. 'When you were a band leader, I mean?'

'Oh my word,' he replied. There was a misty-eyed look on his face.

Twenty-six years before… was it 1967 or was it 1965? He couldn't recall the exact year. But somewhere around those years the George Walsh Big Band was playing a lot of engagements at dance halls and variety theatres throughout the country. The music of the day may have belonged to the pop groups but George went against the grain and as well as playing the old standards of the previous decades he mixed his repertoire. Modern-day pop classics of the 1960s were played by a rousing big band.

George would stand in front of the musicians whilst behind him dancers took to the floor. What a repertoire it was too! Amongst the many tunes the band played there was something for everyone: 'Oh Mein Papa', 'Such a Night', 'Three Coins in a Fountain', 'It's Almost Tomorrow', 'Great Balls of Fire', 'Jailhouse Rock', 'Please Please Me', 'Wayward Wind', 'Glad all Over', 'Mule Train', 'A Whiter Shade of Pale', 'San Francisco', 'Pretty Flamingo', 'Paint it Black'. On some of the old tunes George would take the microphone and deliver the vocals to an old standard such as 'Here in My Heart' or 'Walking Behind You'. When George sang he really did deliver every line from the heart. The tears flowed, the emotions shone through. This man of so many contradictions possessed such a diversity of talent that he brought professionalism to anything he tried.

It was 1967, he recalled. He was definite in that now. The band was playing an engagement at Caesar's Palace in Luton when someone from the club handed George a note in mid-performance. At the end of the number he read the scrawl quickly. His eyes lit up. His face broke into a broad grin. His wife Mary had given birth to his daughter.

'I'm a father, lads!' he proudly announced to the rest of the band members. Some of them stood up, shaking his hand and slapping his back.

From the floor people started to shout. 'More! More!'

George laughed at the joke. He was beside himself with happiness.

'You want more?' he shouted mirthfully. The high spirits in him suddenly flowed in abundance. 'I'll give you more. Ladies and gentlemen. I've just become a dad, folks. My wife has just given birth to a daughter and I'd like to dedicate this next song to her. I couldn't be there with her tonight but she's right here.' George clutched his chest. 'Here in my heart. That's right, and I'm going to sing the Al Martino hit from 1952, "Here in My Heart".'

George sang that song with a voice rich in timbre and the quality of his voice in the way he sustained the high notes was never better. It was a wonderful night. Down on the dance floor, people of all ages danced happily. The girls of the mini-skirt era never looked more attractive. The ladies in their thirties and forties out on the town in stylish clothes and modern make-up looked glamorous, while their escorts appeared equally delighted to be there.

'Oh yes, they were great days,' George recounted to Jimmy and Leonie. 'Big band, swing, rock 'n' roll.'

Alec entered the house quietly. He had wondered just how the three of them would all get on together. Alec need not have worried. George, Jimmy and Leonie looked as if they were heading the rock 'n' roll revival unit. They were all standing up in the kitchen singing the words to 'Rock Around the Clock'!

★★★

Jane was on her way home after having dinner with Carol and Robert. It had been a nice night for Jane. It had been good for Robert too, and the conversation had put Carol in a very romantic and seductive mood.

The lights in the house were turned down low. Their two boys had gone to bed. Very soft, enchanting music rose from a cassette tape. A couple of glasses of wine, and the two were in a relaxed mood. Carol kicked her shoes off, then folded her gorgeous legs as she sat on Robert's lap, kissing him long and lovingly. Robert's senses were aroused as Carol ran her long slender fingers down his back and neck. She rubbed one foot up and down Robert's trouser leg. He was more than a little appreciative.

'I'm very glad Jane came round,' he said softly.

'So am I,' Carol murmured. They paused in their affection and she looked deep into his eyes. 'I was touched that you declared your love for me.' She kissed him passionately. The kiss tasted delicious. 'Well, Robert, who needs a video player or a home computer?'

Robert murmured his reply in between kisses. 'I'd never get a reception like this on satellite television. Just think we could have been watching Cilla Black or Clive James!'

'What a tragedy!' Carol whispered kissing Robert's ear. He returned the gesture with a slow passionate kiss. She expressed her appreciation also. 'Nice… mmm… you haven't lost your touch. Even nicer of you to tell Jane you were a very lucky man to have married me. You'll never know how good that makes me feel.'

'I feel pretty good too,' Robert said with a smile as he anticipated the events of the night ahead.

★★★

Alec had left Marion and Tim in a state of confusion. They had talked for a long time about the merits and minuses of marriage. Marion stood in the kitchen drying dishes. Tim stood in the doorway looking perplexed. The pair were both silent. Neither could think of anything to say.

Marion looked up from the kitchen sink and quickly studied Tim's face. There was a touch of amusement in her eye. She could see that Tim was getting increasingly frustrated, not quite knowing how to deal with the situation.

Tim suddenly raised his finger angrily. 'Look! You!'

Marion turned to face him square on. 'Yes.'

Tim fell to his knees in the kitchen. Marion showed signs of both amusement and surprise. But Tim had more serious matters on his mind.

'Let's be traditional about this, Marion. I love you, I always have. You're the mother of my two children. I need you for the support and love you provide. I would like to ask you to be my wife. I want our love to be blessed in the eyes of God and legally bound so that we may spend the rest of our lives together. Will you marry me?'

'Very nice. I accept.' Marion smiled happily.

Tim looked absolutely relieved. Supposing she had said no, just to be difficult. Oh goodness, he couldn't go all through that again. He stood up and held her tight.

'I'm glad you're happy,' he said.

'You don't have to sleep on the sofa tonight.'

Tim sighed with relief. He had thought he might be banished from the bedroom until he agreed to marry her. No cold nights, he thought. But his relief was short-lived.

'I will instead. Just for tonight,' she told him.

Tim raised his eyes in disgust. She was determined to get him to the altar.

'But when we're married it'll be business as usual,' she added.

★★★

Leonie and Jimmy sat quietly in the lounge room. It was late now and they had enjoyed a very happy evening with George. Now that he had gone home and Alec had gone to bed, they had some much-cherished time to themselves.

'Well it's been a lovely night, Jimmy,' Leonie said in her bubbly, happy, jovial mood. 'My, we did have some fun!'

She was at her most seductive and mischievous. She moved over to sit on his knee, and kissed him.

'It's been a while since I had a lassie on my knee,' Jimmy said with a smile.

'I hope it was me,' Leonie remarked, with a sparkle in her eye.

'So do I,' he replied. 'I've got a job to remember!'

'I just love looking into your deep blue eyes, Jim. They remind me of the colour of sunset over Milton Keynes.'

'That's better than they've been described before. As deep as the colour of the North Sea someone once said.'

Leonie became serious for a moment. 'I just wanted to say, I love you Jim.' Her voice was hushed and sincere. 'I don't say it too often. And I am very happy I married you.'

Jimmy was touched. He had the appearance of being a very hard man, but this camouflaged a soft heart that was always well concealed.

'Of all the guys you could have married, you chose me,' he told her gently. 'I think you gave up so much to marry a craggy old widower like me. I got very lucky when I met you.'

'I was the lucky one, Jimmy. You're an old soulful beggar. I think I'm one of the few people who can really understand you.' In this Leonie was right. Her feminine intuition was correct as always where her husband was concerned. 'When you're with your mates on the building sites you've got a tongue like a blacksmith's anvil and you can appear mean and moody. But that's not the fellow I know. The man I love is a very sensitive fellow beneath all that bravura.'

Jimmy leaned forward and kissed her.

★★★

George took his breakfast alone and laughed to himself at the thought of the previous night. It had been a long time since he had enjoyed himself so much in people's company. Jimmy and Leonie were nice people, who he would enjoy meeting on a social basis from time to time.

He looked up from the breakfast table at a picture of his late wife on the sideboard. 'God bless you,' he whispered. 'I miss you, Mary.'

From the doorway of the kitchen a gentle voice spoke. 'I'm here, Dad.' Jane stood there looking at him.

'I'm just remembering your mum. She gave me so many good years. In all my life no one ever stood by me quite the way your mum did. When I was a coal miner, a soldier, a political leftie, a fisherman, a musician, unemployed or working all hours she was always there for me. Whatever you do in life, Jane don't go through it without a good marriage. A happy marriage is worth more than gold.'

'If it works,' Jane said.

'Make it work. Make it good,' George said, sounding at his most persuasive. 'You know, darling, I made a very nostalgic trip back to Dranthord. I wanted to relive a few old memories.'

The tone of his voice was sad. Red streaks appeared in his eyes. Jane sat down, knowing her father was about to bare his soul.

'Yes it was strange getting off that train at the old station after forty years. I could see the enormous changes that had taken place. I guess it was the thought of you getting married, and I thought of me and your mum when we got wed in the old church at Dranthord. There were still a few remnants of the town I knew. The old colliery was painful to see.'

'I can imagine,' Jane said knowing of her father's painful experiences. George seemed to want to speak about it.

'Ever since the pit collapsed on me and the other lads, I...' His voice broke off as he stumbled to find words to express his feelings. 'I've always slept with the light on, as you know. Darkness frightens me. Being in pitch black nights or places where there is little glimmer or sparkle, or there's not a friendly street light or a welcoming lantern still causes a wave of panic to come over me. I will never forget – even though I've tried, God knows I've tried – how when I lay in the darkness there with a weight on me and the sounds of men gasping for life all around me, the thoughts I had. I thought of your mum and the family.'

He composed himself. 'What I'm saying, Jane, is that at the end of the day the welcome light is the one that's always held by the family. This idea of living together is fine, but it's the bond that counts. Maybe I'm speaking out of turn, perhaps I've got no business speaking my mind, but marriage is an institution that can't be beaten.'

'I respect your opinion, Dad, but it's me. I've always thought about marriage, I've never thought otherwise. At least not until the day I got engaged and then I asked myself: is this it? Is this all I want out of life? Is there more? What have I really done with my life? What more can I do? I was thinking of all that you've done with your life, Dad.'

'I've had a bloody wonderful life, Jane,' George agreed. 'But I've had my share of heartbreak and tragedy, and my mouth has got me into trouble when I spoke my true feelings. You shouldn't compare your life and mine. We're all different. We've all got different abilities and talents, good points and bad points. There's no shame in living an ordinary suburban life, if that's what you want.'

Jane put her arm around her dad. Gruff old bugger that he was, how could anyone not love him?

★★★

The following Saturday, Jane and Alec were out walking, discussing whether to postpone the wedding and live together instead. Alec listened as Jane spoke, unable to make up his own mind.

'Are you still thinking that we should postpone the wedding? At least for a while until we're absolutely certain, until we've no doubts in our minds whatsoever? What do you think Jane? How would you feel about setting up home together?'

'I've been so confused these past few days.' She looked at Alec almost hopefully that he would say something definite about what they would do. It was obvious he wasn't going to lead in this situation. 'One thing I am absolutely certain about is that you're the man for me.'

Alec put his arm around her and pulled her lovingly to his side. He smiled at her warmly.

A little way ahead of them was a church where a wedding was taking place. Cars were parked outside and a small crowd of people were waiting with confetti to throw over the happy couple. AS they approached, the newly married couple emerged from the church. Photographers lined up to take pictures of the newly weds.

'Oh look! Let's stop for a moment Alec.'

Jane and Alec stood still and watched. Alec's face was a picture. He smiled at the married couple posing for their wedding photographs, at the relatives with buttonholes in their jackets, and bridesmaids who looked dazzlingly beautiful. Jane watched too, and it was obvious to anyone just what she was thinking. When confetti was strewn over the couple, Jane appeared entranced. This did not go unnoticed by Alec. The bride's bouquet was thrown into the crowd, and caught by a girl who giggled with embarrassment. The couple then walked to a chauffeur-driven car, waved to their friends and relatives, and were driven away to their reception.

Alec turned to Jane and looked at her, realising that this was exactly what they both wanted. 'Nice,' he said quietly. After some deliberation he added, 'Didn't they look happy?'

'Very happy,' Jane agreed. She looked at him hopefully.

This time he did take the lead. 'That couple had no doubts at all,' he said in a hushed voice.

'None whatsoever,' Jane said in an equally hushed voice.

Alec gazed at her with deep admiration. 'They knew exactly what they were doing,' he said. 'And my, there was love in her eyes for him. I've no doubts any more. Have you?'

'No, not at all, Alec.'

'The first of August. Will that suit you for a white wedding?'

'No.' Alec looked at her in shock. Jane looked back at him but smiled instead. 'The first of July,' she declared with emphasis. 'I want to ensnare you before you change your mind.'

Alec hugged her and grinned broadly. 'The first of July it is then.'

★★★

This was cause for celebration for both the Walsh and the McCutcheon families. After all this vacillating, this pondering of whether to wed or not to, they had finally made the firm decision. It should have all been so simple. Why all the fuss?

Perhaps the real reasons lay in the fact that the mood of the century towards marriage had changed. So many people lived together in the present era. Divorce was common in every street and suburb. Single-parent families were prominent. Also, many people sought adventure and travel while they were young and didn't want to settle down to a life of domesticity too soon.

Before Alec and Jane decided to press ahead with their marriage they really had to work out just what they wanted in life other than wedding bells and bouquets. For both, though, it was clear that a happy marriage was all that they really wanted in life. Anything else would be a fringe benefit.

George was sprucing himself up for the Saturday night engagement party. He was just straightening his tie when the phone rang.

'Hullo?' he said rather reluctantly, fearing Alec and Jane were about to postpone the wedding again.

The voice at the other end introduced itself. 'Tom Fisher. From the AWU. How are you?'

George listened avidly to his friend from the Amalgamated Workers Union. 'So, one of your lads has heard about Denis Miles Engineering going to the wall?' George's expression changed. 'Let's get this right, Tom. You're offering me a job on a full-time basis, working with your boys on the union?' He smiled broadly at the prospect. 'Tom, you've made my day. I'll let you have my acceptance in writing,' he added. 'And you'll find out about work in other factories for folk from our factory?'

George felt delighted that in this hard-hearted era there were still people who cared about the unemployed, even if the Government of the early 1990s gave the impression that it did not. With the good news under his belt, he was sure that he would enjoy this Saturday night.

It was a happy occasion when Alec, Jane, George, Jimmy and Leonie all sat around the table together. Everyone was in fine form. There was plenty of food on the table and wine in everyone's glass. Perhaps no one was more happier than Jimmy that night. He knew his son would honour all of his marital obligations as soon as he had finally made up his mind. Why think that by getting married, one is giving up much in life? Jimmy could not understand people asking themselves this question. He had always believed that when someone got married they gained so much: happiness, security, an emotional warmth, a sense of belonging, someone and something to live for, a purpose, a reason to live, a family, a new way of life. In Jimmy's eyes the benefits of marriage could hardly be questioned.

He decided it was time for some speeches. Slowly he rose to his feet. Jimmy was slightly tipsy, well in control, although beneath his gravelly face there was a little emotion bubbling.

'First of all,' he began, raising his glass as he spoke, 'I'd like to say to you, George, welcome to our house again.'

'Pleasure to be here, Jim,' George, said beaming a very happy smile.

Jimmy was in his element now. 'We enjoy your company, George, and both Leonie and I are agreed that our door is always open for you. Now that Alec and Jane — after a matter of some debate and detailed discussion I might add — have firmly fixed without equivocation a definite marriage date of... well... tell us again, Alec.'

'The first of July,' he replied.

'You better believe it too!' piped up Jane.

'The first of July it is.' Jimmy said the date as if he was pronouncing a judgement, although in reality he spoke with a certain sense of relief. 'Since I'm the most experienced and knowledgeable man regarding marriage, having made the plunge twice, I feel that perhaps I should make the first toast. Is that alright with you, George?'

George responded with a broad grin. 'I think I claim seniority there, having been married to the one woman for well over thirty years. Being father of the bride also carries with it special privileges.'

'I'm a sporting man,' Jimmy replied. 'I'll not disagree with you there.'

George was also a good sport. 'But seeing you're on your feet already, Jim, don't let me stop you.'

'Now there's a true gentleman if ever I saw one,' remarked Leonie.

'Thank you,' Jimmy said, bowing slightly to George. 'Would you please raise your glasses everyone.' Everyone responded to the instruction. 'I'd like to propose a toast to Jane and Alec, a couple who we know will honour the traditions of marriage in every possible sense.' He turned to face his future daughter-in-law. 'Jane, you are a very patient lady and possessed of kindness and a peacefulness about you that I hope will never leave you.' To his son he was more forthcoming. 'Alec, take damn fine care of this girl. They don't come much better. George, I've said my piece. I'll take a seat and let you have the last word.'

George's moment had arrived. He stood up. 'Jim, Leonie. I want to say thanks to you for your friendship. I hope it will extend for many years ahead of us. God bless you. The toast, everyone. To Alec and Jane.'

Jimmy, Leonie and George all spoke in unison. 'Alec and Jane.'

They all clinked glasses and took a sip.

It was Jane, however, who had the final word. She gazed deeply into Alec's eyes. 'To us Alec,' she said quietly. 'An apprehensive couple if ever there was one.'

Also by the Author

Battling Spirits and Kindly Hearts

Colour Sergeant Chesney V.C.

Come Sing with Me My People